Blood Price

PAUL BERNARDI

© Paul Bernardi 2021.

Paul Bernardi has asserted his rights under the Copyright, Design and Patents Act, 1988, to be identified as the author of this work.

First published in 2021 by Sharpe Books.

CONTENTS

Chapters 1 – 30

BLOOD PRICE

ONE

"Behold. The Raven is with us!" Jarl Bjarke pointed at the banner that flapping angrily above their heads in the stiff easterly wind that hurled itself across the marshlands. By his side, Sihtric lifted his eyes to look up to where the square white linen cloth was tethered top and bottom to its long ash shaft, one end of which had been driven into the soft earth around which the centre of the Danish army had formed. The fabric cracked against itself as it twisted and turned in the gale, making a sound not unlike a whip against the hide of a recalcitrant ox.

Sihtric felt a surge of confidence coursing through his chest for the banner had the power to presage victory or defeat for any army over which it was unfurled. Everyone knew that the black raven emblazoned on the banner held their fate in its talons; no one had ever known it to be wrong and none would dare challenge its mystical power. Many was the time that men spoke of it in hushed tones in the feasting halls in the long dark winter evenings. Deep in their cups, they would recall the battles of old and whether the Raven had been with or against them on those days.

Today, it was with them. The bird stood rampant; her wings splayed as if beating against the wind and her talons turned up in readiness to slash at her foe. Today, it threw out its stark challenge to the enemy, the Saxon army led by Eadmund, known as the Iron-sides. All that long summer of 1016 – since the death of King Aethelraed – Knut's Danes had been locked in a bitter struggle with the men of England, led by the king's eldest son. Four times they had done battle over the last six months and each time, no victor had been declared. Men had died in their hundreds and both sides were weary and sick to the stomach of the slaughter. But neither side could put up their swords until the other was defeated. And so, today they would fight once more, even though the year was fast coming to a close.

Winterfylleth, the month of the winter full moon, was already more than halfway done. The hours during which the sun deigned to bestow her presence were dwindling fast and the trees had begun to shed their golden-brown leaves. And the weather? By God, but it was wet. Sihtric could cope with the cold; the winters in Danmark were nothing short of brutal; but here it seemed to rain every day at this time of year. Though he had wintered in England for the last seven years, he was still not used to its privations; he doubted he ever would be.

"The Raven has spoken my friends. Let us fight with courage this day, for no danger threatens us; no enemy can best us. The banner bears witness to the truth of it."

The jarl's words were met with a raucous cheer that spread all the way along to the far ends of the shieldwall, far beyond the wind-borne carry of his words. A few paces beyond Bjarke, Sihtric could see Knut, eldest son of Swein Forkbeard. Now in his twentieth year, the new King of Danmark had come back to complete what his father has begun. Though he had not joined in with the cheering, a grim smile sat upon his face, for he knew the power of the Raven on men's souls.

Though the Danes all now followed the nailed-Christ, they had not long since given up the old ways, and many of them still held true to the ancient superstitions. The banner itself was proof of that; it would be unthinkable to go into battle without it. No amount of praying from the brown-robed monks could hope to replace its power. Had the Raven had not spoken for them, the warriors' hearts would have been downcast before even the first shield was splintered. They would not have shirked their duty or lacked courage for the battle, but they would have awaited their doom. But now the prophecy was with them, they could taste the victory to come.

As the clamour finally subsided, Knut raised his sword above his head and roared. "Forward."

As one, the Danes began to move forward, keeping their shieldwall formation with strict discipline. Each step with the right foot was punctuated with the sound of sword hilts and spear hafts being struck against shield rims; each step with the left was timed to coincide with a cry of "Ut". In this way, the three divisions marched up the hill on top of which the massed ranks of the Saxon host awaited them. Three divisions comprised their host: Knut and his Jomsvikings to the front; the older, more experienced men in the middle and the unblooded, beardless men to the rear, in the hope that they would not be needed.

From his position in the front rank, Sihtric could see what lay ahead of them. If he were a lesser man, one new to the coming sword-slaughter, the sight would have struck terror into his heart. It was hard to estimate numbers but, nonetheless, none could say the English had not come with a mighty host that heavily outnumbered the Danes. This Eadmund with the Ironsides was a man unlike his father. This son commanded the loyalty and obedience of his countryman in a way that Aethelraed never had. Sihtric could not recall, in any of the many battles he had fought, ever seeing so many men gathered to oppose them. He glanced down at his sword; Leggbitr would drink deeply of their blood today.

As they drew closer, Sihtric noticed something odd in the Saxon position. A gap was visible over on the left flank; a gap that split the army into two parts, roughly one third to the left and two thirds to the right. But whether it was laziness on the part of the captains in that part of the shieldwall or indicative of something more portentous, he could not say.

He pushed the thought to the back of his mind for they were close now, fewer than fifty paces apart. Any moment now, those in the rear ranks on both sides would hurl their missiles – light javelins of which each man carried two or three. There was little hope of them dealing death to more than but a few men, but they could disrupt formations, causing men to bunch or cower down behind their shields, opening holes in the shieldwall.

Sihtric looked to his left where Bjarke strode purposefully alongside him. Though he was not small, he was still a good head shorter than his lord. It was by no means a surprise that he was known to all as Bjarke the Tall. His long blond hair escaped from beneath the rim of his helm, reaching down to his shoulders where it was joined by the hair from his beard, swishing from side to side in time with his lurching gait. Both men were well past forty summers, though Sihtric was the older by some years. They had fought together many times and had the scars on their hands, forearms and faces to prove it. Both men yet lived because of the other. Countless times, one had blocked a sword thrust with their shield while the other slashed down on a spear haft just as it was thrust at the other man. They knew each other's strengths and weaknesses, their stances, and favoured moves. It was more than comradeship; rather, it was a deep-rooted friendship, born many years ago when they had first learned battle-craft at the hands of Snorri, the fearsome weapons master, a lifetime ago.

All around him, Sihtric could hear men panting as they toiled up the slope, weighed down by their armour and weapons. Those that had breath to spare hurled insults at their foe. A few puked their guts, the nerves getting the better of them; though none broke pace with their comrades, no matter how great their fear.

"Shields!" Bjarke roared the command. All along the line, men lifted their shields, making sure that they overlapped with their neighbour's. Moments later, the first missiles began to land, thudding against the round linden-wood boards. Most clattered harmlessly to the ground, but a few embedded their steel points in the soft wood, forcing their owners to try to dislodge them as best they could. A few more found their mark, finding flesh in the neck or in the lower leg below the hem of their knee-length mailshirts. Those who could strode on, though, gritting their teeth against the pain. There would be time for healing later, should they survive the day.

Just then, a great shout went up within the enemy ranks. A large section of the Saxon army began to advance towards them, slowly at first but picking up speed until they were running pell-mell down the slope, screaming as they came. Sihtric watched aghast. *How could they be so foolish as to abandon their position on top of the ridge?*

But not all of them had. Those warriors standing to the left of the gap he'd spotted earlier had not moved. But before Sihtric could ponder the significance of this development, the howling Saxons were upon them. The last thing he saw before the ear-splitting crash of shield on shield was that whole third of Eadmund's army turning their backs and marching away.

The first jarring impact took his breath away, but it was not enough to make him fall or even take a single step back. There was iron strength in the serried ranks of warriors around him and it would take more than that to break a Jomswiking shieldwall. Every one of those Danes had the experience of many battles behind them. It was why they formed the front rank, and why they were chosen to face the enemy onslaught first. The code of honour that bound them together was worth another hundred warriors. There were few that could stand against them for long.

Sihtric could feel the hot, rancid breath of the man that faced him; he was that close. The few teeth that remained in his gums were blackened and jutted out in myriad directions. His face was screwed up with the effort of heaving against the Danish shields, but there was also fear in his eyes; fear of the death that stalked the battlefield looking for its next victim to pluck from among the ranks of the living. As time slowed – as it always did at such times – Sihtric found himself idly wondering if it was the warrior's first battle. He was not a young man, by any means, but that did not mean he had been summoned to the king's fyrd before. The smell that assailed his nostrils as the Saxon's bowels opened, lent strength to his belief. The Saxon would not live long, but the end came sooner than he expected. Making good use of his height, Bjarke freed his sword arm from the press of bodies and plunged his blade deep into the man's neck. The blow severed whatever vessels carried the poor soul's lifeblood, causing it to arc in great pulsing gobbets, spattering all those who stood within two or three paces.

There was no time for celebration, though, as the dead man's place was immediately taken by the man from the next rank. And so, it went on for hour after long hour. The sun had been close to its zenith when the first blow had been struck and now, as it dipped towards the western horizon, the battle was no less fierce.

Sihtric's lungs were burning, and his arms ached with the effort required to keep his shield up. His throat was parched, every dry swallow sending a pounding pain into his head. But he knew he could not relax. Those around him depended on him, as much as he depended on them. It would take just one slip for a gap to open, heralding death and disaster in equal measure.

The blade of his sword shone wet with blood and gore. Though its edge was now notched and pitted, Leggbitr had not failed him that day. He had lost count of the number of wounds it had inflicted; it would need many hours of careful repair to restore it to its former state. Though blunted in part, the sword could still serve as a bludgeon. Several times he had hammered down on the helms of those that stood in front of him. Though he might not have killed them, they were – more often than not – rendered insensible, unable to fight on.

Which side was winning was impossible to say. The battle seemed to swing back and forth with neither shieldwall able to secure dominance over the other for more than a few moments. At one point, he had even seen King Eadmund himself close by, leading a surge. It had been at that moment when Sihtric had feared defeat the most. The thrust had come within a hair's breadth of success, but the Raven still watched over them. Just in time, Knut had called forward men from the second wave to shore up their line and Eadmund had been forced back before he could bring his sword to bear on the Danish king.

The end, when it finally came, was both sudden and complete. The sun had finally dipped below the ridge to the west and the twilight was making it difficult to discern friend from foe. The only light came from the near full moon, shining bright in a sky that had at last been cleared of its dread clouds.

Weariness was all that Sihtric felt now. He longed to sink to the ground to sleep. He cared not that bodies littered the grass all around him. He cared not that his boots were sticky with blood and entrails, causing him – on more than one occasion – to almost lose his footing. None of that mattered. He just wanted to close his eyes and rest.

And then, without warning, the pressure against his shield subsided. Where, moments before, there had been a horde of howling humanity pushing against him, there was now nothing but empty space. The Saxons had turned and fled. He had no idea how or where it had started; but like a pebble thrown into a pond, the ripples had spread along Eadmund's shieldwall until it had buckled and broken.

On any other occasion, the Saxon retreat would have been the signal for the Danes to give chase. Oftentimes, many more were killed in the final rout than ever were in the actual battle. But night was falling, and their reserves of energy were exhausted. Sihtric fell to his knees, sucking in great gulps of air to ease his heaving chest. By his side, a laughing Bjarke – his blonde-grey beard stained red with blood – reached down to clap a hand on his shoulder.

"The Raven never lies, my friend. It was but a matter of time until the victory was ours."

Sihtric marvelled at the man. How did he have the strength to remain standing? How was his breathing not as ragged as a cloak snared on a thorn bush?

"It was a close-run thing, though, Lord. The outcome hung in the balance for much of the day. I don't recall being in such a fight in all my born days. I am truly spent."

"Nonsense, Sihtric. It is just the cold finger of old age that taps you on the shoulder, is all. I'd be lying if I said I did not feel her presence as well. Though, I'll grant you that this Eadmund is a worthy opponent. He seems to have all the skills that his father lacked as a war-leader. Perhaps now, however, we have finally bested him? Just look at how many lie dead upon the field. Surely no army can recover from such losses?"

"I hope and pray you are right, Lord, for I fear my fighting days are over. My bones creak and my muscles ache beyond reason. Soon, I will become too slow to block the thrust of a sword and that will be the end of me. Whilst I do not fear a warrior's death – indeed I would welcome it as our ancestors once did – I have a hankering to hang my sword over the hearth and to warm my feet by the fire for a while, before my years are done."

***

"Sihtric, what in God's name are you doing warming your feet by the fire when there is work to be done? Come and help me with these clothes, before Mistress Thorgunnr has my guts for garters. There'll be time for rest later."

The sound of his wife's strident tones penetrated his dreams in the way only Freya could; dragging his mind back from the killing fields of Assandun where he had stood with Jarl Bjarke seven years before. That was the day on which he had killed his last man, swearing to his wife with his hand placed solemnly on the cover of Father Wulfstan's bible, that he would never again take up his sword. Opening his eyes, he smiled up at Freya's frowning, red-cheeked face.

"Gladly, my honeysuckle." He pushed himself up out of his chair, unable to stifle the involuntary grunt that invariably accompanied such an effort these days.

TWO

Sihtric narrowed his eyes 'til they were little more than slits, just enough to maintain his focus, whilst also shielding them from the sparks that shot out from the revolving stone. Whilst many moaned about the tedium that came with sharpening blades, Sihtric rather enjoyed the work. So much so that, along with his own Leggbitr, he also had Jarl Bjarke's sword together with a small pile of others, all stacked against the wall of the barn behind him. He liked nothing more than to sit in the open air, feeling the warm sun on his face as he worked the edges of each intricately patterned blade along the surface of the spinning whetstone. The gentle turning of the wheel and the sound it made as the steel scraped across its surface gave him a sense of comfort and wellbeing that was hard to explain.

Whilst it was still a job that demanded some physical effort – he had to continually pump up and down with his right leg on the flat wooden pedal to keep the stone moving - it was a lot easier now that Ubba the Smith had engineered this fine iron-framed contraption. Housing the large block of sandstone, it allowed it to turn freely at whatever speed you wanted or could manage. Now each sword could be completed in the time it took for a herdsman to milk a brace of cows. A saving of some considerable time.

Though Sihtric had long since hung up his sword - he had not fought again since that blood-soaked battle at Assandun - he still took care of the blade as if it were a religion. In many ways, it was. The warrior's religion. The man who allowed a keen edge to be blunted would not survive to see old age. And so it was that every month, without fail, Sihtric would take Leggbitr down from its place, suspended above their stone hearth. Freya had long since ceased commenting on what she felt to be a waste of his time, for she knew her words fell on deaf ears. Nowadays, she contented herself with a roll of her eyes and a heavy sigh - both of which Sihtric pretended not to notice.

For perhaps the fifth time since he had begun his task, Sihtric lifted the hilt up to his eyes so that he could look along the blade to gauge how true it was. Apart from the odd nick here and there - testament to its long and brutal history - it was now as good as it could be. Grunting with satisfaction, he turned to place the sword on the 'finished' pile on the right, spotting, as he did so, Jarl Bjarke striding towards him, his features as dark as a Blodmonath sky at the onset of winter.

Sihtric was used to his master's foul moods. He had never really been the same man since the death of his first wife, Eadgifu, almost seven winters ago. As happened with so many women, she had died following the birth of their first child - a son who had been christened, Ulf. It had been a devastating blow for Bjarke for he had loved her more than anything. Her death catapulted him into a deep depression that lasted for many moons. It was only the realisation that his son had need of a father that brought him back from the brink of despair.

Though, he had since remarried - to a young, raven-haired beauty from Danmark by the name of Thorgunnr – his new wife could never expunge the sense of loss that he felt. Nevertheless, Bjarke was everything a husband should be: loving, protective, even besotted at times for Thorgunnr was much younger and in the full bloom of her youth. But the spark that had been there with Eadgifu was missing. Not for any failing on the jarl's part, it had to be said. If Sihtric were any judge, which he freely admitted he was not as the wiles of womenfolk were wildly beyond the capacity of his meagre brain - it was Thorgunnr more than her husband who had not the capacity for love.

The match had been made by Thorgunnr's father. Thorveld was a man who yearned for an alliance with a man held high in the king's esteem. With many great tracts of eastern England under his sway, many said Bjarke was second only in power to Knut himself. So Thorveld had given his daughter to secure that alliance, irrespective of her wishes and not caring whether the two were suited to one other. And though Thorgunnr might not love her husband in the same way as Eadgifu had, she made no secret of the fact that she enjoyed the wealth and trappings that went with the life of a woman of her station.

Where Eadgifu had been kindly and thoughtful, knowing

each member of her household by name and always with a pleasant word or gesture for them all, Thorgunnr was the opposite. She was haughty and aloof, unwilling or unable to learn the names of all but a few of those nearest to her and treating all as a means to get what she wanted done in the shortest time possible. The gaiety and laughter that had once characterised Bjarke's hall was now a distant memory. And though things improved when the jarl was at home - his wife making more effort on those days to be the perfect lord's consort - Bjarke was all too often away on Knut's business, not least when the king returned to Danmark as he was wont to do on occasion.

Sihtric put such thoughts out of his mind. Instead, he rose to greet his lord, stretching his back as he did so to ease the aches that came with being slouched over the sharpening wheel for too long.

"Greetings, Lord. I trust the day finds you well?"

"Well enough, old friend. My thanks to you." His tone was gruff, with little warmth to it.

"Please, Sihtric, be about your business. Do not allow me to keep you from your work. You have quite a pile awaiting your attention, I see."

"And with each one comes the promise of a silver penny… save for yours, of course, Lord. That I will gladly do for no charge." he added swiftly.

Bjarke's face broke into a grin. Sihtric was relieved to see his mood lighten so readily. The old master was not lost forever; he just needed coaxing out from the dark corner of the hall in which his mind dwelt from time to time. Spying Leggbitr, the jarl picked up the sword, hefting its weight to test the balance. His eyes sparkled with life as he swished the blade through the air in a series of chopping and thrusting motions, cleaving a host of imaginary enemies in two.

"Ah, but this blade holds many memories, my friend. It has guarded my flank on many occasions and sent many men to Valhalla. Or perhaps, I should say, Hell nowadays, eh? It has earned its name a hundred times over; for I cannot count the number of times it has found its mark beneath the rim of a man's shield."

Sihtric kept his silence, not wishing to disturb Bjarke's reminiscence. Though the jarl was still expected to lead men into battle, as was demanded by his rank and station, Sihtric's fighting years were long behind him, and he was glad of it. He had never been afraid to stand in the shieldwall; he had never shirked his duty or turned his back upon an enemy, but his time was past now. Though he did not doubt he could still handle a sword as well as any man, his promise to Freya would not allow it. Besides, he knew his body could no longer stand the rigours demanded of it in battle. Added to that, his left leg had stiffened as he grew older, a legacy of some distant battle when his leg had been broken beneath the knee.

Sihtric shuddered as he remembered the pain of that day. The break itself had been bad enough, but then when Father Wulfstan had manoeuvred his leg back into position and strapped it tight between two strips of wood, he had passed out, biting clean through the stick that had been shoved between his teeth to protect his tongue. Not even the potion the priest had given him to deaden the pain had made any difference. It had taken most of the winter, but finally his strength had returned. Many more weeks of exercise and training had followed until he was once again able to take his place with the other Jomsvikings. But now, in his twilight years, time had finally caught up with him. The bone still ached from within; it was worse when it was cold or wet. He could still move about well enough, but it never failed to let him know when it had had enough.

The metallic clink when Bjarke placed Leggbitr back against the wall brought him out of his reverie. "You keep a fine blade, Sihtric. It is a credit to you. It pleases me that my own humble weapon will soon have a polish and an edge to match."

"It is a simple task, Lord, but one that brings me pleasure in my dotage. I can think of few better ways to spend an afternoon than to sit here in the sunshine with the smells and sounds of this fine land around me, working the metal against the stone. Not least," he winked conspiratorially, "because it gives me a few hours precious peace away from Freya. Her list of jobs for me is never ending."

Bjarke threw back his head and laughed. Though everyone knew Sihtric loved his wife dearly, the jarl had knowledge of the shared experience of a man taken to task by his wife. "Sometimes, it's like a hen pecking at grains of corn on the barn floor is it not? Or a woodpecker tapping against the bark of a tree until it finally opens a hole for its nest."

Sihtric grinned. "And makes my head hurt in equal measure. But where would we be without our wives, eh?" Too late, Sihtric clamped his mouth shut, cursing himself for his insensitive stupidity.

But the damage had been done. It was like a thick veil had passed in front of the sun. The joy drained from Bjarke's features, leaving him with an expression darker than any rain cloud. Though it had been some years since Eadgifu had died, she was never far from his thoughts. Sihtric knew that all too well and yet he had still invoked her memory, ruining the moment.

To hide his embarrassment, he rubbed his hand over his face, feeling the strands of his thick wiry beard pass through his fingers; a beard that was infused with more and more grey streaks every day. It covered most of his face - save for the gap to the right of his mouth where the stretched white skin shone through, evidence of yet another battle scar. Despite the gravity of the moment, he could not suppress a smile as he recalled how the children in the village would sometimes laugh at him as he passed, saying that his head was on upside down; for as hairy as his chin was, his pate was as bald as a new-born baby's bottom. On warm days, when he had been labouring hard, the sweat made it glisten as if the sun was reflecting off the waters of the nearby lake, adding to the unbridled mirth of one and all.

Bjarke sighed deeply. "What would you do if you were me, my friend?"

"Lord?" Sihtric was caught unawares; he had not expected the question, nor knew to what it referred.

"Thorgunnr. Nothing I do seems to please her, Sihtric. I thought, at first, it was because she was nervous of me, but I have been nothing but caring and respectful. Never once have I raised my hand to her, let alone my voice. And yet she seems to be unhappy all the time."

"Perhaps she yet yearns for her home? Danmark is many days journey from here."

"True, but she does not want for its familiar trappings. She has her maids and two cousins who travelled with her. And you saw how many chests she brought with her. By Christ and all his saints, our chambers are full of reminders of her home. So much so that I had to move much of my stuff out." He smiled ruefully, perhaps a little shame-faced at revealing how little power he had in his own bedchamber.

"Maybe it is because she is young, Lord?" It was true. Though he did not know Thorgunnr's true age, Sihtric reckoned there must be nigh on twenty summers between them. "Perhaps, she sees you more as a father than a husband?"

Bjarke rubbed his forehead as he pondered these words. "Possibly. Though I am sure I have left her in no doubt that she is my wife and not my daughter." A glimmer of a smirk ghosted across his mouth, before he caught himself. Sihtric looked away, caught between masking his own grin and hiding his embarrassment at such a revelation.

"It is on that matter," Bjarke continued, "that I wanted to speak with you today."

Sihtric jerked his head back to face his master. He wasn't sure he liked the sound of where this was heading.

Bjarke chuckled. "Worry not, old friend. It is nothing for you to fear. No, I mean to tell you that the Lady Thorgunnr has only just this morning told me that she is with child."

Sihtric lurched to his feet to grasp his friend by the arm. "My congratulations, Lord, to you both."

Bjarke smiled, his expression one of undisguised pride. "My thanks to you, Sihtric. If I am honest, I am a little surprised as I feared I might be past the age of being able to … you know… But I cannot pretend that it is not news that brings great joy to my heart. Even with Eadgifu, I was not a young man when Ulf was born, and I always thought it a shame that he should have no brother or sister with whom to grow up. You'll know yourself how much brothers can learn about the art of war from scrapping with each other in the dirt."

Sihtric thought back to his own childhood where, as the youngest of four brothers, he'd taken regular beatings until he had grown big enough and strong enough to return the favour. He was the only one left now of the four: the winter sickness had taken one, a ship lost in a storm as it sailed between England and Denmark had taken another, while the third had been killed in the year of battles against Eadmund of the Ironsides.

"Perhaps now I have given her a child, her mood will lighten?"

"I'm sure of it, Lord. What woman would not welcome the joy of motherhood?"

"Well, that remains to be seen, my friend, but I am hopeful. Perhaps this is the missing piece on the tafl board that will complete her? But be that as it may, I tell you this news with but one purpose"

"Name it, Lord. If it is within my power, it shall be so."

Bjarke chucked, "Spoken like a true Jomsviking. Though what I must ask of you should not, I hope, endanger your life as many other of my orders have. I would have you speak with Freya on my behalf. I have need of her skills to watch over Thorgunnr for me. I know…" he paused, as if searching for the right words, "I know that your wife's relationship with Thorgunnr could be said to be somewhat, er… strained - shall we say - but there is none in my service with her experience and skills in matters of this nature. Ask anyone in Hoctune who knows most about the dark art of bringing a new-born child safely into this world, none would name any but Freya."

Sihtric's expression was grave. "You ask much of me, Lord. I think I'd prefer you to order me to attack a Saxon shieldwall on my own."

"I would not ask were it not important. I would have my wife avail herself of the best care possible, and that means Freya. I cannot lose another wife, Sihtric. I beg this of you, in the name of our friendship that has stood for these many years. Please, intercede with your wife on my behalf. Ask her to do it, if not for Thorgunnr, then for me and the child I hope to have."

THREE

"You expect me to eat this?"

Freya froze in the act of clearing away the remains of the previous course. How was she to answer without giving offence? Anxious, she chose a tentative but non-committal response.

"Does it not please you, my Lady?"

Thorgunnr shook her head as if she could not believe what she was hearing. "Have you even tasted it? I would hesitate to offer it to the dogs, for fear of making them ill."

Freya stared at the steaming fish pie that sat before Thorgunnr. Her cheeks reddened, though she could not say whether it was the shame or the anger that was to blame. Before she could speak, though, Ulf bravely came to her rescue.

"Well, I like it. Freya's fish pie is one of my favourites. And father tells me the same was true for my mother also."

With remarkable speed and accuracy, Thorgunnr's hand lashed out, catching the boy flush on his cheek, the sound of the slap leaving no doubt as the strength of the blow. To the boy's credit, he did not cry out, but he was unable to prevent tears of shock and pain flowing down his seven-year-old cheeks.

"What have I told you about speaking when not bidden? And what's more, you know you are not to mention that woman in front of me. I have told you countless times."

"Her name was Eadgifu," Ulf whispered between sniffs.

Thorgunnr glared at him, daring him to utter another word, though she stayed her hand this time.

"Take it away, woman. I find my appetite has deserted me. Bring me wine and fruit in my chambers." With that, she rose sharply, pushing back the heavy wooden chair so fiercely that it rocked back, teetering on its rearmost legs before crashing to the ground. Startled, the two lurchers that had been slumbering by the fire yelped and skittered across the floor, claws desperately scrabbling for purchase in the fresh, loose straw that had been strewn on the densely packed earthen floor.

Without glancing back, Thorgunnr stomped to the far corner of the hall and thrust aside the thick woollen drape that sealed off the entrance to the lord's living quarters. With a final swish of her purple dress, she disappeared from sight, pulling the curtain back into place behind her.

An uneasy silence descended on the hall, broken only by the sound of the dogs whimpering and scratching by the door, still desperate to escape. Freya stood, unmoving, her hands bunching into fists as she fought to control her emotions. For Ulf's sake, she did not want to give full vent to her anger in front of him. Though Thorgunnr was only his stepmother, she still had to be shown the respect due to a woman in her position: the lord's wife and lady of the house.

But, by God, it took every fibre in her body to hold her tongue. The woman was impossible. She could not be more different than Eadgifu if she tried. How she missed Bjarke's first wife. With the lord away on the king's business so often, the two women had become firm friends, despite the gulf in their respective status. But that had been the essence of the woman; she had not allowed such things to form a barrier. She treated everyone equally, asking for - rather than demanding - their help and favour around the estate. But, even then, she was not above taking part in even the most arduous of tasks. She was often to be found down by the river washing clothes, even in the dead of winter when the water chilled your arms to the very bones within moments. And she had a canny knack with the butcher's knife too, paying no heed to the blood and guts that splashed up her arms and clothing as she worked. Yes, the contrast with Thorgunnr could not be starker.

Freya sighed. There was nothing to be done but see to the lady's orders lest she run to her husband telling tales. She very much doubted whether the lord would believe his wife's word against her own, but it was not worth the risk. Thorgunnr could make life very difficult for her with or without his blessing. She came forward to pick up the abandoned pie, wiping her hand on her apron as she walked. There was no sense it going to waste; it would make a fine dinner for Sihtric who knew better than to criticise her cooking.

"I hate her."

Though Ulf had but whispered, she heard him as clear as a bell. Turning to face him, she could see the boy's face, his cheeks still wet with tears but with his little mouth set in a determined grimace. Though he was still a child, he had the demeanour of one much older than his years. And so, it was now. His words were no childish folly, but rather carried the invective that a warrior ready for battle might show. She made a note to herself to speak to her husband. Ulf missed his father and needed a strong hand to guide him, lest he go astray from the path.

"I'm sure she means well enough, Ulf; it can't be easy for her on her own in a different land with no husband by her side for weeks at a time." She hoped that the boy did not see through her facade for she had not meant a single word of it.

"Finish your pie, lad, and then run and find Abbot Ethelstan; it must be time for your lessons."

***

"Bitch!"

Sihtric knew better than to react; he was used to his wife's outbursts. Usually, her ire would be directed at him for some trifling misdemeanour, perceived or actual. But in recent months, he had found himself to be more and more replaced as the target of her tongue by Bjarke's new wife. Whilst on the one hand, he was not displeased by this development, it nevertheless still led to an uncomfortable experience as he had to navigate the turbulent waters of her mind, steering a course between the rocks that lurked beneath the waves, threatening to capsize his leaky craft.

And he could tell that this was just one such occasion. Normally, Freya could be relied upon to get whatever it was off her chest with little or no prompting, leaving Sihtric with no greater duty than to nod or grunt in the right places or to offer suitable, well-timed words of sympathy. But at times, her passion was so great that she stewed in silence, waiting for him to coax forth the words. Sihtric could have sworn she did it deliberately, testing his powers of perception. Already, he knew he had to speak; the silence had already gone on too long.

Another few moments and he risked becoming the new object of her wrath.

"Thorgunnr has angered you, my love?" It was a weak opening, but safe gamble, nonetheless. He hoped it was sufficient to tease apart the logs that had jammed the flow of words.

Freya dropped the soiled dishes on the pitted oak table that formed the centrepiece of the kitchen that abutted the lord's hall. The sound of clattering earthenware pots bouncing off the wooden surface caused Sihtric to wince, hunching his shoulders subconsciously. It would not do to break the jarl's best crockery.

"Whatever gave you that impression, husband?" Throwing her hands into the air, she sighed dramatically. "Is it too much to ask for someone in this world to understand me?"

Shit, Sihtric cursed under his breath. This was going to be a bad one. It could be many hours before this blew itself out. He had no choice but to cling on to the bulwark of his vessel and brave whatever the coming storm could throw at him. With luck, he would emerge unscathed on the other side.

Rising from where he had been whittling a piece of wood into the shape of a deer for young Ulf, he walked over to the barrel of ale in the corner, into which he dipped a cup which he then passed to his wife.

"Why don't you rest your bones, wife, and tell me all that has passed. I'll clean these pots."

Somewhat mollified, Freya grunted her thanks before easing her plump frame onto the three-legged stool that Sihtric placed for her by the fire.

"It's the same story every time, Sihtric. She has to find fault with every little thing I do. I swear she does it just to anger me, to push me to some sort of reaction. I mean, you've tasted my fish pie. There's nothing at all wrong with it is there?"

Sihtric shook his head vigorously, deciding that now was not the time to suggest that a little more salt might not go amiss.

"Exactly. I've been making that pie for years. It's a dish I learned at my mother's knee, and she from her mother before her. It's been a favourite in this household for generations. Why, even Ulf proclaimed his affection for it tonight. But no, it's not good enough for the lady of the house. Said she wouldn't even feed it to the dogs, she did. How dare she?"

Sihtric fought hard to suppress a snigger as he imagined the scene. He would have paid several silver pennies to have seen Freya's face when she'd heard those words. Fortunately, he had his back to her as he bent over the stone trough, in which he was now scrubbing the remains of the food from the rescued crockery.

"Still, her loss is your gain, husband. The pie has hardly been touched so you'll have it for your supper. Waste not, want not, as my mother always used to say."

"My good fortune knows no bounds, good wife." It was fortunate for him that Freya missed the gentle sarcasm in his voice. He needed to catch hold of himself, though, as he had yet to pass on Bjarke's request. He had already left it for a few days, not knowing quite how to broach the subject, far longer than he should have. But earlier that night, he had promised himself that he would do it that evening, come what may. He'd even had a few cups of ale to steel himself. But things could not have got off to a worse start. How on earth would he secure her promise to tend to Thorgunnr's needs now?

"Another cup of ale, Freya? Perhaps you'd like to share the pie with me? You must be hungry, too."

Freya looked up, her brow furrowed in apparent suspicion. "It's not like you to be so thoughtful, husband. You've broken something haven't you, you clumsy oaf? Just don't tell me it's my favourite bowl."

Sihtric laughed, though he could not disguise the note of nervousness in his voice. "Fear not, all your possessions are intact. I merely sought to ease your burden, to take your mind away from the troubles of your day."

"It'll take more than a cup of ale and a slice of pie to do that. But I thank you, nonetheless."

They ate in companionable silence, using the remains of yesterday's bread to wipe up the last of the pie's juices. As he swallowed down the last morsel, Sihtric pushed back his stool and patted his ample stomach, no longer the taut web of muscles that it had once been.

"I swear that is a dish that would be fit to serve to Knut himself, should he ever grace us with his presence."

"Not that he'd have more than a mouthful with you at the table. I swear you eat more and more each day, husband."

"'Tis the fault of the cook, my love. If she were not so skilled, I would not eat half as much."

Freya smiled, her mood seemingly becalmed now she had been fed and watered. "And now you turn to flattery. Are you sure you've not broken anything?"

Sihtric threw his arms wide in mock outrage. "Can a man not praise his wife's food without being accused of some other motive?" He felt his cheeks burn in response to the half-truth, though he felt sure that Abbot Ethelstan would not impose a penance on him on this occasion.

Freya chuckled. "Alright, alright. I believe you. Who could possibly doubt a face as honest as yours? What I can see of it under that unkempt bush you call a beard, that is. Have you checked it recently for nests? A family of mice perhaps?" As she spoke, Freya rose to her feet and danced nimbly over to where he sat before burying her hands deep into the thick strands of his beard. Laughing, she rummaged around as if searching for wildlife before pulling back out of his reach before he could grab her.

"Leave the rest of the crocks 'til the morning and come to bed, you hairy goat."

***

Later, as he lay on his back, his right arm hooked behind his head, Sihtric knew he could not delay any further. He had managed to assuage Freya's passions - in every sense - and now she lay, her head nestling in the crook of his left arm, snuggled beneath the thick furs that lay draped over their bed. If he did not speak soon, she would be fast asleep, snoring loud enough to wake the dead no doubt, and another day would have passed, and his promise to himself rent asunder.

He idly stroked her shoulder, thinking back to the time they had met, a score and a half years ago. It was a source of regret that God had seen fit not to bless them with the gift of children. They had tried often enough but, for some reason that was beyond him, it had not been their fate to be parents. Freya never spoke of it - perhaps for fear of shaming him in some way - but she had made up for her loss by caring for all the new mothers in Hoctune. There was not a child in the last twenty years or so who had not been born into her waiting hands. Yes, some had been lost - coming into the world already dead or surviving no more than a few hours at most - and several mothers had failed to endure the trauma of childbirth too. But there was none who would not agree that Freya was the best there was. Her knowledge, her touch and her care and attention were second to none. As soon as the birthing pains began, Freya was the one they all sent for. And she always came, no matter what time of day or night.

"Do you remember the first child that you ever helped bring into the world?" he asked.

Yawning, she replied. "I remember them all, my love. It was Agatha's boy, Assa. He's married himself now with two fine boys of his own, both of whose births I also attended." Though she was close to sleep, the pride in her voice still shone through.

"Ah, Assa. A good father and a fine warrior, too. I remember fighting with him at Assandun when he was no more than a beardless boy. Though he shit his trews that day, I could see he had skill with spear and shield, even though it was his first battle. No doubt his sons will one day follow their father and find their place in the shieldwall."

"Mmm-hmm."

Glancing down, he could she was losing her battle with sleep. Her eyes were closed and her breathing even and shallow. "It must be several score babies you have held in our hands; over the years, I mean."

"Close to a hundred. Just one short, in fact."

A glimmer of hope shone in his mind, piercing the darkness of their room. "It would be a grand thing to one day make that number, would it not?"

"I daresay the chance will come soon enough; though I know of none who is yet preg…."

Freya's eyes opened and she pushed herself up on one elbow to stare down at her husband's seemingly innocent face. "But wait, there is one who is with child, is there not?"

Sihtric saw no sense in pretending otherwise. "That's right, my love, there is." He was glad her prying eyes could not see the fear in his face.

"Yes, and now it is clear to me where this evening has been heading all along. My, but you're a sly one, husband. Out with it."

"I don't know what you mean, my sweet." Even to him, the nervous timbre of his voice was unmistakable.

"The pie, the ale, the cleaning of the pots and the other. All of it with just one thought in mind. Tell me now or face the consequences."

Though she did not appear to be angry, he knew he was treading a fine line all the same. He knew some battles were best not fought and decided to lay down his arms before any more damage could be done. "It's true I have a favour to ask you, Freya, though I swear all that I have done for you this day has been out of love."

"Will you please just piss or get off the pot." He could sense her patience was wearing thin.

"Jarl Bjarke has asked that you tend to Thorgunnr... when her time comes."

"And that great war leader, that scourge of the Saxons, lacked the balls to ask me himself?" she snorted.

"I think he hoped it would sound better coming from me, though that now seems doubtful. He knows you still carry much love for Eadgifu and that you have not warmed to his new wife. But he also knows that there is none better than you to help a woman deliver her child. He would have no other by his wife's side."

"Even after I could not save Eadgifu?"

"He has never blamed you for her death; you know that. Rather, he knows that you saved his son. That he has Ulf in his life to remind him of his first wife - and to inherit his lands from him when he passes on - is your doing. Yours alone. The child was not breathing when you delivered him from his mother's loins and, but for your quick thinking, he would not have lived. Bjarke will never forget that."

Though it sounded like thinly veiled flattery to his ears, Sihtric knew there was truth in his words. His wife had saved the boy, reacting quickly to clear the blockage that prevented him from drawing breath. When all others panicked and knew not what to do, Freya had remained calm and did what had to be done.

"It was not beyond the wit of man to do what I did."

"Maybe not, but the point is that you did it. You. No one else. And for that - and for all the other children you have successfully delivered - Bjarke wants you by his wife's side."

Freya sighed, perhaps realising that further resistance was futile. "It's late now, husband, and we have to be up with the dawn. Remember you agreed to take Ulf hunting tomorrow."

He had not forgotten, but nor could he leave matters unresolved. "And what answer shall I tell the jarl on his return tomorrow night?"

Freya rolled on to her side, her back towards him as if bringing the conversation to an end. "Tell him that if he has the guts to ask me himself, then I shall consider it right enough."

Sihtric lay on his back, a half-smile playing on his lips. *Why was it that arguing with a woman was always more arduous than untangling a long-abandoned fishing line?* Still, the fact that Freya had not rejected the notion outright was something of a victory; however small.

FOUR

Next morning, Sihtric found Ulf waiting for him when he arrived at the stables. He was not surprised, though; the boy always looked forward to the days they spent together. And, in his own way, the Sihtric had grown very fond of the lad over the years. He was like the son he'd never had, though - in truth - he was more like a grandfather in age. And he flattered himself to think that the boy had some affection for him too. Perhaps it was because his father was so often away with the king's business that he saw Sihtric as something of a substitute, a kindly uncle perhaps. Or was it just that, though still firm, Sihtric was less strict with him than Abbot Ethelstan was. Most likely of all, though, it was because he enjoyed, more than anything, time spent away from his books and his lessons.

Though Ulf was studious enough and possessed a quick brain, he made no secret of the fact that he found the long hours spent poring over Latin texts more boring than anything else imaginable. And Sihtric could not disagree. He had never learned to read, arguing that it was of no use when facing a man over the rim of your shield. What did it matter if you could read the Lord's Prayer if you failed to strike the first blow? It was the priest's job to read prayers over your grave once you were dead; it was no business of his.

But as the lord's son, Ulf had responsibilities. He would, one day, inherit his father's lands and the title that went with them: jarl of the lands of the eastern Angles. His father's word held sway in almost one quarter of the whole of the land of the Aenglesc. And even though the earldom might be the smallest of the four into which the kingdom was divided, it was Bjarke to whom Knut turned to rule in his stead whenever the king returned to the land of his forebears. In those times, it was the jarl of the eastern Angles who ruled, and not those of Wessex, Northumbria or Mercia.

But more than that, a great lord must also be a leader in battle. He must know how to wield sword and shield as well as any other man, if not better. He must study tactics and generalship if men were to trust him to lead them to the gates of hell and back. And for this purpose, Ulf had Sihtric to help him. There was little that the old warrior could not teach the lad about the battle-skills he would one day need. Though he was not as mobile as he once was, though his back ached each morning until he had stretched it and loosened the knotted muscles, and though his left leg still lagged, he was yet matched evenly with the seven-year-old Ulf. He knew there would come a time, though - a few years hence - when the boy's strength and agility would equal and then surpass his own.

It was ever thus, though. The boy grows into a man and takes over from the father, who then dwindles and dies so that the cycle may repeat. Where there is love between father and son - as there was between Bjarke and Ulf - so the transition may run smoothly. Where there is none, then only the gods know what will come to pass. In the case of kings and their sons, the ravens gather and begin to circle, in anticipation of the blood that will soon be shed. Such had been the case between Aethelraed Unraed and his son, Edmund of the iron sides. So divided were they, that the road had been left open for the Danes - first under Svein of the forked beard and then his son, Knut - to march in and take the kingdom.

"Well met, young Ulf. How does the day find you?"

The boy turned to face him, a broad smile forming across his youthful features. "I am well thank you, Sihtric. It is some days since we last spoke."

Sihtric could not help but notice the purple bruise that had formed around Ulf's left eye; he recalled Freya telling him how Thorgunnr had raised her hand to him last evening. It must have been some blow to leave such a mark in its place. He saw no sense in mentioning it, though. He had lost count of the times his own father had found cause to take a belt to his arse; he could almost still feel the burning sensation that persisted long after the beating had ended.

He saw no need to add shame to the already long list of the lad's woes. It was hard for the boy. He had never known his own mother, and his father's second wife had taken against him almost immediately. That was bad enough, but Sihtric could not help but wonder whether Ulf carried a sense of guilt with him. Guilt that it was his birth that had caused his mother's death. Sihtric knew that Bjarke had never said anything of that nature and never would. He loved that boy unreservedly; that much was as plain as the nose on his face.

When Eadgifu had unexpectedly announced one day that she was with child, none had been happier than Bjarke. A child was the one thing that was missing from his life, the one thing that would make him complete. Nothing was too much trouble to make sure Eadgifu was well cared for, no expense was too great to make sure she had all that she might need and more.

The whole of Bjarke's household watched and waited with happy eagerness. All, that was, except Freya. Though she had said nothing to anyone other than her husband, she had fretted about Eadgifu's age. In her experience, the older a woman was, the more likely the chance of some difficultly arising. Though she could not explain why, Freya knew of all the children that came into the world not breathing, most of them were delivered of mothers who had seen more than thirty winters, as was the case with Eadgifu.

So, Freya had prayed every night for the baby to be healthy and strong. And on the night Ulf was born, it seemed that her prayers had been answered for she declared she had never seen a child in as rude health as he. But her joy had proved all too short. All women bled in childbirth; it was expected. But where for most, the flow would soon cease, for Eadgifu it had not. Nothing anyone did could stem the tide. In the end there was no more to be done other than make her last moments as comfortable as they could, before leaving her alone with her husband by her side. He held her hand as she faded, violent sobs wracking his body as he watched, helpless, as his love was wrenched away from him. It was no wonder he had never completely rid himself of the pain. Whilst the jarl cared deeply for Thorgunnr, she lived in the shadow of the woman who came before. It was no surprise that the presence of Ulf in Bjarke's hall was a constant reminder of all that she was not.

"Can we fly the falcons today?"

Sihtric stirred himself from his reverie and smiled. The falcons were ever the boy's favourite. And he could not argue. The birds were a delight to behold on the hand, but even more so when on the wing. Their sleek form, the speeds they reached when diving on their prey. There was simply nothing as majestic or as beautiful in the whole of God's earth. It gave Sihtric huge pleasure that Ulf felt the same way. He had spent many long and happy hours teaching the young lad how to care for the brace of birds that his father kept.

"Gladly, Ulf. But to earn such delights, we must first practise with sword and shield. You need to build muscle and with that will come speed, agility and, finally, skill. Only with all those things will you earn the right to lead men to their deaths in battle. They will not want to follow one who cannot do all that they can and more."

Ulf sniffed but said nothing, the smile vanishing from his face. Sihtric felt stung for a moment; he hated to disappoint the lad, after all. But the fact was that he would be failing in his duty to his master were he not to train the boy in the art of war. The work was often dull and always back-breaking in its intensity, but there could be no short cuts. It would take years for Ulf to become half the warrior his father was. There could be no half measures.

"Come on, lad. The sooner we start, the sooner we can go hunting."

***

It was after noon when they finally trotted out through the wooden gates of Bjarke's estate at Hoctune. It was a new settlement, built in the years since Knut had awarded Bjarke the earldom of the eastern Angles. Apart from the fact that the hall lay close to a large mill that sat on the banks of the fast-flowing river Ouse, the other main reason for its location was its proximity to the great stone abbey at Ramsey, a church that had been founded some two generations before on land that had been donated by a previous lord of the eastern Angles. Since assuming his title, Bjarke had adopted the abbey as his own, richly endowing it with several grants of land in the surrounding area. Eadgifu had been buried within its cemetery too, meaning that Bjarke had good reason to remain close by when not about the king's orders. Several times a year, he would make the ten-mile trip north to pray at the abbey and pay his respects at his wife's grave. In return, the abbot - old white-bearded Ethelstan - would come to the estate each week to teach Ulf his letters. It was an arrangement that suited both men well.

Sihtric and Ulf rode at a gentle pace along the well-trodden path that followed the river as it meandered eastwards. They were heading out to the great meadows that stretched far and wide from the edge of the woods that bordered the fenlands to the north. In his experience, there was never a shortage of rabbits and other small animals to be found there.

Both were mounted on sturdy, sure-footed ponies - Ulf's slightly smaller than Sihtric's - the kind that were common to the flatlands of that part of the country. Whilst their right hands held the reins, they held their left arms out to the side. Each of them wore a thick leather glove with which they gripped on to their falcon's jesses; thin strips of leather that were tied to each bird's legs. The merlins - two of a pair that Sihtric had raised almost from the egg - were hooded so that they remained calm and unperturbed by the sights along the road. The small bells that were attached to their talons jingled with the undulating motion of the horses. Sihtric knew he would be grateful for their reassuring sound soon enough. The birds could fly so high and so fast that it was often hard to keep them in sight. At least they would be able to hear them as well.

In theory, there should be no need for the bells. Sihtric had trained the birds almost daily for the last two years; they knew the sound of his voice and his smell. In truth, they saw him as their mother, for he was all they had known since they were chicks. For the first few months, he had patiently and painstakingly fed them from his hand, getting them used to the idea of taking the meat from him so that they would come to associate his glove with food. Then, and only when he believed them to be ready, did he allow them their freedom, but always with a small piece of chick or mouse ready, so that they could be trained to fly to hand. It was at this stage that he had begun to involve Ulf. The boy would take each bird in turn and place it on a wooden perch that stood at about a man's height. Then Sihtric would walk away, his gloved hand slick with blood from a freshly killed chick. When he was ten paces away, Sihtric would nod for Ulf to release his hold on the jesses and - at the same time - whistling to call the bird to him.

Week after long week they had repeated the exercise, for an hour every day with each bird, slowly but surely increasing the distance between Sihtric and the perch until, eventually, each bird was flying straight and true to his waiting glove. The female had taken to the task the quicker of the two, whereas the male had been prone to distraction. Several times he had spotted a mouse or similar in the grass and veered off to investigate despite Sihtric's urgent and frustrated whistles. But now, two years on, both merlins were as skilled as each other. They were Bjarke's finest birds, the two of which he was most proud. It was to these birds the jarl would turn when he had guests staying whom he wanted to impress. So pleased had he been with Sihtric's work, the lord had gifted him a small gold ring which, even now, he wore on the little finger of his left hand. Its flattened face was engraved with the image of a bird reaching out with its talons as if about to snare its prey.

"How many do you think we'll bag today, Sihtric? Four? Five? Perhaps even as many as ten if we are lucky."

Sihtric laughed. "Ten would be an impressive feat, even for these birds. If I'm not mistaken, six is the most rabbits they have caught in a single afternoon?"

"Yes, that's right. It was last month, wasn't it? I remember it well because it was the day horrid Abbot Ethelstan was too sick to travel, so I had no lessons for once."

"You know, he's not all bad, Ulf. He has your best interests at heart."

"He beats me when I get something wrong, and he smells."

Sihtric could barely suppress his laughter. "I daresay the second is an accusation that could be levelled at me, especially on a warm day such as this. As for the first, if it's what's needed to help you concentrate, then any teacher would do the same, I'm sure. I remember my father would often raise his hand to me if I did not do as I was told. And doubtless you'll do the same when you have children of your own. But when you do, you will at least - thanks to horrid Ethelstan - have the knowledge to be able to teach them their letters. It's more than I ever could."

Ulf sniffed sullenly, as if unwilling to accept the truth of the matter even though he knew Sihtric was right. "How much further?"

"Just over the next rise, and then close by to the woods. The herdsmen tell me that is where they see the most rabbits. With luck and with God's help, we will fill our game sacks twice over. Rabbit stew for supper, eh?"

They rode on in silence, something that had never worried Sihtric. He saw no need to fill the space with empty words. If there was something to be said, he would do so. He saw little value in making idle gossip for the sake of it. Besides, Freya spoke more than enough for the two of them combined. As with many things, Ulf seemed to be cut from similar cloth. He was another who took comfort from his own thoughts. Each word he uttered was measured and had been considered from many angles before it passed his lips. A trait that would serve him well in later years, Sihtric reflected. Passing judgement between two men locked in a bitter dispute would require a level of diligence and care that was beyond most men. One piece of advice he remembered his father had given him more years ago than he cared to remember came to mind. Better to keep your mouth shut and be thought a fool than open it and remove all doubt.

They dismounted and tied the horses to an old birch tree that stood at the edge of the woodland. It grew amidst a patch of lush grass, much to the delight of the two ponies who wasted no time dipping their weary heads to begin cropping at the ripe stalks.

"Here, Ulf. Hold my bird while I unsling my spear."

"Why do we need a spear to hunt rabbit? We have the merlins."

Sihtric smiled with the patience of one given to walking well-trodden ground. "A warrior never goes unprepared into the fray, Ulf. Though our prey may be small compared to us, who knows what we may meet along the way."

Ulf glanced at him sideways, doubt etched on his boyish

features, but did as he was asked. Sihtric removed the spear from the cloth sheath that hung from the pony's flank before leaning it against the trunk of the tree, blade pointing upwards. Then he unpacked the water skin and food bag that Freya had prepared for them, looping the heavier of the two over his shoulder before passing the other to Ulf. It could be several hours before they returned, and they would have need of sustenance in the heat of the late summer's day. Finally, he hitched up his trews - he must be losing weight, he mused - picked up his spear and turned to go.

Ulf sighed with the impatience of a youth who is always made to wait for his elders, but bounded forward nonetheless, almost having to trot to keep pace with the older man's long strides.

The two predators had come alive since they dismounted. Even though they were still hooded, their heads flitted from side to side and bobbed up and down, their keen nostrils sensing the sport to come. Every few yards, one or other of the birds reared up, flapping its wings, causing each of them to hold their arms out further lest they be caught by the flailing feathers.

"They have picked up the scent of their prey. They're eager to be let loose."

"Why do we wait then?"

"Be patient, Ulf. There is an art to flying a hawk. Have I not taught you this? Let us go on a while further until we reach the crest of that ridge ahead of us. From there we'll be able to see over many miles in all directions. It's only a short way ahead."

They stopped midway between the edge of the vast wood to their left and a huge solitary oak tree that stood proud in the middle of the meadow. Its sprawling branches, festooned with leaves, would provide ample shade from the hot sun should they need it, Sihtric thought. The woodland stretched for miles to the north and east, towards the heart of the lands held by the eastern Angles. It was Bjarke's favourite hunting ground for it was rife with deer, boar and other wild animals that could be ridden down by men on horseback. When Ulf was older and bigger - perhaps in two or three years - he, too, would be able to join with his father on such days.

"Remove the hood now, Ulf, as I have showed you." Sihtric began to untie his own, so that Ulf could, if he needed to, copy his actions. The merlin squawked angrily as it twisted its neck round to look behind it towards the trees. When both birds were ready, Sihtric pulled his left arm back, keeping an eye on the boy to see that he was doing it right, before sweeping it forward and releasing his hold on the jesses as he did so.

The two hawks sped away, beating their wings repeatedly to gain height. Soon, they had risen so far that Sihtric - using his hand to shield his eyes from the glare of the sun - could no longer distinguish the blue-grey feathers of their backs from the speckled cream and brown underside.

"Are you not afraid that they will never come back?"

Sihtric did not take his eyes away from the birds as he spoke. "There is always that risk, Ulf, but the bond between us is strong. They have known little but my voice and my smell since they were mere hatchlings and they have come to know that food and shelter are to be found with me. Such is the result of all those hours of training and care. I am like a mother to them."

"You're more of a mother to them than Thorgunnr is to me." Ulf sniffed.

Unsure how best to respond, Sihtric chose silence. Freya would have known what to say to comfort the boy, but he did not. He cursed himself for his clumsiness. For him, comfort came in the form of a spear in one hand and a shield in the other, and the feeling of a warrior's shoulder to either side. His own mother had died when he was but a child, so he had known little of her warmth, few of the hugs a mother reserved for her children. It was the same for Ulf. But he was young yet, still at an age where a such things mattered. That Thorgunnr had no affection for him, no desire to take the place of Eadgifu, just made it worse. But there was nothing he could do to alleviate Ulf's pain. He'd speak to his wife later to seek her advice.

"See." Sihtric pointed, deciding that changing the subject would be for the best. "They have something in their sights."

Both merlins were hovering now, held up in the sky by unseen air currents augmented by occasional beats of their wings. Not for the first time, Sihtric marvelled at their skill and strength as they held station above their prey, waiting for the most opportune moment to strike. It did not take long. Almost simultaneously, the two birds suddenly tucked their wings in close to their bodies and dove from the sky, hurtling their way towards their unwitting target. Sihtric watched unmoving, mesmerised by their grace and beauty. Other than an arrow loosed from a bow, he had never seen anything move as fast.

But then, in a heartbeat, the chase was over. Just before it seemed that they would bury their heads straight into the ground, the falcons pivoted their bodies so that their talons reached out in front and opened their wings wide so that they acted to slow their descent. In tandem, they swooped down onto their prey, twenty or so paces apart, lancing it with their claws as effectively as any spearman might take down a boar.

"Quickly, Ulf." Sihtric began to trot towards where the hawks stood guard over their quarry. They needed to call the birds away, lest they begin to devour their prize. As he ran - doing his best to ignore the pain in his leg - Sihtric reached into his leather hawking bag that hung at his side, its surface stiffened by age and years of grease and blood stains. He grabbed two pieces of newly killed chick flesh and passed one to Ulf who, like him, positioned it carefully between the thumb and forefinger of his hawking glove.

On reaching the birds, he stopped and whistled as calmly and as clearly as his wheezing lungs would allow. Without hesitation, both birds took to the wing once more, before alighting on the familiar smelling gloves where they were rewarded with the morsel of flesh.

Three more times they repeated the exercise until the game bag was empty of rewards but full to bulging instead with eight rabbits. A new record, Ulf had declared, happily. Now they sat in the shade of the oak tree, munching contentedly on the bread and goat's milk cheese that Freya had packed for them. The merlins stood, sentinel-like, a little to one side; their jesses tied to a metal spike that Sihtric had driven into the ground for the purpose of tethering them securely while they ate.

His belly full, Sihtric would have liked nothing more now than to lie back on the soft grass to sleep. Though still hot in the late afternoon sun, there was a cooling breeze which rustled the leaves on the branches above their heads, making for a very pleasant temperature. But he knew that Freya was waiting on them. Jarl Bjarke was due back that evening and she needed the rabbits to prepare the meal for his homecoming. If he failed to return on time, he'd not hear the end of it. With an involuntary grunt, he rose to his feet, brushing the crumbs from his kirtle as he did so.

"Come on, young Ulf. It's time we were away. Gather up the birds for me, will you?"

FIVE

Sihtric turned his back on Ulf to gather up their belongings. He groaned as he bent down to retrieve the various bags and skins that were strewn haphazardly around where they had been sat. It was always the way after he'd been immobile for a while; the muscles in his back and legs stiffened and needed to be coaxed back to life. At least, he mused, they had less to carry on the way home, having polished off most of their food and drink.

"Oh."

His aches forgotten, Sihtric spun round at the sound of Ulf's tremulous voice to see him standing stock still, a single merlin perched on his left hand. Of the other bird, there was no sign.

"I'm sorry, Sihtric. I thought I had hold of him, I really did. But he was struggling to be free and then he scratched me, and I had to let go because it hurt." He held out his forearm to show the angry red welts that already oozed the first drops of blood.

The old warrior bit back on the harsh words that had formed on his lips for he could see that boy was on the verge of tears already. Being angry with him would serve no purpose; Ulf already knew these were his father's best falcons, worth more than a warrior might earn in a year. Bjarke would be sure to have words enough for the pair of them should the bird not be recovered. Instead, he offered an empathetic shrug, or what he hoped passed for one.

"He was ever the daft one, that male. Always played up when I was training him too. Though I thought he had put his silly ways behind him. Now, don't fret, lad, we'll get him back. Did you see which way he went?" He cupped a hand behind his ear, listening for the sound of a bell.

Ulf sniffed and pointed towards the dense woodland away to his right. "I think I saw him alight in the tallest of those birch trees."

"Right you are. Let's be about it then. Make sure you keep tight hold of the other one. In fact, come here and I'll tie the jesses to your glove. We don't want her getting ideas of mischief, too."

As they walked towards the trees, Sihtric tried to spot the bird, but with the trees in full bloom, the thick canopy of leaves made it impossible to see anything much. Inwardly, he prayed they would be successful. He knew not of what he was the more fearful: having to tell Bjarke about the loss of his favourite falcon; or being late with the rabbits for Freya. Both were to be avoided if possible.

"There. Look. I saw him hop to the next tree, further into the woods."

"Odin's blood!" The curse was out before he could stop it. "Excuse me, Ulf. The old ways die hard for one as ancient as me. I'm grateful, though; your young eyes see more keenly than mine, though I wish the damned bird had not decided to lead us on a merry dance."

They entered the trees, and everything was suddenly much cooler and darker. Looking up, Sihtric could no longer see the sky above them, so thick was the foliage. Everything seemed much quieter too; the only sound being their feet as they rustled through the dead leaves and mast amongst the trees. Though the trunks of the trees were not too densely packed, it was still hard to see anything as their eyes adjusted to the gloom and shadows.

Sihtric whistled, but to no end. Whether the bird was out of earshot or simply stubborn, he knew not. "Can you see him, Ulf?"

"I swear I cannot."

"Bastard bird. I'll have his tail feathers for my cap. You see if I don't." They walked on a short while longer, Sihtric whistling every few steps, but to no avail.

"Time is against us, Ulf. Let us split up so we can search twice the area." Ulf, looked uncertain, as if afraid to be alone among the trees. "Don't worry lad. You'll hear me whistling so you will know where I am. You whistle too and stay within earshot. Remember, if you see him, make sure you call out to me and keep an eye on him at the same time."

Sihtric didn't like the idea of leaving the boy alone in the woods, but he had no choice if he wanted to find the bird and return to Hoctune before nightfall. The lad was in no danger, he told himself. There was always the chance that forests such as these might harbour lordless men; men who lived outside the law and who survived by catching what they could or eating nuts and berries. Who knew what they would do to a boy should they stumble across him? Don't be foolish, old man. Surely, there'd be no such brigands this close to Bjarke's hall? You'll be scared of the shadows next, he scoffed at himself. All the same, he unslung his spear and made sure he did not stray too far. Things would go much worse for him if anything were to happen to Ulf. Losing a falcon would mean nothing, were that to happen.

A short distance later, Sihtric stopped. Had he heard something or was his mind playing tricks on him? He took another step. Yes. He definitely heard something that time. His ears were not what they once were, but he was certain. It sounded like someone or something - much bigger and heavier than a small boy - was moving through the trees over to the left… in the direction Ulf had gone. As soon as the realisation hit him, he began to run, his legs pounding heavily, grunting with the effort at every step. *How could you have been so stupid, you old goat?*

Fear lent him the will to overcome the pain in his leg. If it were outlaws, let there not be too many of them that I might hope to save the boy. Though he was old now and had not fought for several years, he reckoned he could still hold his own with a spear. With luck, the sight of him hurtling through the trees would be enough to send them packing. Perhaps, they might even think he was but the first of many such warriors. With that thought, he began to yell orders to his imaginary comrades, hoping to deceive whoever was ahead of him.

Just then, Ulf screamed and Sihtric's heart missed a beat. It was a sound of pure terror, and one that he had not heard for many a year. He forgot about shouting and just barrelled his way through the undergrowth as fast as he could, taking the shortest route possible towards the sound of the scream. He ignored the spiked brambles that tried to pull back on his clothes or which plucked at his flesh; there would be time enough for such trivialities later. Images of the boy's broken and bleeding body filled his mind; followed by another of him carrying the corpse back to his father.

Bursting through the scrub, he arrived in a clearing. There was Ulf, standing a few paces to his left. He seemed to be frozen to the spot but was otherwise unharmed. Of any others, however, there was no sign. So, what had caused the boy to scream? He was just about to ask when the mystery was revealed by a new sound, a deep throated, guttural grunting noise coming from his right. Blowing hard through his cheeks, Sihtric risked a glance in that direction to find his worst fears confirmed: a boar. Not just any boar, mind, but a huge ugly brute of a male with tusks larger than he had ever seen before and carrying the scars of many a scrap on its back and neck. *By Odin's balls, this fellow is a fighter.*

The boar stood about twenty paces away, its front legs splayed firmly, a shoulder's width
 apart. Head bowed, it snorted through its nostrils and pawed at the ground. Sihtric could see that the old sod was about to charge straight at Ulf. And when he did, that would be that. He had no choice, he had to act now. By the looks of it, the beast must weigh as much as a grown man's weight, if not more. And with the power of its heavily muscled shoulders, he was a daunting enemy to face. But he could not wait. It was him or the boy and his own life would not be worth living should anything happen to Ulf. He may as well die fighting the boar, if it meant the lad made it home to his father.

The old feeling gripped him, clawing at his stomach with its icy fingers. He had not felt it since Assandun, but he welcomed it back now, like an old friend he had not seen in years. Part of him wanted to flee, to put as much distance as possible between him and the beast. But the greater part stood firm.

Sihtric reached into his tunic to lift the bear's claw, which hung from an ancient, twisted leather cord around his neck, to his lips. Kissing the charm, he trusted in its power to ward off evil. Abbot Ethelstan might be horrified to see such blasphemy, but it was hard to put the old ways behind him at times like these. Warriors needed every little scrap of luck if they were to survive unscathed.

Then, sucking in one final deep breath, he ran forward to take position in front of Ulf. There, he planted his feet, the left in front, the other at a right angle, behind. Flexing his knees, he jammed the end of the shear shaft against his right instep, while gripping the smooth wood so tightly with both hands that his knuckles shone white through the stretched skin. He would have dearly loved to have a shield for protection, but there was little he could do about that now.

"Run, boy. Away with you." But Ulf didn't move. He was transfixed, terrified; his eyes as round as the wooden platters from which he ate his meals.

"NOW!" Sihtric roared, flecks of spittle spattering the front of his tunic, whose worn wool fabric he knew would offer no protection if the boar's tusks should penetrate his defences.

Whether it was the sound of his voice he'd never know, but the hoary old boar chose that moment to charge. The ground shook as the beast lumbered forward, gaining speed as a heavy boulder might as it tumbled down a grassy slope. Sihtric grimaced, bracing himself for what was to come. He prayed that his old spear would be up to the task; were the ash haft to splinter and break then he was doomed.

The boar was close now, just a few paces away. Its hot breath blowing through its snout as it thundered directly towards Sihtric. The old warrior followed it closely with his eyes, judging the beast's speed and the positioning of his spear point. At the very last moment, he made a tiny final adjustment and gritted his teeth, offering up a silent prayer to any god who might be listening, Christian or otherwise. The impact, when it came, was bone jarring. Every instinct told him to shut his eyes and curl into a little ball, but he forced himself to remain focussed, to leave nothing to chance.

To his delight, he saw the spear point pierce the boar's chest exactly where he had hoped, directly above where he knew the heart to be. The animal's great weight and unstoppable momentum would drive the iron blade deep into the cavity beneath its shoulders and ribs wherein all its vital organs were housed. The sharpened edge would wreak indescribable damage to the soft intestines. Almost immediately, however, his joy turned to horror. Even as it died, the huge beast bore down on him, its vast bulk unstoppable despite the terrible wound that even now was ripping its heart to shreds. There was no time to react though, nor would it have been right to do so. He had to hold his position come what may, trusting in the spear to do its job.

The boar's shoulder struck him hard on his left hip, knocking him to the ground and causing him to lose his grip on the spear as his head collided with the bole of an old oak behind him. A bolt of white light filled his head, and he felt his teeth jar where they were still ground together. He had been lucky, though, for he could easily have bitten clean through his tongue. There was nothing more he could do. His fate, and that of the boy, were out of his hands now. His body finally gave in to the pain and the wave of nausea that engulfed him.

Sihtric woke with a start, his face wet with an unknown liquid. Groggily, he brushed his hand over his forehead, expecting to see it coated red with his own blood, but it was clear. As his blurred vision began to subside, he saw Ulf's pale but smiling face standing over him, an empty water skin in his hand.

"I knew you weren't dead, for I could see your chest moving."

Sihtric chuckled but immediately regretted it. His head felt like a herd of cattle were stampeding around within his skull. Gingerly, he pressed his fingers to the left side of his forehead, wincing as he probed the newly raised mound. It felt the size of a hen's egg. The sensation brought his brain back into the moment. "The boar!"

"Dead, lying not six paces behind you."

Slowly, Sihtric twisted his neck round. The animal lay on its side, his spear still embedded within its flesh, Around the horrific wound, a pool of blood had gathered which, even now, still seeped into the mossy ground.

"By God, but he was a big bugger. I thought he was never going to die. You are unharmed, Ulf?"

The boy nodded; his face was still ashen in shock.

"Well, praise God for that. I know not what I would have done had anything happened to you. At least now I no longer have to worry on that score. But I was wrong to leave you on your own, lad. For that, I apologise. It will not happen again."

Before Ulf could respond, however, the most unexpected thing happened. With a sudden flapping of wings, the missing merlin alighted upon the boar's back, drawn to the scent of the fresh kill.

"Quick, Ulf. Grab the sodding bird."

***

Dusk was falling when the two ponies plodded their way back through Hoctune's main gate. The pace had been slowed by the burden of the boar's carcass which the two sturdy little mounts had dragged behind them from a length of rope that Sihtric had borrowed from a nearby farmer. He had not been inclined to leave a perfectly good prize behind. Though the meat might not be all that succulent - the animal being past its best years - it would still feed a good number of mouths for several days to come.

Ulf was almost asleep in his saddle; his head had been lolling forward for the last half mile or so. And Sihtric was not far behind if truth be told. It had been a long day in the sun, and he wished for nothing more than to dunk his head in a cold barrel of water before collapsing on to his cot. The boar could wait until morning; it wasn't going anywhere, after all.

"What time do you call this?" Having spotted their arrival, Freya had come out to greet them, hands on hips, bristling with indignation. "Because you're so late, I've had to make something other than rabbit stew for the jarl. God only knows what he thought. And-"

"My love," Sihtric began. "It was not of our doing."

"Sihtric almost died," Ulf blurted out, unable to contain himself.

That's not going to help, Sihtric sighed to himself as he dismounted wearily. He turned to face his wife, shrugging ruefully as he did so.

"Oh, did he now? Is that why you're so late, husband? You've been messing about playing warriors with Ulf instead of remembering your chores."

"No, Freya. Sihtric saved my life. It was a huge boar; the biggest I've ever seen. Look, we've brought it back with us."

"What's this? Saved your life?"

Sihtric swallowed hard. He had hoped to speak to Bjarke later once he had composed his thoughts and worked out how best to relay the events of the day. There was no hope of that now, though he did still hope to keep any mention of leaving Ulf on his own out of the story.

"Well, Sihtric? Would you make me wait much longer? Ulf was in your care today, and I would know to what danger you brought him."

"Well met, Lord. I am happy to see you returned safely to your hearth."

Bjarke nodded his acknowledgement of the welcome, but it was clear that he was growing impatient, so Sihtric continued.

"An afternoon spent hunting for rabbit with the merlins, Lord. All was well until the male slipped his jesses and took off for the woods. In searching for it, we were unfortunate enough to disturb this boar," he waved his hand towards the gnarled body, "but - thanks be to God - I was its equal."

Bjarke strode over to inspect the carcass more closely, rubbing his bearded chin as he bent over the beast. "By the saints, but that is a size. I doubt I have seen one larger, not on these shores. Would that I had been with you; it would have made fine sport, I daresay."

Bjarke paced back over to where Sihtric stood and put an arm around his shoulders. "Come, Sihtric. Come share a cup of ale with me. I would hear the tale and relive the thrill of the hunt with you. Ulf, to bed with you."

The two men strode off towards the lord's hall, Sihtric trying not to smile too much for the sake of appearances at least, happy that once again he had avoided rebuke. He could not resist, however, stealing a glance in Freya's direction as he passed, only to see her - hands still on hips - shaking her head in apparent disbelief. *I have more lives than Odin, the cat,* he chuckled to himself. *That's the second time today I've survived the fray.*

SIX

The leaves on the trees that surrounded Bjarke's sprawling village turned slowly from green through gold to brown before finally falling to the ground when plucked from the branches by brisk autumnal winds. During this time, the people of Hoctune busied themselves for long, arduous hours from sun up 'til sun down, gathering in the harvest from the surrounding fields. Men and women, young and old alike, worked side by side scything, packing and loading the wheat, barley and oats into row upon row of rickety wooden wains.

As steward of the village, Sihtric's task was to oversee the unloading of the wains' cargo into the granaries once they arrived back at Bjarke's hall. Ancient custom dictated that the lord stored the entire grain stock - in secure wooden huts, raised on short stilts to keep them dry and to deter rats - on behalf of all the villagers. For, in years when the harvest was poor, it was essential that supplies were managed carefully so that they could be eked out slowly and evenly. Only in that way would none starve. In the worst years, armed warriors would be posted by the doors, day and night, to prevent the most desperate from being tempted to take more than their share.

But hunger would not a problem this year, Sihtric surmised. With several days' work still to go, more than half of the storage space was already full. At the same time, the shepherds and herdsmen were busy preparing their livestock - those that were not needed for milk or to sire the following season's herd - for slaughter. In the Saxon tongue, the name of the month - Blodmonath - reflected the practice. For these were the days when, as winter approached, the bloodletting took place.

It was a time of year that Sihtric hated; the stench of the blood and the cries of the beasts as they smelled their approaching death, filled his soul with misery. He would glad when it was all over. When the blood had been sluiced away and fresh straw lain down once more in the slaughterhouses and when the carcasses had been hung from iron hooks set into the heavy oak cross beams to cure. Some would be eaten over the coming weeks - including the best of the bullocks. That beast would form the centre piece of the great harvest feast in praise of Almighty God, thanking Him for the bounty he had provided. The rest would be butchered before being packed into huge barrels of salt to preserve the meat.

While Sihtric laboured in the granaries, Freya was helping to prepare the great fire, over which the slaughtered bullock would be roasted, its flesh turned on an iron spit for several hours by a couple of kitchen boys whose reward would be a choice cut off of the beast's rump. Large rocks had been placed in a circle between the hall and the church, in the middle of which a small mound of kindling and straw had been carefully constructed. This would be used to start the fire, after which much larger logs would be placed across the top until the fire was burning fiercely and in no danger of going out. Vast piles of seasoned timber had been gathered to one side, ready to be fed into the blaze during the course of the afternoon. Thankfully, the weather promised to be dry with little or no breeze. It would be chilly, no doubt, as the sun went down, but the flames would see to that.

As the next convoy of carts rumbled through the gates, Sihtric wondered whether Thorgunnr would make an appearance. It was expected, of course, that the lady of the village would join in the feast, bestowing small gifts on the worthiest children. But who knew with the raven-haired mistress? She was ever a law unto herself and was rarely more than fleetingly involved with the lives of the ordinary folk. To Sihtric's mind, she believed herself to be above them, as if they were somehow not worthy of her time. Perhaps now, however, as she grew closer to motherhood, she might mellow. Perhaps she would feel more of a connection with the other woman-folk, some of whom were now also with child?

He presumed Thorgunnr must be close to her time now. The bump she carried in front of her could surely not grow any larger without bursting her stomach wide open. But Freya swore she had another three or four weeks to go. And his wife was rarely wrong with these things, he would be the first to admit. It was going to be a race to see which came first: Thorgunnr's child or the feast of Christ's nativity.

An uneasy truce had formed between the two women. Freya had reconciled herself to what she must do, but only through her respect for Bjarke. He was their lord, after all, she'd said, and they owed him for the shelter and protection he provided. It was her duty to do his bidding in return, however distasteful it might be. Though she might not stand in the shieldwall like her husband, there were other ways in which she could serve Bjarke, just as well. For Thorgunnr's part, though she would never admit it, it was plain that she was anxious for her well-being. Wealth and station were no shield to the dangers of childbirth and if she had to swallow her pride to make use of the most skilled woman in the area, then so be it. Either way, Sihtric was pleased, for the mood in his little hut was less toxic than it had been for some time.

It was Ulf he feared for most, though. The boy had become more and more withdrawn with every passing week. It didn't help that his father paid him little heed. If Bjarke was not elsewhere in his earldom, holding court, settling disputes, or enforcing Knut's laws, then all his time was spent with his wife. It was understandable, really. Bjarke had lost his first wife - his beloved Eadgifu - when Ulf had been born, so it was no great mystery that he might fear history repeating itself. Though there was little the jarl could do that was of any practical value, it clearly salved his fears to spend every waking moment tending to her needs.

None of that mattered to Ulf, though. For him, he had lost a mother he had never known, his stepmother hated him and now his father, the one crutch on which he might hope to lean, had seemingly abandoned him in favour of a child that had not yet been born. It was no wonder that the lad was morose. They had not hunted since that late summer's day when they had killed the boar; and only rarely had they even fished in the nearby river. Many was the hour they had spent on its banks in the past, but now the fishing rods did little but gather dust where they were propped in the corner of Sihtric's hut.

He still saw Ulf several times a week, though, but only for

the purpose of continuing his lessons with sword, spear and shield. Even so, the old warrior could see the boy's heart was not in it. He tried to make it as interesting as he could - regaling the lad with tales of bravery and skill from battles in which he had fought - but nothing seemed to be able to break through the barricades Ulf had erected around himself. There were few shieldwalls more effective, Sihtric mused, than the one you raise up around your own mind. At times, it was all he could do not to lose his temper with the boy; and on occasion he failed even that basic task, before quickly stepping back lest he say or do anything he might come to regret.

He could not deny he cared for the boy; no less so than if he had been his own son. It pained him greatly to see Ulf like this, even more so that his father seemed not to care for the boy's plight. Thorgunnr, he knew, would never warm to Ulf. If anything, her antipathy would only become worse should she be delivered of a son in the coming weeks. For if that came to pass, then she would know that her own son would inherit nothing, none of the land, the rents, or the tithes on the mills and rivers. None of it. It would all go to Bjarke's first born son. To Ulf. Who knew how much greater her enmity would be then?

But none of that mattered. There was nothing she could do to change how things stood. As long as Ulf lived, he would be jarl after his father. Nevertheless, as Sihtric bolted the granary door after the last of the wains had been unloaded for the day, he resolved to speak to Bjarke as soon as the opportunity presented itself. He owed it to the boy to speak on his behalf. Whether it would do any good, however, remained to be seen.

***

The hoped-for chance came that night once the last of the roasted bullock had been consumed and the people of Hoctune sat drinking and telling tales around the great fire. Old Abbot Ethelstan had led the prayers, extolling God's munificence and giving thanks now that the harvest had been safely gathered in. But now the old man was deep in his cups, his head resting on his forearms on the trestle table that had been set up for the jarl, his lady and their household. The sound of his snoring carried even as far as Sihtric where he sat with Freya on the other side of the blaze. Thorgunnr had retired early, citing exhaustion, and so Jark Bjarke had taken to wandering amongst the villagers, swapping a few words here and there.

"Well met, Sihtric. I trust you have been fed and watered to your satisfaction."

Sihtric pushed himself to his feet, unable to contain an audible grunt as he did so. "Aye, Lord. That was a rare piece of beef, was it not? I've not tasted finer for many a year."

"And compliments to your wife for that. It was cooked to perfection."

Bjarke made to move on to the next group, but Sihtric tugged him back by his sleeve. "Lord, I would seek a few words with you to discuss a delicate matter."

A frown passed over the jarl's face making Sihtric wonder if he might have already guessed what was on his mind. No matter, he would say what had to be said, regardless. Battles were not won by standing idle on the side-lines.

"You may speak openly with me, friend. The water of many years has flowed between us; your counsel is always valued."

"Long may that be so, Lord. I am ever grateful for it." Sihtric stepped away from the circle around the fire and into the gloom, making Bjarke follow him until they were out of earshot. He shivered for it was immediately much colder away from the burning logs.

"Why all this mummery, Sihtric? What would you have of me?" There was mirth in the jarl's voice, though his eyes gave warning to his thoughts.

Sihtric swallowed, his ears full of the sound of logs crackling and people gossiping. He resolved to delay no longer. "It is Ulf, Lord."

"What of him? What has he done now? If he has been filling Abbot Ethelstan's boots with sheep shit once again, I'll…"

"No, Lord. It's not what he's done - more what you have not done."

The jarl's tone was stark "Your meaning?"

There was no holding back now. "I fear he founders for want of your hand to guide him, Lord. He was never the most joyful of souls - the responsibility of being your heir weighs heavy on his shoulders - but even for him, his mood is worse than ever right now. I have no skill in the art of fatherhood, but I can only say what I see; he pines for your affection. Even if you were to correct him from time to time, just so long as he knows he has your eye." Sihtric paused, afraid he had gone too far. "But then, I am not his father, as I say. Forgive me, Lord. I but care for the boy."

"You're right. You're not his father…" Bjarke bit off his outburst almost as soon as he had uttered it, perhaps in doing so, unwittingly acknowledging the truth in at least some of what his old shieldsman had said.

Then the jarl sighed and slumped down heavily on a nearby bale of straw, gesturing for Sihtric to join him. "Your pardon, my friend. I should not have raised my voice to you. I know you care deeply for the boy. Indeed, in many ways you are the father I fail to be. I lack the patience needed to guide a son to succeed his father, but I know I must look beyond that and do better for him. Perhaps once Thorgunnr is delivered of our child, things will improve…"

He sighed once again. "What little time I have when I am here is eaten up by her demands of me… She is scared, Sihtric. I know your wife tends to her, reassures her that all will be well, but I see it in her eyes. She's too proud to say anything, but I know. Until the baby is born, there is little more I can do. You do understand, don't you?"

Sihtric stared deep into his lord's eyes. Though it was dark where they sat, the light cast by the still raging fire reflected in them, showing that they glistened with newly formed tears. The old warrior swallowed, fearful of allowing his own emotions to take hold of him. Instead, he reached out to grasp Bjarke's forearm with his own calloused hand. He squeezed to show his support in a gesture he knew he could never repeat in front of others. He felt, however, that their many years spent fighting shoulder to shoulder had earned him the right.

"I do, Lord. I have not even a tenth of the responsibility that your shoulders carry so I can only imagine how heavy the burden lies. Will you do me one favour though?"

"Name it, friend."

"Find time to speak to Ulf. If only for a few moments. To know that you still care for him will ease his mind, I'm sure."

Bjarke nodded, the movement of his head enough to dislodge the tear that had gathered in the corner of his eye. Unchecked, it picked a path down his cheek until it found refuge within his beard.

SEVEN

"Freya, come quick. It's the lady's time."

Freya opened one eye, vaguely aware of someone standing by her cot, shaking her by the shoulder. It was still dark, but by the glow of the small candle held in the visitor's left hand, she could just make out that the features belonged to Gisla, one of Thorgunnr's maidservants who had accompanied her from Danmark. The thickly accented words had been enough of a clue, though.

She was a small woman - not much more than a girl in both age and stature with a frame that was not far off skeletal. Unusually for any woman Freya had ever known, she wore her shockingly blond hair short, almost cropped to the scalp. Without any long tresses to frame her face, it only served to draw attention to her striking features; razor sharp cheek bones that were separated by a nose that would have looked at home on an eagle. It shouldn't have worked, but Freya could not help but admit she had a beauty all of her own, unlike any other. Stark but mesmerising, nonetheless.

Yawning, Freya pushed herself up into a sitting position, careful not to wake her gently snoring husband beside her. "What time is it? She whispered, rubbing at her eyes to clear away the last vestiges of sleep.

"I'd say it is an hour or two before dawn. Hurry, Freya, the lady is in great discomfort."

Freya groaned. Every new mother was the same, unprepared for the pain that accompanied the birth of a child. Few had seen Lady Thorgunnr in the last four weeks since the harvest feast, though this was not unusual. As their time drew near, most women of station would take to their chambers to lie in, waiting for the baby to come. It was a luxury that most working women could not afford, especially at harvesting or sowing time. Their families could not do without their help in the fields for such a prolonged period.

A sudden pang of guilt made her catch herself. She

remembered her promise to Bjarke to see his wife safely through this time. *Besides,* she reminded herself, *she is a woman like any other; she will be scared and in need of support.*

"Right, Gisla. I will be there presently. Be sure to have the churls start the fires and have several pots of water boiling as quickly as they can."

The maid turned to go. "Oh, and clean linen. As much as you can find."

It was still dark when Freya followed Gisla outside. Sihtric had stirred but she had urged him to go back to sleep once she had explained what was happening. If Thorgunnr was anything like most new mothers, it would be several hours before it was over. And in that time, there would be much pain, blood, piss and shit before the first cries of the new-born would be heard. As she hurried across the hard-packed frost-bitten ground, she prayed aloud that God would keep mother and child safe, her breath clouding the air in front of her. However much she might dislike the woman, she could not wish ill on her at this time.

Pulling open the door to Bjarke's hall, she was struck by how busy it was within. Despite the early hour, several of the villagers had already arrived. The birth of the lord's child was a big event for the people of Hoctune and word had spread fast by the looks of it. Up by the lord's bench, in the middle of the raised dais, she spied the jarl, deep in conversation with Abbot Ethelstan. Of course, the old priest would be here, Freya smiled. Bjarke would have summoned him to say prayers over his wife; though whether Thorgunnr appreciated his presence was open to question. It was no secret that she still cleaved to the old ways.

"Ah, Freya. Your presence here is a blessing." A hush fell over the room as Freya, carrying her old leather satchel over her right shoulder, made her way forward to where Hoctune's lord waited for her.

"Lord," she curtsied briefly. "I trust the day finds you and the Lady Thorgunnr well?"

"Well enough, thank you, but I shall be much happier once this business is done."

"With God's blessing, all will be well, Lord."

"With you by her side, I have no doubt, Freya. You and your husband shall have a seat at my table for the feast of Christ's nativity next week as a token of my gratitude."

"I'm honoured, Lord. But if it pleases you, I should be about my work." No sooner had she spoken, than a scream echoed through the hall, coming from the sleeping chambers that were screened off from the rest of the building, behind the dais. Despite the gloom, Freya saw Bjarke blanche, a not untypical reaction for any expectant father, in her experience.

"Fear not, Lord. It is natural for a mother to experience great pain at these times. It is no cause for concern. Allow me to go to her."

She made to move away, but Ethelstan moved into her path. She had forgotten the priest also had his duties.

Ethelstan made the sign of the cross over her. "I grant that God gives you his blessings this day, Freya. May He guide your hand and help you watch over both mother and child."

Freya bowed her head. "Amen, Father."

Then Ethelstan held out his leather-bound bible, inviting her to place her hand on its worn, dog-eared cover. "Freya, do you swear, by Almighty God, on this holy book, that you shall remove nothing from the chamber that pertains to the body of the Lady Thorgunnr?"

It was all she could do not to roll her eyes. You'd think by now, after having assisted in so many births over the years, that she could be trusted. But she knew it was pointless to protest. The church had its fears - however irrational she might think them to be - and it had its rules with which it dealt with them. Frankly, there was more chance of Thorgunnr being a witch than her, and she was hardly likely to use her own blood or afterbirth against herself, was she?

With a barely audible sigh, she made the sign of the cross before reaching out to lay her palm on the book. "I do so swear, Lord Abbot."

Satisfied, Ethelstan nodded and stood aside to allow her to pass.

Impatiently, Freya pushed aside the cloth screen that hung across the entrance to the lord's chamber and immediately gagged. The air within was stale; foul and fetid from having been too long enclosed. She saw that the few windows within had been covered with thick woollen drapes so that the smoke arising from the plethora of candles had nowhere to go. Their acrid tang caused her to cough as she breathed in.

"For the love of the Virgin Mary, let in some air. This room is not fit for a dog to birth a litter of pups, let alone the lady of a great lord."

Despite Freya's outburst, Gisla did not rise from her position by Thorgunnr's side. Her piercing blue eyes flashed defiance. "Is it not custom to shut the mother off from the outside world? Should we not prevent evil spirits or bad humours from invading her when she is at her most vulnerable?"

Freya sighed. "Yes, but there are limits, girl. At least uncover the top window there," she pointed above Thorgunnr's head to where a small opening had been cut into the wall about head height above the cot. "The lady needs clean air to breathe, else she will suffocate."

Sullenly, Gisla rose to do her bidding. Freya knew she'd have to watch the girl. If things went badly, she didn't want to have to manage the maidservant as well. It would be a time for clarity of instruction, a time when pleases and thank yous would have to wait. When the blood flowed and the screaming started, there had to be one voice that remained calm and commanding.

Just then, Thorgunnr began to moan once again. It began quietly at first but soon rose to a howling crescendo as the pain took hold of her body. Though the chamber was not unduly warm, Bjarke's wife was bathed in sweat, soaking her thin linen shift so that her distended belly shone through the sodden material. Her eyes were shot with blood through the force of her straining. While her right hand gripped tightly on to the wooden rail that formed the side of the cot, her left grasped the amulet that hung around her neck. Normally hidden beneath her clothing, Freya noted the small piece of iron was fashioned in the shape of a hammer. *So much for her claims to follow the one God,* Freya mused.

"Can't you help her, Freya?" The fear in Gisla's voice resonated around the small room. She was young and inexperienced in matters of childbirth; Freya doubted she would have attended one before now. She would not understand that there was nothing here that was out of the ordinary. Still, Freya knew it would pay to keep Gisla busy, to keep her distracted so that her anxiety did not make matters worse for her mistress.

"Fetch a fresh bowl of cool water, Gisla. And strips of clean linen too, if you please. Then use the cloth, soaked in the water, to mop the lady's face. It will bring her relief between the quickenings. Then, when you have done that, boil some water into which you must add finely chopped parsnips and a little honey. The broth will help ease the pain."

With Gisla sent scurrying from the room, Freya was left in peace to begin the important work of preparing Thorgunnr for the birth. In all this time, she realised she had not yet exchanged one word with her. She cursed herself for her oversight, hoping it would not further sour things between them.

"Blessings be upon you, Lady. I hope I find you in good spirits?"

Thorgunnr's eyes narrowed as she spat her reply. "Does it sound as though I am?" But then, almost immediately, the irritation passed as the pain subsided.

"Your pardon, Freya. The hurt is unlike anything I have experienced before."

Freya nodded. A simple acknowledgement of the apology offered and nothing more. "The quickenings, are they becoming more intense, more frequent? For how long have they been happening?"

"I first felt something odd as I was settling down to sleep last night, but I thought nothing of it; I have had many odd sensations these last weeks, especially if I eat too much cheese. But then the pain woke me a short while later and it's been getting steadily worse ever since. The candle," she nodded to the one standing on the small wooden table by her bed, "has burned down three fingers' breadth in that time."

"Hmmm. If you'll pardon me, Lady, I must examine you to see how soon the baby will come. Do not worry, there will be no pain, I will just take a look."

Before Thorgunnr could object, Freya squatted down on her

haunches and lifted the hem of the damp linen night dress. "Raise your knees please, Lady, and open your legs."

***

Sihtric stumbled into the hall, rubbing his eyes and yawning. He had woken around dawn with the usual sudden and insistent urge to empty his bladder, noticing as he pissed into the clay pot that he kept under his side of the cot, that his wife was not by his side. He had a vague memory of a few snatched words during the night and her rising to leave, but he had assumed that was just part of some dream.

But as the feeling of relief flooded through him and his mind slowly began to focus, he remembered Freya had gone to attend to Thorgunnr. So, rather than go back to sleep, he had decided to go to Bjarke's hall. He knew he would not be allowed into the birthing room - he had no desire to, anyway - and he doubted whether he would be much use to anyone, but it felt like the right thing to do. Perhaps the jarl would have need of him in some way, while he waited for news of the baby.

"Greetings, Sihtric. You've come to welcome my child into the world?" Bjarke hailed him with a grin almost as wide as his face. The Lord of Hoctune showed little sign of fatigue; he was almost bouncing off the walls, such was his fevered state of excitement.

"Aye, Lord. It promises to be a happy day for you and Thorgunnr."

"A happy day for all Hoctune, my friend. And with your good-wife by her side, I have no doubt that mother and child shall be delivered safely from this ordeal. This year the feast of the nativity shall be like no other that has been known in these parts as we will celebrate the birth of two infants."

Abbot Ethelstan, looked askance at the jarl, raising an eyebrow as he did so, perhaps wondering if comparing the birth of Bjarke's second child with that of the Saviour was in some way heretical. He chose to say nothing though, instead turning his smiling countenance upon the steward.

"Blessings be upon you, Sihtric. It is God's work that your wife does. I look forward to baptising the child into the church."

"Hopefully not for a few days, though," Bjarke chided.

Sihtric smiled. He knew the reason Ethelstan lingered in the hall. If all was well, the child would be baptised in church on the next available Sunday - some four days hence. But were the child to be born still, or to die soon after, then the abbot would be on hand to perform the rites immediately. It was important that the child was welcomed into the faith as soon as possible, lest it be condemned to wander the murky world between heaven and earth for eternity.

Ethelstan chuckled nervously. "My thoughts exactly, Lord. We shall celebrate with a full church this Sunday."

Just then, Gisla ran into the hall from the direction of the bed chamber, her face flushed and a wild look in her eyes.

Bjarke flinched before reaching out to grab her as she hurried past, almost oblivious of her surroundings. He must have been desperate for news as it was some hours since Freya had disappeared into the chamber with no word coming forth, save for the periodic wailings of a woman in pain.

"Whoa, Gisla, you look like a startled rabbit. What news is there from within?"

Though the jarl smiled to put Thorgunnr's maidservant at her ease, Sihtric could see the strain behind his eyes, a mixture of exhaustion and worry.

Gisla was breathless in her response. "She is close now… the Lady Thorgunnr. Freya says she can see the baby's head …"

"And all goes well?"

"As far as I know, Lord. Freya is calm and assured in all that she does. There is no panic."

"The Lord be praised for these glad tidings. Now, be about your work, Gisla."

"Well, my friends," Bjarke continued once she had gone, "It seems I shall shortly be a father once again." He then turned to a waiting churl. "Fetch Ulf to me, so that he may greet his new sibling. And fetch ale, too," he shouted at the servant's disappearing back. "For we have much to celebrate."

***

Back in the chamber, Freya was concerned, but not unduly so. The child was taking a long time to arrive, and she was worried that Thorgunnr was becoming too tired to go on. She had known some babies to take even longer; she remembered one mother had taken a whole day - from sunset to sunset - so she was not overly anxious just yet. Not even half a day has passed since she entered the birthing chamber; the weak wintry sun still shone through the window, though it had now begun its slide towards the horizon. Besides, Thorgunnr was young. And strong and healthy due to a diet that was better than many could afford. She stood a better chance than most.

Checking once more - for what must have been the fifth or sixth time in the last hour - she could see a little more of the crown of the baby's head. With every quickening, the baby pushed a little closer to the world; it surely could not be much longer now? Much of the danger had passed and she could do little more than keep the lady's strength up; for which purpose she had dispatched Gisla to bring more of the honeyed parsnip broth from the kitchens. She hoped that the food would replenish Thorgunnr's strength long enough for her to finish her trial.

Thorgunnr's body began to tense again, heralding the fast-approaching next quickening; they were coming with ever increasing regularity now. Her eyes snapped open, her expression a rictus of pain and fear as she sought for confirmation of Freya's reassuring presence. Then her mouth opened, emitting a shriek that seemed to go on without end. As she screamed, so she arched her back, lifting her abdomen high above the cot, whilst seizing great handfuls of the bedding in her fists. Finally, as the suffering abated, she slumped back down, her voice not much more than a whimper. "Make it stop. I can't take any more."

Freya reached out to hold Thorgunnr's hand. "The race is almost run, Lady. The baby's head grows ever more visible; it won't be much longer now. Just a little more effort." Despite her enmity towards the woman, Freya could not prevent feelings of empathy coming to the fore. She saw the woman first and the personality second. She knew how frightened Thorgunnr must be, how exhausted she was. And in that time, she could not bring herself to hate the woman.

"But I am so tired. I have nothing left to give."

"Nonsense," Freya barked at her, using the tone she reserved for those mothers who might otherwise choose to give up in the face of such adversity. "Unless you finish the job, the baby will not live. Now then," she broke off as Gisla returned to the room carrying a steaming bowl of broth, "Set that down over there, Gisla, and help me move the lady onto her hands and knees for the final push."

Together they succeeded in repositioning Thorgunnr onto all fours. She had seen countless sheep, pigs and horses born this way, so it stood to reason that it would work well for women too. She instructed Gisla to kneel by her mistress's side where she could massage her back to help ease the discomfort, whilst she lifted the hem of Thorgunnr's shift, pushing it up over her hips in readiness for the last few shoves. She was just in time, as the young woman began, once again, to thrash and moan as the next wave engulfed her.

"That's it, Lady. Push now; push the baby out. The head is almost free."

Freya positioned herself between Thorgunnr's legs, using her hands to cup the sides of the baby's skull as it emerged. "Well done, Lady, you're nearly done. The hard part is over now; one more push and all will be well."

Moments later, it was over, and Freya held in her hands the fragile form of a new-born baby boy, its pale, almost bluish skin obscured by a thin film of blood and mucus. Thorgunnr had collapsed face forward onto the bed, a spent force, while Gisla stared open-mouthed at the tiny bundle in Freya's arms. Freya knew from experience that she could not relax, though. Not until she had heard the baby cry as that would mean it was able to breath on its own. She had to move fast.

"Quick, girl. Cut the cord, as I showed you."

Used to following commands, Gisla jumped up off the bed and grabbed the knife which had been cleaned and sharpened for this moment. Holding the blade as delicately as she could, Gisla then severed the cord as close to the child's belly as she dared before standing back, her face ashen with worry.

Freya then dug two fingers into the baby's mouth, scooping out the goo from within so that the airway would not be blocked.

Finally, she took tight hold of both legs below the knee and held the baby upside down, whereupon - much to Gisla's shock - she slapped its backside sharply. Almost immediately, the child choked briefly, sucked in a great gulp of air and began to scream with indignation.

Freya finally allowed herself a smile. Another baby had been delivered safely. Whether he survived to adulthood was out of her hands - that would be God's will alone - but her work was done for now. She offered a silent prayer of thanks to the Virgin Mary for having watched over them all, before handing the child to Gisla with orders to wipe off the rest of the mess before wrapping him in clean swaddling clothes. Then she turned to Thorgunnr who had not moved or spoken since the birth.

"Lady, you have a son as healthy as could be hoped for. Now, let's have you cleaned up so that you make take the child to your breast."

Thorgunnr groaned but allowed Freya to remove the sweat-soaked, blood-stained shift which she then bundled into a ball before throwing it into the corner. Along with the sheets from the cot and the afterbirth when it appeared, it would all be burned so that nothing might fall into the hands of any who might wish the mother or child evil. A nonsense superstition, to Freya's mind, but one that had lasted through the ages despite the teachings of the church. As she dressed Thorgunnr in a clean, light blue dress, Freya noted approvingly that her breasts were heavy with milk; at least the child would not go hungry.

While Gisla handed the child to Thorgunnr, Freya went back into the hall to inform Bjarke. She found him seated at a bench along with Abbot Ethelstan and her husband. All three looked pale and haggard, taking it in turns to yawn into their cups of ale. At the sound of her footsteps, the jarl jumped to his feet, displacing his cup as he did so. The pale liquid ran down the myriad grooves and runnels in the grain of the oak tabletop before dripping, ignored, onto the cold stone flags where it pooled in the many shallow undulations on the surface.

"What news, Freya? I cannot wait a moment longer to know; my heart will not take it."

Freya smiled. "You have a fine new son, Lord. A brother for

Ulf. And your wife is well too. Even now, she sits up in bed with the bairn at her breast."

Bjarke bounded over to where Freya stood, wiping the palms of her hands against her stained dress. He wrapped his huge arms around her, pressing her to his chest. "Praise God and all His saints, Freya. I am indebted to you for the skill and care that you have shown them both."

He released her from the crushing embrace and began to move towards the chamber before halting, suddenly. "Er… may I go in now? Is it … er… safe?"

Freya smiled. "It is and you may, Lord."

EIGHT

The winter months passed by in a blur. First the winds came, then the rains, until the rain was replaced by snow, blown by the wind into thick drifts piled high – at times almost as high as the eaves – against Hoctune's many wooden buildings. It was a cold winter, a harsh winter, that year; the sixth in the reign of Knut. It was a winter unlike any other that the villagers could recall in those lands.

Sihtric lost track of how many times he was called upon to help clear snow and ice away from doors and pathways so that folk could be about their business in safety. Each time he thought the worst of the weather had passed, the sky turned leaden grey once again before dumping another thick white blanket over the land.

But despite everything, people were happy. There was plenty of food, for the harvest had been good. The stock of seasoned logs for the fires was plentiful so they wanted not for warmth, either. And on top of everything, the jarl had a new son, a source of great joy and rejoicing in the community. Each day, the women hoped for a glimpse of the boy to see how he grew, the fairness of his complexion and the colour of his hair. The latter was a source of much speculation in view of the lord's fiery mane contrasted with his wife's raven-black hair. But, on the first Sunday after the nativity, when the whole community squeezed into the freezing stone church for the babe's Christening, it seemed as if the mother had won the contest as those wisps of hair that were visible sprouting from the edges of the white linen cap, were more in keeping with her hue than his. It was on that day that the boy was named Erik, a well-chosen name that meant ruler of all in the old tongue.

Later that same day, back in the privacy of their own home, Freya had confided in her husband that she had seen Thorgunnr's hammer amulet around her neck on the day of Erik Bjarkesson's birth. Though Thorgunnr had, of course, been present at the baptism, it was plain that the jarl's wife was not a true Christian. What's more, she wondered whether Bjarke knew of her amulet. Sihtric had nodded but chosen to keep his own counsel. He owned a similar symbol - a small piece of iron in the shape of a crude hammer that he had worn smooth through constant handling. He remembered being given it as a lad by his uncle, his face a mask of solemnity, with a whispered exhortation to always keep it close to his body if he wanted Thunor to protect him from evil. The boy of no more than six summers had nodded, open-mouthed in awe, eyes as big and as round as the wooden platters from which they ate.

Though he had long since stopped wearing it, he still had it somewhere in the depths of the old wooden chest he kept at the end of their bed, wrapped in his old mailshirt. Every now and then, he would take out the heavy shirt, made up of hundreds - if not thousands - of tiny iron rings, sewn together on a leather backing. Though he did not expect to wear it ever again, he could not break the habit of checking it for rust, scraping away any spots he might find and re-oiling it painstakingly, before replacing it in its cloth sack. Good warriors knew the importance of keeping your mailshirt in good condition. He knew it was a ritual he would continue until his dying day. And each time he did so, the little amulet would fall out into his lap, where he would stare at it for a moment before putting it to one side until it was time to be hidden away once again.

But not everyone was content. Bjarke's first son was anything but happy in those early weeks of the new year. Even though Sihtric had raised his concerns with his lord on the night of the harvest feast, it seemed that Bjarke had less time than ever for Ulf now. Such was his neglect that the older boy took to spending long hours - when he wasn't at his lessons with Ethelstan - in Sihtric's house or following him about like a shadow wherever he went. Sihtric told himself he was glad of the help; there was much to do around Hoctune after all. The winter was a time for repair and replenishment; all the little jobs for which they had been too busy during the growing season were stored up for when the ground was too hard or too wet to work. So, there was no shortage of jobs to be done and Ulf, for his part, was a willing helper.

But, in his heart, Sihtric knew he was ignoring what was as

plain as the bulbous, red-veined nose on his face. Since Erik's arrival - and probably since Thorgunnr's if he were honest - Ulf had been slowly, but very deliberately, pushed to one side. Sihtric doubted it was all the jarl's fault, though. Bjarke was often away on Knut's orders and even when he was in Hoctune, there were so many competing demands on his time. But he did seem blind to the needs of his first-born son or, perhaps, he thought that he was well taken care of between Sihtric and Ethelstan. For Thorgunnr, however, he could not help but wonder whether it was her plan to drive a wedge between father and son. Though what good it would do her, he could not fathom. The fact was that, when the time came, Ulf would inherit the land and titles; for he was the eldest living heir.

And then, one spring day, everything changed.

***

It was a day much like any other. The sun was shining, its warmth tempered, though, by a chill breeze that blew from the northeast. The first blossom had returned to the apple trees in the orchard, covering their branches with a cloak of pinkish-white petals, many of which had since fallen to the ground, making it seem - from a distance at least - as if a new blanket of snow had fallen. Soon the blossom would be gone, replaced by the buds that would go on to become the fruit of this year's harvest. Sitting on a flat stone, his back propped against the narrow trunk of one of the trees, Sihtric reflected on the symmetry of it all. Each year, the same cycle began and ended without fail. It was a mystery to him; he would never understand the majesty or purpose of God's works.

Shaking his head, he made a pledge to speak to Abbot Ethelstan about it on the next occasion they met and returned instead to the job in hand. It was time to fashion new snares for the coming season. The old ones had grown weak and brittle through use and exposure to the elements; he doubted they would hold any but the feeblest rabbit. It was delicate work, though, made for fingers nimbler than his great calloused lumps. The one time he was really needed, however, Ulf was nowhere to be seen. Tying the twine to the supple willow twigs would have been easy for one whose eyes and fingers were still young and quick. So, Sihtric struggled on, cursing to himself as - yet again – the intricate knot slipped off its intended home.

So intent on his task was he, that he neither heard nor saw Freya arrive until her shadow passed over his face, blocking the dappled sun light that played over him as the branches swayed in the breeze.

"Well met, husband."

"Good day to you, wife." Sihtric shifted to his left to make room for Freya to sit by his side on the stone. They sat together in silence for a while as Sihtric tried once again to tie the little noose to the snare until, finally, Freya took it from him with a good-natured snort.

"You're all thumbs, my love. A job such as this needs a delicate touch."

Sihtric spread his hands palm upwards before him, noting the lumps and scars that told of a life spent wielding spear, sword and shield. He shrugged. "These hands were made for fouler work, wife. And very good at it they were, too, I might add. I had hoped Ulf might have come to help me, though. His hands would have made short work of it." He winked as Freya finished tying off the twine. "Well done, but there are another six to see to after that one, love" he nodded towards the small pile of twigs and twine by his side.

But, at the mention of the boy's name, he'd seen a shadow pass over Freya's face, though she sought to mask it by bending her head in concentration on the task in hand. Nonetheless, it was a look Sihtric recognised for he had seen it all too often before; usually when she was angered with him over some small offence but would not give him the satisfaction of telling him what it was. Instead, he would be expected to know what it was he had done wrong which - more often than not - was far beyond his limited understanding. He knew better than to allow the silence to fester between them, however; long years of painful experience had taught him that.

"There is something on your mind, wife. As much as I am happy to have your company, I imagine you have better things to do than to sit here with me fixing my snares. What did you come to say?"

A half smile flitted across Freya's lips before being chased away by the return of the frown, just as the sun is suddenly covered by puffy white clouds scudding across the sky. She took a moment to finish fixing the twine before placing the completed snare down on the ground. Then she turned to face him, smoothing down the creases in her woollen dress.

"I'm worried for Ulf."

"As are we both, my love. Since Erik's birth, our lord has had even less time for the boy. But God knows I have tried. I know not what more I can do that won't see me beaten for impudence or cast out of Hoctune."

"No, husband, you misunderstand me. I fear for his safety."

Sihtric paused, looking askance at Freya as if to divine some clue from her features. "How so, woman? 'Tis nought but a phase, is it not? He may never be a favourite of the Lady Thorgunnr, but Bjarke will come to his senses in time. I'm sure of it."

Freya shook her head, her eyes moistening as tears began to form. "That may be, Sihtric, but it is his wife who concerns me more."

"She would not dare harm the lad, wife. No matter how blind Bjarke may be, were anything to happen to his first-born son, he would not hesitate to deal harshly with the culprit. I'd stake my life on it."

***

Freya left her husband snoozing under the apple tree. Though she was glad she had shared her concerns with him, she was not sure she had managed to penetrate his thick skull sufficiently for him to fully appreciate the extent of her fears. But where she should have felt reassured and more at ease with herself, the nagging doubt continued to throb in her chest. She could not point to any one specific thing that had caused her fears to grow; Thorgunnr had neither done nor said anything to cause her any obvious concern. But there was something that triggered Freya's intuitive sense that all was not right.

Since Erik's birth, the jarl's wife had, consciously or otherwise, become less guarded around Freya, perhaps feeling that their shared experience had somehow formed a bond between the two women in her mind. As a token of her gratitude, she had presented the older woman with a pendant that she had sent Gisla to buy from Flemish merchants who had come up from the coast. It was a thing of beauty too, worth far more than Freya could ever afford to buy for herself. A teardrop shaped piece of amber, about the size of her thumb, which had been polished until it shone. When held up to the light, its many facets sparkled, revealing the tiny bubbles of air set within it. At its narrow end, a small hole had been drilled into the stone, through which a delicate silver chain had been threaded, so that it hung around her neck, the stone resting midway between her throat and her chest.

Handing it to her, Thorgunnr said that the stone had come from the far reaches of Norway, where it had been sculpted and burnished by craftsmen whose skills had been passed down since the days of Odin and which were unmatched in the known world. And, despite her misgivings about the woman, Freya's gratitude, and her smile as she accepted the gift, had been genuine enough.

But motherhood had changed Thorgunnr. Of that there was no doubt. No longer was she the haughty, disinterested woman who looked down on all those around her. The baby had transformed her, so that she now seemed a completely different person. Though there was no shortage of help, there was little that the Lady of Hoctune would not do for Erik. Almost every waking hour was taken feeding him, bathing him or playing with him. For most, it was a delight to see a mother so taken with her child. But Freya was unable to shake the sense of unease that had settled over her soul. At every opportunity, Thorgunnr would engage her husband in some discussion about the child or have him watch Erik's latest achievement; something which the proud father was more than happy to indulge.

Though seemingly innocent enough from the outside, Freya could not help but notice a more insidious undercurrent that accompanied such public displays. At first, she scolded herself for her mean-spirited cynicism, but by the time she had witnessed it three or four times in the feasting hall, she was more certain. For, each time Bjarke sought to speak with Ulf on some matter - however trivial - Thorgunnr was sure to interrupt with some thought, real or imagined, concerning Erik.

"Do you think he looks pale?"

"I swear I saw him smile today."

"It won't be long before he begins to crawl."

And rather than anger or otherwise offend his wife, Bjarke would turn away from Ulf to listen to her instead, oblivious to the hurt that he caused his son. The more Freya considered it as she oversaw the serving of the various courses to the family, the more she became certain in her mind that Thorgunnr - under the pretext of her own new motherhood - was seeking to driving a wedge between the jarl and his first born. It was subtle, but unmistakable, nonetheless. Ulf was being pushed to the edge of the family circle as his stepmother did all she could to focus his father's mind on nothing but her and Erik.

On one occasion, Thorgunnr caught Freya staring at her. She shivered inwardly as she recalled how the lady's face had reddened with guilt, or was it anger? She could only hope that her expression had not betrayed the sense of revulsion she had been feeling.

"Is there something troubling you, Freya?" She had smiled, fixing her with her cold green eyes.

N-no, Lady," she had stammered as she hurriedly gathered up the empty platters from in front of them. "I rejoice to see Erik so hale and rosy cheeked."

It had been a calculated deflection and it had worked to perfection. Thorgunnr had beamed with pride as Freya knew she was wont to do whenever anyone complimented her child. As she listened, nodding and smiling at the appropriate moments, she chastised herself for her carelessness. It would not do to reveal her innermost thoughts to this woman. Who knew what she might be capable of? Who knew what she might do in order to see Erik favoured ahead of Ulf?

Though Sihtric might doubt the woman's intent, Freya did not. As much as the thought horrified and appalled her, she genuinely feared that some harm might yet come to the boy. A few days later, her worst fears were confirmed.

NINE

Freya pulled open the door to Bjarke's hall, heaving against the rain and squalling wind which fought to keep the thick wooden boards firmly in place. She was already tired and irritable - the noise of the wind rushing between the roof tiles having kept her awake most of the night - without the very buildings starting to annoy her as well. It was a day for finding work to do indoors. Who in their right mind, she mused, would want to battle their way through a storm such as this? But duty is duty and she had promised to check in on Erik whom, Gisla had told her the previous evening, had been brought low by some ailment. Though she was no healer, Freya did have some small skill with such things and so, next morning, she had packed her small leather satchel and made her way through the village to the lord's hall.

She hauled the door closed behind her, making sure the wooden latch fell securely back into its bed. Her cloak was heavy, sodden with rain, though at least the close-knit woollen fibres had shielded her dress from the worst of the weather. Shrugging herself out of it, she hung it from the iron hook that protruded from one of the central posts, close to the hearth from which a welcoming heat pulsed. With luck it would be dry by the time she was ready to leave. Then she made her way towards the door at the back of the feasting hall that led to Thorgunnr's chamber. As she went, she adjusted her hair, tucking the loose damp strands that had been plucked free by the wind back under the linen coif which she had tied firmly under her chin to prevent it from being blown away.

She was on the point of pulling aside the hanging drape when she stopped. She could not be certain, but something she thought she had heard from within gave her pause. She held her breath, thinking it must be the noise of her lungs. Then she leaned forward, turning her ear so that it was pressed against the slender wall panels. Though it was muffled, she could make out the voices of Gisla and Thorgunnr.

"I know not where to find her, Lady."

"Cwenhild has her dwelling to the north of here. On the road that leads to the Abbey at Ramsey, there lies a village called Broctune. She lives in the forests to the east of that place, by the banks of the river. Go to her and bring back that which I seek."

"Yes, Lady."

With a start, Freya realised that Gisla was now leaving to do her mistress's bidding. There was no time to pull back, no time to pretend she had not been listening at the door. Her heart was beating so hard, she feared it might break free from her chest at any moment. Even should she avoid detection, she could not put what she'd heard out of her mind, and she could only pray her face did not betray that knowledge to Thorgunnr. She had no option but to brazen it out. Pushing the drape to one side with a firmness that spoke of a sense of entitlement and confidence, she came face to face with Gisla, or rather - due to her stature - Gisla came face to chest with Freya. The handmaiden uttered a tiny yelp of shock. Freya knew she had to seize the opportunity presented to her.

Dropping her bag in apparent shock, she exclaimed. "Be careful, girl. I hope for your sake nothing is broken."

"My apologies, Freya. I did not see you." Flustered, the young girl stooped to retrieve the spilled contents, returning them and the bag to Freya. "Everything seems to be in order."

"It is as well for you. Some of these salves and potions are not cheap to source." Stepping to one side, she allowed Gisla to pass. "Now, be away with you, you silly girl, before any more damage is done. And be more watchful in future," she called after her hastily retreating back.

Her composure recovered, Freya moved forward into the room, scanning Thorgunnr's face for any signs of suspicion. The dark-haired woman was sitting on the edge of the bed, her dress pulled down over one shoulder to allow Erik access to her drooping, milk-laden breast. But the child had not settled. Rather, he was grizzling bad-temperedly, his cries interspersed with angry chomping on his mother's teat.

"Ah, Freya, at last. I have need of your skills. Erik is unwell."

"What seems to be the problem, Lady?" Inwardly, she

breathed a sigh of relief; her subterfuge appeared to have worked.

A look of irritation flashed across her face, reminding Freya of Thorgunnr's more normal demeanour before Erik's birth. "How would I know, woman? It is for this reason I have sent for you. He won't sleep, he won't feed; he just seems to be angry all the time. If this goes on much longer, there will be nothing left of my teats for he will have gummed them clean off."

Despite her irritation, Freya detected a note of fear in Thorgunnr's voice. It was the same with all first-time mothers; every experience with the child was new. With no mother or older siblings at hand to explain, she must suffer in ignorance for the wont of someone as skilled as Freya to help.

"May I take him, Lady?" Freya held out her hands to scoop Erik away from his mother, taking care to secure the tiny body in the crook of her left arm so that his head nestled comfortably in the angle formed between her upper arm and her body. Free of her burden, Thorgunnr shrugged her dress back into place before pulling a thick fur shawl around her shoulders. Despite the fire that burned fiercely in its hearth, there was still a spring chill seeping through the room.

"Well?"

"Patience, Lady. Allow me at least to examine the child." It was gloomy with the chamber, hampering Freya's ability to inspect Erik properly, so she carried him over towards the window where the thin light from the watery, cloud-obscured sun did its best to illuminate his features. The poor lad's cheeks, she noted were red and angry. Though this might have been caused by the effort of the wee lad's screams, her experience told her the cause lay elsewhere. With the little finger of her right hand, she formed a v shape, the edge of which she then carefully inserted into the babe's mouth. Immediately, Erik clamped down on her finger and began to grind his gums against her soft flesh.

"See? He's hungry, but why won't he feed from my breast?"

"I'm not sure it is hunger alone that is his problem." Erik was not sucking on her finger; rather he was pressing down hard

"Ouch." She felt a sudden stab of pain from something much harder and sharper than any gum. Removing her finger, she tilted the boy's head back and gently squeezed his nose until he opened his mouth to scream once again, indignant at the rough handling to which he was being subjected. Sure enough, she glimpsed a brief flash of white on the upper half of Erik's mouth before it was obscured once more.

"I suggest you tell me, if you know what the problem is." Thorgunnr's patience was wearing thin. It was obvious she had hardly slept all night. Freya had no idea where her husband was; perhaps Erik's cries had driven him to the tavern where, even now, he still slept in an ale-fuelled haze.

Freya smiled. "It is nothing to be worried about, Lady. Your son is merely breaking his first tooth. This is known to cause babies a lot of discomfort as the teeth force their way through the soft flesh of the gum. See," she held Erik's mouth open for Thorgunnr, "the gum is inflamed. This is the source of his pain. And there," she pointed with her little finger, "you can see the first of his teeth starting to appear. In a few weeks, they will all be through, and Erik can start to eat more solid foods."

"You mean I have to endure sleepless nights for another month?"

Freya smiled. "He will not be in pain all of the time and, when he is, there are treatments you can use. Have him chew on a piece of tree root, stripped and cleaned before being soaked in a mixture of milk and honey. And for the pain, I can prepare some salves to rub on his gums that should reduce the inflammation... unless you have already asked Cwenhild for such remedies?"

The chill room seemed to turn even colder as soon as the words left her mouth. Freya cursed herself for her stupidity. So wrapped up in concern for the child's welfare had she been that she had forgotten the context in which she had overheard the old woman's name.

"Why do you mention Cwenhild?" Thorgunnr's tone was icy cold, her eyes trying to penetrate Freya's soul.

Freya was in trouble. How could she back her way out of this corner? "I... er... thought I heard Gisla saying that is where she was heading when I came in. Was that not the case, Lady?"

"It is true that I have sent Gisla to Cwenhild," her voice was like soft, glutinous honey, but no less dangerous for that. "But not for Erik. I sent her to seek help from the old woman. It is said that she keeps wolfsbane in her garden and I would have use of it."

Freya could not help herself. Wolfsbane, she knew, despite its pretty dark purple flowers could be fatal to any who ingested any part of it. She had learned much plant lore from her mother who had heard it from her own mother before her. There were few plants more deadly. But for what purpose could Thorgunnr have need of it? Her mind reeled with the very worst of thoughts.

"For what would you seek to use wolfsbane, Lady? It is a most dangerous plant if not carefully handled."

"Though I consider it to be little of your business, Freya, your good service to my family demands respect. We have a problem with rats in the hall and I seek to kill them with food soaked in a potion made from the root of the wolfsbane plant. I am told Cwenhild has the skill to distil such a potion."

Freya nodded. There were many things Cwenhild was skilled at. Actual and rumoured. Whilst she undoubtedly had some knowledge of healing, there were many that believed her to be some kind of sorcerer. Many was the time she'd heard folk speak of going to her for some remedy or other. Some sought charms for good fortune to be visited upon their crops; others looked for woe to befall those of their rivals. Some wanted potions that might help them conceive, whilst others hoped to end unwanted pregnancies. The worst of the rumours - though nothing had ever been proved - spoke of potions that could be used to end life. There were those who - in hushed tones over a cup of ale in the darkest corner of the tavern - whispered about unexplained deaths and whether Cwenhild was to blame.

But poison to kill rats? That was an honest use of wolfsbane was it not? She had used it herself on those occasions when the infestation reached such levels that even their dog, Acwel, had been unable to cope. She smiled at the irony. For one whose name meant Killer, the old hunting-hound had once backed-away whimpering from one particularly large and savage family of rodents. The wolfsbane had succeeded where Acwel had not, though she was sure to keep the mutt well apart from the place where she laid the poison. One curious lick would have been the end of him as well as the rats.

"There's nothing better than wolfsbane for rats, Lady. Be sure, though, to keep Erik and Ulf away from any place where it is used. They would perish from a single drop."

***

Walking back to the small wooden cottage that she shared with Sihtric, Freya mulled over what she had heard that day. As a story it was plausible, of course. Rats were a constant problem in Hoctune; there were few who had not - at one time or another - been plagued by the sound of feet scurrying up and down the rafters or, worse still, in amongst the storerooms where they could feast on the sacks of grain if left unchecked. Of course, you would seek a remedy to be rid of them.

So why could she not rid herself of this uneasiness that infested her soul? It had taken hold of her guts, churning them so that they felt like there was an army of worms twisting and turning within her. Even though she told herself she was being ridiculous, the feeling would still not abate. Surely to God she would not dare to do anything to harm Ulf? Thorgunnr would never risk her position and status, for Bjarke's rage would be unquenchable. As she put her hand on the latch to open the door to their home, she resolved to put it from her mind. She was allowing her thoughts to run wild, and it would not do.

TEN

"Ah, there you are, my love. I was beginning to think you had come to blows with the Lady Thorgunnr." Sihtric laughed at his own joke as Freya shrugged off her still damp cloak before stooping to rub Acwel behind the ears. Aside from stealing a meaty bone from the table, it was his most favourite thing and guaranteed to have his tail wagging faster than anything else.

"Don't be ridiculous, Sihtric. Why ever would such a thing come to pass?"

Straightaway, he could tell from the tone of her voice that all was not well. In a rare moment of intuition, however, he surmised that, for once, he was not the cause of her irritation. Whilst that pleased him on the one hand - it saved him from having to guess what he had or had not done - on the other hand, he still had to negotiate a difficult path, beset on either side by bramble thickets ready to claw and rip at his skin as he attempted to navigate to the root of her ire.

"The child, Erik, is well?"

"Well enough," Freya snorted. "The poor wretch cuts his first teeth is all. He will have discomfort for a few weeks, and she will have little sleep, but it will pass soon enough. Honestly, you'd think that she was the first and only mother to encounter such hardship. I have given her some salves and potions to help ease his pain when it is at its worst."

As she spoke the word potion, the frown reappeared on her face once again. Watching her closely from where he sat warming his aching bones close by the fire, Sihtric spotted it immediately.

"But, if not Erik, then there is something else that bothers you, my love?"

Freya sighed and settled herself into her chair on the other side of the hearth. Acwel accepted that her fussing of him was at an end and padded over to lie down in his favoured spot between the two of them, stretched out in front of the fire, his belly turned towards the warmth. Like his master, Sihtric reflected, the old boy looks less like a killer with every passing month. No doubt the old hound would remember the old ways if it were demanded of him but these days, Acwel would much rather sleep by the fire than chase rabbits. Sihtric could not blame him.

"Have you seen Ulf today?"

The question took him by surprise. He had to wrack his brains; some days he struggled to remember what he'd eaten for breakfast. "Why, yes. We spent an hour working with spear and shield and then took the rods down to the river. Reminds me, there's fresh trout for supper."

His wife smiled. Sihtric knew the fish was one of her favourite dishes. *If that doesn't help her mood, then I don't know what will,* he mused inwardly.

"And how did he seem to you?"

He shrugged. "Same as ever. I had to work harder than I should to raise a smile. I remember when I was his age, it was all mud, larks, stealing apples and fighting with my brothers. I don't know what's got into him. I mean, I do my best to be like an uncle to him but…"

Sihtric stopped himself abruptly; he realised he was rambling on, which his wife often told him was his one of his faults. The look on Freya's face told him he had already said more than enough.

"I'm worried for him."

"As am I, love, but I'm sure he will grow out of it. He studies hard and his weapons-craft develops well. I have every hope that he will make his father proud when the time comes for him to take the reins from him."

"If he makes it that far."

Sihtric furrowed his brow. "He may not be the most strapping lad in Hoctune, but he is healthy, nonetheless. Why do you worry so?"

Freya could hold back no more. As the candle burned slowly, inexorably, down to its base, the melted wax pooling in a congealed lump in the bottom of the little earthenware dish in which it stood, she proceeded to unburden herself of all she had seen and heard that day. And Sihtric knew better than to interrupt, contenting himself with nods and grunts as the tale unfolded, until she slumped against the back of her chair, drained of emotion. All thought of the trout had gone from his mind as he struggled to deal with all that he'd heard. He wanted to believe it could all be explained away but - like Freya - there was a part of him that was now filled with doubt.

"Surely, she would not dare harm Ulf. At the very least, Bjarke would put her aside. More likely he'd have her hanged. And then where would she be?"

"Dangling on the end of a rope, I shouldn't wonder. But I fear she is too canny for that, husband."

"What do you mean?"

"Well, as you say, all would be lost were she to be caught in the act of killing Ulf. If she truly intends malice toward the boy, she will find a way to mask the truth."

"But what then can we do? Should I go to the jarl with this?"

"How can we? We have no proof. Were Bjarke to confront his wife about Cwenhild and the wolfsbane, she would merely complain about the rats in the hall. He would have no reason to suspect her and, instead, he might take against us for trying to drive a wedge between them."

"What option do we have then, wife?"

"None, I fear, but to watch over Ulf as closely as we can."

Sihtric nodded, thoughtfully, scratching absentmindedly at an itch deep in his beard. "While we search for more evidence of wrongdoing on her part."

"The time for which could not be shorter."

"How so?"

"Is your head filled with rocks, husband?" The insult was good-natured but stung like a wasp all the same. "Have you forgotten that Bjarke rides for Lundenburh in two days?"

It had not slipped his mind at all. He had spent much of the last week preparing the jarl's war-gear. He'd cleaned his best mailshirt, scrubbing it for hours to remove any last traces of rust, before burnishing and oiling it until it gleamed in the sunlight. So too with his helm. He'd had to replace the nose-guard from where it had been bent beyond repair from its last use. Finally, he had spent a day sharpening the blades of his sword, war-axe and seax over and over again until they were keen enough to slice the wind in two. All so Bjarke could be ready to answer the call of the king who had summoned his many lords and their war-bands to assemble before marching north to face the Scots.

Rumours were rife that King Malcolm - the second of that name - had crossed the border into the ancient kingdom of Bernicia and was threatening the old stronghold of Bebbanburh, built high on a bluff overlooking the sea. Knut could not allow such an insult to go unanswered and so the army would march north. As one of the great lords of the kingdom, and holding the earldom of the eastern Angles, Bjarke was required to attend and to bring his warriors with him, some two hundred or more spears at last count.

But in truth, Sihtric had tried to push all thought of it from his mind, because - for the first time - he would not be going. Notwithstanding his promise to Freya, his body was no longer up to the strains of the shieldwall. It would be the first time he had not marched with his lord since he had been a beardless boy of seventeen summers and he could not pretend it did not hurt his pride to be left behind. Though he knew there would never more be a place for him in the front rank, he still longed to be going with them.

The village had been a hive of activity all week as men, dressed for war, came in from all the outlying estates. Warriors he had not seen for months - some even for years – were gathering within Hoctune's walls. He'd greeted those he knew in turn, some of whom even had their sons with them for the first time. Nervous, pale youths who looked on him with a mixture of awe when introduced by their fathers. For he was one of the old guard; one of those who had stood with Knut when he took the throne of England from Aethelraed and, after him, his son Eadmund of the Iron sides. And before that he had stood with Knut's father - Swein with the forked beard - in countless battles both here and back in their homeland of Danmark. He was one of the few who had lived through it all to reach his dotage. His reputation had been won with his blood and his sweat and was second to none.

Bjarke had seen the hurt in his face as the warriors mustered around him and had made a point of speaking to him.

"This is a sight we have seen a few times, eh? It's just like the old days, my friend."

Sihtric had sniffed. "Not quite, Lord."

Then the jarl, not much younger than him, had laid a hand on Sihtric's shoulder. "I know, my friend. Nothing would please me more than if you were standing at my shoulder in the front rank, your shield overlapping mine as it has done so many times before. But we both know that those days are passed now. The body grows weak with age; it happens to us all. Were I not jarl and expected to lead my men into battle, I too would prefer to rest here with you.

"Besides, I have need of a good man in Hoctune. A leader. One to whom the others can turn for courage and direction should the need arise. There is ever the danger of bandits who might seek to take advantage of the lord's absence. So I need someone I can trust; someone who can rally the farmers to defend their families and their villages. I know you won't fail me in this, Sihtric."

Though it had been meant well, they had both known the words were empty. The risk of bandits was minimal; there had been no raids in these parts for years. Sihtric knew he would not be called on to do anything more than keep the peace between warring neighbours. But for all that, he had not been able to find fault with Bjarke. He had seen the pain behind the smile and had known that his lord spoke the truth. If nothing else there was fate to consider; the jarl had never been defeated in battle when the two of them stood together in the shieldwall.

Sihtric had coughed to hide the emotion in his voice. "I will not fail you, Lord. You may depend on that. You will be back before too long and - God willing - will bring all of these brave warriors back with you."

Turning back to Freya, Sihtric smiled. "Ah, of course. Bjarke heads north with Knut to deal with the Scots. I had not forgotten."

Whether his wife believed his lie he could not tell, for she chose to not to speak. Sihtric knew she was right, though; with the jarl away - probably for several months - it would afford Thorgunnr the opportunity she needed, if malice were, indeed, on her mind.

ELEVEN

For the next few weeks, life continued as normal in Hoctune. The weather grew warmer as the buds returned to the trees and the new-born lambs gambolled in the pastures that surrounded the village. Spring was ever a busy time. Readying the fields for sowing was the work of many men and women over several days in normal circumstances, but with so many of the young men having gone north with Bjarke, there were fewer hands to turn to the ploughs than usual. As steward in charge of the estate, Sihtric had his hands full from dawn to dusk every day of the week, save Sundays, to see that the work was done on time.

After a few days - when it was clear how late they were running - he called upon the younger lads and lasses of the village to help. What they lacked in strength, they more than made up for with energy and enthusiasm which went a long way to compensate for the absence of their older brothers and fathers. Even Ulf was put to work, something he was pleased to do for it meant that Abbot Ethelstan had to excuse him from many of his lessons. Though the lad had not the strength or skill to guide a plough, Sihtric put him to good use running errands. There was so much to do and so many people to coordinate that he was glad of the help; it was more than he could do to keep everything in his mind.

Seeing the boy laughing as he ran from place-to-place warmed Sihtric's heart. He had not known Ulf this happy for many months and it gladdened him beyond words to witness it. Such was the scale of the transformation that, over the days and weeks that followed, he put all thought of Thorgunnr, wolfsbane and Cwenhild from his mind.

For her part, Bjarke's wife was content to leave him to run the estate; matters of agriculture held no interest for her. Nor would she ever deign to allow her fine clothes to be muddied or blackened by manual toil. In any event, she had her hands full with Erik. Though she made ample use of the remedies Freya had given her, the poor lad remained troubled by his teeth for many weeks, bringing his mother to the point of exhaustion, despite whatever Gisla could do to help alleviate the burden.

It was not until one day towards the middle of June, some time after the fields had finally been ploughed, the seeds sown, and the cattle put out to their summer pasture that everything changed. The happy idyll into which Sihtric had woven himself since Jarl Bjarke had departed with the fyrd of the eastern Angles was cruelly and irrevocably torn asunder one foul night in the midst of a thunderstorm that, in days gone by, many would have said was a sign that they had angered mighty Thunor.

***

"Careful, husband, you'll have the door off its hinges. It's not been a week since you had cause to fix it."

Sihtric winced as the already rickety wooden frame bounced off the plastered wall. As ever, she was right. The fix, as she put it, had been no more than a temporary job anyway; he really ought to find the time to replace the whole thing with new planks. She had reminded him often enough, after all.

"I'm sorry, my love, but have you seen the weather?" As if to emphasise the point, he stood there, arms stretched out to the sides, dripping from every stitch of clothing, a pool of water slowly growing around his feet. "It's as if God and all his angels are pissing on us. I'm soaked wet through just walking back from locking up the grain store."

Freya held her hands to her mouth in mock horror. "Don't let Father Wulfstan hear you speak that way. He'll have you doing a penance come Sunday."

Sihtric grunted under his breath, "Hmmmph, it was him that taught me that phrase."

Before Freya could take him to task, however, the door crashed open once again to reveal Gisla, holding a cloak over her head, but equally wet through, nonetheless.

"Thank God, I find you here, Freya. Come quickly, hurry; the mistress has need of you."

Freya was already on her feet, reaching for her cloak and healer's satchel. "What is it? Is Erik sick?"

Dumbly, with tears in her eyes, Gisla shook her head.

***

As she stumbled her way to Bjarke's hall, head bent against the wind and the rain, Freya's mind filled with all manner of awful thoughts. If it were not Erik, then what? Perhaps Thorgunnr herself was ill or had fallen. Maybe she had twisted her ankle. Dear God, let it be that. Anything other than Ulf. She prayed harder than she had ever prayed before and yet she was still filled with a terrifying sense of horror at what she would find.

She followed Gisla into the hall, pausing only to shed her sodden cloak, leaving it where it lay in a soggy heap on the straw-covered floor, her normal fastidiousness forgotten in her haste. Without waiting to see if she followed, Thorgunnr's maid headed straight for the opening in the corner of the wooden screen that separated the feasting hall from the lord's living quarters. Hurrying along the narrow corridor, Freya's heart sank as they passed by the door to Thorgunnr's chamber and stopped instead outside Ulf's room where Gisla now stood to one side, as if unwilling to enter.

Freya swallowed back down the bile that rose in her gorge. Telling herself that she would find nothing more than a mildly sick boy within, she summoned up her lost courage and went inside. A rush of cold air hit her like a slap in the face; the covers had been removed from the window above the bed, allowing the wind to swirl around the room. It took a moment for her eyes to adjust to the gloom within, but when they did, she could see the figure of Bjarke's wife sitting on the edge of Ulf's cot, hunched over the boy.

Hearing her enter, Thorgunnr stood and turned to face Freya. In the thin light coming from the wildly flickering candles in the corner of the room, she could see that the woman's face was ashen-white. Her cheeks were streaked with the tracks of her tears, mixing with the black powder which she was used around her eyes to accentuate her beauty. She must have been crying for some time as her eyes were red-rimmed and her lashes had gathered in little black spikes where the tears had moulded them together.

"Praise God you are here at last, Freya. I know not what is wrong with the boy."

Despite herself, Freya noted that she had invoked the Christian God, even though she knew that the woman yet cleaved to the old Norse gods of her fathers. *Even now, she thinks to mask the truth from me.*

"Tell me what has happened, Lady. Every detail. Leave nothing out for it all may help me to understand what treatment he needs," she paused, "if he yet lives." It occurred to her that she had not seen the boy properly, obscured as he was by Thorgunnr's thin body. Not waiting to be asked, Freya moved towards the bed, pushing Bjarke's wife aside without ceremony. She set her satchel down on the floor beside her and then knelt to examine Ulf.

"Gisla," she shouted so that she might be heard out in the corridor. "Fetch more candles so that I may see. Hurry, girl."

As she bent over the boy, Freya was aware of Thorgunnr's voice, the words only half formed and garbled as they tumbled from her mouth. *Either her shock is genuine, or she is a most convincing liar,* she thought as she listened to her tale. According to her story, all had been well until shortly after dinner when Ulf had gone to bed, complaining of a stabbing pain in his gut. She had thought nothing of it - believing a good night's sleep was all that he needed to be right again - until she had checked on him before retiring for the night herself, finding him writhing on his mattress, soaked in sweat.

Just then, Gisla returned cradling half a dozen candles, each of which was almost as thick as her forearm. Hurriedly, she placed them around the room, with two set close to the bed, before returning with a taper which she carried with one tiny hand cupped around the flame lest the stiff breeze should extinguish it before it could do its job. Duty done, she ran from the room as if she could not bear to be so near to sickness.

With the light now sufficient for Freya to examine the boy properly, she placed two fingers by the side of his neck, recoiling a little at just how cold and clammy his skin felt. She moved her fingertips around for a moment until she found the beat of his blood pumping around his body. She had no need to count to know that all was not well. It pulsed faster than if he had just run from one end of the village to the other and back again. It was a wonder his heart did not burst with the effort.

Ulf moaned in response to her touch, almost as if her fingers were somehow burning his skin. Just then he opened his eyes, grabbed at his stomach with both hands and screamed with pain. No sooner had the sound subsided, then he rolled to one side and spewed the contents of his guts, the effluent splashing noisily off the hard-packed floor.

"Tell me, what did he eat at dinner?"

Thorgunnr paused in her rambling monologue. "Oysters. Gisla bought them from a trader in the market who had come up from Gippeswic yesterday. Ulf was with her, and he insisted on having them. They're his favourite, apparently. My God, it was the oysters, wasn't it? I said to Gisla that I was not sure if they were fresh."

Freya nodded. She had not prepared them herself, else she would have noted their condition and whether they were safe. Oysters that were too old could cause vomiting and loose bowels, but she had not known the effects to be this bad. She doubted whether the shellfish were the whole cause of the problem, but she could not rule it out, just yet. "Did you eat them, Lady? Did Gisla or anyone else?"

"I didn't and I don't believe anyone else did. The trader had only a few left - enough for only one portion, so Gisla told me."

Well, Freya mused, if the oysters were to blame, then at least no one else would be similarly afflicted. "Where is the trader now? I would speak with him."

Gisla, who had been hovering within earshot, answered this. "I fear he has already returned to Gippeswic, madam. He was packing his stall when we came to him, but he agreed to let us be his last customer."

None of this was helping, Freya thought to herself. Ulf was groaning once more, his limbs and torso jerking, convulsing even, as the unseen assailant took hold of his body once more. For all her skill and experience, she felt utterly bereft of ideas. Without knowing the cause of the affliction, she was helpless. As if to emphasise her thoughts, Ulf, rolled onto his side, clutched his knees up to his chest and puked once more, a projectile stream that reached as far as the wall of the room, a good three or four paces from the bed.

"What should we do?" Thorgunnr's tremulous voice had risen several tones, taking on an edge of hysteria. "You must help him, Freya. For his father's sake, if not mine."

"I'm sorry, Lady. Whatever assails Ulf is beyond my skill, I fear. If it were the oysters, then he will recover in a day or so and we need do nothing but feed him water and thin broth to keep his strength up. But this is like no food-induced malady that I have ever seen. I am at a loss as to its cause and, also," her voice sank, "how to treat it. I fear we can do nothing more than trust in Almighty God to save him."

Silence fell over the room, broken only by the sounds of the boy groaning as he twisted and turned on his straw-filled mattress. From the doorway, Gisla sniffed back the snot that was mixing with the tears that flowed freely down her face. "Should I fetch Abbot Ethelstan?"

Thorgunnr said nothing, as if stunned, like a rat suddenly revealed at night in the torch light in the middle of the grain store. None of them was in any doubt as to the meaning of the question. Ethelstan would pray for Ulf's recovery, of course, but his presence would also be needed were it to become necessary to prepare the boy for passing over to the other side, though none dared say as much out loud.

Freya nodded dumbly. "I think that may be wise, Gisla."

***

When Ethelstan arrived from his abbey almost ten miles to the north at Ramsey, his mood was as foul as the weather through which he'd had to ride. So much so that his response to Sihtric's greeting when he met him at the gate was nothing if not abrupt. But by the time some feeling had returned to his fingers in front of the well-stoked fire in the hall's central hearth, his civility had been mostly restored.

"Pray tell me, master Steward, all that has happened. I am led to believe that Ulf has been taken ill. Something to do with oysters?" He continued to rub his fingers vigorously as he spoke, as if trying to force the blood back into them so that they might return to their proper colour.

"In truth, I know not the detail, Lord Abbot, though I fear it to be a grave matter, else they would not have sent for you. It is to be regretted that the boy's father is away."

"There is news from the north?"

"None that I have heard, though any messenger would take several days to reach Lundenburh. So, I don't suppose there is any need to be concerned."

Just then, Freya came through the gap in the screen partition, a look of panicked frustration on her face. "Ah, Lord Abbot, you're here. Sihtric," she turned to scold him, "did I not say you were to send him straight through as soon as he arrived? This is not time to be swapping gossip about battles taking place far away when there are more pressing matters closer at hand."

Ethelstan stepped forward, positioning himself between Freya and her husband. "Forgive him, Goodwife Freya for it is my fault. How is the child? I pray God he improves with every hour?"

"Far from it, Lord Abbot," her voice caught as if fighting to suppress a sob. "I fear he is close to death. I have no skill in this matter; I can do nothing to help."

With that, she grabbed Ethelstan by the sleeve of his habit and pulled him firmly towards the lord's chambers. Sihtric followed dumbly behind, his mind reeling in shock. Until now, he'd not understood just how serious the matter was, how fragile Ulf's grip on life might be. He could not conceive how the lad could be in such danger. Was it not simply a bad gut from eating the wrong thing? Surely, he'd be right in a day or two? But even as he walked, trance-like towards the door, the memory of what Freya had said a few weeks back rushed back into his head like a wave crashing on to a beach. He had forgotten all talk of Thorgunnr, Cwenhild and wolfsbane; he'd been far too busy looking after the estate in Bjarke's absence to worry about things like that. *Bjarke?* Sihtric stopped in his tracks, seized by terror. *What if Ulf should die? How will I tell his father that his son died while under my protection?*

Looking up, he noticed he was now alone in the hall, Freya and Ethelstan having already disappeared through the partitioning wall. Stumbling after them, he fought to bring his breathing back under control. He could not remember ever feeling this scared before. Not in any battle he could recall, for sure. At least in the shieldwall you had staunch lads on either side. Men you had grown up with, lived with, trained for hour after hour with. Right now, he felt very small and very much on his own, a feeling that only became worse when he reached Ulf's room.

The first thing that struck him was the stench; it smelled of death. It was an odour he knew only too well from the battlefield; there was no mistaking it. Looking across at the cot, he caught Freya's eye. Her expression did nothing to reassure him; fear fought for supremacy with anguish, with neither able to achieve dominance. The room was already crowded with five of them not including Ulf, but Sihtric managed to pick his way across the floor, avoiding the discarded scraps of linen and pools of effluent, so that he could stand by his wife's side. He reached down to take her hand in his, feeling her return his grip with an intensity that shocked him.

"Is there no hope?" He whispered so as not to disturb Ethelstan who was already intoning solemn prayers over Ulf's still-shivering form. He had no idea what was being said, for the Abbot spoke in the impenetrable language of the church in which he could only make out the odd word. For all he knew, he could - even now - be chanting the last rites over the boy. If that was the case, then the boy must really be close to death.

Freya shook her head, tears flowing unchecked down her face, adding fresh new tracks on top of those that had already passed that way. Sihtric could feel her body shaking, as if she were struggling to control the sobs to which she longed to succumb. In his helplessness, Sihtric could do no more than place a comforting arm around her shoulders as he stared dumbly down at the scene before him. On the other side of the bed, Thorgunnr was on her knees, Ulf's lifeless hand clutched between hers. Despite the gloom, he could see that her dark green dress, one of her more sumptuous garments as he recalled, was spattered in several places where Ulf had vomited.

Just then, Abbot Ethelstan made the sign of the cross over the boy and rose to his feet. "There is no more I can do. His life is in God's hands now. Join me in a prayer for his soul."

The man of God then bowed his head and began to recite the words of the Lord's Prayer, his voice a quiet monotone as he made his way through the familiar litany. Sihtric found he could not focus. He was aware that his mouth moved in time with the meter of the words, but his mind was elsewhere, filled with images of the times he had spent with Ulf, teaching him how to hunt, how to fight, how to care for his weapons so that he might always rely on them. The many hours they had spent fishing or hawking, lazy days by the side of the river just talking or laughing as the hours sidled past. Ulf has been the closest thing to a son he had ever had, and he could not imagine him no longer being a part of his life.

Then the tears came. He made no effort to stop them or to wipe them away. He was rooted to the spot, struck dumb and immobile by the events unfolding before his eyes. Where, not one day before, there had been a happy lad darting around Hoctune carrying his messages, playing pranks on all those he came across; now there was nothing more than a spent body, still writhing in silent agony, still wrestling with whatever foul beast assailed him. Helpless, all they could do was watch, unable to offer any succour, however small.

Then, without warning, Ulf arched his back - lifting his torso high above the sodden mattress - and screamed. Sihtric shuddered in spite of himself; in all his years, for all the men he'd killed in battle or seen slaughtered around him, he'd never heard such a heart-rending and piteous sound. By his side, Freya - sobbing inconsolably now - leaned forward to try to comfort Ulf in her arms. But it was to no avail. With a final effort, what air remained in his lungs was forced out as his body slumped back down to the sweat- and puke-stained sheets. Ulf moved no more.

With the solemnity due to his station, Ethelstan leaned over the body, placing a hand upon his chest, and turning his ear to his mouth and nose. He held up his other hand for silence for a moment and then sighed. "His pain is at an end for he has departed this world. May God have mercy on his soul."

Rising to his feet, he bowed his head and made the sign of the cross over the now still form. "Lord, receive the soul of this your servant, Ulf, son of Bjarke, Lord of the East Angles. Receive him into your arms and find a place for him in Your kingdom for all eternity."

"Amen." Sihtric mumbled the words, still too shocked to do anything but stare at his feet. With a force of will, he lifted his eyes to look across to where Thorgunnr knelt by her stepson's side. She boasted a pale complexion on the best of days, but the pallor of her face was as white as the snow. Tears rolled down her face as she sat slumped on her haunches, slowly rocking back and forth, her forehead touching Ulf's arm with each move. To his mind, she could not have looked more distraught had she been the boy's own mother.

TWELVE

The people of Hoctune were shocked to their core. Everywhere Sihtric went, carrying out his steward's duties as best he could in the circumstances, people were in mourning, too stunned to do more than nod or grunt in reply to his greeting. Ulf had been well-liked and not just because he was the lord's son. Though a quiet, almost solitary lad at times, he had always shown kindness and respect in his dealings with the people of Hoctune. No one could believe he had passed.

On the evening of the second day, Sihtric met with Abbot Ethelstan in the tavern. The plump old churchman had not yet returned to Ramsey, electing instead to take lodging with the village priest in his little house, just behind the small stone church. Sihtric was near the end of his second cup of ale when the abbot finally squeezed himself on to the bench opposite the old warrior. Allowing the older man to make himself comfortable, adjusting the thick woollen robes that had become entangled around his bare legs, he raised two fingers in the direction of Hamfa, the innkeeper, to indicate he should send over more ale.

"Your pardon, Sihtric. My tardiness is inexcusable. Though in my defence, there is much to be done when it comes to organising a burial of this stature, more than Father Wulfstan can manage on his own." As he spoke, he pressed the flats of both hands into the small of his back, pushing himself forwards to arch his spine. "And it does not help that the bed he has provided for my use would be considered too small for your dog, Acwel."

Sihtric did not smile; he was not in the mood for jesting. "It is about this matter that I wish to speak with you, Lord Abbot."

Ethelstan raised his eyebrows. "The bed or my back?"

Sihtric just about succeeded in keeping the irritation out of his voice. "Neither, Lord. The burial."

"Ah yes, of course. Forgive the wandering mind of an old fool. I fear I remain in shock at the poor boy's passing."

"It has hit us all hard, Lord. It could not have been foreseen."

"Quite, quite. But you must call me Ethelstan in here, my friend. I think we have known each other long enough now to do away with formality. Why, it must be ten years or more since we first set eyes on each other."

Sihtric took a deep draught from the new cup which Hamfa's wife, Saewara, had just placed before him. It was the only way that he could stifle the sigh which had threatened to escape his lips. As ever, the old man was proving hard to keep to the point.

"The burial, Ethelstan. You insist that it must be tomorrow?"

"Indeed so, my boy, indeed so. It does not do to delay the Lord's work. Ulf must be laid to rest in holy ground so that his soul can begin its journey to Heaven. And, besides, there is much for me to do in Ramsey; I cannot tarry here much longer."

There's the truth of the matter, Sihtric thought to himself. The old fox does not like to be away from his housekeeper for too long. If the rumours were true, it was more than her cooking he was missing.

"But should we not wait for Jarl Bjarke? The boy's father should be here to see his son placed into his grave."

"Well, yes, in normal circumstances I would be the first to agree with you, Sihtric. But the jarl is not here, and none can tell when he might return."

"Messengers arrived today. Even now, the army is travelling south to Lundenburh. I have already dispatched a rider to bring Bjarke here first, instead of staying with Knut all the way to the city."

"But, even so, you cannot tell me how far away he is, or how long he may yet be. You'll know as well as I, my friend," Ethelstan leaned in close until his face was no more than a hand's width away, sending a waft of putrid ale breath over the former warrior, "that the longer a body is left in the open air, the more it begins to - shall we say - rot. It would not be fitting for such a fate to befall the esteemed son and heir of the greatest lord in all England."

Annoyingly, Sihtric had to concede the abbot had a point. They probably had a day or two at the most before nature started to take its grip of the body. If the weather had been much warmer, it would have been too late already. Many was the time he had seen, in a battle's aftermath in the height of summer, corpses soon beginning to bloat. Leave them too long and there was a risk that a body could burst. There was no way of knowing when Bjarke might return; though he very much doubted it would be in the next day or two.

"Besides," Ethelstan continued. "It's the Lord's Day tomorrow. What more fitting time could there be for Ulf's body to be committed to the grave?"

Sihtric bowed his head, acknowledging defeat.

"So, it's settled then? You'll send Freya to prepare the body, tonight?"

***

Normally, it would fall to the mother to cleanse and dress the body of their dead child, but with Eadgifu long dead that was not an option. On top of which, Thorgunnr had not been seen since Ulf's death. Apparently consumed with grief, she had retreated to her chamber, not even venturing forth at mealtimes. But there would be no problem. He was sure Freya would gladly step up to the role, giving him one less thing to worry about. He was already wracked with guilt over the boy's death. Although he wished that Bjarke would be home in time for the funeral, an equal part of him hoped for the day of his return to be far away in the future. He still had no idea how he would break the news to his master.

With all these thoughts and more, tumbling through his mind, Sihtric pushed open the door to his home, the sound of its warped planks scrapping across the floor reminding him, yet again, that it was still in desperate need of repair.

"Well, what did he say?"

Freya was sat by the hearth, using a needle and thread to mend his best tunic. Fool that he was, he'd caught the sleeve on a protruding nail as he'd shuffled out through the church's narrow door last Sunday. His wife looked tired and pale, though it was hardly surprising. The last few days had taken their toll on her. If anything, she was just as much an aunt to the boy as he had been an uncle, even though she had spent less time with him. She'd hardly slept since his death; a fact he knew only too well as - wide awake himself - he'd been aware of her restless stirrings next to him each night.

"The burial goes ahead tomorrow."

"He won't wait?"

"No. Though he will not say as much, I know he wishes to return to Ramsey more than anything."

"To lie with his harlot housekeeper, I shouldn't wonder."

Sihtric could not prevent a smirk as he turned his back to hang his cloak on the peg by the door. It never ceased to amuse him the strength of feeling that one woman could have against another whom she perceived to have done wrong. He decided not to indulge her on this occasion.

"To give him his due, I could not find fault when he said that the boy needs to be in the grave before nature begins to take a hand in affairs."

Freya stared at him, a quizzical look playing across her face. To answer her, Sihtric held his thumb and forefinger to his nose while making a face as if recoiling from some foul stench.

"So that is that then?" She said as realisation dawned.

"Not quite, my love. The abbot has asked if you would tend to Ulf this night, so that he may be ready for tomorrow. Thorgunnr is not up to the task; no one has seen or heard from her since…" he left the sentence unfinished, still unable to bring himself to say the words.

"Gladly, husband. I'd consider it an honour to prepare the boy for his final journey to the afterlife. It is fitting that he should be attended by one who cares for his immortal soul."

Sihtric caught the tone of Freya's voice, and it gave him pause.

"Your meaning, wife? You think Thorgunnr cares not for the boy? Did you not see her consumed with grief at his bedside?"

"I don't know what I saw. I would not find it hard to believe that one such as her should be skilled in mummery so that all around her believed her to be as distraught as any true mother would be for the loss of a son. Even a step-son."

"You really suspect her of causing harm to her husband's son?" Sihtric's mind was racing. What if Freya were to voice her concerns to others in Hoctune and word was to reach

Thorgunnr or - worse still - Bjarke? It would be like stepping onto the ice over the duck pond in winter. "There is no proof, woman. You heard what was said; Ulf had eaten his fill of oysters that evening. He would not be the first, nor doubtless the last to succumb to tainted shellfish."

Freya snorted. "We have only Thorgunnr's word for that. Who's to say that she did not cause the poor mite to ingest some foul poison."

"Quiet, woman," he hissed, looking around as if he expected to find others within their home. "To say such things without proof will see you - us - clapped in irons. Even my friendship with the jarl would not be enough to save us. Were such a foul deed to be true - and I dare not believe it - it would be your word against hers. And who do you think Bjarke would side with? At best we would be thrown out of Hoctune to fend for ourselves in the forests with the other outlaws. At worst he would have your tongue and your eyes so that you might never again see or tell of any such thing."

***

Freya stomped her way across to Bjarke's hall, her head a broiling torrent of emotions. Acwel trotted along beside her, his ears and tail pointing down as if all too aware of her dark mood. For her part, Freya knew Sihtric was right on both counts: the unlikely notion that Thorgunnr might be responsible for Ulf's death and the likelihood that - even if she were - Bjarke would hardly be well disposed to listening to the wild ramblings of a bitter old woman who everyone knew had never liked his new wife.

But still the feeling persisted at the back of her mind. Though some weeks had passed, she remembered the words she had overheard as clearly as if it were yesterday. Doubtless, Thorgunnr could point to any number of honest explanations for acquiring wolfsbane from Cwenhild - all of which her husband would willingly accept - but nothing could convince Freya of her innocence. Could it have been an accident? Perhaps she had left the poison in a place where Ulf chanced upon it? It would mean Thorgunnr was innocent of murder, but guilty of a carelessness that she would not care to admit to the boy's father, all the same.

Whatever the cause, she knew she had to put it behind her. Whatever the truth, there was no way it could be proven. Abbot Ethelstan had witnessed the boy's death and it would be written into the records as a surfeit of oysters. There was no more to be done, except to do her duty by the boy to prepare him for his funeral. It was a task that many might baulk at - especially as Ulf were not her own son - but she did not mind. She was inured to the plight of human suffering, the sight and smell of death. Her years serving as Hoctune's midwife had seen to that. She would make sure Ulf was made ready to meet his Maker.

She pushed open the door, standing aside for the lumbering hound to go before her. She left him snuffling about in the straw looking for discarded titbits and, without a backward glance, she pressed on to the back of the hall, pushing aside the heavy drape that led to the lord's living quarters.

Little had changed in Ulf's chamber since his death. The floor had been swabbed clean and the bedding replaced, but no more than that. The boy lay on his back, his eyes staring sightlessly up at the oak beams that formed the sloping roof of his chamber. But he remained dressed in the same puke and sweat-stained linen shift that he had been wearing on the night he died. Inwardly, Freya seethed to see how little care had been afforded the boy in death. More attention had been paid to the room than to Ulf and it saddened her heart to see it. *Still, he's in good hands now,* she told herself.

At least bowls had been placed in the room for her use, with piles of clean linen cloths by their side. Sighing, she put her satchel down by the door and picked up the pitcher. Several trips to the hearth later she had enough hot water from the iron pot that hung over the fire to begin her work. The first time she had gone back to the hall, Acwel had lifted his head from where it rested on his front paws, thinking it might be time to go home. By the fourth trip, however, he did not even deign to open an eye.

Back in Ulf's room, Freya slipped her small seax out from its fleece-lined sheath which hung from her belt. Carefully, she worked the blade under the hem of Ulf's shift just under his chin. Then, gripping tightly onto the fabric with her left hand, she pulled the blade up and along, its razor-sharp edge splitting the strands as if they were not there. The two sides of the cloth drifted apart, revealing the boy's body. Though skinny, she could see how the long hours of battle-craft with her husband had begun to pay dividends. The muscles of his limbs, shoulders and chest were well-defined, though still small. Had he lived, he would soon have started to add bulk to his frame. Doubtless, another ten years would have seen him assume the same stature and build as his father who stood a head taller than most and broad with it.

Shaking her head at the senseless loss of life, Freya took the first cloth from the pile and dipped it in the still-hot water. Wringing it out, she began rubbing the sodden material over Ulf's limbs, rigorously but with the care and respect that the task demanded. She worked her way up from the feet, taking great pains to ensure that all marks of dirt, grime and effluence were expunged until the skin shone white, tinged with a blueish grey where the blood had drained from surface. She had to pay extra attention to Ulf's face as this was where most signs of the violent nature of his death could be seen, most especially around the lower jaw.

Taking a new wet cloth, Freya set about the mouth with renewed vigour. Using strong, downward strokes, she worked around from the right ear towards the left, the sallow skin appearing to stretch with each movement. As she reached the chin, the boy's mouth fell open with a faintly audible click.

"Your pardon, Ulf," she whispered. "I had not meant to treat you so harshly." She was about to push the jaw back into place when something caught her eye. Pulling the nearest candle closer, she turned the boy's head to the side to get a better view. Though she willed it not to be true, there was no mistaking it. How she had not noticed before, she could not say, but there it was as plain as the huge nose on her husband's face. The boy's tongue was tinged a deep shade of purple, not dissimilar to the colour formed when making dye from sea snails. Gently, she pushed her fingers in to widen the mouth a little further, noting that the stain went all the way back to the base of the tongue.

Aside from clothing dye, Freya knew of only one other substance that carried a similar hue: the flowers of the wolfsbane plant. A bolt of fear lanced through her causing her whole body to shudder. All doubt had now been removed in her mind; Thorgunnr had poisoned her stepson and sought to blame his death on diseased shellfish. There could be no other explanation. The wolfsbane she had sent Gisla to acquire from Cwenhild may well have been used for rats, but there was no denying that some of it had ended up in Ulf's belly, causing his horrific and painful death.

Freya sat on the edge of the bed, her head in her hands; she had no idea what to do. Her husband's words rang around her head fighting for space with the myriad other notions that also assailed her mind. Her heart and soul told her that she could not - must not - stay silent. Ulf deserved justice for his foul murder. Thorgunnr would answer to God on the day of her death but that could be many years in the future yet. She must pay for her crime in this world; she must pay the blood price demanded for a crime so heinous. But how? How could she give voice to the innocent?

Sihtric was right. Bjarke was not here and by the time he returned, Ulf would have been buried. And even if he were, what chance would she have to convince the Lord of Hoctune of his wife's guilt? With no solution presenting itself, she could do nothing to prevent the tears of helplessness from flowing.

THIRTEEN

"Why do you wail so, woman? You've woken my child."

Looking up through her tear-stained eyes, Freya saw Thorgunnr standing in the doorway, baby Erik grizzling on her hip. As she stared at the jarl's wife, something snapped within her. She couldn't help herself; her despair for Ulf's death added to the knowledge she had just gained about the cause of his demise combined to produce a reaction that was beyond her control.

"You murderous bitch." She jumped to her feet, rushing forward until her face was no further than a hand's breadth from the other woman, flecks of spittle spattering Thorgunnr's cheeks.

Just for a moment, the jarl's wife was taken aback, shocked by the ferocity of Freya's tirade. But it did not take her long to recover. She had been born into power and was used to commanding others to do her will. She had broken women stronger and more powerful than a lowly steward's wife.

Raising herself to her full and not inconsiderable height, she hissed. "How dare you? How dare you shout such wild and unfounded accusations to my face. I could have you flogged until the bones of your back show through."

"I would not care if you did, for it would not alter the truth. We both know what you have done. And I thank God that you will answer for it come the day of judgement." Freya made the sign of the cross over herself to emphasise her point.

"What are you babbling about, woman? Are you deranged? Your grief for Ulf has destroyed your mind."

The bare-faced denial was too much for Freya to bear. Wheeling round, she strode over to Ulf's body, lowered his chin, and pointed. "Look. Look at his tongue. Do you deny the truth of your eyes? What is this stain if not wolfsbane?"

"Wolfsbane? Why would you say such a thing? Who knows what caused that discolouration? Perhaps it is a symptom of the sickness that took him?"

"You lie! I heard you talking to Gisla not one month ago. You sent her to Cwenhild the witch to acquire wolfsbane. I know my herbs; I recognise the signs. Its leaves are purple. The same hue which you now see before you."

As she spoke, a new and strange look came over Thorgunnr's face. A look that - had she been more in control of her emotions - Freya might have recognised for the danger it portended.

"And what would you propose to do with this knowledge, so recently gained?" Her tone was quiet and silky as if her words were coated with the rich honey made by Abbot Ethelstan's monks at Ramsey.

Without pause, Freya blundered into the trap laid for her. "Why, I will tell Lord Bjarke when he returns. And then we shall see justice done."

Thorgunnr said nothing. Slowly, deliberately, she placed Erik on the floor where he lay contentedly on his back playing with a small, carved wooden horse, a toy which Freya idly recognised as having been made by her husband as a present for the baby. Then, without warning, the younger woman moved with the speed of an otter slithering into the river in pursuit of a fish. In two steps she was in front of Freya and grabbing her by the throat. Her fingers gripped the soft flesh of her neck in a vice-like grip, pushing her back until her body was pressed up hard against the wall.

"Seeing as though you appear to have stumbled upon the truth, Freya, you should be in no doubt as to the position in which you now find yourself. Make no mistake that your fate - and that of your husband - now lies in my hands, to do with as I will. Do not doubt me when I say I could have you killed without a moment's thought. After all, according to you, I murdered my own stepson. Do you really think I would shy away from dealing similarly with you?"

Freya, up on the tips of her toes, fought for breath. For one with such a small and wiry build, Thorgunnr possessed surprising strength. Her bony fingers dug into Freya's skin, forming bruises almost instantaneously. Her green eyes bore into hers with an intensity that shocked her. She could almost taste the venom in her words. Though cowed, however, she was not prepared to dissolve just yet. "But why? What possible reason could you have for wanting to hurt an innocent soul?"

"I would have thought that was obvious." She did not wait for an answer. "My husband is the most powerful man in this land, save for the king himself. He owns vast estates from which he collects huge sums in taxes each year. Nothing is too great an expense for a man such as he. And all this, under the laws that govern this land, would pass to Ulf on his death. My Erik would inherit nothing. For him, the best he could hope for would be a role as some minor captain in Knut's warband or perhaps he might become an Abbot like fat old Ethelstan. Neither of which would be good enough for my son.

"But with Ulf out of the way, Erik now stands to succeed his father; he stands to take the lands, the titles… the wealth. And then there's me. A score or so years younger than my husband. How would Ulf treat me when he became Lord of the Eastern Angles? The stepmother who hates him. I've seen the look in his eyes, the snivelling brat. How soon would I have been cast out of hearth and home when Bjarke passed on? But now, I can look forward to many years of comfort and ease, supported by the largesse of my own son. Who knows, I might even take another husband - a younger man, perhaps - to keep me warm on those cold winter nights."

Freya was aghast. The depth of the woman's depravity had finally been laid bare. God alone knew how long she had been planning this outcome. Since Erik had been born? Or even before that? Perhaps Erik was the missing piece of the puzzle which had now slotted into place. Now Bjarke had a second son, she was free to remove the first; the one that stood between her and her goal.

"You won't succeed, you foul fiend. The truth will out and then you will be sorry."

"But who is going to tell anyone? Who else knows? Only you as far as I see it. Gisla swallowed my story about the rats. It will be a simple enough matter to find a few and poison them with the remains of the wolfsbane. Then there's Sihtric. That old fool has not the wits he was born with anymore. Too many blows to the head, I shouldn't wonder. And even if you were to convince him, what would you do then? No one would believe you. Besides, if I so much as suspect you of breathing a word of this to anyone, you and your idiot husband will be slaughtered. I have warriors here in Hoctune. Men who are loyal to me rather than to my husband. Men who my father gave me from his own warband. They would not hesitate to kill you both. I have but to order it."

Freya was determined not to show the fear that clawed at her soul. She could feel her legs shaking, threatening to buckle beneath her. She ground her teeth together to stop them from chattering and prayed that Thorgunnr would not notice. Her life hung by a thread; she could see no other option but to submit if she wanted to see the sun come up next morning. She knew the men of whom Thorgunnr spoke. Grim, hard-hearted men with evil in their eyes whose arms bore the scars and the gold rings as testimony of their years of battle-craft. She had no doubt that they would do their mistress's bidding without question. Her shoulders slumped in defeat and her head lolled forward as if afraid to meet her tormentor's eye.

"There now. That wasn't so hard, was it?" Victory assured, Thorgunnr's voice assumed a more mellifluous tone. "I am sure in time, we can put this matter behind us, Freya. I have not forgotten how you helped me bring my Erik into this world. A mother remembers such things with fondness."

Freya kept her lips firmly pressed together, not trusting herself to speak. With every bone in her body, she wanted to claw at Thorgunnr's face with her fingernails, to scratch her eyes out if she only could. Anything to remove her smug expression of power and authority. But she knew it was hopeless. Until some unforeseen opportunity presented itself, she knew she had no choice but to acquiesce.

Oblivious to Freya's inner turmoil, Thorgunnr continued. "But there is one last thing I need from you and your husband this night. One last matter to deal with before we can retire to bed. When you have finished preparing Ulf's body, I would have you take him to the meadows to the north of the village and bury him there."

Freya could not hide her astonishment. "B…but… why

would I do such a thing? The funeral is tomorrow. Abbot Ethelstan will bury the boy here in the church - on holy ground - as befits a son of Jarl Bjarke."

"And there will be a funeral. A body will be buried. But it won't be Ulf, and no one need be any the wiser."

"I don't understand." Freya whimpered, her mind wilting under the force of Thorgunnr's iron will. This new development made no sense to her.

"Nor should you have to, old woman. Suffice it to say that if one as dull as you can detect my crime, I can afford to take no further risks. What would happen should my husband choose to have his son exhumed in the weeks or months to come? I would be discovered, and all would be lost. So, you must finish your preparations, wrap Ulf in his burial shroud and then leave. I will send my men to you at midnight. Be sure to be ready. And remember. A word of this to anyone and I'll have them rip your tongue out by its roots; but only after you have watched them slit Sihtric's throat. I hope I have made myself clear?"

FOURTEEN

True to her word, Thorgunnr's men hammered on the door of Sihtric and Freya's homestead a few hours later. By rights, both of them would have been in a deep sleep by now, but such was their state of mind, that slumber was the last things on their minds.

In detail, and leaving no part untold, Freya had recounted everything to her husband. At first Sihtric had refused to believe her; he could not bring himself to accept that Thorgunnr could have contemplated, let alone carried out, the murder of her own stepson. But even he had to concede the truth of it as the tale unfolded. What started out as impotent rage for the fate of the boy had slowly subsided into feelings of fear and anxiety for their own plight. For now, he and Freya would be complicit in the foul deed by being forced to hide the body in the meadows north of the village. Though his wits might not have been as sharp as the blade of his seax, Sihtric could see the workings of Thorgunnr's mind in it. By forcing them to dispose of the body, she was tying them to her fate.

"We must tell someone." Freya had said, her courage having returned somewhat now that she was out of Thorgunnr's physical and mental clutches.

"But do you not see that once we help her to bury Ulf's body, that option closes to us? As hard as it would be to convince Bjarke, or anyone else for that matter, of Thorgunnr's guilt, she knows that we would not dare because she will claim our involvement tonight proves we were party to her plot. She will say that she paid us gold to help her achieve her foul goal."

"But that would be nothing more than wicked lies. There's no gold here and nothing that speaks of it; anyone can see that." Freya had thrown her arms wide, taking in their few possessions arranged on the shelves and cupboards within the single room that they called home. Beyond his old war gear and Freya's cooking and healing pots, they had little else to their name.

"But it would not take much for one of her thugs to hide a

purse filled with a few gold coins somewhere about the place. In the rafters, perhaps? Or dug down under the earth beneath our feet. I'm sure it would soon be discovered in the event of an investigation, especially if you knew where to look."

Freya had said nothing, though he'd seen his words had hit home. Like her, he could see no way out of the stinking bog into which they had blundered. The sodden, shifting soil was scrabbling at their legs, dragging them down, refusing to let them escape. No matter which way they turned, there was nothing on to which they could grip to pull themselves to safety.

The hammering returned for a second time, only this time more violent and insistent. With a sideways glance towards his wife, Sihtric rose and crossed over to the door. From where he lay by the dying embers of the hearth-fire, Acwel's ears pricked up as if sensing that visitors at this time did not augur well.

No sooner had Sihtric lifted the latch, than the wooden panel was propelled back, striking his face before he could react. Dazed, his eyes watering with the sudden pain, he stumbled back a step or two, cursing himself for his stupidity. They had caught him off guard in his own home and the realisation cut him to the bone. *Are you so old and feeble that you could not have foreseen such a thing?* They had come prepared for a fight; he had not. He swore under his breath; he would not allow it to happen again.

Through the now open door, three men barged their way into the room, their size and bulk making the space within seem overcrowded. Sihtric recognised them at once. They hailed from the region of Danmark known as Scania, huscarls who had accompanied Thorgunnr as part of the marriage contract agreed between Bjarke and her father. He knew them to be loutish men, insolent and often drunk, but fierce fighters all the same. As Thorgunnr's men, they had not been summoned to stand in the jarl's shieldwall. Not for them the chance of glory and wealth earned by feat of arms on the battlefield and perhaps it was this knowledge that soured their minds, causing them to resent their station and find different outlets for their strength and aggression.

In another life, Sihtric might have been friends with them.

They could have stood shoulder to shoulder in the front rank, their shields overlapping, battling Bjarke's enemies. But these men had a reputation for being thuggish bullies, one that Sihtric knew was well merited. He could not trust them; he could not rely on any sense of shared comradeship.

Their leader - a man he knew to be called Halfdan - growled at them in his guttural, accented tongue. "You ready?"

Though it was intended to be a question, it sounded more like a demand, the truth of which Halfdan then reinforced by grabbing Sihtric by the collar of his tunic. "And don't think I would hesitate to gut you, old man, should you or your whore wife fail to do exactly as I say. By all accounts, you were once a great warrior, but I'd say that those days are long gone by the looks of you. By the gods, I swear that if you tried to catch me unawares, I'd hear your bones creaking." He laughed at his own joke, a harsh, rasping sound from a voice worn down by countless cups of ale.

"All that matters is that we are three and you are but one - and perhaps not even that, nowadays, eh? It would not go well for either of you should you fail to remember it." Halfdan looked over at Freya. "She's a bit past her best for my liking, but I can't speak for Sibba or Harald here. Maybe she's more to their taste. You wouldn't want to have to watch them take turns before we kill her now, would you?"

For added emphasis, Halfdan punched his left hand into Sihtric's face. It was not a hard blow, intended more to shock than to cause any lasting damage, but it was enough to split the skin of his lower lip, causing a trickle of blood to trace its way down into his beard.

Sensing danger, Acwel rose to his feet and lowered his head as if readying himself to leap, all the while growling deep within his throat. Sihtric knew they would not hesitate to kill the old hound should they think him a threat. Turning his head to one side, he spat to clear his mouth of the mixture of blood and saliva that had gathered.

"Quiet, boy. Lie down."

Acwel did as he was ordered, though not without a whine to express his concern. The beast was well trained and could be useful in a fight. He had taken down more than one boar in his time, but now was not the moment to risk his life needlessly.

Realising what had just happened, Halfdan nodded approvingly. "I can see we'll have no trouble from you this night, Sihtric. I would have hated to have had to end a life as honourably led as yours over something like this. It's better for everyone if this night passes peacefully. Now, let's be on our way."

Outside, they found a simple flat-bedded wain, to which a pair of horses had been attached, each of which was busily munching on a nose bag filled with oats to keep them quiet while they waited. All four wheels had been wound with strips of cloth to muffle any creaks and squeaks as it moved. Though there should be no one around at this hour, it made no sense to risk disturbing anyone. Even though he were the steward and nominally in charge of all matters in Hoctune in Bjarke's absence, he would not be able to prevent the gossipmongers from spreading word of strange nocturnal happenings should they be overheard or seen.

No words were spoken as they walked, the pace dictated by that of the horses, scraggy old beasts that were long past their prime. Sihtric walked alongside Freya, gripping her hand tightly in his to provide what comfort he could. For her part, she had said nothing since Halfdan's arrival, and he had no clue as to her state of mind. She stared straight ahead as she placed one foot in front of the other, looking neither left or right. It was as though she had fallen into a trance, unable to see or hear what was going on around her.

After what Sihtric guessed to be a half hour, they arrived at their destination. Sometime earlier, they had parted company with the road that led north to Ramsey. Instead, they had followed a worn dirt track that meandered its way alongside a small stream in a direction that roughly bisected north and east. A few hundred paces later, they'd turned north again until they had arrived at a large meadow encircled by a host of alder and larch trees that stood tall and silent in the darkness, like sentinels watching over them. A pair of owls, hidden high amongst the branches, hooted with indignation at having their peace disturbed.

"We stop here." Halfdan's tone was brusque, as keen as anyone to have the business done with. He jerked his head towards Sihtric and pointed. "Dig. There."

Sibba and Harald reached up to the cart to retrieve the pick and shovels that had been lain next to Ulf's body, while Sihtric took his seax and began to hack at the soft turf to remove a section that measured roughly two paces by one; plenty of room, he calculated, for the diminutive form of Bjarke's son.

The moon was almost full and the sky empty of clouds, allowing light aplenty by which to complete his unsavoury task. With the grass carefully laid aside in small strips, Sihtric grabbed the pick and began to hack at the soil to loosen it where the winter rains had caused it to harden. Before long, he swapped the pick for the flat-bladed shovel and started to remove great lumps of soil, piling them up to one side.

Though there was a chill to the night air, it was strenuous work and Sihtric had soon worked up a sweat. As he toiled, the perspiration dripping into his eyes, he glowered at the three men who showed no inclination to help. All three leaned against the wain, taking it in turns to swig from a skin which he eyed enviously.

Eventually, Sihtric stood in the bottom of the grave he had dug. The edge of the pit measured just above his waist which he considered deep enough to save Ulf from the ignominy of being unearthed by wild animals. Clambering out of the hole, he walked over to where Freya sat with her back to the bole of the nearest tree. As far as he could tell, she had not moved the whole time he had been working, nor uttered a sound. Gently, he helped her to her feet and guided her to the back of the cart where they carefully eased the shrouded body off and into their arms. Sihtric was amazed at how light Ulf was. True, he had been a slight lad in life, but there was no weight to him at all in death.

They laid him alongside the grave. Sihtric then passed two lengths of stout rope beneath the body, leaving the longer end on the far side of the grave. Finally, with a sympathetic smile towards his wife, he asked. "Ready?"

Nodding, she reached down to take hold of the ropes in each hand, while he did likewise on the far side. Then, at his instruction, they lifted the body, easing it towards Sihtric until it was positioned centrally over the grave. Slowly, respectfully, and without a sound, they lowered the corpse evenly until it came to rest on the cold, damp earth. As he retrieved the ropes, Sihtric fought back the tears that threatened to engulf him once more. How had things come to this? How could a young boy, innocent of everything except the accident of his birth, be made to pay such a price?

"Hurry up now, will you? We must be home before the dawn." Halfdan's gravelly voice broke into Sihtric's consciousness.

"We'll be done when we're done and not before," he growled. He frankly did not care anymore whether they punished him for his insolence or not; he'd had enough of their lack of respect. They cared not that a boy lay dead at the bottom of the pit before them; their minds were focussed only on their beds. To their credit, though, they said nothing; perhaps cowed by his anger.

Taking Freya's hand in his, they stood by the grave, heads bowed in quiet reflection. There would be no sacred rights performed over his body, no priestly benediction would he receive. Worse still, he would not lie in hallowed ground. For him, there would be nothing more than this moment, nothing more than the thoughts of these two people who, whilst they had loved him and cared for him as their own while he lived, could not help but feel they had failed him in death. He swore to himself at that moment, the boy would not go unavenged. Though he knew not how or when he could ever make good on his promise, he would make these bastards pay the price for their deeds with their blood.

For now, however, knowing he had no words adequate for the moment, Sihtric glanced at his wife. "Come on, my love. Let's put an end to this."

He let go of her hand and picked up the shovel. Working methodically, he began to refill the hole from the mound of earth he'd made before. He worked silently, the only sound his laboured breathing as he swung the shovel in an easy rhythm from mound to grave, over and over again. When the soil was back in place, he stomped down hard to make sure it was packed firmly around Ulf's body. Then, taking great care to ensure there was no overt sign of disturbance, Sihtric replaced the turf. Standing back to survey his work, he had to profess himself pleased. If he had not known they had been there, he would never have been able to guess.

Oblivious to his efforts, Halfdan merely grunted. "At last. Perhaps now we can be away? After all, you have to be up early for the funeral tomorrow."

FIFTEEN

None of those present could ever had said that the funeral was anything but properly observed. Abbot Ethelstan officiated, wearing his best robes brought hither from Ramsey. As he intoned the sacred rites in Latin, the villagers who were packed into the stone church maintained a respectful silence, despite the unseasonal mid-spring heat that slowly baked them as it reflected through the several glass windows set high in the stone walls.

All the while, the shrouded form of the body lay on a wooden board, which itself rested on two upturned V-shaped trestles. And none would have ever suspected that the body, so tightly wrapped in strips of white linen, was not Ulf. The form and height were almost identical, certainly close enough to fool all but those who had known him intimately. One such as his father, perhaps? But Bjarke was not there. He had yet to return from campaigning in the north with Knut. No one knew whether the messenger sent to urge him home had even found him yet, let alone whether he was riding hard for Hoctune already.

Only three people in the little church dedicated to Saint Etheldreda knew the truth, and none of them was going to speak out. Thorgunnr's face was a mask; her expression defied any interpretation, though she conducted herself with grace and sobriety as was befitting the stepmother of the deceased. The other two sat holding hands in the second pew, immediately behind the Lady of Hoctune. Many would later say how broken they looked. The people of Hoctune knew that, although Freya and Sihtric had never been blessed with children of their own, they had loved Ulf as much, if not more so, than if he had been their own flesh and blood.

Freya sobbed throughout the service, her body heaving with every breath while, beside her, Sihtric sat stone-faced, his hand clutching hers as if he were afraid to let go. His face - what could be seen of it beneath his bushy grey bread - was ashen, his expression numb and unmoving. No one could ever say that they were not devastated by Ulf's death.

But the most observant among the congregation might have noticed that all was not well. Whilst the tears and grief were genuine, something else was hidden just beneath the surface. Something that spoke of a different kind of pain in the hearts and souls of the old couple. For they knew that the body that lay before them, in front of the cloth-covered altar, was not Bjarke's son. They knew not whose son it was or whence the body had come. Was it even a boy? And what had become of the parents? Did they not mourn for the child, or had they been paid for their silence? All these thoughts and more whirled through their minds as they mouthed the responses required of them as Ethelstan's sombre voice intoned the prayers for the dead.

Later, when the service was over and the body safely interred in a position of honour by the porch, the abbot took his leave. He had made no secret of his desire to be away back north and had waited but a brief time before calling for his entourage. He stood now by his cart, attired once more in his simple monk's habit, as he passed the bag containing his formal robes up to his driver.

"A bad business is any funeral, but a child's even more so, eh? God knows they happen often enough- this life we lead is harsh as we know only too well - but I don't think I will ever become inured to the grief and suffering of parents who have to bury a child."

"It was a shame that his father could not be here to see him on his way, then."

Sihtric started; the tone of his wife's voice did little to disguise the challenge thrown out. Out of the corner of his eye, he could see Halfdan leaning against the wall of the tavern, ale cup in hand, his two henchmen on either side of him. He wondered if they had been ordered to watch them for signs of any weakening of their resolve; something that Thorgunnr doubtless hoped that the sight of the three burly brutes would deter.

"We've discussed this, Freya." Sihtric squeezed her hand in what he hoped would be a signal for caution. "We cannot know when Jarl Bjarke will return and to deny Ulf a Christian burial to ease his quick and safe passage to Heaven for so long would not be fair to the boy."

"Don't forget the stink, Sihtric." The abbot was seemingly oblivious to the sensitivities of others at times. "The weather is warming and that always hastens the decline of the body temporal, whatever the state of the spiritual."

"A Christian burial, indeed. You're right, Lord Abbot. None should be denied such a thing."

This was getting out of hand. Freya's voice was loud, almost shrill. Already, heads were turning as people stopped to witness the exchange, their interest piqued by her obvious distress. It was only a matter of time before Halfdan wandered over to see what was afoot.

Sihtric needed to act quickly; once Halfdan had reported Freya's words to his mistress, it would not be long before some accident befell the pair of them. A fire in the night from a carelessly managed hearth, perhaps. Such things were not uncommon. And whilst people were often able to escape the conflagration, it was not unheard of for occupants to perish in the flames, overcome by smoke in their sleep.

"So, you'll be wanting to be on your way then, Abbot?" Sihtric cupped his hands together to form a foothold to help the old man up into his cart. "The Devil makes work for idle hands, does he not?" It was one of Ethelstan's favourite sayings, forming the cornerstone of many a Sunday sermon as he lambasted his parishioners for the sin of laziness.

"Ah yes, indeed, my son. The Lord's work won't do itself, eh?" With that, he eased himself up onto the bench seat next to the driver. "Send word when Jarl Bjarke arrives, and I will come to see him. Tell him we can pray together for Ulf's soul and perhaps he might see his way to endowing our little foundation in some small way so that we may ensure that prayers are offered for the lad, every day from now until eternity."

Crisis averted, Sihtric allowed himself a brief smile; the abbot was never one to pass up the opportunity for furthering Ramsey's income.

***

Back in the safety of their home, Sihtric rounded on his wife.

"What were you thinking, woman? If you value our lives, none must know the truth. You cannot even hint at it. Ethelstan may be old, but his mind is still sharp. If I had not intervened, God alone knows where your mouth would have gone. It won't take much for him to add the pieces together to make a whole."

"But it's not right," Freya wailed. "Ulf's body lies in an unmarked hole in the ground, far away from any church. No better than if he were a common thief or outlaw." To emphasise her words, Freya grabbed a wooden platter from the table and hurled it at the wall, whence it clattered noisily to the ground.

She was right of course, but what could they do? "I like it no better than you, my love." He took her in his arms, pressing her to him in the way she had always liked, feeling the strength of his shoulders and back enveloping her like a protective cocoon. He prided himself that there was some power yet in his muscles; the daily toil around the estate saw to that.

"But what can we do?" he continued. "You saw Halfdan watching us like one of Bjarke's hawks. Thorgunnr cannot risk word of her crime getting out. She'd sooner have us killed. And if she did not hesitate to murder her own stepson, you can be sure that the death of an old couple such as us would not stain her conscience for long."

"You're a match for him and any like him, husband. Are you not Sihtric blood-spiller? Bjarke's best warrior, rewarded countless times for deeds done in the shieldwall?"

Sihtric laughed. "I have been all these things and more in the past, Freya. But would you now pitch me against men half my age? My leg is always sore, my back aches every morning. I grunt when I stand up or sit down for what reason I know not, and I must get up twice in the night to piss. Halfdan and his mates would make short work of one as ancient as me."

"Put Leggbitr in your hand, though, and it would all come back soon enough."

Sihtric smiled. His heart wanted to believe her. He might still have strength in his shoulders and his muscles would surely remember what to do if called upon, but his speed and endurance were long gone. Thorgunnr's men could toy with him, wearing him down until his lungs were blown and the sword too heavy for his arms to lift. Then they would gut him like some aged boar cornered in the forest.

"A few years ago, maybe, my love. And besides, have you not forgotten the promise I made you?"

"But I can't live the rest of my days knowing what I know and do nothing about it. What will I say to Saint Peter when I stand before him at the gates of Heaven? He will look into my soul, and he will know the truth whether I hide it or no. Perhaps he will exact the blood price for Ulf's death on my soul?"

"I doubt that. He will know the love and tenderness you held for Ulf. He will see that you had no choice but to do what you did for fear of your own life."

"In my heart, though, I will always know that I failed an innocent boy, murdered for no other reason than so his evil bitch of a stepmother could see her own son sat in the jarl's seat."

Sihtric wandered over to the hearth where he bent to pick up the platter. His mind was in turmoil. Like a rabbit caught in one of his snares, he could see no way out. Perhaps his wife had a plan, though; her mind was quicker than his after all.

"So, what do you propose we do?"

"We have but two options as I see it. Either we appeal to Bjarke himself when he returns."

Sihtric's expression must have betrayed the scepticism he felt about such a move as Freya continued without pause.

"Or we go to see Ethelstan and confess all we know. Our souls may be damned, but our consciences will be clear, at least."

"So, we face the bear or the wolf, unarmed and alone. Either would be best avoided if you ask me."

"Well, you asked me and I'm telling you what I think." Freya looked around as if trying to find something else to throw. Finding nothing suitable to hand, she stomped over to the door, flung it open and stormed out into the cool evening air.

Left alone with his thoughts, Sihtric sat on the bench by the wall. Sensing that all was not well, Acwel lifted himself from his spot by the hearth and padded over to him, resting his muzzle on Sihtric's outstretched leg. The old warrior smiled before reaching down to scratch the hound behind the ears. The old boy did not care for the comings and goings of men. As long as he had food in his belly, a warm fire to sleep by and rabbits to chase, he was happy. Not for the first time, Sihtric reflected how life was far simpler for a dog. As if to echo his thoughts, Acwel closed his eyes, yawned and the allowed the ear rubbing to continue.

SIXTEEN

Two weeks later, the day Sihtric had been dreading finally dawned. Bjarke arrived home late in the morning at the head of his warband, its numbers noticeably thinner than before. As if to portend what was to come, the skies had darkened during the preceding days, culminating in incessant, heavy rain. The paths around Hoctune were now little better than a quagmire of mud; no amount of fresh straw could keep the walkways clear and easy to use.

Sihtric had fretted for days about how he would break the tidings of Ulf's death. But now that fateful moment had arrived, he found himself spared the hateful task. As the jarl's mud-spattered horse trudged through the gate, the steward saw Thorgunnr, with little Erik perched on her hip, emerge from the hall to stand under the porch that sheltered the entrance, where she waited for her husband to dismount. He was about to afford her credit for having the courage to take on that duty, until he caught himself. *Well, what else can she do? She must maintain the pretence that the boy's death was no more than an accident. And this way, she gets to plant the seeds of her version of the truth before anyone else can speak.*

Bjarke reined in his exhausted mount in the open space before the hall, handing the bridle to the ostler who was waiting to lead the horse over to the stables. On any other Saturday, the whole area would have been filled with the hustle and bustle of the market, where dozens of merchants would set out their stalls to sell their wares to the townsfolk. But few had ventured forth that morning with the weather as bad as it was and, those who did had soon given up, cursing the rain and mud for keeping folk indoors.

As the weary foot-soldiers began to disperse to their homes, Bjarke swung his leg over the saddle and slid down to the ground, unable to suppress a grunt of fatigue as he did so. Gathering himself, he embraced his wife before then tenderly wiping away the muddy smear he left on her cheek. Next, he bent his head to kiss Erik's forehead promptly reducing the child to tears.

"Greetings, wife. By God it is good to be home at last. Where is Ulf? Why is he not here to welcome home his father? Don't tell me he is sulking somewhere again?" The jarl was unable to keep the irritation from his voice at this apparent show of disrespect from his son.

Thorgunnr took hold of Bjarke's hand, tears now filling her eyes. Sihtric could not help but be impressed by the act that she was putting on for her husband's benefit. All but the hardest heart would be sure to melt.

"Husband," Thorgunnr looked down at the ground in front of her feet, as if afraid to meet his eye. "I have the most awful news. Ulf lies buried in the church these past two weeks."

Bjarke said nothing. He stood rooted to the spot, shaking his head from side to side, unable to believe the words he had heard. Then he looked from his wife to Sihtric and back, hoping for some crumb of comfort. "What game is this, wife? You jest with me. Even now the imp is hiding behind the door of the hall, ready to jump out at me as I go in."

"I wish it were so, Lord. Truly I do," Thorgunnr added a sob to accompany the tears. "He is no more, taken from us by a serving of shellfish that carried some evil humour. Sihtric was there with his wife on the night he passed. Even Freya - with all her great skill - could do nothing to save him."

"Is this true, Steward?" Bjarke roared without diverting his gaze from his wife's face.

Sihtric hesitated, but only for a moment. The urge to tell the truth and throw himself at Bjarke's mercy was almost overwhelming. Had they not been comrades for so many years? Had they not stood side by side in the shieldwall more times than he cared to remember? Had they not also saved each other's lives on countless occasions? Surely, that had to count for something. In the end, however, fear got the better of him. Fear of what the jarl might say or do and fear of his wife. He could feel her piercing blue eyes glaring at him from behind the curtain of her convincingly dishevelled hair.

"It is as Lady Thorgunnr speaks, Lord. Though I wish it were not so with all my heart and soul. There was nothing to be done. I am so very sorry for your loss." He bowed stiffly, partly as a mark of respect but also, so he did not have to look his friend in the eye any longer than necessary.

Silence fell, broken only by Bjarke's horse who whinnied pitifully, nodding his head to tug at the reins held tight in the ostler's hand. Sihtric had not known how the jarl would react to this devastating news, but he had not expected this. The pressure inside his head was almost unbearable; he could feel his temples throbbing with the intensity of the moment. He almost wished that Bjarke would strike him, if only so that the spell would be broken.

Finally, after what seemed an age, Bjarke turned back to his wife, his face a mask that hid his true feelings from all those around him. "Take me to his grave, wife. I would pray over him."

***

Some hours later, Bjarke came to find Sihtric at the smithy where he was tallying the stock of armour and weapons that had been returned for repair. Of the fifty warriors who had formed the jarl's warband from Hoctune, all but eight had returned, though around half of them had injuries of greater or lesser severity. Nearly all, however, had damage to sword, spear, and shield as well as mailshirts and helms that would see Beornfrith the smith and his apprentice sons busy for weeks to come. The business of the estate carries on regardless, Sihtric reflected.

"Ah, Sihtric," The jarl smiled, though it did little to hide the strain in his face or the red rims around his eyes that spoke to the many tears he must have shed.

"Walk with me, old friend."

Without waiting to see whether Sihtric was following, he set forth along the path towards the gate and thence on towards the river. Though the rain had finally ceased, the path was still clogged with mud. Some enterprising soul had lain wooden planks crossways over the worst parts to provide better purchase for those whose business took them outside of their homes, but even these had, in places, sunk beneath the glutinous surface.

Sihtric hurried to catch up with Bjarke's long, rangy stride;

his boots squelching through the mire. He'd ever been a head shorter than the jarl, oftentimes needing two paces to every one just to keep pace. And today was no different as the taller man strode purposefully towards the place where the women would go to wash clothes in the fast-flowing stream. On reaching the water's edge, Bjarke paused to wait for his steward. It did not help matters that Sihtric's back ached from too long spent bending down to help Beornfrith move the piles of weapons and armour into the smithy.

"A bad business this." Bjarke mused once Sihtric finally arrived.

The older man said nothing. It had not sounded as though it were a question that he was required to answer, so he chose to keep his counsel. His father, perhaps knowing that he was not blessed with quick wits, had always advised him that in case of doubt, he should hold his tongue. Better to be thought a fool than to speak and remove all doubt, he would say. Wise words that had stood him in good stead over the years.

"You were there when he died, you say? You saw the effect these oysters had on my boy?"

"I was and I did, Lord. It was like nothing I had seen before."

The jarl raised an eyebrow at that, causing Sihtric to curse inwardly. *Just answer the question and no more, you fool, or you'll land yourself in trouble sooner than the time it takes a thrush to crack a snail shell.*

"You believe the truth of it?"

Sihtric stared into Bjarke's eyes, trying to divine any hidden meaning or intent behind his words. How to reply? He so desperately wanted to bare his soul to his old friend, but he could not be sure how he would react. What he was sure of, however, was that Thorgunnr's retribution would be swift and telling. Moments before, he had sighted Sibba close to the gate, watching him as always; doubtless, word would have already been reported about this conversation. He decided his best option was to answer with a question of his own.

"Do you not, Lord?"

"Well of course I do. Why would I not?"

It was a hurried answer, almost blurted out to cover any doubt in Sihtric's mind. Was Bjarke trying to reach out to him? Did he mistrust his own wife? Even so, he knew he could not risk taking the olive branch, real or imagined. He cared not for himself - he had cheated death on the battlefield on more occasions than he cared to remember - but he could not allow any harm to come to Freya. He would die before he would allow that to happen.

Belatedly, Sihtric realised Bjarke was waiting for a reply. "It is beyond my understanding, Lord. Perhaps Abbot Ethelstan would have the words to explain Ulf's death. Perhaps it is God's will, but I, for one, cannot say why this had to happen." As he spoke, the emotion finally overcame him. He had been holding his grief inside all this time, held at bay by the anger and fear he felt towards Thorgunnr. But now, released from those bonds, he broke down, the tears flowing freely from his eyes. He could not recall the last time he had cried like this; not since he had been a child at any rate.

"You know as well as any, Lord," he sniffed when he had recovered. "I loved that boy. I could not have loved him more even were he mine own. That he is gone and while I was responsible for him pains me more than anything I have ever known - more than any comrade I ever lost in the shieldwall."

Bjarke nodded stiffly, before reaching out to place a comforting hand on the other man's shoulder. "God knows we are no strangers to death, my friend. But death in the front rank is something we can both understand, welcome even. Though it is brutal, there is an honour and purpose to it, nonetheless. But this? This has no meaning; this has no sense. Ulf had not even seen eight winters whereas I have well over forty to my name and stand victor in countless battles. Why would God not take me instead if someone had to die? What purpose can He have had to take one as young as my boy?"

"I cannot explain it, Lord, for all those reasons and more." Sihtric fell silent, unable to offer any more crumbs of comfort. His insides burned with the secret they held, like an acid eating away at him.

The two men stood, side by side, as they had so many times before, staring out across the river - each lost in his own thoughts - until, eventually, Sihtric spoke.

"And what of the Lady Thorgunnr? How does she fare?" He had not intended to ask, but he thought it might be seen as odd were he not to.

Bjarke sighed. "She is strong that one, my friend. Though perhaps it helps that she has had several more days to become accustomed to it. And she has Erik to take her mind off things. She dotes on that boy, and it pleases me to see her so happy with him."

Sihtric could not help himself. "Aye it's a blessing you have another son to succeed you when the time comes."

The jarl turned away from Sihtric. No longer able to see his face, the old warrior wondered whether he had overstepped the mark. He had not intended for it to sound so blunt, so unfeeling, but his mind was filled with conflicting thoughts, and it was as much as he could do to keep them in some sense of order. Knowing what he did, it sounded to his ears as if he had almost accused his lord of being complicit in his wife's crime. A notion almost as ridiculous as the foul deed itself.

When he spoke, Bjarke's words were slow, almost hesitant, as if they had been chosen carefully after much consideration. "It had not escaped my notice, Sihtric, that I have a second son on whom to bestow my inheritance and I am grateful to my wife for having borne me Erik. But do not think that this fact in any way lessens the pain that I feel for Ulf. I am cursed that I was not here for him when he needed me most; I shall bear that guilt with me for the rest of my days. Nor was I even here to see him placed in his grave, to say prayers over his dead body." The jarl's voice was rising with each word, choking with a potent mixture of grief and rage.

"But none of this gives you the right to doubt me on this matter, Sihtric. Our association and my love for you go back many years and are known to everyone here in Hoctune, and many more besides. But you should not presume that my love and favour will protect you through all things. I have my limits, my friend; I have a line which must not be crossed, and you should know that you are perilously close to finding it."

Sihtric hung his head. The rebuke had been earned in full and he could have no complaints. He knew his position was both privileged and vulnerable in equal measure. Many was the lord who would have dismissed him out of hand simply for having not prevented the death of their child. At least Bjarke was a fair man; a fact which made it all the harder to keep the truth hidden from him.

SEVENTEEN

With little time to dwell on the sad events of the past, the people of Hoctune slowly returned to normal; the business of running the estate stood still for no one. There was much to do, either tending the fields or herding the livestock out to the summer pastures where they would spend the long daylight hours happily munching on the lush, thick grass, a welcome change from the hay they had been used to over the winter.

Sihtric went about his duties as if nothing had changed; he could not afford to do otherwise. From the outside, none would have noticed any change in his demeanour but, beneath the surface, he was beset with worry. For one, he had not exchanged more than a dozen words with Bjarke since they had spoken, and all of those had been little more than single word responses to enquiries about estate business. It pained him to think that his relationship with his lord had been damaged to this extent. He even began to suspect the hand of Thorgunnr might be involved. Perhaps the jarl had discussed the matter with her and now she whispered in his ear when they lay together at night.

Then there was the fact that everywhere he or Freya went, there was Halfdan, Sibba or Harald taking it in turns to watch them. Sometimes they chose to conceal themselves behind a cart or round a corner but, more often than not, they stood in plain sight, making it obvious that the couple could not afford to relax. They could go nowhere and say nothing without being observed or heard. For him, he could grin and bear it; little he said or did was that interesting after all. But it was wearing for Freya. Though she would not speak of it, he could see the strain in her eyes. Her normally ruddy cheeks were pale and sallow despite the warmth of the season.

And above all, there was the burden of the truth hanging over them, weighing them down like a heavy millstone had been placed on their shoulders. There was no escaping it. It was the first thought in his mind when he opened his eyes each day and it was his last thought as he closed them again each night. Even with his reputation for stoic endurance in the face of hardship, he was being slowly ground down into the dirt. It was worse still for Freya; he wondered for how long she would cope.

The answer came two days later. Far sooner than he would have hoped.

***

"I swear if I have to go on like this for another day, I shall throw myself into the river." Freya slammed the door behind her, rattling the wooden frame so hard that Sihtric feared it would shatter. He'd only just finally fixed it the previous Sunday, but he doubted his repairs would be able to withstand such treatment for long.

Though he was well used to his wife's outbursts, this was worse than normal. She dropped the basket of cheeses and apples she had been carrying and threw herself face-first down on to the low cot in the far corner of their one-roomed house; the goose feather pillow doing little to mask the sound of her sobs.

Sihtric went to sit on the edge of the bed, gently patting her back for want of any better gesture of comfort. "What ails thee, wife?" He knew it was a foolhardy question, worthy of a caustic reproach but, to his surprise, Freya was so upset that she could not even bring herself to take him to task over it. Indeed, it was some time before she had recovered her composure sufficiently to be able to look in his direction.

"How much longer will we have to endure this torture, husband?"

Sihtric stared at his feet, his hand idly stroking her shoulder. He had no answer, for there was none to be had.

"Everywhere I go, I feel their eyes on me. Nowhere in Hoctune is safe from her thugs. I even wonder if they watch when I piss."

"It'll pass in time, my love. You see if it doesn't." He wasn't sure he believed it, though.

"But when? I'm not a young woman, Sihtric. I don't know how much longer I can stand it. I've a good mind to speak to Father Wulfstan; to tell him everything. Perhaps he will know what to do."

Sihtric's heart began to beat faster. "You can't my love. It would not be safe."

"Don't be silly, husband. What sort of priest would he be were he to betray everything that people told him?"

She was right in principle; priests were supposed to keep what they heard in confidence. But Sihtric also knew that Wulfstan had a liking for ale. And when he was deep in his cups, there was no telling what he might say. Many was the time he had overheard him in the tavern, telling anyone who would listen some juicy titbit of gossip with which he had just been entrusted. No, telling anything to Wulfstan was only a good idea if you wanted the whole of Hoctune to know your business within a day.

"You know as well as any that he cannot be trusted to keep a secret. How many times have you told me something that you'd heard from someone who'd heard it from Wulfstan?"

Freya was sitting on the edge of the bed now, her head in her hands. "But I must tell someone, Sihtric. I'm burning up inside with the weight of this knowledge."

He put his arm around her shoulder and pulled her to him tightly. "We have to be strong, wife. The danger is too great. If word gets back to Thorgunnr that either of us have spoken out of turn, I promise you Halfdan and his mates will come a-knocking; except they won't wait for us to answer the door this time."

***

Sihtric sat alone on his little three-legged stool by the hearth, holding his hands out to enjoy what warmth remained from the embers that still glowed a dull red. It was late, the sun having long since set. By his side, Acwel lay flat on his side, his legs and belly facing the fire as usual, while his head rested on Sihtric's left foot. The house was quiet now. Freya slept on the cot, exhausted by her outburst. The only sound was the slow rhythmic breathing of both wife and dog, mirroring each other on either side of the room. He reached down to scratch Acwel behind his ear causing him to raise his head expectantly.

"Sorry, old boy," he whispered. "I've nothing for you tonight." The dog lay his head down once more, with a noise that Sihtric could have sworn sounded like a sigh. He chuckled despite his inner turmoil. *That dog understands more than he lets on.*

He had sat there for longer than he cared to think, mulling over Freya's words, pushing them back and forth in his mind. But every which way they twisted and turned, no solution to their predicament presented itself. He knew that speaking to Wulfstan was not the answer but nor could he think of any other answer to the problem. Whilst he could hide the truth, presenting an iron-clad face to the rest of Hoctune, it was his wife he worried for. With every day that passed, he could see Freya becoming more and more fraught. She was jumpy, quick to anger and constantly tired, traits that were also noticeable to others around the village. Already, a few of their closer acquaintances had taken him to one side to ask whether she was ill; and these were people that knew them well enough to ask the question. God alone knew what the others must think.

He picked up his seax from where it lay on the table beside him. Absentmindedly, he ran his thumb along the edge, testing its sharpness, and winced as the first few spots of blood welled up from the resulting cut. Sucking his thumb, he wondered whether they should talk to the abbot? For all his faults, Ethelstan was a good man, a godly man. Surely, he could be trusted to protect them, to know what to do? He'd suggest as much to Freya on the morrow. Perhaps she would see the sense of it more than talking to the priest. But for now, he needed sleep. He had to be up with the sun tomorrow to take Bjarke and several of his thegns on a hunt deep into the forests to the west. Rumour had it that wolves had been seen in the trees. Not only would they provide good sport for the spear, but it was as well to deal with them before they attacked the livestock.

He yawned and stretched his arms above and behind his head, feeling the bones crack and the muscles groan in protest. Sitting hunched over for so long in the same place was not good for his back; it always seized up and yet he never seemed to learn. 'Twas ever thus with him, Freya would say. Always just putting his head down and barrelling forward to reach his goal, no matter what lay in his way. But this time it was different. This time he could see nothing but obstacles and no hint of what lay on the other side. All he knew was that the storm clouds were gathering.

EIGHTEEN

Sihtric stifled a yawn as they trotted in single file along the old forest path. It had been a long, hot day following hard on the heels of night with little sleep. Up before the dawn, he had left Freya, still sleeping in bed, to make ready for the day's hunt. Saddling all the horses and arranging sufficient supplies of food and ale were tasks that could not be taken lightly. He knew where the blame would lie should one of the lord's guests - or, even worse, Bjarke himself - find their seat was loose or discover they lacked some essential item when they came to look for it. And then there were the spears. Each one needed to be checked to ensure the head was securely fixed to the shaft, and that the blade had been sharpened to a keen edge. Both would be critical when facing down a wounded or cornered beast. And though there were many hands to help with the work, he could not rest easy until he had checked everything himself, at least twice.

But the day had gone well. In no small measure - he liked to think - due to his diligence. The lads he had sent out at sunrise had tracked their quarry through the forest and had succeeded in driving two brace of wolves towards the hunting party where they had been dispatched following a long chase. To cap off a fine hunt, Bjarke himself had brought down the largest animal. The old greybeard of the family, though none the less powerful and agile for his advancing years.

"A fine day, Sihtric. I commend you."

Startled from his thoughts, Sihtric swung round to see Bjarke had nudged his horse alongside his. His long hair, flecked with grey at the temples, lay matted and plastered to his head from the sweat brought on by the exertion of riding down the old wolf. The beast had led them a merry dance through the trees, unwilling to give his life away cheaply, until finally he could run no more and had turned to face his pursuers, fangs bared and growling his defiance. It had been a brave show which had counted for nought when the jarl's spear had taken him deep in the chest.

Sihtric nodded warily, still unsure of his standing.

Unperturbed, Bjarke continued. "It was a day much needed. One that helped put other thoughts and feelings to one side, at least for a while. I am grateful to have had something else to think about, to enjoy the company of my fellows and the thrill of the chase once more. God knows there has been all too little by way of amusement these last several days."

"It is ever my honour and my duty to serve you, Lord."

Bjarke chuckled, slapping Sihtric on the arm. "Don't be so stiff, you old goat. Is this the same man who stood next to me in battle, staring down the snarling hordes who would spit us on their spears as readily as I did dispatch that wolf? Have we not stood knee dip in blood, guts, piss and shit at the end of a battle, thanking God and each other that we yet live?"

"None can deny it, Lord." Sihtric could not prevent a smile forming on his lips as his mind brought those images to mind. The fear, the terror, the bloodlust descending over them like a fog envelopes a valley floor. Mixed with the excitement, elation almost, of thrusting your steel blade into the neck or guts of the snarling fiend facing you, feeling their hot blood splash over your arm, your face. Over and over again, building a rhythm - block, thrust, parry - until one side can take no more. Few were the times when it had been they who turned and ran. Standing victorious, cheeks blowing, lungs ready to burst, they would watch as the young bloods chased the enemy from the field, slashing at their backs. Those who had not experienced such days could hope to understand what they meant to those who had. How such days bound a man together with his comrades, with ties of loyalty and honour that were tighter - more unbreakable - than any knots of twine or rope.

"Well then. We should remember that and not allow anything else to come between us. Our past is stronger than our present, Sihtric. We should not forget that. Let's not allow this matter to divide us any longer."

"Nothing would please me more, Lord." And he meant it, fervently. But, in truth, Sihtric was torn. His years of service with the jarl and his father before him, stood for so much. They defined his life, gave it meaning. In as much as anyone would remember him after he was gone - and, with no son to follow him, all too few would - they would refer to him first and foremost as Bjarke's man, a warrior, with the courage of a boar and the strength of a bear. It was a hard-won reputation and not to be discarded lightly.

But set against that, his honour and his integrity still gnawed at him. Did his respect for Bjarke, the duty he owed him, not mean that he must tell him what burned away at his soul? Would not unburdening himself of the truth give him the relief he needed, like the steam that rises when the smith plunges the newly forged red-hot blade into a barrel of water?

As they talked, they reached the edge of the woods to see the welcoming sight of Hoctune in the distance. Dusk was falling and Sihtric could see the watch fires high on the palisade that encircled the settlement. He decided to wait for another day; he needed more time to search his soul and to pray for guidance. There was still the option to petition Abbot Ethelstan at Ramsey, of course. Perhaps he should find some pretext to make the short trip on some business or other of the jarl's?

Bjarke leaned over to slap Sihtric on the shoulder. "'Til the morrow then, friend. We'll talk some more over a cup of ale. Relive the old days, eh? And I can tell you about the campaign against Malcolm and his Scots. By God, and I thought the Welsh were strange fellows."

Before he could reply, the jarl dug his heels into his mount's flanks, urging it into a gallop, whooping in delight as he did so. All around him, his call was answered with a chorus of shouts and yells as the dozen or so thegns took flight, each eager to be first in the race for the gate.

***

His duties done at last, Sihtric trudged back through the village to his home. By now it was dark, save for the orange glow emanating from several braziers positioned at regular intervals around the perimeter. All was quiet within the walls, everyone else having long since retired to their beds. Somewhere on his left, beyond the walls, an owl was hooting, its long, haunting call, soon answered by its mate further off still. He knew that over in the woods that surrounded the village, the creatures of the night would be stirring, coming out to find prey to feed their young. Hunting was hard enough, he mused, without being cold and unable to see your quarry as well.

Grinning to himself, he pushed open the door to his home. The smell of his wife's cooking greeted him like an old friend as he hung up his cloak on the peg by the door. Twitching his nostrils, however, he noticed another, less familiar scent.

"Freya, my love. Is something burning?"

No reply. *Perhaps she has fallen asleep waiting for me to return*? He knew he was later than he'd hoped but that was no excuse. Falling asleep with food cooking in the hearth was foolhardy to say the least. How many times had a home burned down in such circumstances? With a sharp rebuke forming on his tongue, he turned to face the room and stopped short.

Of Freya there was no sign. Unusual enough on its own, it was not the most disconcerting sight that befell his eyes. The interior of his home was a mess; it looked as if a fierce storm had blown through it. The table had been overturned, the clay pots that rested upon it were strewn across the floor, many of them shattered beyond repair. The two stools which were usually tucked tidily away beneath the table had met a similar fate, from what he could see. One of them had been broken into several pieces as if something heavy - a body perhaps - had fallen on top of it. Over in the far corner, the bed had also been up ended and the mattress ripped. Straw had spilled out on all sides, adding to the confusion and carnage within the room. *What in God's name has happened here*?

Just then his thoughts were interrupted by the sound of a whimper coming from the far side of the room, near the bed. Acwel! Sihtric bounded across the room, shoving aside the table in his haste to reach the hound. Lifting the ruined mattress, he found his dog. The poor animal was trying to get up, but his movements were feeble, hindered greatly by the heavy wooden frame of the bed which appeared to be trapping him across his shoulders.

"Easy, boy." Sihtric stroked his flank to calm him. Acwel's whole body was shivering, most likely with shock and pain as it was not cold in the house. From where he crouched by the dog's side, he could not tell if he were injured or not. He feared the worst, though; nothing would normally prevent Acwel from jumping up to greet him on his return.

Gently, he lifted the bed and pushed it over to one side where it clattered noisily to the floor. He cared not, though. His only thought was for Acwel; even Freya had been relegated to the margins of his mind for the time being. Though no longer encumbered, still the hound did not move. Carefully, so as not to discomfort the petrified beast any further, Sihtric used his fingers to probe his limbs and back, feeling for a break in the bones, all the while watching closely to see if there were any reaction. There was none.

"I can feel no injury, boy, and yet still you do not jump up." He stroked Acwel's head as he spoke, rubbing behind his ear. As he did so, he felt a sticky wetness. Holding his hand out to the light cast by the hearth, he saw that the ends of his fingers were stained red. All now became clear. Lifting the dog away from the corner, Sihtric turned him over so that he might expose the wound for closer inspection.

"Who did this to you, boy?"

The question was rhetorical; he had already added the pieces together in his mind and the picture he painted filled his heart with a potent mix of fear and rage.

With Acwel settled on his side in front of the fire, Sihtric was able to see the extent of the damage. Thankfully, it did not look as bad as he first feared. The dog must have been clubbed unconscious by one of the assailants who had come into the house, most probably with the leg of the stool. It stood to reason; they would have been afraid of him not least because of his size - he stood almost waist high to most men - but also because he would have been barking, snarling, fangs exposed and ready to rip into flesh. In many ways, he was surprised that the ruckus had not brought people running. As it was, he could at least hope the old boy had managed to inflict some damage before he was knocked out of the fight.

The poor hound had stopped whimpering. His breathing, if a little laboured, was even as he closed his eyes and began to snore. His skull felt intact but any more than that, Sihtric could not say. He would have to wait to see how he was in the morning, praying that a good night's sleep would do much to restore him to his former self.

At last, he allowed his thoughts to turn to Freya. He had no clue where she might be, nor even whether she yet lived. There were no other traces of blood in the room that he could see, for which he was thankful. All he could really say for certain was that she must have been taken by Halfdan and his cronies. But for what purpose? All he could think was that Thorgunnr had simply decided to remove all risk by killing the witnesses? Perhaps she had sensed Freya's deteriorating state of mind and decided to act before it was too late.

If that were true, then they would be coming for him next. Or did they hope to lure him out into the forests in search of his wife, perhaps wary of trying to tackle him within Hoctune itself. He glanced towards the space above the fireplace and was reassured to see Leggbitr still there. That old sword had seen him through worse times than this, he mused, and whoever had taken his wife might come to regret not having also taken his blade. If it were a trap, then it was one he was willing to walk into if it was the only way to save Freya.

But for now, he needed sleep. There was no sense blundering around in the dark like a boar being chased through the forest. He needed his wits about him; he needed to see what tracks might be found around his house, and for that he needed daylight and strength. His body ached from the day's exertions and his leg had stiffened through excessive use. If he was going to pick up his sword once more - and in doing so, break his solemn promise to his wife - he would need his body to be sturdy. An old man, hobbling around on one leg would be easy prey to the likes of Halfdan.

NINETEEN

The dawn light streaming through the narrow gaps between the wooden slats that made up the wall of his house was enough to wake Sihtric from the light sleep to which he had eventually succumbed. Rolling on to his side, he put his arm out across the bed. The lack of a reassuring lump where normally Freya would be, caused him to open his eyes and sit up. The sight of the broken furniture brought his memory flooding back in an instant.

He swung his legs out of bed and pushed himself upright, testing, as he did so, his full weight on his left leg. Though the battle wound had long since healed, the pain never fully receded. It was worse in the cold or - like now - when he had asked too much of the limb the previous day. He winced as a sharp stab of pain lanced through his shin, but it passed soon enough, and the leg held firm. Feeling more confident, he stood on the tips of his toes, bouncing lightly up and down, feeling the satisfying burning sensation from the muscles in the back of his lower leg. He would need them to respond at a moment's notice if it came to a fight.

Eschewing breakfast, he dressed quickly and prepared to leave. Ever a creature of routine, Acwel lifted himself from where he had been dozing and padded over to where Sihtric stood by the door, stretching his front and rear legs in turn, arching his back and then finally shaking his head vigorously. Though a little more lethargic than normal, the hound appeared to be unaffected by his ordeal. As if it were any other morning, he stood by the door, tail wagging, waiting to be allowed out to sniff the morning as was his wont.

"Come on then, boy." Sihtric ruffled his ears playfully, taking care to stay well clear of where he had been bludgeoned. "Let's see what we can find, eh?"

Outside, the air was cold but fresh, clearing his brain of the fatigue and fear that had enveloped him since waking. He gave thanks that, as the hour was still early, there was no one in sight;

no one to ask awkward questions about what he was doing. He halted on the threshold, eager not to add any further confusion to what tracks might still be visible. But it was useless. The ground around his doorway was thickly trampled with all the comings and goings over the past days and weeks. There was no way he could make sense of the confused crisscrossing of the many different sized feet: human and animal.

He began to scout the area more widely, gradually moving away from the house in a series of arcs, five paces apart. It was on the third such sweep that he spotted the first possible clue: a pair of rutted, parallel lines roughly two short paces apart that headed off in a straight line towards Bjarke's hall. They looked fresh too, having very few, if any, footprints cutting into their uniform lines.

A cart has stood here recently, he thought to himself. He now had the answer to the question of how Freya had been taken, but not where. A few more moments spent searching the ground revealed no further clues. It was now several hours since his wife had been seized and who knew whether she still lived? And even if she did, what manner of unspeakable atrocities were being visited upon her person while he dallied?

Even as he tried to banish such thoughts from his mind, he felt a searing anger starting to boil in the base of gut once again, rising inexorably through his body and threatening to subsume him in its steely grip. It was like an old friend. One who he'd not seen for several years, not since that day at Assandun when the two shieldwalls clashed at the top of the rise. He'd welcomed it then, knowing it added to his strength and battle-fury. Men had recoiled from him then, recognising him as one lost to the gods of war. But for now, he knew he needed control over his emotions. He needed what wits he possessed to find where they had taken Freya. Later, there would be time aplenty to unleash the berserk fiend that lurked within.

He began to follow the tracks, focussing on the rutted lines to distract his mind. He soon passed Bjarke's hall on his right with no sign that the cart had halted there. As he expected, the tracks made a turn to the left taking the path between the church on one side and the granary on the other. A few people had stirred by this time, but he was oblivious to them all the same. One or two hailed him, wishing him the best of the day, but they were ignored, their voices failing to penetrate his consciousness. They shook their heads and muttered to themselves before passing on their way.

Before long, he arrived at the main gate, finding it still shut and barred at that early hour. Shielding his eyes against the low sun that now peeked over the palisade, he looked up to the walkway where he could see the night-watchman staring out towards the forest.

"Hail, Fortha."

The sentry turned about. "Hail, Sihtric. Wait there, friend, I'll come down. It's time to open the gate for the day, anyway."

Moments later, Fortha stood before him, gripping him by the forearm in the warrior's greeting. Fortha was another of the old lads of the jarl's warband but was also now - like Sihtric - too old to stand in the shieldwall. He'd always been a stout fellow, with legs as thick as tree-trunks, and now he had the belly to match. Without the need to train each day, the beer and food had taken its toll on his waist. But Sihtric did not begrudge him that. To have fought in as many battles as he had, the man had twice over earned his rest and the right to spend it any way he pleased. It was said Fortha had never once taken a step back in battle. Sihtric thought it an unlikely claim, but it had earned the old warrior the nickname of Oaken-Legs. Where he planted his feet, there he stood, unmovable until the day was done one way or another.

"What can I help you with, my friend?" Fortha's voice was deep and gravelly, almost lost within the beard that obscured the greater part of his craggy face.

"Have you been on watch all night?"

"Aye, what of it?" His tone had assumed a defensive air as if Sihtric was about to accuse him of some dereliction of duty.

Ignoring him, Sihtric continued. "Anything to report? Any unusual comings or goings during the night?"

The other man paused for a moment, casting his mind back while Sihtric waited, impatient for an answer. "No... No... Wait. Now you mention it, a cart did head out not long after I came up to the wall."

"And?" It was not just the man's legs that are oaken, Sihtric mused, wondering how long it would take to drag the information from him.

"And what?"

"Who was with the cart? What were they carrying and what reason did they give to be on the road at night? Were they not afraid of bandits?"

"Hmmph, these boys had little to fear, I'd say. Burly bastards, the three of them and with faces only a mother could love."

"Did you know them?" His patience was just about worn out. It was as much as he could do not to grab Fortha by the throat and shake some sense of urgency into him.

"I knew one of them. Halfdan, I think his name is. Lady Thorgunnr's man. Didn't know the other two, but I'm sure I've seen the three of them together before."

There it was. Though Sihtric could not consider himself surprised. As soon as he had found Freya missing, he suspected their hand in it. Halfdan and his mates had been watching them both ever since his wife had confronted the jarl's lady.

"And where did they claim to be heading?"

"South to Lundenburh. On the lord's business they said. Wanted to get as far as they could before sundown, hence the early start."

Sihtric snorted. A lie for certain, but one that was sufficiently bold to convince the night's watch to open the gate for them. He'd heard enough. He needed to be on his way if he were to have any hope of catching up with them. He thanked Fortha and turned to go noting, as he did so, that the old warrior was rubbing at his chin through his wiry brush of a beard, as if trying to recall some further detail.

"Wait."

Sihtric turned back, an expectant look on his face.

"I knew there was something else. Something that struck me as odd at the time."

"Well?"

"Though they said they were heading south, they took the north road towards Ramsey."

"You're sure of this?"

"Aye. I watched them take the path towards the trees but when they reached the main road, they turned to the right. They must have thought themselves far enough away to be out of sight, but the fools carried a torch to light their way. I distinctly saw its flame heading to the north."

Now this was something worth knowing. He clapped his old comrade on the back and began walking back to his house. It was time to be about his business.

Fortha called after him. "Is there anything I can do to help? My duty has finished now."

Sihtric pondered this before answering. It might be useful to have a stout fellow alongside him. Odds of three against one were not to his liking, but could he really put such a burden on his old comrade? Besides, it would mean having to take old Oaken-Legs into his confidence. Decision made, he stepped back up close to Fortha, so that his face was not far from the other man's ear.

"I believe they had Freya in that cart and that they mean her harm."

Fortha's mouth fell open in astonishment. "But… why?" was all he could muster.

"The story is long and the time to tell it is not now. If it is true, I must find her before it is too late."

"Wait here, Sihtric. I'll fetch my spear and shield. It'll be like old times, eh?"

Sihtric placed a hand on Fortha's shoulder. "My thanks to you, old friend. On any other day, I would gladly welcome your offer, but I cannot ask this of you. You have served your time in the shieldwall; none can say otherwise. You have earned your peace and I would not have your death on my conscience for this is no one's fight but mine. But you can do me one service."

"Name it, friend." Fortha could not hide the relief on his face, made worse by his eagerness to fulfil whatever favour Sihtric might ask of him instead.

"Should I not return, be sure to tell Jarl Bjarke where I have gone and why."

Fortha pulled Sihtric to him and clasped him in a firm

embrace. "It shall be so, Sihtric. May God watch over you. Bring Freya home safe and teach those Dane bastards some manners at the same time."

***

Back in his house, Sihtric knew he could waste no more time. Halfdan and his friends already had several hours' start on him and it was going to be a tall order to claw it back. But he had to be prepared. He could not blunder in blindly, not if he hoped to save his wife's life. If she had not been killed already of course. His only hope was that they needed her alive in order to lure him out to save her, thereby trapping two rabbits in a single snare.

He strode over to the wooden chest that stood at the foot of their bed. It was some time since he'd opened it, but he knew that what lay within would be in order. Once a warrior, always a warrior, he grinned; and no warrior worth his weight in salt would allow his equipment to fall into disrepair. He grunted as he lifted out the heavy package which he then laid carefully on the floor. Kneeling before it, he unwrapped the oiled hide covers to reveal his byrnie, the knitted iron links gleaming in the sunlight that streamed across the room. Deftly, he unfolded the mailshirt, rubbing his calloused hands over its familiar rings. Here and there, patches stood out that were newer than the rest, testament to blows long since forgotten and the painstaking repairs he had laboured over afterwards. This old shirt had seen him through some tough scrapes, keeping him alive on more than one occasion. He had thought - hoped even - that its days of service were long done. But if that was not to be its fate, then so be it.

He pulled the cumbersome garment over his head, noting with pride how there was not a single patch of rust to be seen. It felt heavier than he remembered, though he had not yet cinched it into place with his belt, so all the weight was pulling down on his shoulders. *You're getting old, Sihtric. In days gone by, you would not have noticed the burden. At Assandun, you fought all day without a word of complaint.*

With the byrnie now snugly in place, he returned to the chest to retrieve his helm. For a moment, he considered leaving it behind - its extra weight might slow his progress. But the protection it offered was not to be taken for granted. Many was the time his skull had been saved from being cleaved in two because of it. Like his mailshirt, the helm showed several signs of age and tear. The nose-guard had been replaced more than once while the metal panels had several small dints to mark where blows had struck. Many warriors might have done away with one as worn as this, but it was comfortable and fitted as well as any glove. Besides, such things did not come cheap and without the chance of booty to be taken in battle, Sihtric could not afford to be choosy. Glancing back in the chest, he saw his old amulet and paused. He knew he should not take it, but what could it hurt? He needed all the luck he could muster. Squatting down he lifted the small iron hammer to his lips before slipping the leather cord over his neck. Pushing it out of sight beneath his byrnie, he patted the spot over his heart where it came to rest.

Finally, Sihtric made his way over to the hearth, where Leggbitr hung proudly over the fireplace. For a few moments, he stared at the blade, reminiscing about the battles it had seen and the blood it had spilt. Then, he lifted it from the fittings that held it to the wall. As he hefted it in his hand, remembering its weight and balance, his thoughts turned once again to his wife. *Forgive me, Freya, for I must break the promise I made to you.* He had no choice. If he were to rescue her from her captors, he would need to be prepared to deal death once again.

He slid the blade into its fleece-lined scabbard that hung from his belt, easing it back and forwards to ensure it ran smooth and did not snag. Then he pushed his seax into its own sheath and grabbed his shield from where it stood against the wall. He was ready. It was time to walk the path of the warrior one more time.

TWENTY

Young Chad the stable boy dared ask no questions of Sihtric as he saddled up the steward's pony. One look at the old warrior dressed in his war gear was enough to still his tongue. Everyone in Hoctune knew of the promise he had made to Freya. Even Chad and his friends who often whispered in awe of the greybeard whenever he passed by. Many was the man who had joked of it in the tavern, but only when Sihtric was not in earshot or when their wits had been dulled by too many cups of ale. When strong drink lent men courage, there were those who might have said that it was the wife that wore the trews in that house. But none would have dared say that to his face, even when drunk, for he was a man to be feared still, despite his advancing years. The great bear of Bjarke's war-band, the rock on which his shieldwall was built, still commanded respect amongst the people of the town.

Chad would have a tale to tell his father when he got home, though. His eagerness to do so was tempered, however, by the chilly morning air that caused his fingers to fumble with the leather straps of the saddle and harness. To make matters worse, he was very aware of Sihtric standing behind him, tapping his foot impatiently against the straw-covered floor of the stable. Knowing the old steward was growing impatient caused Chad's cheeks to flush red with shame and embarrassment. With the task finally completed, the stable boy led the pony outside to the mounting block, where the indignant beast stood snorting and blowing steam impudently from her nostrils in protest at being taken from her warm stall.

Struggling to maintaining an even temper, Sihtric followed the boy. Stepping up on to the block, he took hold of the leather pommel at the front of the saddle and then swung himself up. He took a moment to shuffle himself into a more comfortable position before slotting his booted feet into the stirrups that hung loosely on each side. Finally, he nodded his thanks to the boy and - against his better judgement - flicked him a silver penny from his purse for his troubles.

Dipping his heels into the pony's flanks, he coaxed the beast into a reluctant walk. At the sound of the hooves thudding along the hard-packed earth, Acwel came bounding out from the stable where he'd been snuffling happily amongst the piles of night-soiled straw. Sihtric smiled to see the hound looking something more akin to his normal self and gave thanks that his injury appeared to be no worse than a sore head. He would be glad of the company on his quest. Who knew? The old boy might yet serve a greater purpose.

He passed through the gate a few moments later, acknowledging Fortha's arm which was raised in salute with a wave of his own. For a brief heartbeat, he reconsidered asking old oaken-legs to come with him, but he had already delayed long enough. He could not afford to wait for the heavy-set man to waddle back home to fetch his gear. And besides, this was no one else's fight but his own. He could not have another man's death on his conscience. In truth, the odds scared him, but the thought of what might happen to Freya scared him more. He was not afraid to die, but to lose his honour should he not at least try to save her was unconscionable. He had never stepped away from a fight, and this would not be the day to start.

His jaw set in a determined grimace, he pushed on along the path that headed towards the trees that circled the little village. A hundred or so paces saw him come to the junction where the road turned to the left and south or right and north. As Fortha had said, he could see the clear imprint of the cart's wheels heading off to the north.

If the tracks stayed like this, Sihtric mused, he should have no difficulty following them. If not, then he'd have no chance of finding them; he had no idea where Halfdan might have taken Freya. Surely, he would not take her as far as Ramsey. What would be the point? It was more likely that he would take her deep into the forests that covered the land between Hoctune and the abbey ten or so miles to the north, for no other purpose than to kill her, before then coming back for him or to keep her captive until he came looking for her.

In his favour, though, was the fact that Sihtric knew the

woods well; he had hunted in them many times over the years. He also knew - with disheartening certainty - that there were dozens of little huts dotted among them. Some used by herders to shelter from storms, others used by hunters to sleep overnight. A few were even homes to people who lived beyond the law, by choice or necessity. People like Cwenhild, the so-called witch. The enormity of the task facing him caused his gut to wrench. With a word of encouragement, he urged Modig into a trot.

***

By the time the sun had climbed high into the searingly blue sky, Sihtric still had not found anything resembling a clue as to Halfdan's whereabouts. With every passing hour, he was growing more and more anxious. He knew that the longer this went on, the less chance there would be of finding his wife alive. Nevertheless, even though he had no way of knowing, something deep in his soul told him she yet lived. It sounded a ridiculous notion, but he felt he would know if she were dead. Some shadow would have fallen over his heart should her life have been snuffed out. And that hope, however vain, kept him plodding forward mile after mile.

Several times - fancying he had seen some small sign, real or imagined - he had turned Modig's head aside to follow one of the smaller paths into those places where the trees were more thickly gathered. On each occasion, Acwel would bound off into the distance, running hither and thither, sniffing every tree and bush. But each time he failed to find any recognisable scent to follow and would slowly lope back to Sihtric, his ears flat against his head and his tail between his legs.

But then, just as despair was starting to take a firm hold of him, Acwel let out a sharp bark. Looking down, Sihtric saw the hound had frozen in place, one front paw raised in the act of stepping forward, his tail stock still and pointing sky-wards.

"What is it, boy?"

Acwel looked up at Sihtric, his head cocked to one side, before turning back to face the same direction. Something had spooked him, that much was certain. As the day had worn on, the ground had dried and hardened, making it more and more difficult to track the cart's progress. And this spot was no different. He could see no clear path through the trees and there were no tell-tale tracks to follow. Still, it was not like Acwel to act up for no reason. He would have to investigate.

The old warrior eased himself out of the saddle and slipped down to the ground, landing on his worrisome leg with a muted grunt. Straightening up, he pushed his hands into the small of his back and twisted his hips back and forth, loosening the muscles in his lower back which had stiffened from so long hunched in the saddle. Then, taking hold of the bridle, he led Modig forward at a slow walk, scanning the ground to the left and right as he went. Acwel prowled at his side, snuffling at every scent, desperate to be let loose. But it was a risk he could not take, lest the hound should prematurely alert Thorgunnr's men to his presence.

Every ten or so paces, Sihtric stopped. Each time, he cupped his hands behind his ears to better funnel the sound as he swivelled his head from side to side. Nothing. Just a deep stillness formed by the ancient, densely packed trees. There was not even a breeze to cause the leaf-laden branches to rustle overhead.

Though he was out of the sun, the heat under the thick canopy of foliage was still oppressive. The lack of air made him want to gasp to fill his lungs. He could feel the sweat trickling down his back, soaking the waist band of his trews beneath the padded jerkin he wore for comfort beneath his mailshirt. He might be glad of its protection later but, for now, he cursed its sodden burden.

He pressed on a further ten paces. Then something caught his eye. A colour lighter than the browns and greens of the lichen-covered twigs and branches. A colour that was out of place in its surroundings. Dropping to his knees, he used his hands to part the prickly branches of a bramble bush, cursing under his breath as he felt more than one vicious spike lance into his fingers. Then he saw it again. A small piece of blue cloth, snagged on the prickly thorns. It was not proof of anything in itself, but it showed that someone had passed this way, carelessly allowing their garment to catch and tear on the bramble. Sihtric could picture the man pulling impatiently at the cloak as it dragged him back. Either in too much of a hurry or not caring for the material to take the time to gently unpick it from its spiny captor. *More fool you, my friend. For now, I know you followed this path.*

Sihtric led his pony back to a point midway between the bush and the road. Finding a suitable tree, he tethered the bridle securely so that Modig could not wander. Not that she appeared to have any such inclination, preferring to lower his neck to chomp contentedly on the lush grass that grew in abundance around his hooves. With the pony thus distracted, Sihtric untied his shield from where it had been secured behind the saddle. Slinging it across his back, he rubbed the beast's nose as a tender parting gesture. "I'll be back for you soon, girl." He hoped it was a promise he could keep.

From here on, he would need stealth and cunning. Though he could not risk Modig whinnying in fright or annoyance, Acwel, on the other hand, he could trust. A strong bond had formed between them over the years, such that he knew the dog would obey his commands without the slightest hesitation. And with Acwel there, he did not feel truly alone.

As if to seek reassurance, Sihtric bent to scratch the dog behind his ears, whispering as he did so. "Stay close to me, boy. I don't want you getting another clout round the head. Be ready, though. When the time comes, I may have need of your teeth."

Acwel licked his hand, yawned, and then went back to sniffing the ground. Sihtric chuckled. Who knew what went on in that thick head?

Preparations made, he set off, pausing only to unsheathe his sword; it would not do to be caught unawares. At first, there was nothing to be seen or heard; even the birds seemed to have deserted the trees. Either that or they perched silent and unseen in the branches high above him, frozen by fear of the death-bringing man who stalked the forest floor beneath them.

Every step he took was carefully planned. Though it slowed his progress to little more than a snail's pace, he could not risk snapping a dry twig. Even if the trees helped to muffle the sound, it would still carry further than the eyes could see, providing ample warning to any that lay in wait up ahead.

His mouth had taken on the familiar dry feeling that came before the promise of battle. Several times, he had to ease his tongue away from the roof of his mouth and work his gums from side to side to tease some saliva from his parched mouth. A small knot had formed in his stomach as it always did; the sensation flowing through him, sharpening his senses as of old. He prayed his limbs and muscles would be similarly sharp when he had need of them.

By his calculation, he had walked about two hundred paces from where he had left Modig, when he saw it. About thirty paces to his front, partially obscured by trees, the incongruous sight of right-angled lines came into view. Another few steps confirmed that he had happened upon one of the many huts secreted throughout the woods. Any doubt that he might have held over whether he had found his quarry was dispelled shortly after as, circling to his right, the form of a four-wheeled wain - with horse attached - came into view, pulled up on the far side of the hut.

A little further to his right still, he found a clump of shrubs clustered between two huge oak trees. Crouching down behind them, he found that he could, through the maze of leaves and berries, keep watch on the door of the hut whilst being confident that he could not be seen. He settled in to wait, his mind racing, torn between the desire to charge in to rescue Freya as quickly as possible, and the need for caution. Blundering in blindly might well achieve little but his own death and a guarantee of a foul end for his wife. He needed a plan.

He lost track of time as he sat there thinking. The heat made his eyes droop, reminding him just how tired he was. His brain was awash with thoughts, none of which amounted to anything even remotely resembling a plan that bore any chance of success. With the three of them inside and him without, the odds were heavily stacked in their favour. He knew he would have a greater chance outside, with room to swing his sword and use his shield; but how could he entice them out without losing the advantage of surprise?

So far, there had been no sound or movement from within; he

had begun to doubt whether anyone was even inside. It occurred to him that they might simply have dumped the cart and gone further into the woods on foot. The trees did become more densely packed beyond the building, so perhaps they had abandoned the cart for that reason? If that were the case, he knew not what he would do. He had wasted too much time already sat behind these damned shrubs and, all the while, Freya could have been subjected to God knows what atrocities at the hands of these Dane bastards.

A sudden rustling nearby jerked him back to the moment. His hand dropped to the hilt of his seax as he rolled on to his side, ready to confront whatever had managed to creep up on him. He was just in time to see a squirrel disappearing into the upper reaches of the oak tree to his left, its mouth bulging with acorns. Disturbed by the sudden movement, Acwel lifted his head from where it had been resting on his front legs as he dozed. He sniffed the air, disinterestedly, before resuming his position. Sihtric chuckled, relieved that it had been a false alarm. The hound had learned long ago that chasing squirrels rarely ended in anything other than disappointment and humiliation.

Just then, another noise - this time from the direction of the hut - made him freeze in the act of resuming his seated position. Easing himself down gently, Sihtric peered through the screen of leaves and spikes. He was just in time to see the door open, from which the stocky form of Harald emerged with Halfdan's shouted instructions following him.

"Make sure you go far enough away. I don't want to have to smell your shit wafting over us all day. It's bad enough having Sihtric's bitch in here with us. I swear on Odin's eye that she's pissed herself in fright."

Harald muttered something unintelligible by way of reply, before stomping off in the direction of the trees.

Grinning to himself, Sihtric knew that not only was his wife alive within, but that he had also been granted the opportunity for which he had been waiting. Where he had been unable to devise a plan of his own, one had now been gifted to him. A call of nature had improved his odds by separating the three men. But he would have to act quickly if he were to take advantage of this unforeseen manna from heaven. Offering a silent prayer of thanks, he rose into a crouching position, ignoring the protests coming from his knees, and watched to see what path Harald took.

Placing his sword and shield down, Sihtric began to track the Dane's path. As luck would have it, the big lumbering oaf had headed to where the trees and undergrowth grew thickest. Whether it was in deference to Halfdan's parting instructions or whether the Dane sought a greater measure of privacy from those inside, Sihtric cared not. Instead, he concentrated on following at a distance that was close enough to keep him in sight but far enough away to stay out of earshot. He was helped in this endeavour by Harald's tuneless but carefree whistling; the man clearly had no clue that his life was nearing its end.

Nevertheless, Sihtric timed each of his steps to coincide with those of his prey, another small but effective ploy to reduce the risk of his approach being detected. As he stalked his unwitting victim, he reflected on the good fortune that had seen Harald leave the hut to void his bowels. Taking a shit would take longer than a mere piss and would also see Harald at a significant disadvantage as he squatted. No man could defend himself with any great agility with his trews around his ankles and his arse bared to the world.

He would not take stupid risks, though. Many a man had been tricked into thinking his opponent was beaten only to find himself on the wrong end of a sword or seax point. Besides, though they had gone some distance from the hut, a yell from Harald could yet bring the others running. He needed to be quiet and precise, to dispatch the Dane before he had a chance to call out in fear or pain.

Sihtric switched his knife to his left hand so that he could wipe his palm against the rough wool of his trews. Sweat from the heat and anxiety had made the skin clammy and he could not afford to lose his grip on the bone handle at the vital moment.

Eventually, Harald stooped to grab a handful of dock leaves before stepping behind a huge oak. Without pause, he began to fumble with the drawstring that held up his trews. Sihtric was no more than ten paces away now and hidden from view by the vast, sprawling bole of the tree. As he drew closer to the trunk's gnarled bark, he could hear Harald straining to be free of his burden; several earthy farts presaged the onset of something altogether more solid.

A small part of him sympathised with the Dane; no man deserved to be sent to the afterlife in such a way. But he had no choice if he wanted to save Freya. Besides, he had no doubt Harald would show him no mercy had their roles been reversed.

With a final glance behind him to be sure that neither Halfdan nor Sibba had emerged from the hut, Sihtric inched his way around the tree. As soon as the back of Harald's head came into view, he lunged forward, plunging his seax deep into the exposed flesh of the Dane's neck with all the force he could muster. The momentum of the blow knocked Harald over, losing his balance as his legs became tangled in the clothes bunched around his ankles. So deep did the blade penetrate that some vital vessel must have been severed for blood gushed from the gaping wound in a great arc that Sihtric recoiled to avoid. For a moment, he panicked lest Harald should cry out, but he need not have worried. Blood flooded his throat and lungs, drowning him before he had a chance to make any sound greater than a pathetic gurgling as he clawed at his throat, gasping for the air that could no longer find its way into his lungs.

As his life slowly ebbed away into the soil, Harald finally lost control of his guts, emptying his bowels in a seemingly unending stream of effluence. The stench was enough to cause Sihtric to gag. Holding his left hand over his nose, he pushed himself up and away, but only once he was certain that Harald breathed no more.

"By God man, between your blood and your shit you did your best to ruin my mailshirt, you bastard." He aimed a final kick at Harald's face as a last act of retribution. "Though if I find my Freya has been harmed or interfered with in any way, you will thank your Gods that your end was swift. For I promise you it will go less well for your friends."

TWENTY-ONE

Sihtric paused only long enough to wipe the blood from his seax before returning to where he had left his sword and shield. He needed to move fast; it wouldn't take long for Halfdan and Sibba to begin wondering where Harald was. He contemplated letting that play out; would it not work in his favour were one or both of them to come looking for their companion? But he soon dismissed the idea. Had their roles been reversed, he would assume the worst and come out prepared for a fight. And who knew what they might do to Freya if they feared an attack? Better for him to move now, while they were least expecting it.

He pushed his left hand through the worn leather straps of his shield, hefting its familiar weight up and down to warm up the muscles in his shoulder. Then he grabbed the hilt of his sword and set off towards the hut, taking care to stay out of sight of the single, small window. Leggbitr felt comfortable in his right hand, its weight and balance so familiar to him after all these years.

As he walked, he rolled his wrist to twist the blade around, recalling all the old moves: parry and thrust, parry and thrust. It felt good, comforting even, to have the weapon back in his grasp. He just prayed he still had the speed, agility and - most of all - luck to beat the two men who waited for him; two men who were half his age. It was of no matter, though; he had no choice. His jaw set, he resigned himself to whatever fate might hold in store for him. By his side, Acwel trotted along, looking up at him expectantly.

He had no plan to speak of. He would just barge through the door - smashing it down if necessary - with as much noise and uproar as possible. He hoped the ensuing chaos might buy him precious time to assess what he faced. If the two Danes had any inkling of his approach, then he was doomed for sure. With luck, his sudden appearance would prompt Halfdan and Sibba to advance towards him, like bees to a flower. Such an outcome would allow Freya ample time and space to escape before the killing began.

Sihtric covered the last few paces in silence, taking inordinate care over where he placed his feet. Any inadvertent sound now and the game would be over before it had even begun. Reaching the hut, he paused with his back to the wall, his ear pressed against the planks to try to hear what was going on within. He was thankful that whoever owned the hut had taken good care of it, stuffing the gaps between the slats with moss to keep out the draught. It also had the welcome effect of masking any sight of him from within. The slats themselves, though sound, were grey from years of exposure to the elements. Here and there, they were streaked with dark trails where sap had long ago oozed from the joints before being frozen in time, like a permanent amber icicle.

Slowly, as he filtered out the noise of the woodland around him, he became aware of voices. Low and muffled as they were, he could, nevertheless, make out the sound of two men conversing. Though indistinct at first, the tone of their voices seemed calm. As far as he could tell, his presence was, so far, unknown. But all that was about to change.

"Where's he got to?"

With a start, Sihtric realised that Sibba had moved close to the window.

"Patience, friend. You know he likes to take his time over a shit."

Sibba grunted. "Can't we just be on our way? Slit her throat and dump her deep in the forest? I've had enough of her incessant moaning. I don't know how her bastard husband puts up with it."

Sihtric felt a lump form in his throat. His wife might still live, but her fate hung in the balance. He tightened his grip on his sword, readying himself for the fray.

"You heard Lady Thorgunnr. Keep her alive until she comes, or until Sihtric finds his way here. If that happens, which I doubt given how dull-witted he is, then we kill them both. Just think about the coin waiting for us on our return."

"At least let me have some fun while I wait. Give her something to really moan about."

"Suit yourself. I care not."

His mind made up, Sihtric eased himself away from the wall to take up position facing the door. It was time to act. He had to save Freya from whatever foul deed Sibba had planned for her.

Standing stock still for a few moments, he weighed up the strength of the door. It looked old and in need of repair; he felt sure it would not withstand a brutal assault. He realised he was breathing hard. His heart was pounding in his chest as it always did in the moments before battle. Apart from the boar that had nearly killed Ulf the previous year, the last time he had felt this sensation was back in the shieldwall at Assandun as the two armies closed together. He took several deep breaths, filling his lungs with air. He felt them expand, filling the space beneath his mailshirt, before slowly exhaling through his nose. With a final heft of both sword and shield, he launched himself forward, raising his right leg so that the flat of his boot smashed through the dilapidated planks.

The door seemed to fold in on itself before splintering into several pieces. Sihtric didn't wait to admire his handiwork, though; he could not afford to give the two Danes any time in which to recover their senses. Roaring incoherent curses that would likely earn admonishment from Father Wulfstan had he been there to hear them, he barged into the one-roomed building, his shield clearing what remained of the door as he passed. Released at last, Acwel hurtled past him barking, snarling and growling, seemingly all at the same time.

It was gloomy inside the hut, but what he saw sent him into a rage, the likes of which he had not experienced before, not even amid the fiercest battle. He could feel himself losing control, as if a veil was being drawn over his mind. The sound of blood rushing through his ears was like a torrent, drowning out all other sounds. He knew at that moment, there could be no mercy. These men would die here.

Over in the far corner lay some crude mattress - nothing more than an old piece of sacking, in truth, stuffed with straw and roughly sewn so that several loose stalks protruded through its myriad holes. In the middle of the mattress lay Freya, on her back with her dress shoved up to her waist. Kneeling between her legs, Sibba was busy fumbling with his clothing, readying himself to assault her, while Halfdan leaned over her torso, pinning her arms down to stop her from struggling. A piece of rag had been shoved in her mouth to stop her from screaming, but the fear Sihtric saw in her eyes spoke louder than any words.

"Bastards!" Sihtric howled, tears springing to his eyes with the force of anger that welled up inside of him. Casting aside all thoughts of any plan, he lowered his head and charged forward, ramming the top of his iron helm directly into Halfdan's chin as he was halfway back to his feet. The force of the impact snapped the man's neck back, smashing his unprotected head against the wall with a sickening thud. The Dane's eyes rolled back up into his skull, as his legs gave way beneath him, leaving him in a crumpled heap by the side of the bed.

Turning his head, he caught a blur of movement in the corner of his eye. He threw up his shield as quickly as he could. It was a reaction based on instinct - nothing more - learned on the field of battle long ago, where a blow could reach out and take you from any direction, at any moment. It was an instinct that had saved him many times before and it did so again now. But the passage of time meant he was no longer the man he had once been. Though his strength had yet to fail him, he did not have the same speed of movement. So it was that his shield was only partially raised when the blow landed. Sibba's sword hit the narrow iron rim that wound its way around the edge of his shield, holding the alder wood planks together. With a shower of sparks, the blade travelled along the metal casing before connecting with the side of his head, no more than two fingers' breadth above the rim of his helm.

It was his good fortune, however, that the blow had been hurried. A snap reaction to his sudden appearance. It lacked the full force of Sibba's body behind it, and the shield served to dull its weight yet further. But it was still enough to daze Sihtric. He staggered back a few paces, bright flashes of light exploding behind his eyes. He shook his head from side to side, desperate to clear the fug so that he could focus once more, but it was futile. Blindly, he held the shield in front of him, knowing it was of little use. Sibba had but to follow up his attack and he was finished. He had failed Freya when she needed him most, and now they would show her no pity; they would make her pay for his actions.

But he had reckoned without Acwel. How could he have forgotten about his faithful companion? Seeing his master in danger, the hound did the only thing he could, using the only weapon he had. Ignoring the cruelly sharp blade in Sibba's hand, Acwel leapt forward, closing the distance to the Dane in a heartbeat, before clamping his jaws around Sibba's wrist. The woollen sleeve of his tunic did nothing to prevent the razor-sharp teeth from biting deep into his flesh.

Howling with shock and agony, Sibba dropped his sword, the long metal blade clattering heavily against the wooden floorboards. Frantically, he began shaking his arm to try to force the dog to release its hold, punching at the hound's head with his weaker left hand. This only served to anger Acwel, however, so that he clamped his jaws together more tightly than ever. At the same time, the hound's claws scrabbled against the wooden floor, seeking greater purchase as he hauled back on the shrieking Dane's arm. And all the while, Acwel shook his head from side to side in his fury, as though he were trying to remove the arm from its socket.

Sibba was starting to panic. Not only must the pain in his wrist be unbearable, but he would also have known that it was only a matter of time until Sihtric recovered his wits sufficiently to finish him. Shaking his arm had not worked, nor had punching the beast. In his desperation, he did the only thing he could. Reaching awkwardly across his body with his left hand, he drew his seax from its sheath. His face contorted with rage and pain, he then stabbed down as hard as he could into the dog's flank.

Instantly, Acwel released his grip, yelping in pain. He seemed to curl in on himself, his tail and ears flattened against his body as he crawled away into a corner where he slumped to the ground, doing his best to stop the flow of blood by licking at the wound.

Acwel's sacrifice had not been in vain though. His selfless act of devotion had saved his master, giving Sihtric the time he needed to regain his senses. The old warrior might not have been able to protect his faithful hound, but he would not allow him to go unavenged.

With fresh tears stinging his eyes, Sihtric threw back his head and roared; pain and anguish filled his soul, taking over his senses. All aches and bruises forgotten, Sihtric bore down on the Dane who was frantically trying to retrieve his sword. Holding it awkwardly in his left hand - for his right hung uselessly by his side, blood dripping freely from several puncture wounds – Sibba dared his opponent to come on.

Sihtric needed no second invitation. He slashed Leggbitr sharply to his right, swatting Sibba's sword away as if it were nothing more annoying than a horsefly. Then he stepped inside the Dane's reach and punched his shield's iron boss straight into his snarling face with every ounce of strength he possessed. To his credit, Sibba did not fall. Swaying unsteadily on his feet, he spat blood and broken teeth from his ruined mouth.

But Sihtric was in no mood to show mercy. He cared not that Sibba was insensible, defenceless; he saw only death, a death that the Dane had earned twice over for what he had done to Acwel and for what he had been about to do to Freya. He could not, would not, allow the bastard to live a moment longer. He stepped in close to the other man, close enough to feel his hot breath on his face, to fill his nostrils with its fetid reek. Baring his teeth, he hissed at Sibba, speckles of saliva mixing with the blood and snot on the Dane's face.

"This is your last moment on God's earth, you hairy-arsed pig-shagger. Even now, Harald - who I sent on before you - prepares a space for you amid the fire pits of hell. And, in your turn, so you will prepare a seat for Halfdan who will surely follow you there before the sun sets on this day."

He had no idea whether his words had penetrated Sibba's addled brain, but nor did he care. Sihtric hawked and spat a great gobbet of phlegm at Sibba's feet. Then, pulling back his sword he stabbed it deep into his enemy's belly. Sibba gasped in pain as he folded in on himself as a wine sack does when pressed hard in its middle. Hot blood gushed from the wound, soaking Sihtric's sword hand. Slowly, Sibba sank to his knees, his life ebbing away into an ever-widening pool that spread across the floor, until he finally fell on to his back.

With a snort of disgust, Sihtric stamped his foot down hard on the dead man's chest, working Leggbitr from side to side to ease its passage from the cloying flesh that seemed reluctant to release its hold. With one last heave, the steel point of his sword finally pulled clear of Sibba's body, the sudden lack of resistance causing Sihtric to stagger backwards over the corner of the mattress. A sudden jolt of pain shot up his spine as he landed on his arse, driving the air from his lungs with a whoosh.

Halfdan chose that precise moment to attack. Sihtric heard him coming, lumbering across the room, shoving obstacles out of his way as he came. But he could not react; the big man was upon him before he could even move. He could only watch in horror as the Dane - his face contorted and red-faced - stumbled towards him to aim a kick at his face. All Sihtric could do, at the very last moment, was shift his head slightly to one side. It shielded him from the worst of the blow, but no more than that.

Halfdan's boot connected with his head just by his right ear. Despite the protection afforded by the metal helm, his head still exploded in blinding pain. Had the Dane not himself still been groggy from where his own head had been smashed into the wall, the blow might have been enough to snap Sihtric's neck. As it was, he was fortunate to still be conscious.

Dazed, Sihtric fumbled for a weapon, but found none. He had dropped Leggbitr when he fell and now - with stars bursting behind his eyes - he could not see where she lay. Nor did he have time to scrabble around on the floor in the hope his hand would alight upon her familiar features. His head was thumping, and his body was screaming at his brain to be allowed to rest. He knew to do so, however, would mean death for him and his wife.

Ignoring his body's many protests, Sihtric forced himself into a crouch. Nearby, he was vaguely aware of Halfdan readying himself to attack once more. Though his form was indistinct, blurred by the half-light and the continuing turmoil in his head, he could see that the Dane had a knife in his right hand. He tried to stand, but his legs buckled beneath him as a wave of nausea flooded through his head. *This is it,* he realised. *Survivor of countless battles only to be killed on my knees in some godforsaken hovel.*

In his last moments, an image of Freya filled his mind. It was fitting that it would be the last thing he saw. It was a vision so clear that it could almost have been real…

Screaming like a banshee, his wife threw herself at Halfdan, clinging to his back, and desperately trying to claw at his eyes. The sudden, unexpected onslaught forced the Dane to shift his attention away from Sihtric to deal with this new threat; it was a final opportunity that Sihtric could not afford to waste.

Bunching his hands into fists, he lurched forward, ignoring the agonising pain lancing through his head. His right shoulder connected with the younger man's gut, causing him to double over and throwing Freya to the floor. Sihtric didn't stop, though; he kept pounding his legs, using the muscles in his thighs to drive his opponent back until he toppled to the ground with Sihtric on top, his knee in the other man's chest.

He gave Halfdan no respite, not even a moment to catch his breath. Instead, he began pummelling the younger man's face and head with a flurry of punches, their speed making up for what they lacked in power and precision. Halfdan's nose split after half a dozen blows, covering his twisted features with blood. Two more blows and his left eye began to puff up. Sihtric could feel the other man wriggling beneath him, in a frantic effort to free himself before he lost consciousness. He must have known that his life hung in the balance and that knowledge lent him the strength to resist.

Before Sihtric could react, Halfdan managed to free his right arm from where it had been pinioned to the ground. Though he did not have room to swing a proper punch, he was able, nonetheless, to bludgeon the side of Sihtric's head, in the same spot where he had kicked him earlier. The blow caught Sihtric off guard, causing him to topple over to one side. Halfdan was on him in a heartbeat, his knees on his chest as he closed his bear-like hands around his neck, choking the life out of him.

Sihtric was now struggling. His throat burned as he tried to gasp huge mouthfuls of air. He could feel himself fading; waves of nausea flowing over him threatening to swamp his consciousness. He had a matter of moments before it would be over.

Just then, his right hand - flailing around on the floor - came into contact with something familiar. Arching his back, he extended his reach to its fullest until he felt his fingers close around the hilt of a discarded knife. It was Halfdan's, dropped when he'd fallen to the ground.

Offering a silent prayer to whichever saint watched over him at that moment, Sihtric tightened his grip. He had little room for manoeuvre, and time was running out. He would have but one chance. Twisting his wrist inwards, he stabbed down as hard as he could, the blade punching its way into the fleshiest part of the Dane's thigh.

Halfdan screamed. A shrill, high-pitched sound that pierced Sihtric's ears, adding new layers to the already excruciating agony inside his head. Almost immediately, though, the pressure on his upper body was gone as the Dane rolled to one side, clutching at the knife that remained embedded deep in his flesh. Lurching to his feet, Halfdan pulled the knife out, keening with pain as he did so. Then, with his trews soaked with his own blood, he limped through the door, leaving a dark trail behind him.

TWENTY-TWO

Sihtric didn't have the strength to pursue his foe. Chest heaving, head thumping, he collapsed on to his back, his right hand now sticky with Halfdan's blood. He doubted the wound would be fatal, but the bastard would most likely carry a limp for the rest of his days. Still, at least he could console himself that he had sent two of the whoresons to hell. *Not bad for a decrepit old man, eh?* he smiled to himself, grimacing through the aches that threaten to overwhelm him.

Freya came to kneel beside him, doing her best to hug him and kiss him as he lay, exhausted on the hard floor. Opening one eye, he smiled up at her, pleased to see that she looked none the worse for her ordeal.

"I'm sorry, my love."

"For what, you foolish old goat? You just saved me from the jaws of death."

"Yes, but in doing so, I have broken my promise to you that I would never again don armour or pick up sword and shield."

Despite the maelstrom of emotions that must have been coursing through her veins, Freya laughed. It was a happy sound that spoke of relief at her deliverance from the hands of the Danes. From having been at their mercy, facing God alone knows what horrors, she was safe once more. Just then, a feeble whimper interrupted the moment.

"Acwel!" Sihtric forced himself to his feet and staggered over to where the dog lay on his side, mortally wounded. A small puddle of blood had gathered where he had been stabbed. So weak was he now that he no longer had the strength to even lick at the wound. He barely even reacted when his master dropped to his knees by his side, managing only to flap his tale once, thudding weakly against the floor.

Sihtric lifted Acwel's head so that it rested in his lap. Looking at the gash in his flank, he could see there was nothing to be done. As gently as he could, he rubbed the dying hound behind his ears, hoping it would bring him some comfort in his last moments. Many was the time he had watched over a mortally wounded warrior, holding his hand and speaking soothing words as they made ready to pass to the other side. It should be no different for his dog, an animal as steadfast and as loyal as any shieldsman had ever been. He felt the tears come, splashing on to Acwel's limp body where they mixed with his fur. Sihtric's throat burned with raw emotion, as though it were filled with a lump of hot coal that he could not swallow.

"I'm sorry, boy," he whispered close to Acwel's ear. "I will never forget that your last service to me, was to save my life and that of Freya too. For this act alone, you will always command a place in my heart."

Freya came to sit beside him, draping an arm around his shoulder. As she rested her head against his, Sihtric could feel that her face was also wet. Though Acwel had always been his dog, following him around the estate, on hunts and whatever else Bjarke would have him do, she had always - in her own way - been fond of him too. Though she would often curse the beast for getting under her feet or for leaving muddy paw prints on her newly cleaned floor, Sihtric had often seen her, when she thought he was not watching, feed him scraps of meat from the table.

Looking down, he noticed that the shallow rise and fall of Acwel's chest had finally ceased. "He's gone," he whispered.

"His suffering is over, my love."

They buried him behind the hut, using a shovel that Sihtric found in the back of the wain in which Freya had been abducted from Hoctune. While he laboured, Freya explained how Halfdan and his men had come for her while he was out hunting. They had taken her by surprise, clamping a hand over her mouth from behind so she could not scream. She'd had no choice but to go with them, though she prided herself on managing to gouge Harald's cheek with her nails when he foolishly allowed her arm to be free for a moment. Sihtric grunted; he recalled seeing a row of three angry red welts on the man's cheek as he'd killed him. To know this was Freya's work gave him no small amount of pleasure.

"But they did not mistreat you, wife?" He could not bring

himself to say the words, hoping that his meaning was clear. He paused in his task leaning on the handle as he searched his wife's face for any hidden signs.

"No, my love. Though they handled me roughly to get me in and out of the cart, they otherwise caused me no physical harm. Though that would have changed had you not arrived when you did. I fear they had grown bored of their task and sought some enjoyment before killing me."

"That was their plan? To murder you here?" He had been wondering that ever since he'd found her gone from the house. The presence of the shovel in the back of the cart had been a clue as to their intent, but now Freya had confirmed it.

"I heard them say as much and they didn't care that I knew it, either. They hoped that by taking me, it would draw you out too, hence they did not worry about covering their tracks too much. Then with both of us out of the way, Thorgunnr would have nothing to worry about."

They fell silent as Sihtric finished digging the grave, both contemplating the lengths to which Bjarke's wife was prepared to go to silence them. Once the hole was deep enough, they carried Acwel's body from the hut, having wrapped the body in Sibba's cloak so that he might be warm and comfortable in the cold earth. Finally, once Sihtric had shovelled the soil back into the grave and tramped it down hard, they stood, heads bowed, in silent reflection.

Eventually, Sihtric coughed to clear his throat. "Run free, old boy. If there is any justice, you will hereafter catch all the squirrels you want."

Freya squeezed Sihtric's hand and turned to face him. "What now, husband?"

The same thought had been in the back of his mind for some time. In truth, though, he had little idea. "Well, we can't stay here. We have already dallied too long. Though it will take time for Halfdan to hobble back to Hoctune, rest assured he will soon gather more men and come after us."

"So, we can't go home either?"

"No. That will be the first place they look for us. They cannot allow us to live now."

"Well, what then? Are we now outlaws? Destined to roam the woods until our dying day?"

It was a fair question and one to which Sihtric was not sure he had an answer. After some moments spent pondering their fate, he alighted upon the only course he could see that remained open to them.

"We keep going north. To Ramsey."

"Whatever for?" The look on Freya's face showed she was anything but convinced.

"Because, if I am honest, I have no better suggestion."

"But why Ramsey?"

"Abbot Ethelstan is there. Whatever you may think of him, he is an honest man of God. And that means we can trust him more than anyone else we know. Things have gone too far now for us to manage this on our own. We need help if we are to survive and if we are to have justice for Ulf. Who better to turn to in our hour of need than the Abbot?"

Freya looked askance at her husband as if he were mad but said nothing.

"If you have another idea, then I would hear it, wife." Though curt, his words were not meant unkindly. He genuinely did not know what else to do and would have gladly heard counsel greater than his own. But Freya had none and so they resolved to follow that path; though what they would say to the Abbot when they arrived, neither one of them knew.

TWENTY-THREE

Midday had long since passed when they set off. Sihtric had wanted to leave much earlier, but Freya had insisted he rest for a while. She was worried, she said, about the blows he had taken to the head.

"Though with that thick skull of yours, I doubt it could have done too much damage. And, besides, they can't have knocked much sense out of you as you had very little to start with."

But despite her jocular barbs, he could tell she was concerned. He compromised by insisting they leave the hut but that they would stop further along the stream that ran nearby. Once there, he allowed her to wash the blood from his clothes and skin as best she could, while he sat with his back against a large rock and closed his eyes.

He had no idea how long he slept, but he woke with a raging thirst that was soon sated from the cool, fresh running waters of the brook that babbled its noisy way around and over a rocky bed on its meandering route south. Though his head still pounded, it was much improved; the sleep had done him some good, at least. For a moment, he had no memory of all that had gone before. But that brief period of blissful ignorance was shattered when he turned his head to see Freya sitting a few paces away, her expression one of worry and concern. Then - like having a pale of ice-cold water thrown over him - he shivered as everything came flooding back to him. The fight, Acwel's sacrifice... It was as if a black cloud had passed in front of the sun on a summer's day.

"You are well, husband?"

"Well enough, thank you." It was but a small lie. Aside from his throbbing head, his leg was stiff, though that was nothing unusual. It seemed to have seized up while he'd been asleep, and he knew it would hurt like the devil when he tried to put any weight on it. On top of that, his muscles ached. It had been a good few years since he'd put them to use in a proper scrap and they weren't happy with it if their loud protests were anything to go by. He smiled at Freya, nevertheless; she needed him to be strong if they were to come through this alive.

"I think it's time we were away, my love. A few hours of daylight remain to us; we can cover several miles in that time if we walk briskly."

Freya got to her feet, using her hands to smooth down the folds of her thick woollen dress. "How long before we arrive at the abbey?"

Sihtric shrugged. "Depending on our pace and assuming we find no trouble along the way, then I'd say no later than midday tomorrow. Though we will have to sleep under the stars tonight should we not happen across another hut."

But the pace was slower than Sihtric hoped, but not because of Freya. Every step he took sent stabs of pain through his leg, making the going much harder than it should have been. Shame-faced, he knew it was not his wife who held them back. The weight of his shield and mailshirt did not help, either, nor the undulation of the ground as they picked their way around small boulders and grassy hummocks as they followed the stream ever northward. At least he knew that if they kept going in that rough direction, they should pick up the path that led to Ramsey, eventually.

And now that the sun was starting to set, they would soon have to stop for the night, lest they risk losing their way in the dark. Ramsey was, to all intents and purposes, a small island set within the vast waterlogged land of the fens that stretched for miles to the north and east. It was only within the last two or three generations that a causeway had been built linking the island to the rest of the area. A feat of engineering that coincided with the foundation of the abbey. Before then, the only way to cross over was by boat. Either side of the causeway, the land was, in places, boggy marshland at best. Should they stray from the path, there was every chance of blundering into one of the many bogs, from which there would be little hope of escape.

He reckoned they had covered little more than four miles. Less than halfway, if his calculations were correct. They had been following an ancient track, the width of no more than one person, which seemed to follow the course of the stream. Most of the time it twisted and turned in tune with the flow of the water but, every now and then, it took itself off in a completely different direction, only to return to the water a hundred or so paces later.

Of other people there had been no sign thus far. The dense woodland all around them was silent and oppressive, save for the occasional rabbit or squirrel who stopped to stare at the couple as they passed by, judging them insufficient of a threat to be worth scurrying for the safety of their burrows or drays. Sihtric did not mind, though; with no huts or people, there was less chance of them being discovered. Sleeping among the trees also held no fear for him. He'd lost count of the times he had done so in the past. Freya was less used to such hardship, admittedly, but the day had been warm and the wind light. There would be little or no chance of rain so they should be neither cold nor wet. The greatest risk to their safety was Halfdan. Who knew what mischief he might yet cause?

"We should rest here for the night," he grunted.

"Surely, we should press on to reach the safety of the abbey as quickly as possible?"

"No, my love. Night's drawing near and I don't dare miss the path. The way is dangerous with many bogs and pools into which we might fall. And there will be no moon to light our way tonight."

Freya nodded, accepting the wisdom of her husband's words. Settling into a comfortable position with her back against an alder tree, she pulled her cloak around her shoulders more tightly. "At least we'll not be too discomfited here, eh?"

Sihtric smiled. "I saw some mushrooms and berries not far back. You wait here while I go fetch some for our supper."

Freya yawned, stretching her arms high above her head. "It'll make a nice change you preparing the meal for once, husband."

***

Sihtric lay awake, staring up at the sky through the canopy of leaves above his head. With no cloud to speak of, he could see little pinpricks of light dotted here and there from the plethora of stars that shone through intermittently as the gentle breeze rustled the leaves to and fro. Other than the foliage and the sound of Freya's slow, but even breathing by his side, there was little to be heard, save for the occasional hoot of an owl.

He longed for sleep to take him, but he could not stop his mind from racing. Thoughts and fears tumbled over themselves as they jostled for ascendancy in his head. In the end, though, they all boiled down to one simple question: what would become of them?

Normally, their recourse would be to seek the protection of their lord to whom they were oath-sworn; there was none other to whom a man could turn. An oath, once given, was not lightly discarded. And in return, the lord was duty-bound to defend the oath-giver in all matters of justice and wrong-doing. But when the source of their persecution was Bjarke's own wife, then where did that leave them? No matter which way he looked at it, he could see no way out. They could not have been more lost than if they had fallen into one of the many marshy pools hereabouts. Their only hope would be to reach out to grab a branch, by which they might haul themselves to safety. Ethelstan was that branch and Ramsey Abbey was the route by which to reach it.

A noise nearby broke into his thoughts, but he dismissed it, cursing himself for being so jumpy. Most likely a boar or rabbit, snuffling about in the undergrowth. But then…. What would such an animal be doing abroad this late at night? A badger perhaps? Instantly on the alert, he twisted round as quietly as he could so that he lay flat on his front, facing the direction from which the sound had come. He could see nothing, hear nothing. Perhaps it was his mind playing tricks on him, as if it did not have enough to do already. Should he wake Freya? Not if it were a false alarm; she would not thank him for interrupting her sleep. But what if it were Halfdan returned with new men?

Then, he heard it again. A twig breaking underfoot? But how far away, he could not say. Sound travelled further at night, so it could be a hundred paces or more away. Was that a light? Over there, off to his right? By the saints, it was. Flickering, coming in and out of sight as it passed among the tree trunks. There was another, possibly a third too. Who else could it be but Halfdan? Out looking for them. There was not a moment to lose.

Gently he placed a grubby hand over Freya's mouth while shaking her shoulder in what he hoped was a reassuring gesture. Despite the gloom, he saw the panic in his wife's eyes as she woke. Leaning in close, he whispered in her ear.

"The bastard's found us. We must go. But be sure to make no noise; they are close by."

Composed, his wife nodded and began to rise. He was impressed to see how quickly her fear had been replaced by a grim determination. Her fortitude was a marvel. He took a last look over his shoulder to check on the progress of the enemy, and then struck out in the opposite direction, a route that was not far off his intended course from what he could remember of their position.

He wanted to run, to put as much distance as he could between them and their pursuers, but he knew that would have meant their doom. It was too dark to see where they were going, and they would be sure to blunder into danger or disturb some wildlife and give away their position. For Halfdan and his mates, there would be no such hindrance. They had no need of stealth or silence, for they were the hunters.

The couple crept on, deeper and deeper into the forest, further and further away from the path they had been on. All the while, he feared they were moving closer to the fens and the perils they posed. For now, the ground felt firm enough underfoot, but for how much longer would that last? When he started to feel the ground oozing up around his boot, then he'd know they were in trouble. But by then, it could be too late.

He'd slung his shield across his back so that he could hold out his left hand to guide his wife. In his right hand he held his seax, ready to defend himself. Using a combination of his shoulders and his right arm, he pushed his way through the undergrowth, choosing the paths where it grew thickest to better obscure them from their followers. It made their progress slower than he would have liked but that was outweighed by the benefit of the added seclusion. He had to remember to hold back the branches with their wickedly sharp thorns so that they did not ping back into Freya's face as she passed.

After a few hundred or so paces, he paused, holding a finger to his lips as a warning. Standing stock still, he placed a hand behind his ear and slowly turned his head from side to side, trying to funnel any sound. Sure enough, he could still hear them, crashing their way through the woods, calling to each other as they went to avoid getting lost. Although it was harder to see the light from the torches in this denser part of the forest, the men's voices - he could make out no more than three - seemed, if anything, closer than they had been before. They were too far away to discern what was being said but, by their tone, he doubted whether they realised just how close their quarry was. Nevertheless, the sad truth of it was they were not going to be able to outrun them. The hunters had youth on their side and no need for secrecy. They would catch up with them in time. With a sinking feeling, Sihtric knew they had no choice now but to hide and put their faith in God that their pursuers passed by in the dark.

Pressing his mouth up to Freya's ear, he told her of his plan. He felt her stiffen with fear but, to her credit, she made no sound, merely nodded her understanding. Taking her hand once more, he guided her towards a patch of brambles that grew thickly and unchecked in a small hollow that was ringed by trees that stood guard like night watchmen.

Pulling Freya down to the ground, he began to crawl, inching himself slowly forward. He had to keep his face down to avoid the clawing of the tangled branches but, as he had hoped, once you had passed the first few inches, there was room aplenty within. So ancient and overgrown was the bramble thicket, that it had spread with wild abandon on all sides from a central clump where the roots were. It was tight but it was as good a hiding place as they were likely to find. They should be invisible here but for the most observant of hunters.

Carefully, Sihtric twisted round so that he was facing back out the way they had come. A short while later, a man appeared to his left. By the light of his flaming torch, Sihtric had a good view of his features, but it was no one he recognised from Hoctune. He began to wonder whether it was them that the man sought, but he could think of no other reason for his presence at that time. Perhaps Halfdan had called upon men from outside of the jarl's estate to help, the offer of coin being enough to tempt lawless, desperate men to his cause.

With his right hand the man was swishing his sword haphazardly at the undergrowth as he walked. It seemed less like a concerted effort to clear the way and rather, the actions of a man with nothing better to do. *Coin might buy you the body, but it rarely buys you the soul,* Sihtric thought to himself. *The man has no loyalty to this quest; he cares nought for it as long he has adequate recompense in his purse come the end of it.*

With every step, the swordsman came closer and closer to where Sihtric and Freya hid. Nothing about his attitude or demeanour indicated he had any inkling how near his quarry lay. He was no more than twenty paces away now, whistling some tuneless dirge that Sihtric vaguely recognised. It was a bawdy drinking song favoured by Frankish sailors who frequented the trading ports of the Anglian coast, to the east of Hoctune. At least, that explained why he had not seen the fellow before, though it did nothing to allay his fears. The Franks had a reputation as fierce and brutal fighters who'd think nothing of slitting your throat for the slightest argument over a game of chance. Sihtric didn't think much of the company Halfdan was keeping.

"Anything?"

Sihtric recognised Halfdan's voice, shouting from several yards away to his right. So, the bastard was fit enough to walk then. He swore to himself he'd make a better fist of it should he be granted a second bite of the apple.

"Nothing. You sure they came this way? I'm tired and you're keeping me away from the innkeeper's daughter."

The accent was thick, guttural even. It confirmed his suspicions; this man came from across the whale road. It also confirmed his suspicions that the man's heart was not in it.

"Shut up, Lothar. You're being paid well enough to give her up for the night. Just keep your wits about you. He's a hard bastard, this Sihtric. He's shit better men than you for breakfast and another for lunch for good measure."

Lothar grunted, unimpressed. "You only say that because he

got the better of three of you earlier today." Sihtric doubted Halfdan would have heard him, though, as Lothar's reply was little more than a whisper.

"But Agnes knows how to make a man happy, Halfdan. And those puddings she has under her dress, you could go deaf for a month were you to put your head between them."

"Well, just think how pleased she will be to see you with a purse full of coin to spend on her. Now be quiet and keep looking. You saw the tracks back by the stream; they're heading this way, I tell you. On their way to the abbey, I'll be bound. Should we fail to stop them, you won't need to worry about Agnes anymore. I will see to that."

Lothar muttered something inaudible but otherwise held his counsel. Instead, he carried on walking, still wafting his sword casually from side to side. A few paces later, he took a slight turn around an ancient yew tree and set off in a direction that - Sihtric realised in horror - would take him very close to their hiding place. He turned his head to face Freya, imploring her with his eyes to make no sound or else they were lost.

On he came, seemingly in no hurry and Sihtric's feelings of panic increased with every step. He had no idea what to do should Lothar see them. In the time it took to free himself from under the brambles, the Frank would have no difficulty in sticking him with the end of his sword. He sent a silent prayer heavenward, promising he'd make some small donation to the abbey should they survive this ordeal.

Just then, Lothar halted. He'd reached the edge of the cluster of bushes under which they hid. Sihtric could see his leather boots, scuffed and muddy from loading and unloading boats down by the wharves, not two paces from where they lay. He held his breath, just in case the sound of his lungs expanding and contracting betrayed them.

Lothar pushed the point of his sword into the soft earth by his side, so that it stood proud, on its own. Sihtric then heard a rustle of cloth, a brief pause followed by the sound of a stream of urine splashing off the leaves and twigs all around him, accompanied by a heartfelt sigh of relief.

Repulsed by the stench of the hot liquid, Sihtric could do

nothing but lower his head and accept his lot. Better to smell like a cesspit than be dead. He'd be able to bathe when he got to the abbey.

Lothar's piss seemed to go on forever, his bladder doubtless filled with ale from the tavern in which Halfdan had hired him. Eventually, he finished; the last few drops tumbling down as he shook himself dry before stuffing his cock back in his trews. He grabbed his sword, not bothering to clean the soil from its blade, and stomped off, oblivious to how close he had been to earning his pay.

Sihtric could not move or speak for several moments, even though he knew Lothar was no longer within earshot. It took an age for his heartbeat to return to normal; in truth, he'd been surprised that the Frank sailor had not heard it. To his own ears, it had been like the rhythmic boom of thunder in his ears, accompanied by the rushing torrent of blood pumping around his head. Eventually, he turned to Freya and whispered.

"That was close, but I think we are safe now."

"I knew it." Freya hissed.

"Knew what, my love?" he was genuinely puzzled.

"That Agnes. I knew she was a harlot who'd let any man have a feel of her tits for a silver penny."

Sihtric had to stifle a laugh. Though they were in mortal fear for their lives, all Freya could think about was a tasty morsel of gossip for the next time she sat down with her cronies in Hoctune. Should there ever be a next time.

TWENTY-FOUR

They saw no further sign of Halfdan, Lothar or, indeed, anyone for the rest of that long night. Well hidden, warm and comfortable, they decided to stay where there were; they considered it unlikely that Lothar would retrace his steps after all. Even so, Sihtric dared not fall asleep just in case. By dawn, he was tired but not ruinously so. These days, he found he needed less sleep anyway, so it proved no great hardship to stay awake and watchful for one night.

As the sun began to rise through the trees, Sihtric gently shook his wife by the shoulder; it was time for them to complete their journey. They still had a few miles to cover to reach Ramsey Abbey and the sooner they were on the path, the sooner they would be safe. Surely none would dare risk God's wrath by breaking the Holy law of sanctuary.

They quickly finished what was left of the mushrooms and berries, accompanied by the remains of the bread Freya had found in the back of the cart the previous day. Thus fortified, they set off.

Sihtric was pleased to see that his sense of direction had not deserted him in the dark. They had not strayed far from their path at all. So, with the sun positioned on his right-hand side, he set off, shield and sword at the ready. He was hopeful that the hunters had given up and returned to Hoctune or wherever they hailed from, but he could not be sure of it. He would remain on his guard until they were safely within the abbey walls. Now Halfdan knew what he was up against, Sihtric doubted he would be able to repeat the success of the previous day, but he might at least hold them up long enough for Freya to escape.

But they saw and heard no one. The further they went, the more confident Sihtric became. He did not dare sheath his sword or sling his shield, but with each passing mile, he began to believe they might make it after all. Even Freya's mood had lightened as they neared the end of their journey. For her, reaching Ethelstan would signal an end to their problems. The old abbot would know what to do. Sihtric was less certain, less sure of his faith in God, but then he had no other plan.

The sun had almost reached its zenith when they finally emerged from the thick woodland. Pleasingly, Sihtric found that his navigational skills had not let him down, for in front of them was the road that led to the causeway to the island. And there, in the distance and in the centre of that island, he could see the white stones of Ramsey abbey gleaming in the sunlight.

The abbey complex - of which the church itself was the centre point - was huge. At any time, upwards of eighty monks lived there, working the land and caring for the sick and also for the pilgrims on their way to the nearby cathedral at Ely or to the shrine of St Edmund the Martyr at Bury. On top of that, there were all the servants. Ethelstan never tired of telling anyone who would listen that it was the fourth biggest abbey in England and Sihtric could well believe it. The land surrounding the abbey extended over many acres. What was not given over to the various outbuildings needed by the abbey was taken up by fields of barley, wheat and oats or by pasture for the grazing of sheep and pens for the abbey's vast herd of pigs.

It was a bustling community, the size of any moderate town at least, built on land which had been gifted to the abbey's founders by good King Edgar some fifty years before. Even from this distance, Sihtric could see several brown-robed monks scurrying about their business out in the fields or hurrying between the various workshops or other monastic buildings. He smiled to himself; they were almost there. He turned to Freya to share the news but, as he did so, he froze in shock.

"Duck!"

The warning came just in time. Freya threw herself face down in the dirt, just as the axe flew past where her head had been moments before. As it turned end over end, Sihtric recognised it for what it was. A short-handed throwing axe, with a wickedly sharp blade, favoured for generations by the Franks. That could mean only one thing: Lothar, or another of his compatriots was here.

Sure enough, there he was, no more than forty paces away. It had been a long throw with little chance of success, but the man was clearly skilled in its use as the blade would surely have cleaved his wife's skull in two but for his shout. His face now contorted in rage at having been thwarted, Lothar drew his sword and began to run.

"Flee, Freya. Flee for the abbey. Don't stop, no matter what occurs. Do you hear me?"

She didn't need telling twice. Scrambling to her feet, Freya set off towards the causeway, not daring to look behind her. Sihtric prayed she would make it; she was not a fit woman and no longer in any flush of youth. He knew he'd have to hold Lothar up long enough for her to reach the church, and hope that no other hunters were nearby, or else all would be lost.

Sihtric positioned himself between the Frank and his wife. Rolling his shoulder muscles, he planted his feet shoulder width apart with his left side turned to face the enemy. In his mind, he was back in the shieldwall; his knees slightly bent, shield held so that the upper rim ended just beneath his nose. In his right hand, he held Leggbitr, his elbow angled so that its deadly point protruded just past the upper edge of the iron-rimmed board. He would have dearly loved to have a trusted warrior on either side of him, though.

He took stock of Lothar as he came on. He had not appreciated just how big the man was when he was being pissed on from above, but now - in the clear light of day - he could see that the Frank was huge. Years spent working the trading boats between Frankia and England had rendered him muscles the size of which he had rarely seen before. He wore no armour to speak of, just a jerkin made of boiled leather. He wore his long dark hair in a tail, tied with a thin leather thong at the side of his head, so that it bounced as he ran. He made no sound as he came, just grinned triumphantly at the prospect of wetting his blade in Sihtric's flesh.

Lothar appeared to be alone, making Sihtric wonder whether his attack was brave or foolhardy. Perhaps he felt the old man was not to be feared, or - worse still – he had comrades not too far distant. If that were true, then there was no hope for either of them. Even so, he noted that Lothar did not call out to anyone. He had the courage of the young, a belief in his own invulnerability. And Sihtric intended to prove him wrong.

As he ran, Lothar lifted his sword high over his head, aiming a blow at Sihtric's neck which, if it landed, would sever his head clean from its shoulders. But the old warrior had no intention of allowing that to happen. Just before the moment of impact, Sihtric took a step to one side whilst, at the same time, jabbing his sword down around the Frank's ankles. It was an old move and an easy one to spot if you had your wits about you, and yet Sihtric was amazed how often it bore fruit. And Lothar was no different. Though he might be useful in a tavern brawl, he had no battle-craft, and was no match for the war-hardened warrior.

A look of shock, which soon turned to fear, spread over the Frank's features as he felt his legs go from under him as they tangled with the rigid blade. He landed face first in the dirt, a grunt of pain escaping his lips. Incredibly, though, he did not lose hold of his sword and was now already trying to regain his feet. Sihtric gave him no chance, though. As Lothar placed his left hand to push himself upright, Sihtric hacked down with his sword, its keen edge slicing through the bone and sinew of his forearm as easily as if it had been made of butter.

Lothar screamed as a great gout of blood spurted from the ruined stump, all the while staring uncomprehendingly at the severed hand that lay, useless, on the ground. Dropping his sword, he clutched at the stump, tears of pain springing from his eyes. With a final glare at Sihtric, he stumbled back towards the woods. If he were lucky and found help soon, his life might be saved, but Sihtric thought it more likely that he would bleed to death in the woods. He would lose no sleep over it, though.

Turning towards Ramsey, he sought out Freya. She was about two hundred paces ahead of him now, perhaps halfway to the abbey and still running. He began to lumber after her, slowed down by the weight of his shield and armour and the jolting pain each time he placed his weight on his right leg. Steeling his mind against it, he put his head down and followed his wife as quickly as he could.

But just as he thought their ordeal might be over, two more men burst from the trees ahead of him and to the right, roughly midway between him and Freya. *By God, Lothar was not alone after all!* By the looks of them they were also Franks; their bulk and their features were so similar, in fact, that all three might have been brothers. Heaven help him, he thought to himself, if they'd seen what he'd done to their sibling.

Judging by their location, it would be a close call whether they would cut him off before he made it to the causeway. Fear lent him a new burst of energy, giving him the strength to redouble his efforts. He longed to throw his shield away, but his honour would not allow it. In all his battles - victory, and defeat - he had never once discarded it. He always remembered the words his father had spoken to him on the eve of his first battle - words he'd claimed had come down through the ages from some long-lost source - "Come back with your shield, or on it." It was a mantra he was not about to reject now.

With a growing sense of dread, he watched as the two men separated; one ran for Freya, while the other turned to intercept him. *Clever bastards,* he thought, grudgingly. It was what he would have done had he been in their position. They had to stop both Sihtric and Freya from reaching the abbey and this move gave them the best chance of success. Whatever happened, whether he was able to overcome the first man or not, Sihtric knew that he would not have time to reach the second man before the whoreson caught up to his wife.

Rage starting to burn within him, presaging the onset of the familiar bloodlust that would soon descend over him. If his fate was to die in this place, on this day, then he would die with his sword in his hand, fighting for Freya. He could think of no better death. He would make the Frank scum pay as best he could before he died.

Roaring with incoherent rage, he threw himself at his opponent, the two shields smashing into each other with a noise like a clap of thunder. The Frank was a big man and stood his ground, but - like his brother - he too was no soldier. Whilst his enemy stood still, Sihtric was already stepping to his left, opening his stance to launch a hacking blow with his sword.

The sailor managed to block Sihtric's blade with his shield, but his angles were all wrong. Leggbitr sliced its way through the planks that formed the linden board, splitting the wood along its grain, cleaving the shield into two parts.

The Frank yelped in pain as the sword bit into the hand that held the shield. Although most of the power and long since gone, soaked up by the wood, it was a painful blow, nonetheless. But it was far from debilitating. As if to emphasise the point, the Frank slipped his wounded hand from the grip and hurled the ruined fragments at Sihtric. The jagged edge of the smaller part struck him hard on his upper arm before he could react, numbing the muscles and making Leggbitr feel like no more than a heavy lump of iron in his hand.

Seizing his opportunity, the younger man leapt forward, swinging his sword and howling in triumph. Sihtric lifted his shield, feeling it shake as it took the full force of the blow. Again and again, the Frank hacked at him. Now shieldless, he could use both hands to add extra weight to each strike. There was little technique involved, no finesse to it, but each cut forced Sihtric backward. What he lacked in sword-skill, he more than made up for with brute strength.

With his right arm swinging uselessly by his side, Sihtric could do no more than retreat, keeping his shield squarely between the two of them, all the while trying to coax life back into his stunned limb. If he could just stay out of reach for a little while longer, he was confident that the big man would start to tire. No one could maintain such a furious onslaught for long; many years of battle experience told him that.

And the Frank proved to be no different. Already he was blowing hard, his cheeks reddened with exertion. He had no concept of what it took to win a fight such as this; he had no plan other than to batter the other man until he succumbed. As he lifted the sword above his head for yet another crushing blow, Sihtric jumped backward out of range. It was a risky move as he did not know what was behind him, whether he might trip over some rock or fallen bough, but it paid off. As his sword swished harmlessly through the air, the Frank could not stop himself from stumbling unexpectedly forward into the empty space left by Sihtric. Though he did well to keep his feet, he was now off-balance and off his guard.

Sihtric did not waste the chance he had been given. With his opponent almost bent double before him, he grabbed the back of the sailor's head and pulled him down. At the same time, he brought his knee up sharply into his face, feeling the satisfying crunch of bone as his nose split. The dazed man dropped to his knees, his face bloodied, spitting out teeth and phlegm. Taking a couple of steps back, Sihtric launched a kick, backed with every ounce of strength he possessed. It connected with the Frank's chin, snapping his neck back with a horrifying click. His eyes rolled back up into his head as he toppled over on to his side.

Sihtric did not have time to check whether he was dead, for his thoughts had turned once again to Freya's plight. He had lost precious time in what he already knew to be a race he could not hope to win. Regardless, he began to run, his lungs once more heaving at the effort.

Although some feeling had at last returned to his sword arm, it mattered not for he would be too late to use it. Ahead of him, his worst fears were confirmed as he saw that Freya still had some way to go to reach the causeway. She was no longer running, though. Such was her exhausted state that she stumbled along, struggling to keep her feet among the uneven tussocks of grass that sprouted up through the boggy ground that surrounded the island. He was amazed she had not fallen already.

And all the time, her pursuer was gaining on her with every stride. Though he, too, was hampered by the undulating land, his stride was longer and surer than his wife's. It was obvious that he would overtake her several yards before she reached the safety of the abbey grounds. He roared in impotent rage. There was nothing he could do to save her. If only he hadn't sent her on ahead, he might perhaps have saved her.

Tears of frustration sprang to his eyes. He wanted to turn away; he did not want to watch her cut down before his eyes. But he could not do that to her. After a score and ten years or more spent together, he owed her that much at least. He would be there at her end, to bear witness to her murder.

He promised her two things through his tears: first, he would kill the man that ended her life. There was no debate; the bastard would not live to boast of his foul deed. Second, he would see justice done for her. No matter the personal cost, he would go to Bjarke and explain everything. He did not care whether his lord believed him or not, he would have his say. If need be, he would demand the right to trial by combat to prove that he spoke the truth. There was a blood price to be paid - for her and for Ulf. God would not desert him in his hour of need. No sooner had the thought entered his head, though, than he was struck by its irony. Where was God now? Why had he abandoned them to their fate? Was he not meant to protect the innocent?

All these thoughts and more swirled around his head as he ran, sobbing now, towards the causeway. He saw Freya had now finally reached the road, the improved surface allowing her to increase her pace a little. But it wasn't going to be enough. The Frank was no more than twenty paces behind her now. As soon as he reached the path, he would overhaul her in no time at all.

Just then he heard a shout. *My God, there's more of the bastards.*

But no! The shout came from the direction of the abbey. Looking up, he could see a group of a dozen or so men running through the gate in the compound wall. Each one was clad in long black robes that flapped comically around their skinny bare legs as they skittled their way along the roadway. Monks. Each of them carried some sort of farm implement: a couple of long handled scythes, a shovel, rakes. All manner of makeshift weapons.

Sihtric's heart leapt. Perhaps God had not abandoned them after all. Even now, the monks were charging across the causeway, as fearsome as any Norse raiding party to his streaming eyes. Though he doubted their fighting skill, there was enough of them, at least, to make even the doughtiest warrior pause.

And so it proved. Seeing them hurtling towards him, the Frank slowed, clearly wondering what he should do. And then he stopped. Just as the men of God reached Sihtric's wife, he took flight, bounding off into the trees on the far side of the road, chased by half of the brothers, the other half having stopped to stand guard over Freya.

Sihtric sank to his knees, dropping his shield and sword on to the soft ground by his side. His lungs felt as if they would burst as he sucked in vast mouthfuls of air. He felt like he might never move again; he could not recall ever being as tired as he was now. And still the tears flowed unchecked; but now, at least, they spoke of relief, of deliverance from the very gates of hell.

TWENTY-FIVE

"I find it beyond the bounds of belief, if I am honest." Abbot Ethelstan shook his head, while pressing the ends of his thin, bony fingers against his temples as if trying to massage the information he'd just been given into some sort of order in his mind.

"This cannot be so; I held a funeral for the boy," he continued. "I recited the sacred rites over his body. You were both there."

"An imposter," Sihtric confirmed. "Some poor lad who had died a day or two earlier, no doubt. He was substituted for Ulf to hide the evidence of the poisoning."

"But I knew the boy well. I'd taught him his lessons for many a year. I had no reason to suspect that the body that was laid in the ground was not his."

"But you did not see his face or, indeed, any part of his body. Thorgunnr chose well; she found a corpse of a similar size and shape to Ulf, knowing that you would not stop to question it. Your eyes only registered what your mind told them to see."

"Freya's right," Sihtric continued. "I daresay that if we searched long enough, we'd find a poor family down by the wharves whose pockets are now filled with coin in payment. Perhaps they were promised a good Christian burial for their son; something they could not have afforded on their own."

"And Thorgunnr planned this all along, you say?"

Sihtric could see that the old man's resolve was wavering. At first, he had been incredulous - angry even - that they should seek to level such heinous accusations against Bjarke's wife. He'd told them they must be motivated by the devil or by the result of wild grief for the loss of one they had treated as their own son. But, as Sihtric began to explain what had happened to them since Freya had discovered the evidence of Ulf's murder, he had begun to soften. Nevertheless, the look on his face made it plain that he still found it hard to believe that so much evil could live within another's soul.

"It would seem so, Abbot. It appears that the lengths a mother will go to in order to see her son inherit great wealth and power know no bounds."

The abbot shook his head again, lost in thought. Sihtric silently implored him to hurry. It would not be long before word reached Thorgunnr that they had reached Ramsey. She would lose no time taking steps to secure her position. Though what she would do, he knew not. Eventually, he lost patience.

"We've come here to place our lives in your hands, Abbot. We submit our souls to God's mercy. Guide us, Lord. Help us navigate these stormy waters to find a safe harbour."

Ethelstan looked up. "What's that you say? Ah yes, of course. We must find a path through this mess. If what you say is true, there must be justice for Ulf and the Christian burial that has been denied him. Buried in a meadow to the north of Hoctune you say?" He shook his head once more.

"But first, join me in prayer, for we must seek God's guidance."

***

"So, when will the bishop arrive?"

"Patience, my dear Sihtric, is a virtue with which you seem ill acquainted." Ethelstan chuckled at his own jest but stopped when he saw the look on the other man's face. "Ahem, it is a journey of four days from here to Dorchester by the Thamesis, so, if we are to allow Aethelric time to gather himself and his retinue, I would hope to see him here within ten days."

Sihtric looked perplexed. "But what are we to do until then?"

"Well, you must stay here, of course. If what you say is true, it would not be safe for you to venture forth from these walls. No man - Dane, Frank or otherwise - would dare violate the sanctity of holy land. And fear not, for we have plenty of work to keep you both busy, so you'll not be needing to pay coin for your keep."

"I can't say I was overly concerned on that front, Lord Abbot."

"I can see that you do not wholly accept my solution to your ills, but I can see little else we can do. Bjarke is the king's man in England. None is above him in standing when Knut is away from these shores. And when he is gone, the king lets it be known that Bjarke speaks for him here. How can I, a mere abbot, challenge the word of one as high in rank as he? If we are to accuse his wife of murder, then we must do so with a power higher than that which I possess. Hence, I must defer to the bishop for he is second only to Aethelnoth in Canterbury. And I would have petitioned him had he not gone to Rome to receive his pallium of office.

"But you should trust in Aethelric and in God, my son. The bishop is a good man, a fair man, who holds nothing more sacred than justice and honesty. If anyone can find the path of truth and righteousness, it will be him."

Sihtric allowed his shoulders to slump. He knew the abbot was right, but he hated the thought of waiting here in Ramsey for so long. Despite their predicament, his mind was already turning to his duties at Hoctune, duties that were no doubt going untended in his absence. His sense of honour and loyalty to Bjarke was not so easily set aside, despite all that had passed.

But then he chided himself for his stupidity. If things went badly, he'd have no role to return to anyway, let alone a house. At best they would be outlawed, but most likely they would be hanged or - at least - mutilated. The thought of spending the rest of his life with no hands or no tongue or, worse still, having his eyes put out that he may not see or speak evil lies ever again, filled him with dread. Such was the danger of standing up to a lord of Bjarke's stature in a court of law. Lose, and you'd lose everything.

TWENTY-SIX

The days merged into one long, interminably anxious wait. It was not until late on the tenth day when Sihtric finally caught sight of a great cavalcade heading towards the causeway. Leaning on the long ash shaft of the scythe he'd been using, he watched them come, shielding his eyes from the low sun to the west. Using a piece of rag he had stuffed into his belt for the purpose, he mopped his brow, stopping the beads of sweat from dripping into his eyes. His view was obscured by a vast cloud of dust had formed over the road, but that told him that a sizeable group of travellers, many of whom were on horseback, was heading their way.

He felt his pulse quicken; what if they were mounted warriors? Had Thorgunnr lost patience and sent a small army to drag him and his wife from the abbey? He wouldn't put it past her. She had little allegiance to the Christian God, so what would she care if she were threatened with eternal damnation by Ethelstan? Doubtless, she would also have no problem finding warriors to do her bidding, men who cared more for her coin than they did for their souls.

His fears abated, however, as the party drew closer, for it soon became clear that Bishop Aethelric had finally arrived. And with him came a huge entourage, for - in Sihtric's admittedly limited experience - no bishop liked to travel without all the trappings of his office. It was the same with kings, he reflected. Wherever they went, they took the best part of their household with them. Whilst it was a great privilege when the king or one of his great men came to stay with you, it could also be a curse as they consumed vast quantities of food and ale wherever they went. It looked like Aethelric was no different. Fully three dozen monks, servants and other hangers-on crossed the causeway and rattled through the gates into the abbey compound, followed by two ox-drawn carts piled high with all manner of things that a bishop might need.

As the convoy passed, Sihtric went back to work. He guessed

it would be some time before he was summoned to appear. Bishops and abbots would have much to discuss before turning to his matter, for running an abbey was a business much like any other. There were rents to review, new land charters to discuss, even spiritual matters on which to opine. He imagined it would be some hours before they had time for him; they might not even see him until the next day.

In fact, he could not have been more wrong. He had worked no more than one narrow strip of the field before a kitchen boy ran up to him, breathlessly urging him to make haste to come to the abbot's lodgings for his presence had been requested.

He followed the young lad back through the gate, skirting the great stone church that was the centrepiece of the island, before heading to the dormitory building where the monks lived. Whilst the brothers occupied a pair of elongated rooms with bunks spaced evenly along each of the long walls, Ethelstan had his own quarters as a mark of his rank. Although his bedroom would have been given over for the bishop's use, he would still have access to his antechamber which he used to conduct the business of the abbey.

Arriving in the small, sparsely furnished room, Sihtric found a small party already waiting for him. Along with Aethelric and Ethelstan, there was Freya and another man who sat at a small desk in the corner with a sheet of parchment in front of him, apparently ready to make a record of the meeting.

"Ah, Sihtric, it's good of you to join us so quickly." Ethelstan rose to welcome him, reaching out to clasp his hand as he did so. His fingers were long, cold and bony, and Sihtric had to be careful not to crush them in his bear paw of a hand, its skin rough and calloused from a lifetime of manual work. The bishop remained seated, as befitted his rank and his great age, but allowed himself a smile and a nod in greeting.

"May I introduce you to his grace, Bishop Aethelric of Dorchester?"

Sihtric went down on one knee, grunt involuntarily as he did so, so that he might take the hand that was proffered to him, whereupon he brushed the ring of office with his lips. Obeisance done, he settled himself on the one empty stool.

Ethelstan continued. "Your charming wife here," he nodded to where Freya sat on another stool over by the window, "has explained to the bishop all that has happened since the night poor Ulf was taken from this world. Now Aethelric is most keen to discuss what must now be done."

Where Ethelstan was thin to the point of emaciation, Bishop Aethelric was anything but. A portly man whose generous paunch bulged over the cord that was tied around his waist, he had the look of someone who enjoyed the perks of his office to the full. Not for him, Sihtric mused, the meagre rations enjoyed by the monks at Ramsey who followed the strict order of Saint Benedict.

It was well known that Aethelric had begun his career in the church at this very abbey, but that was many years in the past. Nevertheless, he had never forgotten his time at Ramsey for rarely a year went by without a visit. Many times, he had bestowed gifts of relics or grants of land to help the abbey grow to the size where there were now few houses greater in wealth and importance in the whole kingdom. Several stories were still told in these parts of the young novice's time at Ramsey, and he was remembered fondly by those who were there with him at the time. He had also made no secret of his desire to be buried in the abbey church when the time came.

"It seems to me," the bishop began, "that we must tread carefully, as though we were crossing a newly frozen river in winter. Who knows the thickness of the ice, whether it will hold our weight or whether cracks might appear? There are few in this kingdom favoured more than Jarl Bjarke. He and Knut have been friends since their youth, fighting together as Jomsvikings in Scania. Much of what the king holds today, he owes to Bjarke and his family. Furthermore, Scania holds the key to the throne of Danmark. Keep Scania and you keep Danmark. Keep Danmark and you keep England. Knut will not willingly abandon such a powerful pillar of his realm."

Sihtric nodded dumbly, unfamiliar with matters of politics. For him, life was ruled by a much simpler code. You took an oath to a lord. He gave you protection and the chance for reward. In return you gave him rent and service. You pointed your sword at whomever he commanded you to and continued to do so until you were either dead or there were none left to face you. Whilst the bishop's words had meaning to him, their subtlety was largely lost. Nevertheless, a thought penetrated his skull, nagging at the back of his mind.

"So, you think we have lost before we begin? That Bjarke is too powerful to be called to account? But it is not he who has caused us injury; he has never been anything but a fair lord and a friend to me. It is his wife with whom our grievance rests."

Aethelric smiled benignly, as if schooling a particularly slow child. "Attack the wife and you attack the husband too, for is she not his possession, as assuredly as is his hall or his livestock? However fair Bjarke may have been to you in the past, Sihtric, however much renown you may have earned in his service - and believe me, there are few in these parts who have not heard of your feats in the shieldwall - do you think he would side with you before his wife? No man would. Would you? Would you defend your lord ahead of Freya here?"

Sihtric saw the bishop was right. If he were honest with himself, he had long known that this path - should they chose to follow it to its bitter end - would bring him into conflict with the jarl. He had hoped that Aethelric would be able to find a way around that hurdle, but it seemed it was not to be.

"So, we are confounded then? We have nought but a life of outlawry to look forward to. Unless Abbot Ethelstan finds work and lodgings for us here until our dying day?" He asked, hopefully, casting a sideways look at the white-haired churchman.

"Hush now, Sihtric. Do not be so keen to be measured for your monk's habit just yet. I have not said that every path is closed to us. Just that whatever path we chose will be beset by thorns and brambles on all sides. But we should not be afraid to tread that road, should it be God's will that we do so. He will provide for us in his mercy, I'm sure."

"What the bishop is trying to say," Ethelstan intervened, "is that he feels your case has merit and deserves to be pursued. I know of none with a greater sense of justice than my Lord Aethelric. Indeed, it was why I summoned him hither to hear you. He will not stand by and see this crime against God go unpunished."

The bishop nodded sagely; his fingertips pressed together to form a steeple in front of his face. Sihtric noted, with interest, that the veins on the side of his bald head throbbed alarmingly, perhaps with the effort of divining a way forward.

Eventually, after what seemed an age, Aethelric sighed and rose to his feet. "Forgive me, but I must retire to rest. The journey here was arduous for one as old as me. God has not yet granted me the sight to see through this maze, so I must pray for His guidance. Let us speak once more on the morrow, after breakfast."

***

"Thanks be to God," Bishop Aethelric closed his eyes and lifted his face heavenward. "For He has heard my prayers, eased my suffering and shown me the way to the light."

"Amen." Ethelstan bowed his head in prayer.

Sihtric coughed gently into the prevailing silence. He had nothing but respect for these men of the church, but he came from a world of action, where decisions and their repercussions were measured in heartbeats rather than hours. Freya, standing by his side, head also bowed in reverence, aimed a kick in his direction, connecting painfully with his shin and forcing a barely stifled groan from his lips.

Ethelstan looked up, noted the look of annoyance on Freya's face and smiled. "Quite. So, pray tell us, Lord Bishop, how should we proceed?"

"Although Jarl Bjarke may have Knut's authority while the king is away, we should not forget that no man - however powerful - can set himself above the law. To my mind, this case is sufficiently grievous as to demand that it be heard and answered in a court of law. Ulf deserves justice if it can be proven he was poisoned. And no man, from the mightiest jarl to the lowliest farmer, can deny him that. But we must, nevertheless, respect the fact that Bjarke is the most powerful man in England after the king, so it is fitting that any summons must come from one such as me, the most senior man of God after the bishop of Canterbury."

"You think this will work?" Sihtric had his doubts. What would there be to stop Bjarke ignoring a demand from the bishop to present himself before a court?

"He would not dare defy the rule of the king's law. I have no doubt of it."

"But the king is overseas and who knows when he might return?" Freya's face betrayed the misery that she felt. "And besides, even if he were to allow his wife to appear before a judge, who would believe the word of a foolish old woman against a lady of noble birth? Who would there be to speak for us? Who would pledge an oath to the truth we speak? I fear we are destined to lose."

Sihtric saw a fleeting frown play across the bishop's face before it was replaced by a benign mask of reassurance. He knew what the churchman was thinking. It was rare for any court to find against one as powerful as a jarl. The resources he could bring to bear, the number of people he could command to give oaths in support of his wife's innocence far outweighed anything he or Freya could muster. His gut told him their chances were minimal at best and now he suspected that the bishop also held that view.

He could not understand why Aethelric would be willing to commence legal proceedings, but then he had no knowledge of politics. Perhaps the old man saw benefit in defeat as well as victory if it meant that Bjarke's power might be weakened in some way. From where Sihtric stood, though, it was like facing a horde of Vikings who outnumbered you by ten men to every one of yours. He was not afraid of a fight, but even he would baulk at those odds.

"We will worry about that soon enough, my dear. For now, however, we must focus our energies on bringing the jarl in front of the court. Should we fail in that, then there will be no trial at all."

TWENTY-SEVEN

Three weeks later, Bishop Aethelric returned to Ramsey with the news they had been dreading. The summons had been served on Jarl Bjarke in his lodgings in the city of Lundenburh, but he had chosen to ignore it.

"What did he say, exactly?" Abbot Ethelstan enquired.

"That his son died from diseased shellfish and that he beseeched us to let his son rest in peace in his grave. He also added that we should desist from such frivolous enterprises as he has far too much to do by way of governing the kingdom on behalf of King Knut, than be bothered by spiteful actions such as these."

"He used the word, 'spiteful'?"

"I am assured that he did, Sihtric."

"So, we have failed in our enterprise? There'll be no justice for Ulf."

"I did not say as much, Freya. This was but the first hurdle, and I half expected it to fail. Simply put, we must now redouble our efforts."

Sihtric toyed with the idea that Aethelric might be lying to ease their suffering. It sounded a little too convenient to his ears, but he would not call him out on it for fear of causing offence.

"So, whither now, Lord?"

"Fear not. A messenger has already been dispatched to issue a new summons. This one makes it plain that he must attend or be in contempt of the law. If he thought that we were not serious in our endeavour, this second letter will disavow him of that notion. I have given orders for him to return here with Jarl Bjarke's response. I expect him to arrive within the week. Until then, I shall stay here to acquaint myself with the latest additions to your excellent library, Ethelstan. I hear you have a copy of Pope Gregory's *Dialogues*. I have long wanted to read this; you must tell me whence you acquired it."

"Do you believe him?" Freya cut in.

"Do I believe what, my dear?" The bishop turned to Freya,

genuinely puzzled.

"When he says that Ulf died from eating bad shellfish and that he is buried in Hoctune church? I know both of these things to be lies. I saw the boy's tongue; I saw the purple mark of the wolfsbane there. I heard Thorgunnr tell Gisla to buy the poison from Cwenhild. And Sihtric and I buried the boy in the meadow at Lolworth. Does he hide these truths to protect his wife, or does he truly believe Thorgunnr's lies?"

"It's hard to know, Freya. A man in thrall to his wife will believe almost anything that she tells him. Would you not say, Sihtric?" Aethelric arched an eyebrow in his direction.

Sihtric found himself chuckling despite the seriousness of the discussion. "I think those days are long behind us, Lord Bishop."

***

But the second summons proved to be as toothless as the first. Still Bjarke refused to accept the bishop's authority and still he denied any wrongdoing had occurred. But this time, a separate rider - one of Bjarke's own men - accompanied the messenger, carrying a message for Sihtric.

In it, the jarl begged his steward to return to Hoctune to resume his duties, for the estate suffered without his steadying hand on the tiller. He implored him to put this disagreeable nonsense behind them, to not let a thing such as this come between them and their comradeship. They were both mourning Ulf, and grief caused people to do and say things that were out of character; things that they would later come to regret if not soonest mended. He ended by asking Sihtric to send his reply with the rider.

"What do you think?"

Freya frowned. "I don't know, husband. It seems to me that he has swallowed Thorgunnr's lies whole, though; else he seeks to entice us back with honeyed words so that we may be trapped like flies on his wife's evil web."

"You think Jarl Bjarke could be so devious?"

"Perhaps I do him a disservice. Until now, he has ever been a fair and honest man from my dealings with him. He can he strict when he needs to, but you need that in a lord when there are misdemeanours to be punished. I can only conclude that he has been bewitched by his wife. She has a power over men, that one; I would not be surprised if she is touched by witchcraft."

Sihtric grunted. Personally, he didn't think Thorgunnr cavorted naked in the forests of Hoctune under a full moon covered in the blood of chickens. For him, her hold over her husband had more to do with the allure of her body. She was a good fifteen or twenty summers younger than her husband and possessed a beauty that would entrance any man. Still muttering to himself, he went back outside to find the waiting messenger, telling him to be on his way to inform Bjarke that he promised to consider his words most carefully but that he begged more time to search his conscience before making his decision. Mollified, the messenger jumped back onto his horse, turning his head back across the causeway and south.

Later, back in Ethelstan's rooms, the four of them met to review their position.

"I, for one, am not prepared to step back from the cliff-edge at this late stage." Despite his advancing years, the bishop's voice was firm. "This is a matter of principle now. Should word spread that a jarl can hold himself above the law, then who knows where that might lead? The nation has not long since recovered from the tyranny and chaos of King Aethelraed's reign and, were we to do nothing, we would risk a return to the iniquities of those days."

"But what - in all good conscience - can we do now? If Bjarke continues to ignore us, what recourse do we have? He is a great noble, with many hundreds of spears at his command. We cannot not force him to submit for we are but few and armed only with cross and cowl in place of helm and shield."

"Worry not, good Ethelstan. I had hoped to avoid this, but I fear we have no choice but to resort to more drastic means."

Sihtric, ever the man of action, was growing impatient once more. Taking a step to one side, just out of range of Freya's boot, he demanded. "Speak plainly, I beg of you, Lord Bishop. Every day we delay is a day closer to death for Freya and me. It is only a matter of time before Thorgunnr finds an assassin willing to breach God's law and kill us here at the abbey. We need to resolve this affair and soon."

Aethelric's expression suggested that he doubted such a thing could come to pass. "Rest assured you will be kept safe here, my son. None will harm either one of you, I swear it. As to what we shall do. Well, I plan to appeal directly to Knut. He needs to be made aware that his rule of law is being flouted by the very man to whom he has entrusted the dispensation of justice in his name. If I know Knut, he will not allow such an insult to his authority to stand. You will recall what happened to Eadric the Streona these few years past? Everyone thought him too mighty to be brought low"

Sihtric nodded; he had not been there, but everyone had heard how Knut had ordered Jarl Eric Haaskonsson to strike Eadric's head off with his axe in the middle of his palace at Lundenburh. His body had then been flung over the wall and left to rot in the surrounding ditch, but not before his head had been stuck on a long spear and displayed from the highest part of the city wall as a warning to others.

Aethelric continued. "Well, you can be sure that Bjarke will not have forgotten either. He would do well not to risk Knut's wrath, lest the same fate befall him. There was no trial, no hearing of evidence. Just a man pushed to the point of uncontrollable rage, determined to be rid of one who had been revealed to have defied the king's word once too often."

"But Knut is in Danmark,"

"Indeed he is, my dear woman. But a swift ship and a fast horse will see the letter safely to his court there within a week. I'm sure of it. With luck we will have the response back with us before Lammas. And then we shall see what we shall see."

***

The days passed slowly for Sihtric and Freya. Though there was plenty of work for them in the fields around the abbey, it could only take their mind off things for so long. The long evenings, after they had shared a meal with the monks in the refectory along with all the other servants and farmhands who worked for the abbey, went by slowly with little to occupy them but thoughts of what could be.

To make matters worse, neither of them felt they could leave the compound. Though they saw no sign of Halfdan or his mercenary Franks, they agreed it was not worth the risk. For all they knew, Thorgunnr might have men hiding in the forests around the island, waiting to pounce should they be foolhardy enough to wander further afield. So, though their lot was not overly onerous, Sihtric could not escape the feeling of being imprisoned. Something, he thought ruefully, they might have to get used to should things go awry for them. That was always assuming, of course, that they did not feel the biting edge of a seax between the ribs before then.

But, fifteen days after the bishop's messenger had set off for the coast, he returned, his horse kicking up great clouds of dust as he pounded across the sun-baked packed earth of the raised path across the boggy fenland that surrounded the abbey.

"Finally." Sihtric muttered under his breath as he began to trudge towards the abbot's lodgings, stopping only to place his scythe back in the tool-shed. As he walked, he spotted his wife drawing water from the well and hailed her to join him. Together, they entered Ethelstan's rooms to find the messenger, still wearing his dirt- and sweat-stained travelling cloak, slugging back a cup of ale with which to sluice the dust of the road from his mouth. Meanwhile, over by the abbot's writing desk, Bishop Aethelric was smoothing flat a parchment that was covered with characters scrawled in black ink. Not for the first time, Sihtric wished he had the gift of being able to read. To him, it looked like a family of spiders had scuttled across the surface having first dipped each of their eight legs in the inkwell.

Eventually, having waited for what seemed an age, Sihtric spoke. "Is it from the king? What does it say?"

The bishop held up a hand and smiled. "Hold fast, Sihtric. My eyes are not what they once were. I need a moment to decipher the script. It looks to have been written in a hurry, and in poor Latin too."

The old man hummed absentmindedly to himself as he traced his finger across the script, following the words. At last, he cleared his throat and turned to face the others. The smile on his face had Sihtric's heart beating faster.

"It is a cleverly worded admonishment that, as far as I can interpret, both supports Jarl Bjarke in his position as governor of the kingdom whilst, at the same time, criticises him for his lax approach to upholding the law. I must confess; I am impressed with the skill Knut has shown."

"Go on... read us what it says." Even Ethelstan was becoming impatient now.

"Hmm, so I'll cut straight to the key text if I may; there's quite a bit of flowery language before Knut arrives at the point. But kings were ever thus, eh?"

And bishops even more so, thought Sihtric.

"*Furthermore, if anyone - be they ecclesiastic or layman, Dane or Aenglesc - is so presumptuous as to defy God's law and my royal authority, or the secular law, and he will not make amends and desist according to the direction of my bishops, I then pray, and command, Jarl Bjarke, if he can, to cause the evil-doer to do right. And if he cannot, then it's my will that with the power of us both, he shall destroy him in the land or drive him out of the land, whether he be of high rank or low.*"

Aethelric paused, looking at each of them in turn, a triumphant look etched upon his wizened features. "Do you not see what he has done there?"

Silence echoed across the room, the only sound the heavy breathing from the messenger who still fought to control his heartbeat. With no answer forthcoming, the bishop sighed and shook his head in the manner of an exasperated teacher faced with a particularly slow class of pupils.

"Without naming Jarl Bjarke specifically - doubtless to avoid undermining the power of the man he left in charge of his kingdom - Knut has told him that he, too, must abide by the king's law. That he should desist from his current course and submit himself to the direction of his bishops - in this case, meaning me. It is all I could have hoped for and more," he beamed, "and I have no doubt that we shall see the jarl and his wife in front of us before very much longer."

"How can you be so certain?" Freya looked far less confident than the bishop.

"Because not only do these words leave him no room to

misunderstand the king's intent, Knut ends by stating that he will be returning to England before the end of the summer to see that his commands have been observed. Bjarke has no choice but to obey now, or risk open conflict with his king."

TWENTY-EIGHT

And so it proved. No more than a week later, yet another messenger clattered into the abbey's main courtyard in the middle of a violent downpour, the heavy drops of rain bouncing off the cobbles as the horse's hooves splashed muddy water from the myriad puddles. Almost before his mount had come to a halt, the bedraggled man leapt to the ground, his lank, blond hair plastered tightly to his face. Looking about him, he hailed a nearby monk who happened to be hurrying across the yard from the scriptorium to the refectory, head bowed and face almost entirely covered by his woollen cowl which he had pulled down as far as it would go.

"You there. Inform Bishop Aethelric a messenger has arrived from Jarl Bjarke. And be quick about it, so I can be on my way home and out of this god-damned pissing rain."

From where he stood, under the patchy shelter of the smithy's thatched roof, Sihtric chuckled. The man seemed to care nought for his surroundings. He wondered, idly, if he would go to hell for taking the Lord's name in vain within the abbey compound. He'd certainly have a job on his hands explaining that one to Saint Peter when he arrived at heaven's gate. Still smiling, he pushed himself away from the stout, oaken post that formed one corner of the open sided building and sauntered over to where the messenger stood waiting for the monk to return.

"Well met, fellow. If it pleases you, I can take you to the bishop. I imagine the news you carry concerns me anyway."

"And who the hell are…", The messenger stopped dead in his tracks as he looked Sihtric up and down as if measuring the man before him. A look of dread flashed across his face forcing him to cast his eyes downward rather than hold the older man's steely gaze for another moment.

"Yes, I am Sihtric Leggbitr, shieldsman and huscarl of Jarl Bjarke. I see you have heard of me."

Still the messenger would not meet his eye. "Your pardon, Sihtric. I knew not to whom I was speaking."

"Whether you knew or not, a little civility would cost you no coin. You'd do well to remember that, as you never know when you might need a friend." He paused to let that sink in. "So, will you follow me to the bishop's lodgings?"

Without waiting for a reply, Sihtric turned on his heel and trudged off across the yard, ignoring the downpour but taking care to avoid the worst of the puddles. He pushed open the door to Ethelstan's rooms, the bottom edge scraping noisily across the stone doorstep, showing how much the wood had already swollen in the rain. Inside, the abbot was deep in conversation with Aethelric, but broke off hurriedly at the interruption, a look of anger passing fleetingly across his face until he saw who it was who had disturbed them.

"Ah, Sihtric. You have tidings this foul day?"

"Aye, Lord Abbot. A rider comes with news for the bishop." He stepped aside to allow the messenger to enter the room where he bowed to the two churchmen, his manners seemingly restored. Reaching inside his cloak, he withdrew a sealed parchment from within a leather sack which was slung across his shoulder by a thin twine strap.

"I bring word from Jarl Bjarke, Lord Bishop." He stepped forward to proffer the message, before bowing once more and shuffling backwards. Sihtric congratulated himself on managing to suppress a snort of amusement but could not keep a wicked smirk from his face.

Ignoring Sihtric, Aethelric lost no time breaking the seal with his fingers. Quickly, he scanned the words, using the index finger on his right hand to trace his way across the closely written lines of text. Looking up when he reached the end, he smiled at Sihtric.

"The jarl has acceded to our demands for a hearing."

"That's wonderful." Ethelstan sprang to his feet to hug Sihtric, showing surprising agility for a man of his vintage. Unused to such overt displays of affection - even from Freya - Sihtric knew not how to react. In the end, he stood there grinning stupidly, his arms hanging limply by his sides.

Releasing him, the abbot turned back to Aethelric. "So, what happens now, Lord Bishop?" Does the letter tell us more?"

"Not much, admittedly. He has invited us to set the time and place for the court and he swears he will attend with Thorgunnr. He finishes by saying that he hopes the matter may then be brought to a swift and satisfactory conclusion." He coughed politely into his hand, as if to hide his embarrassment. "It would appear that my letter has had the intended result."

Sihtric nodded. "And I think I know where best the court might be convened."

***

That evening, Abbot Ethelstan came to see Sihtric, long after the evening meal had been cleared away. The old warrior looked up from where he sat, polishing his mailshirt. He noted with amusement the look of astonishment on the monk's face.

"You surely don't expect to need that do you?"

"A good warrior takes care of his equipment in both peace and war, Abbot. Just as you tend to your flock, so do I to mine." He indicated his sword and helm sitting on the table by his side, awaiting their turn.

Ethelstan nodded absentmindedly, his mind apparently already distracted by some other thought.

"Sit, Father. You have some business to discuss with us? A cup of watered ale perhaps?"

The abbot took the stool by Sihtric's side, waving away with a smile the cup that Freya held out to him. "I've been meaning to talk with the pair of you for some days now. It is a matter of some import."

Sihtric exchanged a glance with his wife, her face showing the same mix of anxiety and confusion that he felt. "Speak freely, Ethelstan. We are friends here."

The abbot sat in silence for a while, gathering his thoughts. Finally, he cleared his throat. "I'll come straight to the point. I fear there are forces at work in the shadows that may yet stand between us and justice for Ulf."

Sihtric opened his mouth to speak but stopped himself, judging that he might best be served by allowing Ethelstan to continue at his own pace.

"As you know, Bjarke holds vast estates in these parts as Jarl of the Eastern Angles. He commands many hundreds of warriors. Who knows, Bjarke might even rival Knut himself on a battlefield should it come to it."

"Should it come to it?"

"Aye."

"Abbot. I do my thinking with sword and shield. My brain does little but wonder what I'll next have to eat. Do me the favour of speaking as if to a child so I might grasp your meaning."

Ethelstan laughed. "Simply put, dear boy, should the court find against Thorgunnr - which is a significant doubt in itself given the resources Bjarke can bring to bear - then Knut may find his hands tied when it comes to enforcing punishment." Seeing the blank look that remained on Sihtric's face, he pressed on. "Knut places a huge reliance on the jarl and the warriors he commands. Should the king deal with him too harshly, then he risks losing that support. These fragile alliances are all that keep the kingdoms of England and Danmark united. The slightest imbalance could see the whole thing collapse as if it were built on sand. It's no secret that Norway ever looks enviously towards its neighbours.

"Already there is talk of its king, Olaf Haraldsson - gathering an army to invade Danmark. With the men that Olaf can muster, Knut would be hard pressed to defeat him, even with Bjarke by his side. But should the jarl be tempted to fight for Olaf - say, because he has fallen from favour here - then Knut knows he could be finished. Do you see now? Is that plain enough?"

Sihtric burned with a frustration that spread like a heath fire in a dry summer. He had always distanced himself from the world of politics and, in return, it had largely left him in peace too. It had always been enough to follow the orders of his lord and not worry too much about whence came those commands or why. He knew if he did his duty to the man who gave him land and protection, then none could besmirch his honour. It had stood him in good stead for many a year - throughout his whole warrior life, in fact. But now it looked as if it might have finally caught up with him.

"That is as may be, Lord Abbot. But I, for one, care little for the machinations of the high and mighty. My sword is straight and true and that is how I live my life. I will not deviate from the path of justice no matter what."

"And nor should you, my friend. I merely seek to warn you that the outcome may not be all that you hoped for. Were this simply a dispute between two neighbours over the boundary between their lands, then we would not have a care, for justice would be swift and simple. But when you seek to put the wife of one of the greatest men of the land before the judge, then you must be prepared for the path to be beset by obstacles."

Sihtric took Freya's hand and squeezed hard. "So be it, Abbot. We are ready to take that chance. Let God's will be done."

TWENTY-NINE

The day of the trial dawned bright but mild. But, before too long, the sun began to climb high into a cloudless blue sky, spreading its warmth over the golden sheaves of wheat and barley that grew in the fields surrounding the abbey. Sihtric was not a man given to displays of religious fervour, but on days like these, he truly believed he could feel God's power reaching out to touch the land. It filled him with a sense of optimism that he hoped would sustain him through whatever the day might bring.

As soon as breakfast was done, they set off. Though the distance to the location chosen for the trial was not great, their pace was going to be slow as neither Aethelric nor Ethelstan were confident horsemen. To reduce the risk of accident as much as possible, they had been given the most sturdy and docile of ponies; beasts who would do little more than a steady walk.

Sihtric plodded along near the rear of the group, alongside his wife. Neither of them had slept much; they were both too full of concern as to what the morrow might bring. Though they should be looking forward to the prospect of an end to their troubles, Sihtric could not forget the abbot's cautionary words. Would they see justice snatched from them at the final reckoning? Would Ulf continue to lie alone and uncared for in an unmarked plot of land to the north of Hoctune? What would become of them?

He had decided not to tell Freya about his conversation with Ethelstan. Her mind was already beset with worry and to add to it seemed to be the least charitable thing he could do. Besides, she knew as well as he did how courts worked. The burden of proof often mattered less than the standing of the individuals involved. And there could be few cases where there was a greater gulf between the opposing sides.

He might carry renown and respect amongst his fellows, his reputation formed in the front rank of the shieldwall over many years and through many battles, but he had no wealth to speak of. He could not pay coin to command the voice of numerous oath-helpers: men and women who would speak for your character and honesty before the judge. They would have no one to vouch for them, no witnesses to say what they had seen or heard. They would be alone before God's judgement.

Thorgunnr, by contrast, had her husband and all his resources standing behind her. She would not want for any of number of people to swear to her innocence. People who had taken Bjarke's coin to speak the words they had been told. Whichever way he looked at it, the scales of justice were weighed heavily against them.

His thoughts were interrupted by the sudden realisation that those in front had stopped, his own mount halting of its own accord without waiting to be told. Craning his neck, he realised they had arrived. So engrossed had he been in his thoughts, that he had not noticed the passage of time. A journey of some hours had passed by in the blink of an eye. Smiling encouragingly, he reached out to take hold of his wife's hand.

"Well, here we are, my love. Let's see what the day shall bring, eh?"

Freya's face was ashen, her features drawn as if the skin were being pulled tight across her cheek bones. Nodding weakly, she squeezed his hand in acknowledgement. Though his own guts were knotted with worry, Sihtric felt sure that it was nothing compared to what his wife must be feeling. All the pain, fear, injury and anger of the last several weeks were at last drawn together in one time and place: Lolworth meadow.

Though it had been dark the last time they were here - that evil night when Halfdan and his thugs had forced them to bury poor Ulf – the memories came flooding back in the daylight. Straightaway, his eyes strayed to the far reaches of the clearing, close to where the cluster of alders stood. That was where they had dug the grave, where they had gently laid the poor murdered boy's body to rest before covering him over with soil. There he lay still, unknown and uncared for. No priest had performed the funeral rites over him, no prayers had been spoken, no mourners had wrung their hands or wept over him. Worse still, his own father knew it not.

He felt a lump form in his throat, causing him to swallow hard to force it back down. It was a day for calm, for logic and strategy. He would need to keep his emotions in check if they were to have any hope of success. His horse began to move again, taking its lead from the one in front. As they emerged from the tree-lined path into the wide-open space of the meadow, he could see that the jarl's party was yet to arrive.

So far, all had gone to plan. Once he had shared his idea about where to hold the trial, Ethelstan and Aethelric had taken to it with enthusiasm, recognising the bare bones of a plan that - with a bit of added flesh - might yet tip the balance in their favour. Though they had set the time of the trial for midday, they had made certain to arrive a good while earlier, affording them plentiful time to set the stage to their advantage, as a group of players might prepare for a performance in the king's hall.

Once all was ready, there was nothing to do but wait. The bishop sat in the abbot's wooden chair in the shade of a great oak tree so that he might be protected from the heat. Two sweating servants had manhandled the cumbersome piece of furniture from the back of the wain that had brought it hither from Ramsey. Though he'd known it would slow their progress, Sihtric had agreed it worth bringing. It lent an air of gravitas to proceedings.

Otherwise, the court was set plain. The players would have to stand before the bishop, exposed to the sun's full glare, adding to their discomfort. Not that Aethelric would be the sole judge. Courts such as these were held for the people and by the people. Decisions were made mostly by acclamation. The assembly would decide - on the balance of the evidence provided and on the credibility of the oath-helpers who spoke for either side - which party mostly likely spoke the truth. It could be a boisterous and unruly affair at the best of times so the bishop's role would be to see that order was maintained. There would be few who would dare defy his authority.

Placed in front of Aethelric's chair was a table - no more than a wooden board resting on two trestles in truth - but covered in an ornate and intricately woven altar cloth borrowed from the abbey for this very purpose. On it were positioned three small wooden caskets, each containing the relics of saints that had long been venerated at the abbey and which had been the inspiration for many miracles over the years. The two on either side housed the remains of the brothers, Aethelraed and Aethelberht; two princes who had suffered martyrdom for their faith, centuries before. The casket in the centre, however, housed the remains of Saint Felix, the first bishop of the eastern Angles. He had come to England from Rome with Saint Augustine over four hundred years previously. When overseeing the loading of the caskets that morning, Abbot Ethelstan has proudly asserted that such auspicious and revered relics would guarantee that none would dare bear false witness that day. Sihtric wanted to believe him but could not help but wonder whether Thorgunnr would be in any way moved by their presence.

Shortly before midday, people began to arrive. It was no more than a trickle at first, ones and twos coming in from the outlying hamlets. But the trickle soon became a flow before, finally, a flood. Whilst courts such as these were not infrequent, it was rare that they involved matters as weighty, or people so lofty, as the alleged murder of a lord's son. News had spread fast, and it seemed that everyone who lived within a half day's journey wanted to be there to witness proceedings.

It had been another factor in favour of using Lolworth meadow; its wide expanse of soft, luxuriant grass afforded ample room for people to gather in large numbers. Already, many had settled themselves down on the ground in small family groups, the womenfolk breaking open sacks filled with bread, cheese and fruit, while the men passed round skins of ale. It was a day off from labouring in the fields and most, it seemed, were happy to treat it as if it were a holy day. The anticipated entertainment of the court case to come was just another bonus to add to the glorious weather and fine company.

To Sihtric's eyes, from where he stood close to the bishop, it seemed that the whole of Hoctune had turned out. Everywhere he turned, there were faces he recognised. Most nodded to him as he caught their eye, their association going back many years and not lightly thrown away. Many of the older menfolk were former warriors who had fought alongside him. In these men, Sihtric thought, he would find support and compassion. They knew him to be honest and stalwart, characteristics which they held dear and which they also espoused in themselves.

But many others looked away, unwilling or not daring to hold his gaze or even admit to knowing him. In the main, these were younger folk, those with whom he had not stood in battle before. Folk who perhaps knew him less well and who would take the side of the jarl if only for their own preservation. He knew to expect little in the way of help from that quarter.

As he surveyed the huge crowd, he realised that a hush was spreading across them. Then, like a field of barley waves in the wind, row upon row of heads turned towards the path that led into the meadow. Following their gaze, Sihtric saw Jarl Bjarke. He sat atop a huge black stallion, a beast larger than any he'd seen before. And, if that weren't enough to strike awe into the hearts of the crowd, he wore a fine crimson cloak over a mailshirt that had been burnished until it shone, causing those caught in its glare to shield their eyes. He sat proud and erect, his chin raised so that he appeared to stare over the heads of those assembled, as if unaware of their presence.

By his side, the Lady Thorgunnr rode. Her slight, diminutive form perched on the back of a chestnut brown mare, was dwarfed by her husband's mount. Yet people still gasped as she passed, for never had she looked more stunning than she did at that moment. Her pale skin, kept shielded from the sun, was in stark contrast to her jet-black hair which hung halfway down her back. She had eschewed the usual headscarf that married women were expected to wear, in favour of allowing herself to be seen unfettered. It was a bold move, but one calculated to add to her aura of beauty. It was clever, Sihtric mused; how could any believe a woman as beautiful and as poised as she could be in any way guilty of murder?

They were followed by what appeared to be a small army. A dozen or so fully armoured huscarls from the jarl's personal retinue, rode in a column of twos, after whom came a larger group of men and women of varying ages and status. *Those must be Thorgunnr's oath-helpers,* Sihtric thought to himself.

Judging by how many had come, nothing was being left to chance. A dozen more warriors brought up the rear. It made for an impressive, if not imposing sight.

As they drew closer, Sihtric spotted Halfdan amongst the first group of riders. It pleased the old warrior to see that the Dane still wore a piece of white cloth tied tightly around his leg, a reminder of their encounter in the forest hut. With luck, Sihtric smiled to himself, it would be a wound he would carry with him for the rest of his days. He would never again know what it was to be free of pain. The knowledge gave him some small crumb of comfort in what was, otherwise, a depressing display of power and wealth.

He realised that Halfdan was staring at him. A baleful look of impotent rage on his face was evidence enough of what he would like to do should he have the chance. Sihtric returned his stare, his expression blank as if ignorant of his identity; a move he reckoned would only add to the other man's ire.

The jarl's party halted in the open space at the centre of the meadow, whereupon Bjarke leapt to the ground in one sweeping movement before striding over to his wife's pony to help her dismount. The jarl knew his audience, knew they wanted spectacle, and so this was all part of the theatre of the occasion. The effect was powerful and only marginally spoiled by Halfdan who, as he slid down from his saddle, grunted in pain and dropped to one knee as his wounded leg buckled under his weight. Laughter echoed around the crowd, causing Bjarke to glare at the shame-faced Dane. Downcast, Halfdan mumbled something by way of apology before excusing himself to see to the horses.

Amid the continued merriment, Bishop Aethelric rose to his feet, brushing aside a young monk's proffered arm. "Welcome, Jarl Bjarke, Lady Thorgunnr. If all is well, then shall we begin?"

He paused long enough for Bjarke to nod, stiffly.

"Very well." He cleared his throat.

"People of Hoctune," he began, his voice strong and clear so that it carried to all corners of the crowd with ease. "This court is convened in the sight of Almighty God and in the presence of the relics of these most holy saints," he waved his hand over the caskets before making the sign of the cross, "to hear a most disturbing case." He paused, allowing time for the excited chatter to dissipate.

Sihtric looked at Freya by his side and gave her a conspiratorial wink. It seemed that the jarl was not the only one who knew how to manage a crowd; the bishop would doubtless prove to be an effective foil to whatever chicanery Bjarke might muster.

Then Aethelric pointed at the jarl's wife, raising his voice as he would when haranguing his congregation from the pulpit, bringing down God's judgement upon them. "The Lady Thorgunnr stands here before you, accused of murder. That she did cause poison to be ingested by Jarl Bjarke's son, Ulf, and that he did die from it." He paused once more, to let the gravity of the charge sink in. By now, all chatter had ceased; everyone's attention was focussed on the bishop, eager to hear what he would say next. Here and there, Sihtric noted, some had even paused, with hands holding food or drink halfway to their mouths.

Eventually, the bishop lowered his arm and looked around. "Who here brings this charge against Lady Thorgunnr?"

With timid steps and with her hands clasped firmly before her, Freya shuffled forward into the centre of the clearing. "I, Lord Bishop. Freya of Hoctune, daughter of Folkwin, do so accuse her." Though clearly petrified, her voice was firm, betraying little of nerves she must have felt.

Aethelric nodded and smiled kindly at her. Few outside the ranks of lords and churchmen were used to speaking in front of such large numbers; it could be a daunting prospect to say the least.

"And now, Freya of Hoctune, you must state your case against her. Leave nothing out in the telling."

Hesitantly at first, but growing in confidence, Freya told her story; how Thorgunnr had never warmed to the boy and had often treated him harshly, a situation that had only worsened once her own son, Erik, was born. She went on to describe how she'd overheard her sending Gisla to buy wolfsbane from Cwenhild and how Ulf had died in agony after eating shellfish that had been laced with it. As she described his death, her voice cracked and she broke down, the emotion finally getting the better of her.

Aethelric waited for her to recover her composure, sending one of the young monks to her with a cup of water. Meanwhile, Sihtric watched his wife with pride. She had done the boy proud with her testimony. Though he was not here to speak for himself, Ulf could not have wanted for a more eloquent and credible representative. She finished her tale by explaining how she had found the purple stain on Ulf's tongue and how she had confronted Thorgunnr with the evidence.

"And what happened then, my dear?"

"She threatened to kill me and my husband unless we held our tongues."

"Lies! The old witch is lying." Thorgunnr had managed to restrain herself throughout Freya's speech, but she'd finally lost control. Her eyes blazed with hatred as she pointed accusingly at Freya.

The bishop rose to his feet. "Lady Thorgunnr. I must ask you to remain silent. You will have your turn to speak in good time." Turing back to Freya, he continued. "Pray finish your tale, goodwife."

Freya then recounted her abduction by Halfdan and Sihtric's role in her rescue. As she explained how he had killed Sibba and Harald and wounded Halfdan, a good number of his old comrades nodded appreciatively. They knew his reputation in battle. They also knew that if they had been in his place, they too would have done likewise to defend their own. If he were honest, Sihtric would have liked to have told the tale himself, as if he were sat by the hearth-fire late at night when old men swapped stories of battles past and deeds done. But Freya had been there, and she did the tale justice. She ended with a flourish, pointing to where Halfdan stood leaning against a tree to keep the weight off his bandaged leg.

"I thank you for your courage, Freya of Hoctune. I think we can all see the evidence of the struggle you so vividly described," he nodded in Halfdan's direction. "But that on its own does not prove Thorgunnr's guilt. What other evidence do you have to prove the truth of your words? Are there witnesses that you can call upon?"

"There are none, excepting Gisla, Lord Bishop. Lady Thorgunnr's maid."

Aethelric turned to Bjarke's wife. "Well, Lady? Is this Gisla here with us today? Please have her come forward to give us her testimony."

But it was Bjarke who spoke instead. "Your pardon, Lord Bishop, but Gisla has returned to her home in Danmark to care for her ailing mother. Had I but known that she would be required to speak here today, I would have forbidden her to go."

"That is disappointing, to say the least, Lord. And - some might also say - fortuitous. Without Gisla, there is no one to back up Freya's story. Is there anyone else here who wishes to add their name in support of Freya?"

Sihtric raged helplessly into the ensuing silence; he could do nothing to intervene. How could the two of them hope to defeat the wealth and influence that Jarl Bjarke could command? Freya's testimony had been strong - she could have done no more - but there was no one to stand with them; no one to give evidence in support of their case.

Just then, a movement to his left caught his eye as people began to shuffle to one side, forming a path through which someone was now moving. With a glimmer of hope, Sihtric saw it was old Fortha Oaken Legs. He had not seen him since that day, several weeks ago now, when he had left Hoctune in search of his wife.

The old shieldsman barged his way to the front and then stood in front of the bishop, planting his legs shoulder-width apart with his hands on his hips; a stance from which a whole army of Danes could not have shifted him. Sihtric saw him in a new light, then. That he was prepared to step forward and speak for them touched him greatly and showed the true value of friendships formed in the shieldwall.

"I speak for Freya." His voice boomed across the clearing.

Aethelric nodded. "State your name and make your case."

"I am Fortha, son of Frithuwald, watchman of Hoctune. I did not see or hear the events of which Freya speaks concerning

Ulf's death, but I did see Halfdan and his two cronies leave through the main gate with a covered wain during the night. It happened as Freya said. And then, the next morning, I spoke with Sihtric, who told me his wife had been taken and that he meant to get her back. I offered to go with him - as two men are better than one and we have stood together in Bjarke's warband many times - but he bade me not to. Rather, he told me that, should he not return, I should tell my story so that all may know what had befallen him and why.

"I should have known he would not need my help, even against three of these womanly Danes," he spat in Halfdan's direction. "But I now fulfil my promise to Sihtric, and I state here in front of everyone that I believe Freya speaks the truth." Fortha then folded his arms across his chest, thrusting his chin forward, as if daring anyone to challenge his word. At that moment, Sihtric could have hugged his old comrade in arms. Though it might not tip the balance, at least they were not alone. A hush fell over the crowd as folk murmured to each other, quietly discussing what they had heard.

Eventually, the bishop rose to his feet.

"You have spoken well, Fortha" Aethelric smiled. "I thank you for such stalwart words. I believe that closes the case against Thorgunnr, and we must now invite her to have her say as is her right."

Now we will see how we stand, Sihtric thought. He still had one piece left to play in the game, but he hoped not to have to use it, for it was a piece that - once played - could not be taken back.

Meanwhile, Thorgunnr shuffled forward timidly. It was as if her recent outburst had never happened; that she was somehow cowed and frightened by the proceedings and the great throng of onlookers. Knowing her as he did, Sihtric saw through it for the act it was, thinly veiled and calculating, designed only to evoke the sympathy of the crowd. Finally, after having smoothed down the folds of her dress and adjusted her hair, she indicated that she was ready.

Aethelric nodded. "In your own words, my child, you may now respond to the accusations levelled against you by Freya of

Hoctune."

Glancing from abbot to bishop to husband, she stammered. "It's all been a dreadful mistake. I don't know why Freya says these things against me. She knows my poor Ulf died after the oysters made him sick. Freya was there; she saw how he vomited and cried out in pain, clutching his stomach. How else could he have died if not from this?"

Freya snorted with derision. "Anyone infected with wolfsbane would die in this way. Besides, how do you explain the stain on his tongue?"

Aethelric held up his hand for silence, his face a scowl of irritation. "Freya, you have had your turn to speak and now you must stay silent so Thorgunnr may state her case unmolested." He turned back to Bjarke's wife whose cheeks were, by now, wet with tears. "Nevertheless, Lady, the point is valid. Vomiting alone is not prove that Ulf died from food he had eaten. What of the purple mark on the tongue? Do you deny it was there?"

"I do not, Lord Bishop. But it is no more sinister than the juice of blackberries. Ulf had spent the afternoon picking them from the bushes that grow to the south of Hoctune. He had eaten some in his room before he went to bed. Freya must have found their stain on his tongue, but in her haste to condemn me, did she think to check his fingers? If she had, she would have seen the same mark there."

Sihtric scowled. It was a lie; he knew it. But it was a good one. It sounded plausible and would cast doubt in peoples' minds where before they might have been certain. They would ask themselves: could she really have wanted to kill her stepson? Could she really have been so callous?

"But, if you had nothing to hide, why abduct Freya in the middle of the night? What could you hope to achieve?"

Thorgunnr shrugged, her face a mask of innocence. "I did not give that order. I cannot explain how it happened. Freya helped deliver my child, Erik, into this world. Beyond this silly misunderstanding, I have nothing but love and respect for her."

"I find this hard to believe, if I am honest."

"I am sorry, Lord Bishop, but I know not what else to say. Perhaps Halfdan overheard me talking to my husband about

Freya's accusation. Perhaps he acted on instinct, somehow thinking that he could help me in some way. Such men think only with their swords, I am sure you will agree. I truly wish he had not, that we could go back to before it happened. After all, two men have paid for it with their lives and Halfdan himself has been grievously wounded. None can say they have not paid the price for their foolishness."

When she had finished, Aethelric turned to address the crowd. "You have heard Lady Thorgunnr's reply to the accusation made against her. Who here speaks for her?"

It was the signal they had been waiting for. The two-dozen folk who had arrived with Bjarke and Thorgunnr then, one after another, dutifully repeated the words they had been given to say. Each of them recounted how the Lady Thorgunnr had always been a kind and considerate mistress, how they had never been mistreated by her and how they had never seen her mistreat anyone else, especially Ulf.

As each one spoke, their words so alike to the one before to make it almost farcical, Sihtric wondered how much they had been paid for their services. A few extra coins in their purse would come in handy for the winter. Had Thorgunnr paid for them from her own coin or had her husband dipped into his own reserves? He still did not really know what Bjarke believed about his wife's actions. Did he really trust in her innocence? Or had she told him the truth, hoping his love for her would spare her the noose?

As if reading his mind, Freya reached for his hand, squeezing his fingers hard in a vice-like grip. With a start, Sihtric realised the last of the oath-helpers had spoken and the bishop was on his feet once more, to begin his summary. His heart rate quickened, thumping against his chest like the smith's hammer on the anvil.

"People of Hoctune, you have heard the case against Lady Thorgunnr and her own explanation for the events which led to the death of her stepson, Ulf. What is not in doubt is that the boy is dead; he lies buried in the church of Saint Edmund in the town. What does need to be decided, however, is whether his death was the result of accident - tainted oysters no less - or whether it was by the hand of the boy's stepmother, by means of wolfsbane acquired from Cwenhild the healer. And that she did this for the purpose of enabling her own son, Erik, to accede to his father's titles and lands when the time comes. I leave it in your hands to decide by acclamation." He paused, surveying the crowd with a glare so stern that there could be no doubt in their minds as to the importance of their duty. "All those here who believe the Lady Thorgunnr guilty of murder raise your hand and say 'Aye'".

Here and there, a few hands went up - Fortha among them - accompanied by shouts of 'Aye', but it wasn't nearly enough. Sihtric saw a few had started to move only to hold back, perhaps waiting to see how many of their peers acted first. When they saw how few spoke up, they changed their minds, keeping their arms by their sides. As the result became clear, Freya gasped as the enormity of the situation struck home. They had lost. They had not even come close to proving that Thorgunnr had murdered Ulf.

"Very well." Aethelric signalled to the scribe who sat to his left. "Let the record show that Lady Thorgunnr was found to be not guilty of her stepson' murder. Let that be an end to the matter so that he may now rest in peace in Saint Edmund's church for ever more. Amen." He made the sign of the cross once more.

"But what if I could prove Ulf's body does not lie in the church as you say?" Sihtric stepped forward into the centre of the clearing. It was time for the final piece in the game to be played. He had hoped it would not be needed, but he knew that there was no other choice now; not if he hoped to avoid a life of outlawry.

"He lies!" Thorgunnr screamed in anger, her carefully fabricated facade cast off for good this time, as though removing a cloak when stepping in from the cold.

"How so, Lady? You have not heard what he has to say? How can you be sure he lies unless you know what he is in his mind...?"

Silenced, she stared at Bjarke, as if imploring him to intervene.

On cue, the jarl moved towards Sihtric, his arms held out in a placatory gesture. "The court has made its decision, my friend. Would it not be better for all if we were to put this matter behind us? Can we not return to our lives now? I know how much you and Freya cared for Ulf and how devastated you both were by his death. Why drag out the pain any longer than necessary? Nothing can bring him back to us. He lies buried in the church in Hoctune. Let that be an end to it."

"Only I know he doesn't, Jarl Bjarke."

His old friend and comrade stopped in his tracks, visibly shaken. The crowd was in uproar; everyone was either discussing Sihtric's outburst or passing it on to those behind who had not heard. At length, Aethelric had to stand to appeal for calm.

"This is very irregular, Sihtric, but then nothing about this day has been what I would call normal. We shall hear what you have to say, but" and he fixed Sihtric with a stare that would have had a weaker man quaking in fear of God's wrath, "be sure you have the evidence to support your claim or stand in disgrace before the Almighty."

Sihtric strode over to where the carts stood to the rear of the bishop's chair. Once there, he grabbed a pick and shovel before then walking back to a spot about ten paces to the right of Aethelric, shooing people out of the way as he went. Halting, he threw the tools on the ground and pointed to the two nearest men, farmers he recognised from Hoctune.

"Dig."

The farmers looked at each other, unsure what to do and embarrassed to have been thrust into the centre of everyone's attention.

"What is the meaning of this?" Bjarke took a step forward, his composure recovered. As he spoke, his hand strayed to the hilt of his sword.

Ignoring him, Sihtric repeated his command. "Dig here. Now."

Shrugging, the two men spat on their hands, picked up a handle each and set about the turf, having first sought confirmation that they were in the right spot. Though the ground had been baked hard by the summer heat, the men were strong and the tools sharp, helping them to make short work of the top layer. With sweat pouring from their bodies, they were soon down to depth of about two feet.

"Careful now. Go gently from here."

Dropping to their knees, they began scraping away the loose dark soil with their hands, visibly afraid of what they might find. As they went on further and further, Sihtric began to doubt himself. Had he mistaken the place? Worse still, had someone come back and moved the body? His stomach lurched as he realised that such an outcome was more than likely. But then, suddenly the man on the left - Osric he recalled his name was - called out.

"Look here."

As people surged forward to see, Osric gently brushed away the remaining earth to reveal a patch of stained linen which grew with every moment until there was no doubt it was a shroud wrapped around a body.

No one spoke. Heads turned between Sihtric, Aethelric and Bjarke, waiting to see who would speak or act next. Then Sihtric motioned for Osric and his companion to leave the trench whereupon he stepped down, wincing at the familiar pain in his leg as his weight bore down on it. Pulling out his seax, he deftly cut open the cloth around the head and pulled it back.

Those close enough to see recoiled, gasps of shock and revulsion spewing forth from their lips. Whilst parts of the flesh had decayed, there was no mistaking that it was Ulf. The wavy fair hair and a chipped front tooth where he had been kicked by an angry horse the previous year, were proof enough.

Turning to Thorgunnr, Bishop Aethelric drew himself up to his full height, crossed himself and pointed at her. "Murderer! Freya spoke the truth. Ulf's body lying here condemns you beyond doubt."

THIRTY

Everyone was shouting all at once. Aethelric and Ethelstan tried hard to restore some semblance of order, instructing the monks to move through the crowd, parting those who showed signs of anger. Nevertheless, some scuffles did break out here and there, as arguments between supporters of either side descended into blows. From where he stood, Sihtric could see Thorgunnr, her skin almost as white as newly fallen snow, her face a mix of fear and rage. Bjarke was attempting to comfort her, but she was beyond reason, shaking and screaming incoherently, her once finely coiffured hair now dishevelled and wild.

In contrast, Freya stood silent but open-mouthed, too shocked by the turn events to speak. From certain defeat to complete uncertainty in the matter of a few heartbeats. Sihtric could see that she wanted to believe, wanted to cast off the despair that had gripped her just moments before, but who knew what would now happen?

Eventually, with the help of the monks, Bishop Aethelric managed to silence the crowd. "Jarl Bjarke, I command you by the power invested in me as head of this court to place your wife in chains. She must answer for her crimes."

Bjarke looked up from where he stood, his arms wrapped around his wife's narrow frame forming a protective barrier. Releasing his grip, he stepped in front of her and roared. "I will not. I swear she is innocent of this crime." To emphasise his point, he grabbed a great handful of his beard and yelled at the top of his voice. "I swear by the beard on my chin that she has done no wrong."

The crowd fell silent, stunned. For the ancient oath carried untold weight and meaning. Though it hailed back to a time before the message of the nailed-God had reached the northern lands, there were many who still behoved to the old traditions despite that. For a man to swear by his beard was as portentous as it could be. By these words, Bjarke had issued a challenge; a challenge that could only be answered in blood. Should any now want to call him liar they must come take his bear and with it, therefore, his head.

The silence endured as no one - not even Aethelric - seemed to know what to do or say in response. The only sound was the rustling of the leaves, gently disturbed by the light summer breeze. Even the birds had stilled their song as if stopping to watch the human drama play out beneath them. The sheriff's men, who had been on the point of seizing Thorgunnr, stopped midway across the clearing, none of them wishing to enrage the jarl further.

With a sudden sense of certainty, though, Sihtric realised what he must do. He turned to hug Freya, her eyes widening in fear as she guessed what was on his mind. But before she could form the words to stop him, he turned and pushed his way through the throng until he stood before his friend.

"I, Sihtric of Hoctune, call you liar, Jarl Bjarke. And I am willing to prove the truth of it with my body and my sword. I claim the blood price for your son, Ulf, even if you will not."

A look of infinite sadness passed over Bjarke's features, as his shoulders slumped. "Really, Sihtric? Has it come to this? Must we - old comrades in arms as we are - cross swords to settle this matter? Does our friendship, the respect we have for each other, earned over many years, mean so little that you would chance it on the roll of a dice?"

"If you are as unwilling to abandon your wife, as I am to abandon mine, then I fear we must. I know Freya speaks the truth; I will gladly stake my life on it and trust in God to smile upon the righteous. Can you say the same, Jarl? Will you risk God's wrath and fight with me here today?"

"Sihtric, you are old. Your leg troubles you; I cannot recall a time when you did not walk without a limp. God knows you were ever one of my best warriors - never bested in the shieldwall to my knowledge - but those days are long past. I would not consider it a fair fight to pit myself against you."

Sihtric planted his feet in front of Bjarke, puffing out his chest in a show of proud defiance. "Fear not, Lord. The bones may creak, and the flesh may groan, but the brain is still sharp enough and Leggbitr's edge remains keen. Perhaps you should ask Halfdan how well I can still fight? You could ask Sibba and Harald too, were they still alive."

The jarl sighed, accepting defeat. "So be it then, old friend. Let it be known that I would have done anything to avoid this outcome but, if you will not withdraw your accusation, then honour demands that I answer you in kind."

***

An hour later, the two men took their places on opposite sides of the clearing. Both were clad in mailshirt and helm, and each was equipped with sword and shield. Sihtric rested his shield against his leg and handed his sword to Fortha so that he could adjust the strap on his helm to a more comfortable position; it would not do to have it slip during the fight for fear that the rim might obscure his vision. Satisfied, he picked up his shield once more, threading his forearm through the leather straps, welcoming the feel of the familiar weight of the hide-bound linden boards.

Nodding his thanks to his old companion, he stepped forward only to be stopped by Freya who pulled him round by his upper arm.

"Are you sure about this, husband?"

Sihtric brushed some loose hairs away from her face; a small but tender gesture that said far more. "I see no other way if we are to have peace, wife. Should the worse come to pass, stay close to Ethelstan; he will see you safely housed at the abbey."

Freya smiled, though her eyes had filled with tears. "I would rather stay married to you than to God. I will pray for you; I shall beseech God and His saints to protect the righteous." With that, she leaned forward to kiss his cheek.

Sihtric had to cough to fight down his emotions. Squaring his shoulders, he walked on, lunging down on to his haunches every few steps, to test the strength of his leg. The old twinge was there as always, but there was little pain to go with it. It was always more bearable in the summer months as if the muscles were strengthened by the heat of the sun, just as an apple ripens on the tree. He prayed it would not let him down if the fight wore on too long.

He halted a dozen or so paces from Bjarke. The younger man - the jarl had almost ten summers on Sihtric - was a good head taller and had the extra reach in his sword arm that went with it. Sihtric knew from the times they had trained together that he would need to move in close. He had to negate that advantage as much as possible. As he stared at his opponent, watching the other man's face intently, he tried to think ahead, to imagine how the fight might unfold.

With both men now ready, the bishop rose to his feet. "I must ask you both once again; is this a path on which you are both agreed? It is not too late to call a halt."

"You must ask Sihtric. If he will withdraw his accusation, then I will gladly step aside."

"Well?" Aethelric turned to the old warrior.

Sihtric said nothing, but simply shook his head.

"So be it then. The fight will end when either one of you is dead or when one drops his sword and calls for mercy. May God see that justice is done." With that, Aethelric made the sign of the cross over both men before resuming his seat, a look of infinite sadness on his face.

But Sihtric ignored the churchman's feelings. His mind, his whole body, was focussed entirely on his opponent. He was oblivious, even, to the crowd of onlookers who had erupted into howls of encouragement. This had turned out to be a day to surpass all expectations. First there had been the taut excitement of the trial followed by the unexpected twist, and now there was the prospect of blood; a contest between the jarl, no less - the most powerful man in the land after the king - and his stalwart steward. A warrior whose martial reputation had surpassed most others.

The two men began to circle each other, side stepping so that they remained facing one another while they each searched for an opening or a weakness. Though they often trained in this way, it was rare for warriors to find themselves one on one in battle; most conflicts began as two solid walls of men pressed hard against each other and ended with one side in full flight. Fights such as these were the stuff of legend, the subject of songs sung by scops around the hearth on the long winter nights, where facts counted less than dramatic embellishments.

Suddenly, Bjarke was on the move, hurling himself towards Sihtric. He held his sword held high above his head as he roared a battle cry of old, covering the short distance between them with incredible speed. The older man had little time to adjust. Despairingly, Sihtric flung his shield up, hoping it would be enough. A heartbeat later, his whole arm shook with the impact of the jarl's sword as it smashed against his shield. So savage was the blow that a narrow shard of wood, about a foot long, sheared off the edge, sending splinters of wood into his face and narrowly missing his eyes.

But he had no time to enjoy his luck, for Bjarke was attacking once more. Swirling round from his initial assault, the jarl launched into a flurry of hacking cuts and thrusts, each as brutal as the last. But rather than try to penetrate Sihtric's defences, they were all deliberately aimed at the shield, trying to exploit the damage that had already been done. For now, the remaining boards held firm, though his arm and shoulder were almost numb from blocking blow after crushing blow.

All the time, however, he was being forced back, step by painful step. He was vaguely aware of people behind him now scrambling to get out of the way, several tripping over the remains of the food and drink they had brought, in their haste to be away from danger.

And still the blows came, each one hammering down on his shield like the smith's hammer strikes the anvil. Sihtric wondered how long Bjarke could keep up the intensity of his attack. Surely, he had to pause for breath soon. Although he was not working as hard physically, he could feel his own lungs beginning to heave with the effort of keeping his opponent at bay.

Then, without warning, Bjarke suddenly changed the angle of his attack, springing to one side to aim a vicious thrust at Sihtric's unprotected right flank. Nothing but blind instinct saved him; the reactions of a man who had fought countless battles in his long years. Flinging his sword arm to the side, he managed to parry the thrust, blocking the jarl's weapon just inches before it connected.

The momentum of Bjarke's blow brought the two men closer to each other, their swords screeching in protest as their notched edges scraped together until, eventually, the cross-guards intervened, preventing them from coming into direct contact. Even so, they were so close now that Sihtric could smell the foul reek of the younger man's breath and feel its heat on his cheek.

Unperturbed, he held Bjarke's gaze, both men breathing hard, grateful for the temporary respite. The younger man glared with the wild abandon of a man fighting for his life, all grip on normality temporarily set aside. Then, without taking his eyes off him, Sihtric pulled his head back before ramming it forward, taking the jarl completely by surprise.

For once, his lack of height worked in his favour as he heard the crunch of bone splintering as the top of his iron helm crushed the bridge of Bjarke's nose. His opponent staggered back, his eyes streaming with tears, while blood and snot flowed from his ruined nostrils. Dazed, he shook his head before wiping his sleeve across his mouth, spreading the gore yet further across his face and lending him a demonic appearance.

Now the jarl's blood lust exploded, the pain helping to fuel an incoherent rage. Blinded by tears of pain and anger, Bjarke threw himself forward, spitting foul obscenities at his former friend.

But this time, Sihtric was ready. This time, he did not stand and wait for the onslaught. Instead, he crouched down into a ball of muscle and sinew, all the while keeping one eye on the jarl's sword, watching and waiting for the right moment. Just as he saw the blade begin its downward arc towards his head, Sihtric ducked under its trajectory. He then straightened up and, in the same movement, jabbed his shield into Bjarke's chest, noting with satisfaction the sound of air being expelled from the taller man's lungs. Without pause, he then punched his right arm forward, smashing his gloved fist into the jarl's face, adding to the damage his helm had already wrought. Had he had room to use Leggbitr's blade, the contest would have been over there and then, but the range was too tight. He need not have worried though.

Bjarke stumbled back a couple of paces, his arms hanging

uselessly by his side, while his legs wobbled like those of a newborn foal. Another step and he fell to his knees, his limbs no longer equal to their task. Keen to press home his advantage, Sihtric launched a kick at the side of the head, sending the jarl sprawling to the ground.

With a gleam of victory in his eyes, Sihtric stood over the prostrate man. Raising his face skyward, he yelled, the sound a mixture of relief and triumph. Then he too dropped to his knees, astride his beaten opponent's chest, letting go of his sword and shield in the process. He stayed that way for a moment, his chest heaving as he sucked air into his lungs. Then he reached down to unsheathe his seax. Reversing the blade, he held it so that its point hovered menacingly over Bjarke's throat. His mind was in turmoil; emotion fought with sanity for dominance of his head. Images of Ulf's horrific last night on earth filled his mind, choking him with their intensity. There was a debt to settle, a blood price to be paid. But was it really Bjarke's debt to pay?

A scream rang out from the crowd. Fearing some new attack, Sihtric looked up to see Thorgunnr, the architect of all their troubles, facing him. She was frozen to the spot, her pale skin almost wax-like. In her arms she held Erik who, frightened by the tumult around him, was crying hysterically.

Glancing back down at the jarl, Sihtric hesitated. Had he really been about to end Bjarke's life? The man who had been his friend as well as his lord. The man who had offered him his protection for so many years. He had lost count of the number of gifts he had received over the years, the spoils of broken enemies given in grateful recompense for his service. Is this how he wanted it to end?

As he wavered, he became aware once more of the crowd. The noise they made - now that it had finally penetrated his senses - was louder than any battle he had experienced. With all those eyes upon him, he was struck by an unbearable feeling of melancholy. What was the point of it all? A child was dead. Why now add to it with the life of his father? What would that achieve? The pent-up emotion of all that had gone before now rose up in his gorge, overwhelming him like waves crashing on a beach. Then the tears came, misting his eyes and blurring his vision. He cared not who saw them, though, as his shoulders slumped with exhaustion.

The jarl stared up at him, barely conscious, yet aware that his fate was held in the other man's hands. To his credit, he showed no fear. Rather, he set his jaw in an expression of grim determination. Like the true warrior he was, he had prepared himself for the journey to come. With his right hand, he scrabbled around for the sword he had dropped, his fingers finally closing over the pommel. He made no attempt to use it though; but a warrior must set off on his path to the afterlife suitably equipped.

Dragging himself back to the present, Sihtric made his decision. Ignoring the shouts and screams around him, he reached forward with his left hand. Grabbing a handful of Bjarke's beard, he hacked through it with the blade of his seax. Then, rising to his feet he marched over to where Thorgunnr stood, still sobbing.

Throwing the clump of hair at her feet, he shouted. "There's your truth, fiend. May you rot in hell for your crime."

Then, without a backward glance, he limped away, the crowd parting silently before him.

EPILOGUE

Sihtric leaned back against the wall of the barn, angling his face towards the late afternoon sun, revelling in the feeling of its warmth on his skin. The harsh grating noise of the spinning sharpening stone in front of him slowed and eventually stopped as he lifted his foot from the pedal. There were few things finer, he reflected as he closed his eyes, than a short nap in the sunshine of an afternoon. His chores were done for the day; taking care of Leggbitr - keeping her edge keen - was an act of love rather than a duty.

"I hope you're not thinking of using that thing again, are you?"

He opened his eyes to see Freya standing over him, her buxom form blocking out the sunlight and casting a shadow over him.

"Now then, my love," he smiled, a knowing glint in his eye. "You know I have promised never again to wield her in anger."

"Not unless the occasion should arise, that is," she corrected.

He chuckled along with his wife. What had once been forbidden to him had now been caveated. Halfdan and his cronies had seen to that. Having said that, he was very conscious of the fact that, in his fight against Jarl Bjarke, he had not managed to land a single blow with his sword. So ferociously had the jarl fought, he'd had neither time nor opportunity.

A lot had happened in the weeks since the trial, and not all of it for the best. But finally, he and Freya had felt safe enough to return to Hoctune and resume something approaching a normal life. One or two of the townsfolk remained wary of them but, on balance, that was a small price to pay after what they had been through. Things had gone worse for Bjarke and his wife, after all. Though not as badly as many might have expected.

Bishop Aethelric had written to the king, placing the facts of the court before him: that Lady Thorgunnr had murdered Ulf and then sought to conceal the truth by having him buried in unconsecrated ground, while substituting another body in his place in the church. But if they had thought that Thorgunnr would be punished for her crimes, then they were to be sorely disappointed.

"It's a question of politics, my boy. Just as I feared." Aethelric had explained after receiving Knut's letter in reply. "Bjarke is simply too powerful to be slighted. He could raise almost as many warriors as the king, should it come to a reckoning between them. And when you also think of the vast territories he holds back in Danmark, Knut dare not risk open conflict with the jarl. He needs him by his side."

Seeing the look on Sihtric's face, however, the bishop had continued. "But fear not, for all is not lost. I hear that the king flew into a rage on hearing of this matter. Whatever their station, Knut cannot have his greatest lords treating the law as if it were nothing but a minor inconvenience – like stepping around a puddle to avoid muddying your shoes."

"So, what has he decreed?"

The bishop scanned the final few lines of the letter. "He has banished the jarl from these shores for the passing of a year."

And so it was that Bjarke had left Hoctune within a week. He sailed back to his homelands in Danmark from the port at Gippeswic, taking Thorgunnr and Erik with him. An in the absence of any new lord being appointed in his place, Sihtric had resumed his role, reaffirmed in his position as steward by the king's own hand.

Sihtric's first act, a day after his return, had been to arrange for Ulf's body to be recovered and reburied in its rightful place. He was buried by Bishop Aethelric with full ceremony alongside the body that had been placed in his stead. No one thought it right to move the poor unfortunate soul who had been an unwitting piece on the game board, after all. After the service, Abbot Ethelstan had declared an end to the whole sorry saga at last.

"Budge up, you old goat." Freya flopped down on the bench beside him, barely waiting for him to shuffle along to make room.

Yawning, Sihtric stretched his arms above his head before bringing one down around her shoulders. In turn, she lent her head against his shoulder, settling into his stocky frame.

"I suppose things turned out for the best in the end." She said sleepily.

"They most certainly could have been worse, for sure. Though I do have one regret, if I am honest. One thing I would change if I could."

Freya gave him a squeeze. "But you didn't lose me, and those Dane bastards never had the chance to defile me before you turned up."

"Eh? I was talking about Acwel. Truth is, I miss the old hound."

Laughing, he ducked to avoid the slap that she aimed at his face.

THE END

Historical Note

The inspiration for this story came from - of all things - a podcast on a dog walk: specifically, the British History Podcast (very much worth a listen if that's your kind of thing). In discussing political machinations during the reign of King Knut in the early 1020s, the host narrated a tale, found in the pages of the Chronicles of the Abbey of Ramsey, about a man named Thorkel who had sworn on his beard that his second wife was innocent of the murder of her stepson - his son by his first wife who had died in childbirth.

By the end of the thirty-minute episode, I was hooked, almost dragging my dog back to the house in my eagerness to start making notes. It made for a compelling story, and one which I felt could - with a little effort - be massaged into an intriguing medieval murder mystery. At its core is a story as old as the hills: jealousy. It was a jealousy that led to the murder of an innocent child followed by a quest to bring the killer to justice.

In writing the story, some dramatic licence has had to be taken; the monks' account was annoyingly sparse, after all. I have changed the father's name - it was simply too alike that of the lead character in my Huscarl Chronicles series for comfort. I have also made Bjarke the Jarl (the Danish equivalent of earl) of East Anglia. In the Ramsey Chronicle, there is some doubt as to whether the man concerned is Thorkel the Tall, who was Lord of that territory and second only in power in England to the king; or whether he was just a local man who happened to have the same name. For the story to carry the weight it needed, however, I decided that Bjarke would have to be a man of power and influence for the story to make sense.

One fact that might tip the balance in favour of it being Earl Thorkel, however, is that the Anglo-Saxon Chronicle does record that he was banished from England at some point in the mid-1020s. Frustratingly - as is so often the case with the ASC - it neglects to tell us why. How tantalising is it, though, to imagine that the cause of the rift might be found in a disagreement between king and earl over the behaviour of the latter's second wife?

An early working title for this book was going to be: *Bjarke's Beard*. I chose this to reflect the importance of the oath that Bjarke swore at his trial. It features in the pages of the Ramsey Abbey Chronicle as the climax of the court proceedings. Rather than have his wife subjected to interrogation, the earl stepped forward and swore on his beard that she was innocent. And in taking this oath, Thorkel yanked hard on his beard - to demonstrate the strength of his word - and, you've guessed it, it came off in his hand.

Clearly, this serves only as a literary flourish, a device by which the abbey monks could give credit to the power of God. Surely it can't have happened like that. But whatever the truth of it, it was too good a detail to leave out of the story all together. Hence, with a bit of nifty footwork, we see our hero Sihtric - with the trial going against his wife - challenge his lord and protector to trial by combat to decide who was telling the truth. And in this way, we arrived at the actual title - suggested by my wonderful publisher at Sharpe Books - of *Blood Price*.

It was a long-held tradition in pre-conquest times for a man to make good on some misdemeanour by paying a fine - or wergild (literally: man payment). Its purpose was to prevent bloody feuds from wiping out multiple generations of warring families, as each sought vengeance for a wrong committed by the other. Instead, you could be brought before the court and made to pay a fine, the value varying according to station. Killing an earl's son, for example, would be a whole lot more expensive than killing a lowly herdsman.

Having Sihtric win the fight, but then pull back from slaughtering his erstwhile friend and simply cut off his beard instead, seemed to be a neat way to bring the story to a close as well as work in the apocryphal beard falling out story from the Chronicle in a more realistic way.

Finally, I can't finish this note without a nod in the direction of my dog, Pepper. My constant companion on long walks in the Cheshire countryside, during which I do much of my best plot thinking, she is the inspiration for Acwel in this story.

Though I doubt she would ever manage to equal Acwel's feats in the forest hut (unless she were to lick Sibba to death), she does at least share similar prowess when it comes to chasing squirrels. Never managed to catch one yet.

Printed in Great Britain
by Amazon

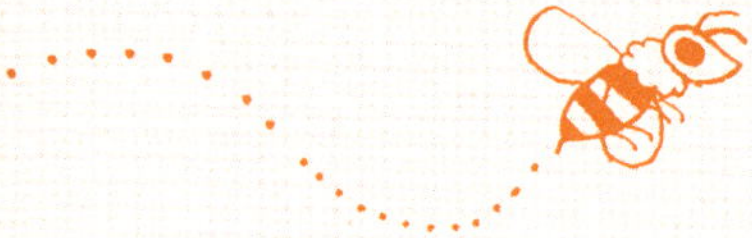

ひとさじの
はちみつ

自然がくれた家庭医薬品の知恵

Spoonful of
Honey

前田京子

maeda kyoko

マガジンハウス

マヌカ

クローバー

菩提樹
ぼだいじゅ

アカシア

Spoonful
of
Honey

甘露蜜
かんろみつ

そば

高千穂産の百花蜜
たかちほ　ひゃっかみつ

対馬産の百花蜜
つしま

ひとさじの はちみつ

お気に入りのはちみつが手に入ったら、はちみつ用のスプーンをそろえるのも楽しい。「これ！」という一本を決めてもいいが、毎日のことだから、気分によって、使い分けて遊ぶのも悪くない（27ページより）。

ガラスのスプーン

鹿の角のスプーン
つの

ステンレスの薬さじ

木のスプーン

● はちみつの歯みがき 2種（60ページ）

● はちみつの胃薬
（132ページ）

はちみつとはっかの
歯みがき（62ページ）

はちみつとシナモンの
歯みがき（64ページ）

はちみつの
スキンケア

肌の表面をつるんつるんにしてくれるその即効性に
は、「おおっ」と人知れず感動するのである（10ページより）。

● はちみつの化粧水
（82ページ）

● はちみつのクレンジング（106ページ）／
　はちみつのトリートメント（109ページ）

● バスハニー
　＜はちみつの入浴剤＞
（86ページ）

● はちみつのフェイシャルパック（109ページ）

はちみつは おいしい 医薬品

「このひとさじで元気になる」と思いつつ、なめるはちみつの美味しさは格別。医薬品としてのはちみつの一番の得意分野は、傷ついた細胞、特に粘膜の修復だ（27ページより）。

● はちみつの軟膏と
絆創膏（95ページ）

● はちみつの目薬
（120ページ）

● ハニーレモンキャンディ
＜はちみつとビタミンＣ＞（150ページ）

（はちみつとビタミンＣを一緒に
摂ると理想的なサプリになる）

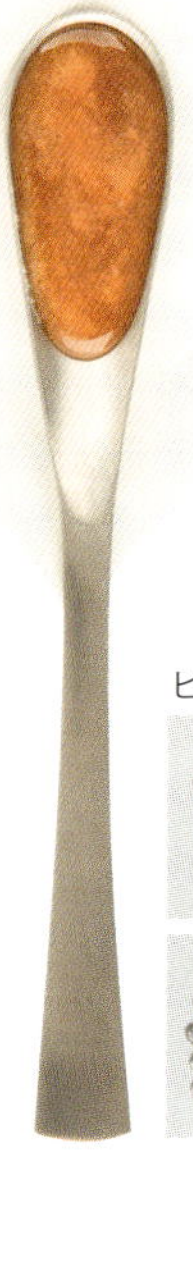

オプションとして……
● はちみつ緑茶
キャンディ（46ページ）

（ビタミンＣの豊富な粗挽き
緑茶や抹茶を加えても）

粗挽き緑茶

ビタミンＣ原末
（アスコルビン酸）

ビタミンＣ原末（ア
スコルビン酸）は、
遮光びんで保存。

ビタミンＣの量を調整

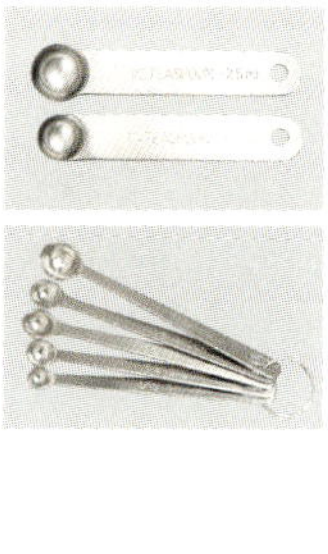

● はちみつ水／
ハニーウォーターDD
＜手作りイオン飲料＞
（72ページ・172ページ）

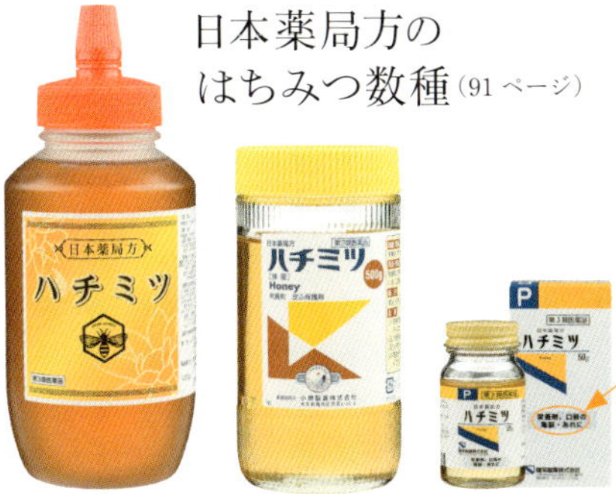

日本薬局方の
はちみつ数種（91ページ）

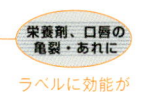

知らなかった はちみつの 世界

栄養剤、口唇の
亀裂・あれに
ラベルに効能が
記されている

ちょっと珍しいメディカル系はちみつ＆はちみつ製品

ニュージーランド産

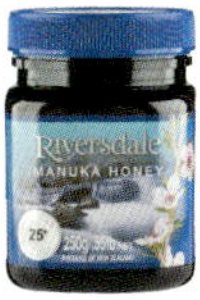

● 活性マヌカはちみつ
特定有効成分の活性度25＋の表
示は飛びぬけた効能の高さを示す
（表示のしくみについては、127・128
ページ脚注参照）。

● レワレワの花（ニュージー
ランドスイカズラ）のはちみつ
特有有効成分特定の研究が進め
られている（38ページ脚注参照）。

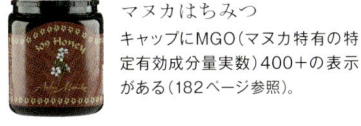

● 309ロード沿いの活性
マヌカはちみつ
キャップにMGO（マヌカ特有の特
定有効成分量実数）400＋の表示
がある（182ページ参照）。

● 南島原生林の甘露蜜
（honeydew honey）
特有有効成分特定の研究が進めら
れている（37ページ参照）。

● ハチ毒入活性
マヌカはちみつ
内服用痛み止めとして使われる（37
ページ参照）。

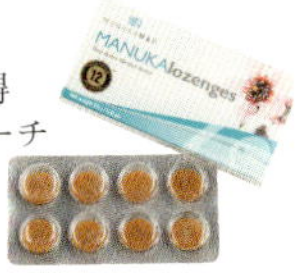

● 医薬品の国際標準規格取得
の活性マヌカはちみつのトローチ
医療機関で使われる。

● ハチ毒入活性マヌカ
はちみつ軟膏
外用痛み止めとして使われる。

オーストラリア産

● 活性ジェリーブッシュはちみつ
「オーストラリアのマヌカ」と呼ばれ、同様
に検査機関で活性度が検査される。写真
のものは特定有効成分活性度20＋かつ
MGO800＋、と表示（39ページ参照）。

● 活性ジャラ（ユーカ
リの一種）はちみつ
写真のものはTA（はちみ
つ全体の活性度）30＋と
表示（39ページ参照）。

ひとさじのはちみつ

自然がくれた家庭医薬品の知恵

もくじ

まえがき

✤ はちみつと私 009

✤ 「医療用はちみつ」＝「メディカルハニー」との出会い 011

✤ はちみつの食べ方にもコツがある 015

Spoonful of Honey 1

ひとさじのはちみつを寝る前に 019

✤ 場所や時代を超えた、はちみつへの熱い想い 022

✤ 効用のあるはちみつの条件 024

✤ ひとさじのはちみつを摂るのにベストな時間 027

Spoonful of Honey 2

もうひとさじのはちみつは、目覚めのお茶とともに 031

✤ 寝覚めのはちみつは脳に効く 034

✤ はちみつは今や、自然療法のスーパースター 037

✤ 「はちみつはビタミンCと一緒に」がコツ 039

✤ シナモンとはちみつも黄金のコンビネーション 041

Spoonful of Honey 3

ひとびんのはちみつは、理想的な非常・保存食 043

✤ はちみつは、ほぼ完全な栄養剤 046

✤ ピンチはチャンス、空腹は幸運かも 048

✤ 常温で腐らないはちみつは、非常時のための備蓄に最適 050

✤ 食卓の喜びは精神の備蓄 052

Spoonful of Honey 4

はちみつで歯を磨こう 055

✤ はちみつは虫歯菌を退治する 059

✤ はちみつとはっかの歯みがきで、歯はつるつる、息はぴかぴか 060

✤ あなたはジョリジョリ派？ それともトローリ派？ 062

✤ はちみつとシナモンの組み合わせは、古代エジプトの歯槽膿漏の処方箋 064

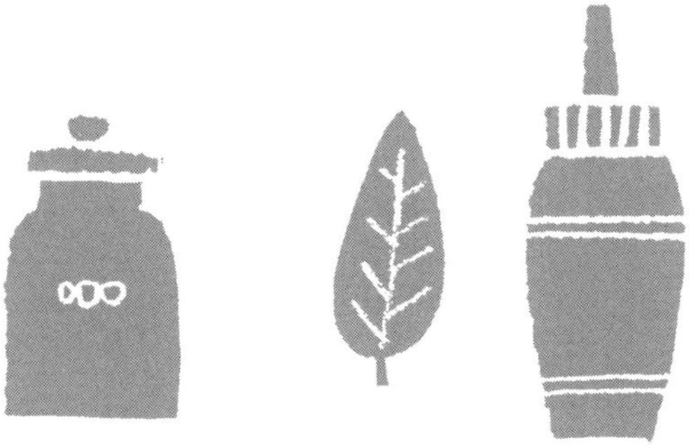

Spoonful of Honey 5

大汗かいたら「はちみつ水」（手作りイオン飲料） 067

✢ イオン飲料の材料として理想的なはちみつ 071

✢ とっても便利な日本薬局方のビタミンC 074

✢ 季節や体調によって、好みの味を楽しもう 076

Spoonful of Honey 6

はちみつ化粧水とはちみつのお風呂 079

✢ 日焼けの手入れに、はちみつを 082

✢ 化粧水で、はちみつの香りを愉しむ 085

✢ 紫外線ケアには、はちみつとラベンダーのお風呂 086

Spoonful of Honey 7

はちみつ軟膏とはちみつの絆創膏 089

✢ はちみつが特に効く傷・やけど 093

✢ はちみつの抗菌作用の仕組み 096

✢ 抗生物質が、効かなくなった耐性菌をやっつけるはちみつパワー 098

Spoonful of Honey 8

はちみつパックと
はちみつクレンジング
101

✤ 悪玉菌を殺し、肌を清浄にするはちみつ

✤ とてもシンプルなはちみつクレンジングの方法ふたつ
104

✤ はちみつが、しみ、そばかすに効き、
肌を白くすると言われてきたわけは？
106

✤ はちみつフェイシャルパックの即効性と
お風呂でのはちみつトリートメント
108

109

Spoonful of Honey 9

はちみつ目薬
111

✤ 白内障、角膜炎、結膜炎の治療報告、
そして目の老化現象や充血、疲れ目に
115

✤ 目に湿布をしたような気持ちよさ
119

✤ 自分の涙で目を洗う
121

Spoonful of Honey 10

はちみつの胃薬

✢ 日本のはちみつ博士はいずこ
129

✢ ただの消化不良や胃もたれにも
132

✢ 夢見る日本のメディカルハニー
133

125

Spoonful of Honey 11

はちみつとビタミンCで、見えない敵と闘う——*1*

135

✢ 「病気の予防や治療にビタミンC」という一般的な習慣
138

✢ ビタミンCの「適量」は自分で見つける
141

✢ はちみつを通して再会したビタミンC
145

✢ はちみつとビタミンCは同じ武器を手に
ウイルスやがん細胞をやっつける
148

✢ はちみつとビタミンCを混ぜた
「ハニーレモンキャンディ」は最強のサプリメント
150

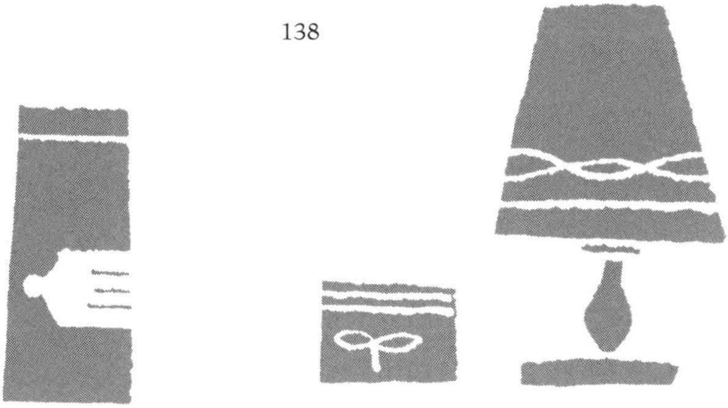

Spoonful of Honey 12

はちみつとビタミンCで、見えない敵と闘う──2　155

✤なぜ、おかしな循環が止まらないのか　158

✤「ビタミンCを摂りなさい」　160

✤紫外線対策と放射線対策の共通点　163

✤まず自分が健やかになること　165

Spoonful of Honey 13

はちみつでおなかすっきり　167

✤はちみつ水でデトックス　170

✤断食クリニックで学んだことと、お腹の畑の土作り　175

あとがき

✤はちみつミルクか、はちみつワインでおやすみなさい　181

主要参考文献　189

装丁・本文デザイン
こやまたかこ

イラスト
谷山彩子

撮影
千葉 諭

編集
島口典子

まえがき

はちみつと私

はちみつは長年、私の暮らしの中にあたりまえのようにあった。
料理に使ったり、パンやお菓子に焼き込んだり、ヨーグルトやわらび餅
にとろりとかけたり、ちょっと口寂しいときにひとさじすくって、そのま
まペロリとなめたり。

産地の違うさまざまな蜜源のはちみつのひとくちをゆっくりと味わいな
がら、その土地の風景を思い浮かべるのは、ちょっとした旅行気分だ。珍
しい花のはちみつに出会うと、その絵や写真を探して眺めるのも楽しい。

これまでも書いてきたことだけれど、はちみつを入浴剤としてお風呂に
持ち込むこともしょっちゅうだ。大さじ2、3杯を湯船に溶かし入れるの

だが、べたべたせずに、すばらしくさらりとした極上の保湿力。お風呂上

がりはいつもご機嫌だ。

イタリア産のオレンジのはちみつに、オレンジの花の精油*1とオリーブオ

イルを数滴合わせるなど、その日のお風呂素材の組み合わせを夕食の献立

のように考える。疲れたときの何よりのレクリエーションである。

すぐに出かけなくてはならないのに肌がちょっとまずい状態だったら、

大急ぎでひとさじのはちみつにお気に入りの植物油を美容オイルとして1

滴垂らして混ぜ、1、2分のはちみつパックをする。

毎度のことなのに、肌の表面をつるんつるんにしてくれるその即効性に

は、ばたばたしながらでも、「おおっ」と、人知れず感動するのである。

「はちみつと私」を英語で言うと、「Honey & I」となる。これは恋人や

夫婦の間の甘ーい言い回しで、「あなたと私」という意味だ。実は、去年

私は、「はっか油」への恋文を本にしたところなのだが、相手が素材なら、

長年の恋人が何人いてもかまわない。

実を言うと、子どもの頃からもう何十年のつきあいだったはちみつとの

*1 芳香療法（アロマ
テラピー）で使用される、
植物の花、葉、茎、枝、
樹脂などから採取された
芳香成分。古くから医療、
美容に利用される。

Spoonful of Honey　010

関係に、数年前、革命的変化があった。そのことが、これまでのはちみつとのつきあい方をふりかえり、この本をまとめるきっかけとなったと言っていい。

「医療用はちみつ」＝「メディカルハニー」との出会い

ある時期、突然しつこい喉のイガイガに悩まされるようになった。

それまでだったら原因が何であれ、寝る前に、マグカップに熱いお湯を入れ、はっか油を垂らして喉にかざすスチームバスのトリートメントをすれば、翌日か翌々日にはすっきりと元通り。

ところが、どんなのど飴よりも頼りになっていたはずのはっか油なのに、今度ばかりは喉のイガイガが何日経っても治らない。いったいどうしたことなのか。

そこでふと思い出したのは、「はちみつが傷んだ肌や粘膜の修復を助ける」ということだ。あれた肌の修復に、いつもの顔のはちみつパックがあ

れだけ効くことを考えたら、はちみつをもっと早く喉に試さなかったのは不覚であった。

さっそく、そのとき手元にあった中から、温かい日向のような味の大好きなクローバーのクリームはちみつを選び、寝る前にひとさじなめて床につく。そうしたら翌日は、数日ぶりに快適な目覚めがやってきた。万歳！

ところがその後しばらく、何とも不思議な感覚が続いた。どうもイガイガの原因は完全に取り除かれているわけではないようなのだ。はちみつをなめているかぎり、症状をある程度抑えることはできるのだけど、「イガイガ」や「ひりひり」が、くすぐったいような「ちりちり」になるぐらいで、完全に喉のことを忘れ去ることができない日が多い。体調が悪いということがめったになくて、そのことに対して耐性というか、がまんの修行が全くない人なので、生まれて初めてと言っていい長期にわたる喉の違和感が気になって、他の何にも集中できないようなそわそわした気分に苦しめられた。

そんなとき、ハッと思い出したのが、十年ほど前、ニュージーランドに

*2 天然はちみつを、生化学的有効成分を損ねないように温度管理しながら、ごく細かい結晶にして、なめらかなクリーム状に仕上げたもの。

*3 ニュージーランド全域に自生するフトモモ科の常緑樹。白、ピンク、赤などの梅のような花を咲かせる。抗菌有効成分を最も多く含むのは白い花とされる。マヌカはマオリ語で、古くからその葉が薬草として使われた。はちみつを採るようになったのは、ミツバチと養蜂技術が入って来た1840年頃以降のこと。庭木とされることも多いが、日本でも園芸で扱われ、ギョリュウバイと呼ばれる。

Spoonful of Honey

住んでいる大学時代の友人が電話をかけてきてくれたときに聞いた、ある
はちみつの話である。

「あのね、マヌカハニーっていうの、知ってる？　マヌカっていう植物は、
ティートリー[*4]に似ているんだけど、やっぱりちょっと違うの。こっちでは
ね、はちみつというとマヌカなのよ」

私が精油やはちみつに目がないことを知っていた友人は、そのはちみつ
の話をした後すぐに、香りがとっても似ているというマヌカの仲間の植物、
カヌカ[*5]の精油をペーパータオルに染みこませ、手紙といっしょに送ってく
れた。興味津々でいそいそ封を切ると、濃いエメラルドグリーンの強い海
風のような香りがあふれ出た。

なんでもマヌカのはちみつは、れっきとした病院でお医者さんたちが難
病の治療にまで使うもので、効き目の強さによって数種類のグレードに分
類されているのだという。

2002年当時、日本でも、ほんとうにちらほらとマヌカハニーという
名前を聞き始めた頃だったので、友人から聞いた後、さっそく輸入食品店
でひとびん手に入れて私も味わってみた。はちみつというより、濃いキャ

*4　オーストラリア東
部に自生するフトモモ科
の常緑樹。精油は高い抗
菌作用を持ち、世界的に
アロマテラピーで最も広
く使われるもののひと
つ。キャプテン・クック
がその葉をお茶にしたこ
とから、「ティートリー」
と呼ばれる。

*5　ニュージーランド
に自生するマヌカと同じ
フトモモ科の常緑樹。マ
ヌカより樹高は高く、白
い花の花径は小さく、強
い芳香がある。はちみつ
の性質はかなり違う。

013　　　　まえがき

ラメルのような感じ。自分としてはとっても好みの味で美味しい。

でも、難病どころか体調不良とも縁遠かった私は、「薬として使われるらしい」ことはあまり気にもとめず、トーストに塗ったりしながら、ひたすらペロペロ美味しく食べてしまったのだった。

「そうだ、そうだ。あのはちみつをこの喉に試してみよう」

そう思った私は、さっそく、いろいろと資料を探し始めた。そうしたら、すばらしく興味深いことに、あれからマヌカハニーの研究はさらに進んでいて、それは世界で他のはちみつの医学的研究をも促し、なんといまや「メディカルハニー」とでも言うべき「医療用はちみつ」の分野が確立しつつあるらしいぞということが、段々わかってきたのだ。

「マヌカハニー」の効き目の理由となる特殊な成分は『UMF＝ユニークマヌカファクター*6』と名付けられている」と知ったときには感動し、途端に喉の憂鬱が吹っ飛び、一瞬それだけでひりひりまでなくなった気がしたほどだ。

それまでいろいろな植物オイルの効能を使い分けては、肌の調子やタイ

*6　38ページ参照。

Spoonful of Honey　　014

プに合わせて石けんや美容クリームのレシピを作ってきたけれど、オイル
と同じように、いろいろなはちみつも効能をねらって使い分けられるよう
になってきたのか、と思ったら、小躍りしたい気分になった。
　いや〜、年をとるのも、たまに喉が痛いのも悪くない。長生きというの
はするものです。

はちみつの食べ方にもコツがある

　というわけで、その後、メディカルハニーの世界にどっぷり足を踏み入
れたら、それまでのはちみつ人生の次元がぐぐっと広がり、楽しみ方が、
何倍にも膨らんだ。
　それまでのように、いろいろな種類のはちみつを味わい分けるのも面白
いけれど、不調に対する「効き目」ということを真剣に考えたら、はちみ
つのひとさじの食べ方、選び方にも、実はいろいろコツがあるということ
も段々わかってきた。
　で、肝心の喉のイガイガひりひりはどうなったかって？

詳しいことはあとで書くけれど、うれしさと驚きのあまり、どうしても原生林で満開のマヌカの花とハチたちの飛び交う様子が見たくなり、春のニュージーランドに自分も飛んで行ってしまったぐらいなのです。

普段の体調不良や体力作りに、はちみつが幾通りにも役に立つということを知ると、はちみつを常備しておくということは、大げさではなく、家にちょっとした薬局があることに等しいとわかる。

はちみつのどんな成分が、どう効くのかということにもふれながら、この本では実際に試してみた、楽しくて具体的な使い方を、ちょっとした工夫も織り交ぜつつ、ご紹介したいと思う。

今や世界中に、はちみつをなめて胃のピロリ菌を退治している人はずいぶんいる。従来の病院でもらった通常の抗生物質などの薬を飲んでも、ずうっと効かなくてあきらめていた人たちだ。

もともと病院に行ったわけじゃないけど、うわさを聞きつけた人たちの中にも、はちみつがそんなに胃にいいのならと、手放せなかった市販の胃薬をやめて、朝晩ひとさじのはちみつに切り替える人たちも増えた。

Spoonful of Honey　016

ひどい白内障には外科手術が第一の手段とされているが、予防や軽い症状の治療なら、はちみつを使うという方法もある。はちみつは古来、眼病の薬で、最近は、はちみつの目薬も開発されるようになった。普段の疲れ目を和らげるのに、私自身も今では、たまのはちみつ点眼が欠かせない。

そして面白いことに、何の症状から入ったとしても、一度はちみつを試してその効果を体感した人が、進んで元の市販薬に戻ることは、あまりないようだ。

それはきっと、上手に使ったとき、はちみつがからだの不調を緩和するだけでなく、ほんとうの元気をくれるということを実感できるからだと思う。

まずはお気に入りのひとさじを探す旅に出てみませんか？

017　　まえがき

Spoonful of Honey 1

ひとさじの
はちみつを寝る前に

「1匹のハチが一生に集める
はちみつの量は、小さじ1杯」って知ってた?

——ジョーン・モンテリエ

お風呂や着替えも済ませて寝る準備が整ったところで、いそいそとキッチンへ。

ティースプーンを取り出して、はちみつをすくい、びんの外に垂れてこぼれないよう注意しながら、ぺろーり、きれいになめ取る。

口の中に伸びやかにじんわり広がっていく夢心地の甘みをゆっくりと味わうひとときが、安らかな眠りへの玄関口だ。

ミツバチの一生ってどんなものなんだろう？　と、ミツバチに関する本や資料を当たると、「働きバチは一生の間にひとさじのはちみつを集める」という内容の記述が出てくることが多い。でも、10年ほど前に住んでいたアメリカ・ワシントン州の田舎町で、モンテリエ・チーズ農園の女主人、ジョーンさんからそう聞くまでは、私はそのことを知らなかった。

彼女が作る飛びきりのチーズやバターは青空市場の花形だ。材料のミルクのために山羊を数十頭飼っているのだが、その他に農場で野菜を作り、鶏を放し飼いにし、ミツバチの巣箱をいくつか置いている。はちみつは売りものではなくて、自家用、または贈り物用だったが、私が家で作る石けんを気に入ってくれていた彼女は、たまにはちみつのびんを持って我が家

021　🥄　1　ひとさじのはちみつを寝る前に

を訪れ、石けんとの交換を申し出た。

「ミツバチが幸せに暮らしていないと農場とは言えないでしょ」と言うジョーンさんは、いつも、卵を産むメンドリや、蜜を集める働きバチのことを、My girls（「私の娘たち」）と呼んでいた。

そう、働きバチも、実はみんなメスなんですね。そのことも私は知らないわけではなかったのだけど、実はあまり意識したことがなかった。ジョーンさんの「娘さんたち」がせっせと花から集蜜し、熟成させて作りあげたはちみつのひとさじをすくいとって味わうまでは。

◼️ 場所や時代を超えた、はちみつへの熱い想い ◼️

女ミツバチ1匹が一生働いてできあがる美味なひとさじは、大家族を養っていかなければならないハチたちにとって貴重な食料だ。だがそれは私たち人にとっても、味覚の愉しみを超えて、この上なくありがたい恵みである。

日々の体調を整えるのに、寝る前のひとさじがどんなに役立つかを、私

Spoonful of Honey　　022

自身も体験的に実感するようになって久しい。

はちみつは昔から健康、長寿の鍵とされてきた。

古代エジプトの古文書でも、インドの伝統医学「アーユルヴェーダ」でも、はちみつは医薬として扱われていて、さまざまな処方が伝えられている。

古代ローマの大博物学者プリニウスの著述の中にも、はちみつを常食する養蜂家がたくさんいる村には、百歳を超える長寿の人がとっても多いというくだりがある。納税台帳の記録によると、なんとローマのその地域（アペニン山脈とポー川の間）には、百歳どころか、１３５歳以上の人だって、ひとりやふたりではないというのだ！ ＊１

ところ変わって中国の薬学書の中で最も大部で重要なものとされる明朝の『本草綱目（ほんぞうこうもく）』でも、「十二臓腑の病に宜（よろ）しからずというものなし」と、はちみつは、眼病、皮膚病、呼吸器、消化器なんでもござれ。ほぼ万能薬認定の勢いだ。

まあ、１２０を超えて生きるとか、万病を治すとか、はちみつのびんを握りしめてそこまで怖れ知らずの野心を掲（かか）げようと思わないにしても、現代になって、科学的に成分が分析される結果などを見ていると、歴史上の

＊１ プリニウスが納税台帳で人々の寿命を調査したとき、養蜂家の長寿に感心したのは確かなようだが、中には１５０歳を超える記録もあったとされる。はちみつだけでなく台帳管理の鷹揚（おうよう）さも手伝った可能性は否定できないのでは……。

023　　🥄　　1 ひとさじのはちみつを寝る前に

はちみつ讃歌にも、いろいろなずける点があるかも、と思えるのもまた確かだろう。

なにしろはちみつは、各種ビタミンやミネラル、酵素、抗酸化物質の宝庫で、真菌や細菌に対する殺菌力もめっぽう強い。明治期に始まった日本薬局方[*2]にも指定され、今でも薬局方のはちみつというものが医薬品としてちゃんとあるし、それは栄養剤としての他、口内炎や口角炎に効くとされている。

そんな歴史をあれこれ考えたら、はちみつを単なる砂糖代わりの甘味料や嗜好品と思う人が多くなってしまっていた昨今は、人類とはちみつの歴史の中では、もしかすると例外中の例外なのかも、とさえ思えてくる。

効用のあるはちみつの条件

はちみつが、世の中で「お砂糖代わり」のような扱いになりかけた理由は、もしかすると、純粋はちみつではない加工はちみつが大量に出回ってしまい、本来の良さが伝わらなくなってしまったことと関係あるのかもし

*2 生薬、製剤、試験法などの基準を定めた医薬品の規格書。国、地域ごとに制定されている。「日本薬局方」初版は、1886年（明治19年）に公布され、2015年現在、第16改正日本薬局方が公示されている。

Spoonful of Honey　024

れないという気もする。

精製、加糖、加熱などの加工をされたはちみつには、巣のかけらなどの不純物を濾過しただけの天然の純粋はちみつが持つ医薬品としての効能などはほぼ期待できないし、栄養価も大きく損なわれているからだ。

たとえば、栗やそば、菩提樹（シナノキ）など、色の黒くて風味の強いはちみつほど、鉄や銅などのミネラルが特にたっぷり含まれていて、造血作用が豊かとされている。健康的なはちみつなので、ドイツやフランス、朝鮮半島などでは昔から人気が高いが、日本やアメリカではあまり好まれず、脱色脱臭精製してミネラルを取り去ってしまってから、製品として使うことも多いらしい。

でも、白パン白米全盛の時代を経て、今では日本やアメリカでも全粒粉のパンや玄米が人気になってきたから、黒いはちみつのファンもそのうちだんだん増えてくるかもしれず、はちみつ精製の状況も変わってくるかも、と期待をこめて思ったりする。

また、純粋なはちみつの場合、働きバチが花の蜜を集めてくるだけで、はちみつになるわけではない。ハチは運んできた蜜を巣に帰ってから吐き

025　　1　ひとさじのはちみつを寝る前に

出して唾液の酵素と混ぜ、それを受け取る係のハチに引き渡す。蜜の蔗糖（しょとう）はハチの持つ酵素でブドウ糖と果糖に分解されるのだ。花蜜は巣房（すぼう）に詰め込まれるが、働きバチの姉様たちは、せっせと羽ばたいて水分を飛ばし、蜜を濃縮していく。十分に濃縮されたらその後巣房はふたをされ、その中でゆっくり時間を過ごした蜜は次第に熟成されていく。

だが、早く製品にしたいからと自然の摂理を待ちきれず、急いで収穫したはちみつは完成しきっていないので水っぽい。

そこで、濃度を上げるために水あめや、「人工転化糖」（蔗糖をブドウ糖と果糖に人工的に転化させたもの）を混ぜた「加糖はちみつ」、水分を飛ばすために加熱した「加熱はちみつ」が作られるというわけだ。また、かさ増しのために水あめなどが加えられることもあるだろう。

いずれにしても加工はちみつの場合、他のものを加えたり加熱することによって、本来持つ栄養素の分量が減ったり変質してしまっていて、古来ほめたたえられてきたはちみつのめざましい効能は、見るかげもなくなってしまっているのである。

だから、はちみつを美味な「薬」として使おうとするなら、精製や加糖、

Spoonful of Honey　026

加熱のない、天然の純粋な生はちみつを選ぶことが、まずは基本と言っていい。

ひとさじのはちみつを摂るのにベストな時間

お気に入りのはちみつが手に入ったら、はちみつ用のスプーンをそろえるのも楽しい。「これ！」という一本を決めてもいいが、毎日のことだから、気分によって使い分けて遊ぶのも悪くない。

金属がはちみつにふれると変質するので、必ず木のスプーンを使った方がいいと言う人もいる。はちみつは酸性なので、確かにアルミのスプーンなどは避けた方がいいかもしれない。私は木やガラス、陶器などのスプーンも使うが、長めの薬さじを使ってはちみつをなめるのも大好きで、ステンレスなら大丈夫と思うことにしている。いずれにしても「このひとさじで元気になる」と思いつつ、なめるはちみつの美味しさは格別だ。

医薬品としてのはちみつの一番の得意分野は、傷ついた細胞、特に粘膜

の修復だ。

そこで考えてみると、からだが細胞を修復させ、新しい細胞を生み出す時間帯は、夜の10時から午前2時までだという（だからその時間によい睡眠を取ることが健康や美容の秘訣であるとは、よく言われることだ）。だとすれば、喉が痛いときも、胃の調子がよくない場合も、「寝る前に、はちみつを患部にぬりのばすつもりで、ゆっくり飲み込んでから休めば回復が早い」というのは、わかりやすい自然の理と言っていいだろう。

最近は、市販の咳止めシロップより、ひとさじのそばはちみつの方が、よく効いて眠れる可能性が高いという論文もあるほどだ。[*3]

喉が痛いときや咳が出るときなどは、上を向いてゆっくり頭をまわし、はちみつが喉の患部に当たるように意識しながら時間をかけて飲み込む。

はちみつが当たったところは湿布を当てたかのようにひりひりとして、「ああ、きくきく！」という感じである。

寝る前に歯を磨いたそのあとで、はちみつみたいな甘いもの、なめちゃって大丈夫なの？　と思われるかもしれない。ところがどっこい大丈夫などころか、はちみつを口中に広げることが、虫歯や歯周病の予防になると

*3　「咳をする子どもとその親の睡眠の質に及ぼす、はちみつ、デキストロメトルファン、無治療の場合の効果の比較」。2007年にアメリカで発表された研究論文。主要参考文献⑯。

Spoonful of Honey　028

いう。*4これは昔ながらの使い方のようなのだが「甘いものはみな歯に悪い」

と思い込んでいたから、初めて知ったときには、私もたまげた。

実際、「歯みがき後、寝る前のひとさじ」を始めてみると、朝起きたと

きの口の衛生状態が格段にアップしていることに、すぐ気づくと思う。

はちみつを寝る前に摂るといいもうひとつの理由は、はちみつの主成分

がブドウ糖や果糖などの単糖類*5なので、これ以上消化する必要がないから

胃に優しく、すぐに吸収されて頭にもからだにも速効の疲労回復剤となる

のが大きいのだろう。

用があり、ストレスを取り除く安眠剤でもあるからだ。はちみつに鎮静作

今日のひと口の蜜源となった花が咲き群れ、ハチたちが飛び回っていた

のはどんなところだろうと想像する間に、一日の緊張はゆるりとほぐれ、

ビタミンやミネラルがからだにしみこんでいく。

昼間の戦いを終え、傷んで疲れた細胞が癒やされ、慰められていく様子

を思い浮かべつつ、ハチの羽音を聞き、あたりを満たす花の香りに包まれ、

口中の甘い後味を楽しみながら、そしていつしか……。

ＺＺＺ……と穏やかなときが訪れるのである。

*4 「はちみつで歯を
磨こう」(55ページ参照)。

*5 それ以上分解され
ない糖類。

もうひとさじの
はちみつは、
目覚めのお茶とともに

Spoonful
of
Honey
2

緑茶とマヌカはちみつを組み合わせると、私たちの免疫システムは、実戦に役立つ仲間ふたりを、味方につけることになる。

——デトレフ・ミックス『マヌカはちみつ』より

もともと朝型という人がうらやましい。

暗いうちに起き出すのは嫌なようだが、お日さまが到着するやいなや、機嫌よくコケコッコーと寝床を飛び出すことができる。子どもの頃から半世紀の間、ずっと変わらないと言うのだから、そういうタイプとしか言いようがない。私はといえば、寝起きの鈍さは折り紙付きで、弟は昔から、私を「寝ぼすけ」と呼んでいた。

一番頭が冴えて活動的になるのは、夜の9時から午前3時までの6時間ほどだ。

小学生の頃、目が悪くなるから寝ながら本を読んではいけません、と、しょっちゅう言われて、見つからないようにふとんの中に懐中電灯を持ち込んだりしていたから、押しも押されもせぬ立派な近眼になってしまった。時にはこっそり起き出して、皆が寝静まった台所でひとり、昼間の思いつきをあれこれ試してみたものだ。大人になってからもずっと、ものを考えたり書いたり、お菓子や石けんの新レシピを試したりするには、夜のしじまが一番だった。

ところがこの頃、寄る年波のせいか、夜の10時から午前2時の睡眠の貴

重さが、身にしみるようになってきた。疲労回復の度合いや起きたときの肌の調子から鑑みて、この黄金の時間帯の30分の睡眠は、それ以外の1時間の効き目にゆうに匹敵するというのが、つくづく最近の実感なのだ。

というわけで、夜型の体質をなんとか朝型に変えていこうとするようになってから、一番の助けになっているのが、目覚めのはちみつのひとさじなのである。

寝覚めのはちみつは脳に効く

体質というのは不思議なもので、一朝一夕には変わらない。たとえ習慣を改めて黄金の時間に睡眠を取り、めでたく疲労回復をなしとげて寝床から出ても、起き抜けの私の脳細胞は、すぐには目覚めてくれないのだ。さくさく行動を開始している夫を横目で見ながら、どこかぼーっとして、手足の動きもめっぽう鈍い。

ところが、歯みがきを済ませてひとさじのはちみつを口にすると、頭の中に朝の日光がすすーっと射し込んでくる。甘みが口の中に広がっていく

Spoonful of Honey　034

様子はまるで、日陰の地面が端から段々明るくなっていくところを見ているようだ。

健康のために、一日にひとさじだけはちみつを摂ろうというのなら、はちみつと睡眠の細胞再生、修復作用の仕組みを生かすために、寝る前が一番いい。*1。

だが、それに加えてもうひとさじを「薬」のつもりで摂るのならやはり、起きて最初のひと口としてというのが、断然いいだろう。

なぜなら、はちみつの糖分は、砂糖と違ってそのほとんどが、すでにブドウ糖と果糖に分解されているから、寝ぼけた脳の細胞にすばやくダイレクトに燃料を投下してくれる。

しかも、はちみつは、各種栄養素をからだに吸収されやすい形で含んでいる栄養爆弾だ。クエン酸、グルコン酸、コハク酸などの有機酸やアミラーゼ、グルコースオキシダーゼなどの酵素類、ビタミンB_1、B_2、B_6、ニコチン酸、葉酸、パントテン酸、コリンなどのビタミンB群だけでなく、さまざまなビタミンをバランスよく含んでいる。アミノ酸を全20種類、カルシウム、鉄、銅、マンガン、カリウム、マグネシウムなどのミネラルを全

*1 はちみつ小さじ1杯は約20キロカロリー（砂糖の約3分の2）であることを意識するとよい。寝る前のはちみつは安眠、熟睡を誘い、寝ている間の脂肪燃焼の効率を良くするとも言われる。

27種類、それにポリフェノールなどの各種抗酸化物などなど。一日を始めるにあたっての栄養補給としては、まことに理想的なのである。

脳に活を入れる「薬として」のつもりでまずはひとさじなめたら、その

あと「朝食の一部として」はちみつを食べる楽しみも多い。

朝、はちみつを摂るのが昔からの習慣だったフランスでは、宿の朝食にはちみつの小びんが、ジャムなどと一緒に、よりどりみどりという感じで何種類も出てくる。

「朝ご飯は常にしっかり食べなくちゃ」と思い込んでいた若い頃には、旅先でベーコンやハム、卵などが盛りだくさんのアメリカやイギリス式のブレックファーストが楽しくてお得に思えたものだが、大人になるにつれ、目覚めのコーヒーや紅茶に少しのパンと天然はちみつだけといった大陸式の習慣にも、なかなか優れた理があるということが、飲み込めてきた。

今朝はどれにしようかな、とためつすがめつ、自家製のヨーグルトにその日かけるはちみつを選ぶのは、起きかけの脳みそにとっては格好のエクササイズだ。

中国には、屋台でおやつに豆腐を売る地方があって、ふわふわとろりの

Spoonful of Honey　　036

なめらかな豆腐にはちみつをかけて食べるのが人気らしい。家でやってみるとこれは、冷たい豆腐だけでなく、温かくてもおいしくて、冷えたヨーグルトが食べにくい寒い季節の朝には、お腹にやさしい選択肢である。

ちょっと黒蜜のような風味がするミネラルたっぷりのそばや栗、甘露蜜（かんろみつ）のはちみつ（honeydew honey *2 ハニーデュー・ハニー）などをとろーりまわしかけ、すりごまやきなこ、抹茶を好みでふりかけていただけば、栄養満点の立派な朝食で、しかも胃にやさしい。

はちみつは今や、自然療法のスーパースター

最初に引用した『マヌカはちみつ』（Manuka-Honig）という本は、2014年にドイツで出版されたマヌカハニーの専門書である。著者のデトレフ・ミックス氏は、長年、医師たちと共同で病気治療の実践と研究に取り組んできた「ドイツ蜂療法協会」の療法士だ。

ヨーロッパには昔から、はちみつや花粉（ポーレン *4）、プロポリス *5、ロイヤルゼリー *6、蜂針 *7 などを使って病気の治療をする蜂療法の伝統がある。

*2 小さな昆虫が樹液を吸って露（dew）のように分泌する甘い体液をミツバチが集めたもので、酵素の働きにより抗酸化作用の非常に高い、濃厚な味わいの蜜となる。近年、医療用はちみつとしての効果が注目され研究が進んでいる。ヨーロッパでは昔から人気がある。口絵参照。

*3 主要参考文献②。

*4 働きバチが集めた花粉に酵素を混ぜて丸め、蜜を塗り、貯蔵して発酵させたもの。良質のタンパク質、アミノ酸、酵素、ビタミン、ミネラルの塊で、ハチパン（ビーブレッド）とも呼ばれ、はちみつ同様ミツバチが作る大切な食料。人にとってもミラクルフードとされる。

037　2 もうひとさじのはちみつは、目覚めのお茶とともに

そしてその療法の根幹となる一番大事な基本的「医薬品」がはちみつだ。

1980年代にニュージーランドで、「マヌカハニーには、何かはわからないが、他のはちみつにはない独自の抗菌、治癒成分があるぞ」ということが発見され、その有効成分が「UMF＝ユニークマヌカファクター」と90年代に名付けられた。そして、その抜群の抗菌作用のしくみが科学的に解明されることになってから、はちみつを使った病気治療全般の研究が活気づいた。

さらに、マヌカハニーの、この有効成分の正体が、「MGO＝メチルグリオキサール」という物質だったということが2008年にドイツの研究機関で突き止められて発表されたものだから、さあ大変。はちみつは、医薬品としてさらなる脚光を浴びるようになったのだ。

「もしかして、うちの近所で採れるはちみつにだって、何か特別なユニークファクターがあるかもしれないじゃないか」と思う人たちがいっぱい出てきたのは、ごく自然なことだろう。だって、はちみつは、それこそ昔から「薬」とされてきたのだから。*8。

ところで、ニュージーランドはちみつ界の偉業に触発され、次に続け！　と開発を

*5　元々は植物が芽を守るために出す樹液で、働きバチはそれを集めて分泌液を混ぜ、プロポリスを作り、巣の入り口や隙間を埋めて外敵や細菌などから守る。

*6　「王乳」ともいい、働きバチが分泌する乳白色の粘液。女王バチのためだけの特別食。

*7　患部やツボに蜂針を刺して蜂毒の薬理効果により血行を良くし炎症や痛みを抑える技術が蜂療法の中にある。

*8　ニュージーランドでは、地元に自生する植物の、はちみつの特有な効能成分を解明しようとする研究にはずみがついた。レワレワ（ニュージーランドスイカズラ）などはその代表的なもの。口絵参照。

進めたのが、お隣のオーストラリアだ。東部の海岸地帯に生えるジェリーブッシュ＊9のはちみつや、西部の原生林となっているジャラ＊10の樹にも、マヌカと同じような強い抗菌作用があることを数値でつきとめた。

糖尿病で足に難治性の感染症を起こし、切断以外に方法がないとされていた患者たちが、それらのはちみつを傷口に当てる治療で次々切断を免れたという臨床記録とともに、オーストラリアからも、マヌカに続く「医療用はちみつ」がいくつか、いち早く名乗りをあげたのだ。

この勢いでは、そのうち世界中のいろんな花のはちみつが、われもわれもと独自の効能を声高らかに謳ってくれるようになるのではないかと思うと楽しみで、私はその結果を早く見届けたくてわくわくしているのである。

「はちみつはビタミンCと一緒に」がコツ

実は、はちみつと同じように、今、世界的にその治癒効果が注目を浴びているものがある。緑茶である。

ミツバチ療法の専門家デトレフ・ミックス氏の本で、治療の根幹となる

＊9　オーストラリアのマヌカと呼ばれ、有効成分の種類も同じだが、はちみつの味わいや見た目は全く違う。口絵参照。

＊10　オーストラリア西部に自生するユーカリの一種。従来、腐食に強い上質な木材として重用されてきたが、最近は医療用はちみつとして脚光を浴びている。口絵参照。

はちみつと組み合わせて使ったとき、からだの免疫力を高めてくれて、病気の治癒効果が特に高くなる6つの素材として、1. プロポリス、2. 花粉（ポーレン）、3. ロイヤルゼリーの次の4番目に、なんと緑茶があげられている。あとの2つは、アロエ・ヴェラとシナモンだ。

緑茶に含まれるカテキンの名声は世界にとどろいていて、この本でも解説されているけれど、目覚めの一杯として、はちみつと同時にお茶を飲むのが理にかなっているわけは、なんと言っても、緑茶がビタミンCたっぷりであることらしい。[11]というのも、ビタミン豊富なはちみつに、唯一不足気味なのが、ビタミンCだからである。

「はちみつ＋牛乳」で、ほぼ完全食品だからと、1日に、はちみつ100グラム、牛乳1・2リットル弱だけで、3ヵ月間過ごしてみるという実験をした冒険心旺盛な学者さんがアメリカにいた。ぴんぴん元気で3ヵ月過ごしたが、検査をしてみたらビタミンCだけ、わずかに足りない状態だったらしい[12]（オレンジジュースを摂ることで問題はすぐに解消したという）。

朝一番の天然活性ビタミンCはとっても吸収がいいそうだから、寝覚めのはちみつや緑茶はビタミン補給にぴったりなのだが、カフェインがほし

*11 タンニンを含むお茶は、はちみつの鉄分の吸収を妨げるので、2つを同時に摂らない方がいいという説もある。その場合、間を30分ほどあけるように勧められることが多いようだ。

*12 「成人による牛乳とはちみつのみのダイエットについての臨床的生化学的研究」。1944年にアメリカで発表された研究論文。主要参考文献㊺。

Spoonful of Honey　040

くないというときには、ローズヒップやハイビスカス、柿の葉茶などもいいだろう。

シナモンとはちみつも黄金のコンビネーション

ところで朝食つながりのお話をもうひとつ。

緑茶と同じように、はちみつとシナモンも免疫増強に最強の組み合わせで様々な病気を治すサプリメントになるとして、デトレフ・ミックス氏は、小さじ1杯のシナモンパウダーを大さじ1杯のマヌカハニーで練ったペーストを自分の好みに合わせて、体調を整えるために少しずつ、適宜摂ることをすすめている。[*13]

だとしたら、きっと、はちみつをかけたシナモントーストも、健康的な朝食メニューと言えるだろう。

美味しいバターを塗ったパンに、好みの量のシナモンパウダーをぱっぱとふりかけてトーストする。あるいは、焼いたパンにバターを塗ってから、

*13 実はこれは、歯みがき剤にもなる。66ページ参照。

シナモンパウダーをふってもいい。

ただ今日的なはちみつ使いとしては、酵素を生きたまま摂りたいので、はちみつだけは加熱せず、焼きたてのパンにたっぷり塗ってそのままかぶりつくのが王道だ。

そういえば昔から、伝統的なお菓子のレシピにシナモンとはちみつの組み合わせは多い。が、このシナモントーストならお菓子を作るより簡単だ。

中医学ではシナモン（肉桂）は補腎薬で、ぜんそくや更年期障害などにいいとされているが、はちみつと同様、血糖値の調整作用があることがはっきりしてきて、昨今ドイツでも糖尿病の治療に使われるようになってきたらしい。きっとそのことも、はちみつとシナモンがゴールデンコンビとされる理由なのだろう。

こんがり焼けたパン。シナモンとバターとはちみつ。

その香りだけで、今日一日がうまくいきそうな気がしませんか。

＊14　主要参考文献②

Spoonful of Honey　042

ひとびんのはちみつは、
理想的な非常・保存食

Spoonful
of
Honey
3

蜜蜂は自分たちが集めた蜜を誰が食べるのか知らない。
同様に、私たちが宇宙に導き入れる精神の力を
誰が利用することになるのか、私たちは知らない。

——モーリス・メーテルリンク　『蜜蜂の生活』より

日本は世界に名だたる自然災害国。地震、台風、火山噴火と、どこかでほぼ毎日のように、山は煙をあげるわ、地面はぐらぐら揺れるわ、滝のような雨に雹の嵐。にぎやかなこと、この上ない。

いきなりドカンとおおごとになり、物資の供給路が断たれることなきにしもあらず、最低限の食料や水の備蓄、救急箱の準備ぐらい、ひと通りしておかなければ、とは、今日日、誰もが思うことだ。

我が家では備蓄品の中に、家族ひとり当たり1・8キロのはちみつを用意している。非常のときこそ、家族のみんなが大好物のとっておきの品である。

ほっぺたが落ちるおいしさの高千穂や対馬産日本ミツバチの百花蜜。奥深く豊かな風味の北海道の菩提樹（シナノキ）、そば、アカシアのはちみつ。

それに、とろけるキャラメルのようなニュージーランド産医療グレードのマヌカハニーなど。

この美味な備蓄がどん、とあるだけで百人力。

「来るなら来い！」と大船に乗った気になれる。

045　　3 ひとびんのはちみつは、理想的な非常・保存食

はちみつは、ほぼ完全な栄養剤

前にも書いたが、3ヵ月をはちみつと牛乳だけでゆうゆうと生活したという人がいる。はちみつは栄養剤としては、ほぼ無敵なのだ。

はちみつの糖分はブドウ糖や果糖なので、消化器に負担をかけることなくスムーズに吸収され、すばやくエネルギーとなる。からだが必要とする各種ビタミン、ミネラル類が、バランスよく含まれている。

ビタミンCだけは、はちみつだけに頼っているとやや不足するので補った方がいいとされているから、そのために備蓄品の中には、葉や茎を丸ごと粉に挽いた緑茶も入れてある。こんなお茶なら水やお湯をそのまますだけですぐ飲めるし、ゴミも出ない。

繊維も葉緑素も丸ごと摂れるので、野菜がすぐに手に入らないときも、オタオタしなくていいし、緑茶の粉をはちみつにふりかけたり、混ぜ合わせて食べても、和菓子のようで美味しい（「はちみつ緑茶キャンディ」口絵参照）。

Spoonful of Honey　　046

我が家でひとり当たり1・8キロのはちみつを備蓄しているのは、こういうわけだ。食品成分表によると、はちみつの熱量は、100グラムで294キロカロリーとなっている。ものによってやや差があるとはいえ、ほぼ、100グラム＝300キロカロリーと思っていいだろう。1日に必要なエネルギーが1800キロカロリーとして、それを満たすためには1日当たり600グラムのはちみつがいる。1・8キロのはちみつがあれば、3日間は安心ということだ。

もちろん非常時だとしても、1日をはちみつ600グラムだけで過ごすのは味覚の点からも厳しいだろうし、備蓄品がはちみつだけというわけではない。けれども、ガスも電気も水道も使えない状態のとき、何もせずにふたを開けただけで食べられ、洗いものもゴミも出ず、それだけでエネルギーとビタミンとミネラルがばっちり摂れるものが、「キロ単位で、で――んと目の前にある」状態は、すばらしく心強い。

東日本大震災の日は電車が止まり、仕事の打ち合わせのあった横浜駅から自宅まで、連絡のつかない家族が本棚の下敷きになっている様子を思い浮かべながら、25キロほどを、ずっと小走りで帰った。くねくねとひどい

047　3 ひとびんのはちみつは、理想的な非常・保存食

回り道の途中でおなかがぺこぺこになって、開いていたパン屋さんに飛び込み、カイザーロールをふたつ買ったっけ。

それ以来、「なんだか今日は大きめの地震が来るかも」という気がするが、電車に乗って遠くへ行かなくてはならない日には、大びんはまさか持ち出せないが、軽いプラスチックの遮光容器入りの250グラムのはちみつをスプーンと一緒に袋にまとめ、かばんに入れて行くこともある。

ま、準備があってもなくてもいざとなったら、何とかなることもあるし、全然どうにもならないこともあるだろう。

が、はちみつは確実に、普段の暮らしの不安をはらうお守りにはなるのである。

ピンチはチャンス、空腹は幸運かも

とはいえ、いざというときのために意識しておくようにしているのだが、そもそも、人は毎日3食、1800キロカロリーを必ず摂らなければ生きていけないというわけでもない。

Spoonful of Honey　048

ある年の春休みに夫婦ふたりで興味津々、断食クリニックへ行き、試しに2週間過ごしてみた。その経験のビフォー、アフターで一番変わったのは、体調よりも何よりも、

「人って、5日間何にも食べなくても大丈夫。水だけでも別に死にはしない！」ということを、身をもって納得できたことだった。

その時のプログラムは、数日間かけて食事量を減らしていき、丸5日何も食べず石清水を飲むだけで過ごし、それから数日かけてゆっくりと普通食に戻すというものだったのである。

何が原因であっても、1日、2日普通のご飯が食べられないからといって、そのことだけで慌てたり不安になる必要は全然ない。それを知ることは、からだと心にとって大発見で、ちょっぴり大げさかもしれないが、人生からひとつの恐怖がきれいに消えてなくなるような、心地よい開放感を伴った素敵な感覚だった。

いざというときのために頭をひねり備蓄に励むのも大事かもしれないが、そもそも非常時なんて、どこでどんなふうに遭遇するかわからない。

「腹が減っては戦ができぬ」というのは一面の真実ではあるけれど、そう

思い込んでしまったら、お腹がぐうっと鳴ったとたんに気力が失せてしまうということもあり得る。いざとなったら、

「空腹でお腹が鳴るのは健康の証拠。すごく気持ちのいいことなんです。お腹がすいたらそれは、内臓が消化活動から解放されてゆっくり休めるってことなんだから、心の底から感謝して喜ばないといけないんですよ」

と教えてくださったクリニックの先生のことばを思い出し「これを機会にデトックス」ほどの気持ちで、ゆったり鷹揚に構えようと思っている。

その上で、もしそのとき大事にとっておいた、ひとさじのはちみつを口に入れることができたら、たぶん天上の美味が味わえて、豊かな滋養成分がからだのすみずみにまでゆきわたるに違いない。

常温で腐らないはちみつは、非常時のための備蓄に最適

はちみつが非常食、保存食として優れている理由は他にもある。

強い抗菌作用を持つはちみつの中では、ばい菌が繁殖することはできな

Spoonful of Honey　050

いので、常温で保管してもいつまでも腐るということがない。もちろん生のはちみつの場合でもそうなのだ。賞味期限が切れるため、定期的に食品備蓄の入れ替えをするという必要がないはちみつは、面倒くさがりやには、とってもありがたい。

油と同じように光には弱いので、涼しくて暗い所にふたをきっちり締めておく。そうして一度備えてしまえば、基本的に何年も放りっぱなしで忘れておける。[*1]。

何しろミイラの保存に使われたというはちみつだ。その抗菌作用、効能が長持ちなことにかけては、折り紙付きなわけである。

——のはずなのですが、実際には、「とっておき」というのは、時々誘惑にかられて、ついつい出してきてしまうものなのですね。

大変な非常時にこそ、元気を出さなくてはいけないからと考えて、とっておきのはちみつを備蓄しているはずなのだけれど……。

急なお客のときなどに「あ、お菓子が何にもないけど、食後のデザートどうしよう！」などというのは、備蓄に手をつける上等の言い訳として最適の機会だ。

*1　ただし、日本ミツバチのはちみつは、西洋ミツバチのはちみつより巣の中で長期の熟成を経ているので、酵素が特に多く、発酵しやすい。そのため、必ず冷暗所での保管が必要で、場所の条件によっては、夏は冷蔵庫保存が必要な場合もあるので注意。

051　　3　ひとびんのはちみつは、理想的な非常・保存食

まあこれって、ある意味確かに、非常時だとも言えるわけでしょう？

食卓の喜びは精神の備蓄

ボードの上にはちみつのびんを何本か並べ、その種類の数だけスプーンをひとりひとりに配る。とっておきのはちみつならば、ひとさじずつ順番にゆっくり味わうだけで、十分立派なデザートだ。くるみやアーモンドなどの木の実や、なめると美味しい塩を少しばかり、小皿に添えてもいい。

買い置きのパルメザンやコンテ、チェダーなどのハードチーズを拍子木に切ってはちみつの数だけ並べ、生のはちみつをとろーりかけるだけでも、新たにデザートが一品できあがる。生のチーズやはちみつの酵素が消化を助けてくれるので、食後の胃にもやさしい。コーヒー、紅茶、ハーブティーに緑茶、ワイン、ブランデーと、食後の飲み物にもよく合う。

その他にも、小さな湯飲みにささっとそば粉を熱湯でといて小ぶりのそばがきにし、ソースとして好みの味のはちみつを探すのも楽しいし、粉をゆるくといて、フライパンでそば粉のひと口クレープを何枚も作り、熱々

にはちみつをかけてもいい。

することはシンプルきわまりなくても、産地や花の種類を味わいくらべながら、あれこれおしゃべりするだけで、飛びきりのご馳走だ。

備蓄に手をつけつつ、こうして大切な人たちと時間を愉快に過ごすのは、どこかで非常時に思いを馳せることに通じているかしら、と時に思う。

働きバチは一度の飛翔で、それに消費する約50倍のエネルギーの花蜜を巣に持ち帰るのだという。

メーテルリンクが言ったように、ミツバチは自分たちが集めた蜜を誰が食べるのか知らない。同様に、私たちは、今日こうして彼女たちから受け取り、笑いのうちに培ったエネルギーが、宇宙に解き放たれてどこに行くのか知らない。

何事もなく過ぎた今日という日の気の遠くなるようなありがたさ。

こうしてひとさじずつ、美味しくて幸せな思いを積み重ねていくことが、逆境への何よりの備蓄かな、と信じているわけなのです。

まあ、基本は食いしん坊の言い訳なのかもしれないけれど……。

053　　3 ひとびんのはちみつは、理想的な非常・保存食

はちみつで歯を磨こう

Spoonful
of
Honey
4

歯茎の潰瘍を除去する薬。
シナモン（一）、ゴム（一）、
はちみつ（一）、油か油脂（一）

——『エベルスの医学パピルス』[*1]

「甘いものを食べたらすぐに歯をみがきなさい」

「甘いものは歯に悪いから、あんまり食べると虫歯になりますよ」

家や学校で、そう教わらなかったという人はいないのではないだろうか。

もちろん私も子どもの頃からそう言い聞かされて、何の疑いも持たずに育った。だから、人生半ばに差し掛かろうかともいう頃になって、ヨーロッパの、あるはちみつの本を読んでいたら、はちみつを食べる話の中で、

さらりと、

「はちみつで虫歯を防ぐ」

とあるのを見つけたときには、ソファから転げ落ちそうになるほど驚いた。「そんな、まさかねえ!」というのが、正直なところだった。

実はそれまで何年もの間、重曹とはっか油とグリセリンを使った自家製歯みがきペースト、*2 それに、シナモンとクローブパウダーを加えたもうひとつのバージョンを、*3 私は愛用し続けていた。

それらのレシピの使い心地には自信があったし、作り方や使い方を、本で詳しく紹介したこともあった。行きつけの歯医者さんにも、歯の状態をほめられて、「歯や歯茎の健康」については(ひとりで密かに「ウッフ

*1　紀元前1550年頃の古代エジプト最古の重要な医学文献。

*2　「ミントの歯みがき」。重曹大さじ1杯半、薬局方グリセリン大さじ1杯、薬局方はっか油5滴を混ぜ合わせたもの。

*3　「クローブとシナモンの歯みがき」。重曹大さじ1杯半、薬局方グリセリン大さじ1杯、薬局方はっか油5滴、クローブパウダー小さじ4分の1杯、シナモンパウダー小さじ4分の1杯を混ぜ合わせたもの。

4　はちみつで歯を磨こう

フ……」と)、いくばくかの自負があったのである。

研磨材として「重曹や塩で歯をみがく」のは、大昔から歯みがき界の王道だ。他方で最近、

「歯をみがくのは、歯と歯周ポケットの中のかすをブラシで取り除くのがポイントなんだから、歯みがき剤なんてなにもつける必要はない」という主張も聞いたことがある。

しかし、よりにもよって砂糖の約1・5倍もの甘みがあるというはちみつで、虫歯を防ぐとはこれいかに？

もしかすると、万能薬といわれるはちみつには、食べる以外にも、オーラルケアに使って、虫歯を防ぐ方法があるというのだろうか。

激しく興味をそそられ、やってみたい！　と思ったのだったが、具体的にどうすればいいのか、その本には肝心のそのことが書いてないので、やり方がわからない。そのページの話の中心は、はちみつを使ったシナモン風味の焼き菓子の作り方のことだったから、

「お菓子なんて、余計に虫歯によくないんじゃないの？」と私は混乱した。

しかしですよ、もしも自家製歯みがきペーストに、はちみつが使えたと

したらどうだろう？　フッ素が虫歯を防ぐとか、いやいや毒だとか。そんな優雅とは言えない議論が絶えないこの時代、甘くて美味しいはちみつで虫歯を防ごうなんて言ったら、それは夢のような話である。うーむ、やってみるべきか。

いや、でも、理屈や分量、使い方がはっきりわからないまま、我が身を挺して実験し、もし虫歯だらけになったら怖すぎる。

はちみつは虫歯菌を退治する

ところが、ややあって、拍子抜けするほどあっさりと雲間の晴れる日がやってきた。

別のはちみつ治療法の資料を見ていたら、今度は、養蜂家でもありミツバチ療法の専門家でもある日本のお医者さんが、はちみつそのもので歯をみがくこと、はちみつ大さじ1杯をコップ1杯の水に溶かしてうがいし、歯槽膿漏や虫歯を予防して、口臭を防ぐことをすすめていらっしゃるではないか。

059 　4　はちみつで歯を磨こう

「はちみつはミュータンス菌の活動を抑えるため、虫歯を作りません」

と、そこには書かれている。なるほど、化膿したひどい外傷にも効くといういうはちみつの名高い殺菌力は、口の中の悪玉菌をも退治してくれるものらしい。

西洋医学を修めた医学博士で医師でもあるその方は養蜂家の二代目でもあり、ドイツのはちみつ療法学会員としても研究をされている。そして何より説得力があったのは、はちみつが腹痛にも歯痛にもやけどにも使われる非常に優れた食品、および医薬品であることを、子どもの頃からの実体験を通じて知っていると語られていたことだ。[*4]

ほんとうにいいかどうかは実際にしばらくやってみないとわからない。

でもやってみることに対しての迷いは、これですっかり吹き飛んだ。

はちみつとはっかの歯みがきで、歯はつるつる、息はぴかぴか

まずはシンプルに、はちみつだけで歯をみがいてみることにする。

[*4] 主要参考文献⑳。

Spoonful of Honey　　060

いろいろな種類のはちみつが手元にあるなかで、どのはちみつがいいか
と迷ったが、使い勝手をいろいろと考えた末、一年を通して透明のまま、
とろーり固まらないアカシア蜜を小さなからしスプーンを使って歯ブラシ
にのせてみた。

トーストの上で見慣れたものを歯ブラシにのせて口に入れるのは不思議
だけど、なんだかちょっぴり楽しいね、と思いつつ歯ブラシを動かす。

あたりまえのことだが、甘くてとっても美味しい。驚いたのは重曹のよ
うな研磨剤がないのに、みがいた歯の表面がすぐにつるんつるんになって
いく感覚だ。使い心地でまず言うならば、歯みがき剤として全然悪くない！
で、その時以来、はちみつ歯みがきにどっぷりはまり、あれこれといろ
いろ試してみた。

長ーい話を端折って言うと、はちみつには、確かに口の中のばい菌を退
治してくれる強力なパワーがあるようなのだ。

歯みがきで口をすすいだ後、口臭・虫歯予防のダメ押しに、はちみつを
追加でなめて、あらためて口中に広げてもいいくらいなのである。あるい
は逆に、歯みがき前に口をよくすすいでから、はちみつで歯みがきしたら、

もう、うがいしなくてもいいほどだ。もしかすると「甘いものがすべて歯に悪い」というわけではなくて、「歯に悪いのは砂糖」ということだったのかしらん？

とにかく、口の中の善玉菌を助けて、悪玉菌を退治してくれるかどうかが鍵なのだ。緊急時の非常食にはちみつがあったら、食べものとしてだけでなく、オーラルケアにも使えるなんて、すばらしすぎてミツバチにはもう、一生頭が上がらない。

あなたはジョリジョリ派？ それともトローリ派？

一年を通じて歯をみがくことを考えるとき、結晶にならないタイプのちみつを選んだのには理由がある。はちみつにはっか油を混ぜ合わせて、「はちみつとはっかの歯みがき」にしたかったからだ。

虫歯菌に対する抗菌力や口臭予防のことだけ考えたら、生のままのはちみつで効能は十分。けれども和種のはっかの精油である「はっか油」を合

Spoonful of Honey　062

わせると、はちみつの甘みにはっかの辛みを合わせ、後味をよりさっぱりと清涼にすることができる。メントールとの相乗効果で、抗菌作用もうんと高まる。そして、はちみつとはっか油をまんべんなく混ぜ合わせるには、一年中固まらないはちみつの方が、断然扱いやすいというわけだ。

大さじ2杯のはちみつに、はっか油5、6滴を垂らしてよく混ぜ合わせたらできあがり。密閉容器に保存して、使うときには小さなスプーンでとろりと歯ブラシにのせる。はっか油のおかげで、みがいた後の息のさわやかさは折り紙付きである。

初めの頃、もしかすると結晶がジョリジョリしている方が研磨剤にもなっていいかもと、レンゲやそばのはちみつの結晶部分を歯ブラシにのせてみたりもした。

ジョリジョリの感覚は悪くはないが、重曹の研磨剤に比べると、粒が粗くてちょっとざらつく。それに、研磨剤がなくても、はちみつなら問題なくつるつるにみがけるということがわかったので、私は今では歯みがき用はもっぱら扱いやすいアカシアだ。

でも、大好きな味のはちみつがあって、それがたまたまジョリジョリ型

はちみつとシナモンの組み合わせは、
古代エジプトの歯槽膿漏の処方箋

古代エジプト人たちは、はちみつを医療、美容に文字通り、「使い倒した」

で、ミント味にしなくてもいい、ぜひそれで歯をみがきたいという方は、迷わず試してみてください。歯茎の病気には良質なミネラル補給が大事ともされているから、そばのはちみつみたいにジョリジョリしても、色の濃いものが向いているかもしれないのだから。

はちみつが寒い季節に結晶して固まるか固まらないかは、ブドウ糖と果糖の割合で決まる。果糖の割合が多いアカシアのような蜜は一年中固まらず、ブドウ糖の多いそばのようなはちみつは、冬になると固まりやすい。

固まった結晶を溶かしたいというときはゆっくりと弱火で湯煎にかければいいのだが、医薬品としての効果を持つ純粋な生のはちみつは、はちみつ自体が40度以上になると生きた酵素がだんだん死んでしまうので、びんをつけるお湯の温度が60度を超えないように、どうか細心の注意を。

と言っていい。クレオパトラがその美をみがくのに、お風呂にはちみつと
ミルクを入れていたのも有名な話である。

そこで、古代エジプト植物誌研究の本の中で、オーラルケアにはちみつ
を使ったものがないかと探してみたら、おお！　歯茎の潰瘍を治すという、
冒頭にあげた薬の処方が見つかった。歯茎の潰瘍といえば、歯肉炎や歯周
病のひどいのに違いない。

これは歯みがき剤ではなく、歯茎にぬる軟膏みたいなもののようだ。ゴ
ム（樹脂？）と脂肪は基剤のようなものだから、薬効成分は、はちみつと
シナモンにあると見ていい。

なるほど、はちみつが歯や歯茎の健康にいいということは、すでに古代
に自明の理であったのか。はちみつを歯につけることをためらっていた私
は、いったい何にしばられていたのだろう。

この処方ではちみつと組み合わされているシナモンだが、オーラルケア
にとてもいいということは、「びわの葉が肩こりにいい」というぐらいに
アメリカやヨーロッパで常識になっている。重曹の歯みがきペーストやマ
ウスウォッシュのレシピにはそれまで私も使っていたから、はちみつの歯

065　4　はちみつで歯を磨こう

みがきも、はっか味だけでなく、シナモン味も作ろう、となるのは自然の成り行きであった。

大さじ1杯のはちみつに小さじ1杯のシナモンパウダーを合わせて、スプーンでよく混ぜ合わせてできあがり。歯茎や歯周ポケットのケアに直球の歯みがき剤だ（「はちみつとシナモンの歯みがき」口絵参照）。

しかもこれって、直球でお菓子の味ではないですか？

「良薬は口に苦し」ということわざをクレオパトラは聞いたことがあったのだろうか。

大汗かいたら、
「はちみつ水」（手作りイオン飲料）

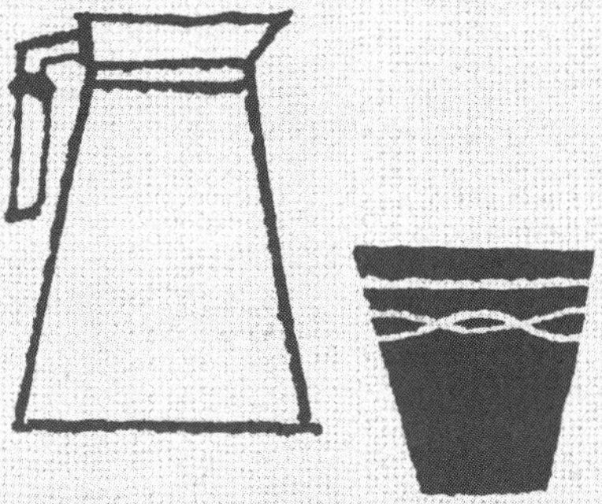

Spoonful
of
Honey
5

「炎天下のはちみつ水は命綱。畑でできる点滴だよ！」

——エフラン・メザ

アメリカ西部のワシントン州東側とオレゴン州の境のあたりは高品質のワイン産地として注目を集めていて、年々ワイン用の葡萄畑と醸造所が増えていく。

エフランは、そんな飛びきりのワインを産み出す農園の畑で働くメキシコ人の青年だ。この農場では化学肥料や農薬、除草剤を一切使わない。

彼の仕事は、4ヘクタールほどの葡萄畑の列の間を2頭の耕作馬で鋤き返す土の手入れと馬の世話で、実はこれが美味しいワイン造りの生命線だ。

畑には、フランスのローヌ地方、シャトー・ヌフ・デュ・パプ[*1]みたいに、こぶし大の丸い石がゴロゴロしている。古風な鉄製の鋤を使ってその表面を返していくのは、馬にとっても、操る人にとっても大変な重労働なのだが、その仕事のおかげで、土には定期的に草と新鮮な空気が混ぜ込まれる。

健康な香りを立ち上らせる畑の土は、いつも柔らかでふかふかだ。

初夏のある朝、シラー種[*2]の葡萄畑は花が満開で、きらきらした朝日の中で、ミツバチがぶんぶんと忙しく飛び回っていた。どっしりとたくましい耕作馬のゼッポは、ひと仕事を終えて、からだから湯気を立てている。ゼッポの後ろで鋤を操っていたエフランは、息をつくとラベルのないペット

*1 強い陽ざしと土ぼこり、石ころ、自生のハーブなどの風土を反映した力強い風味のワインを産むフランス南部のワイン地方。

*2 フランス南部ローヌ地方で主要な赤ワイン用葡萄の一品種。

ボトルを取り出した。

そして、汗に濡れるぴかぴかの笑顔で「はちみつ水！」とひとこと言うなり、ごくごくと一気に半分ほど飲み干した。

「毎日うちで作ってくるの？」ときくとそうだという。

「はちみつに塩をひとつまみ、水で溶かしてライムをしぼって、前の晩に冷凍庫に入れておく。葡萄畑を耕し終わる頃にちょうど半分ぐらい溶けてるんだ。ゼッポにえさをやってから、今度は野菜畑や動物たちの世話をする。そのうち残りもうまい具合に溶けて、1日に2リットルぐらいは、畑ではちみつ水を飲んでるね」

ットルのボトルが2本分なくなるよ。1日に2リットルぐらいで500ミリ

農場や醸造所で働く人たちが毎日食べる野菜や卵、牛乳、時には肉なども、ここでは作っている。最終的に作って売るのがワインだからといって、ワイン用の葡萄だけを単一栽培するのは、自然で健康的なワインを産み出すことにつながらない、という考え方からだ。そんな自家用農場の切り盛りもエフランの仕事である。その労働を支えている命綱が「はちみつ水」だと言うのだ。

Spoonful of Honey　070

イオン飲料の材料として理想的なはちみつ

エフランのはちみつ水の材料をよく見てみると、熱中症予防や高熱時の水分栄養補給のためのイオン飲料、またはいわゆるスポーツドリンクとして、理想的な組み合わせだということがわかる。

彼がボトルからこれをごくごくと飲むときの元気な喉の動きを見ていると、このはちみつ水が彼のからだとその運動に与えるエネルギーがそのまま、耕す畑の土に注入され、パワーと旨みがみなぎった葡萄を実らせることにつながっていくのが、目に見えるような気がする。

はちみつは、エネルギー源となるが、同時にミネラル、ビタミン類の宝庫だ。

ビタミンCだけは、それだけで十分とは言えないので足した方がいいとされるわけだが、エフランはライムやレモンで、ちゃんとそこを補ってもいる。

天然塩を加えることで、汗をかいたときに失われるナトリウムやその他

071　　5　大汗かいたら、「はちみつ水」（手作りイオン飲料）

のミネラルをさらにプラスする。

「ふーむ、なるほど！」と感心しているうちに面白くなってきて、塩分や糖分、ビタミンCの分量をあらためて計算しながら、簡単にできて美味しい「手作りイオン飲料」のレシピを自分でも作ってみることにした。で、いろいろ試してみた結果、定番となったのがこれである。

- ・水　　５００ミリリットル
- ・天然はちみつ　大さじ２杯（または約40グラム）
- ・天然塩　小さじ４分の１杯（または1・5グラム）
- ・新鮮なレモン（またはライム）果汁
　　大さじ1杯（15ミリリットル）
　あるいはビタミンCの原末（アスコルビン酸）*3
　　小さじ4分の１〜２分の1杯

多くの市販のイオン飲料には砂糖が使われていて、からだにいいと思って常時飲むクセがついてしまうと糖分過多になり、子どもでも糖尿病を誘

*3　上のレシピをレモンで作った場合は、吸収されやすい活性ビタミンCが約15ミリグラム摂れる。アスコルビン酸で作った場合は、活性ビタミンCではないが、120０ミリグラムから240０ミリグラム摂れる。アスコルビン酸の場合、調整しながらたっぷりと量を摂りやすい。

Spoonful of Honey　　072

発することもあるので要注意であるとされる。

だが、はちみつに含まれる果糖や麦芽糖はすい臓に負担をかけない。はちみつの場合、血糖値を一定限度以上には高めない自動的な調節作用が働くとされているのだ。

その点、血糖値が気になる人は果糖の多い、結晶化しにくいタイプのはちみつ（代表的なものはアカシア）を選べば特に安心だし、水にも溶けやすいので作るのも楽だ。

ミネラル類、特に鉄分の補給などを優先したい場合には、色の黒い天然はちみつ（代表的なものは、そばや栗など）を選ぶといいだろう。

「果糖とブドウ糖の割合は『結晶の状態』で見極め、ミネラルの量は『色』で見極める」という基本を頭に入れておくのが、効用をとことん享受するために長年のうちに身についた、はちみつ使いのコツである。

それには、くれぐれも、固まらないようにするために水あめなどの糖分を添加したり、加熱したりしていない、天然の生はちみつを選ぶことが大事だ。

このレシピは、運動や発熱により、大量の発汗をした場合の上限の塩分

量なので、その時の体調などに合わせて調整するといいだろう（170ペ
ージ参照）。

とっても便利な日本薬局方のビタミンC

はちみつ水は、フレッシュなレモンやライムをしぼった果汁を入れて作
るのが、なんといっても美味しい。作ったその日いっぱい、味にいきいき
とした躍動感がみなぎる。果皮からほとばしる天然の芳香成分と、生きた
ビタミンのなせる業だ。

だからといって、いつも新鮮なレモンやライムが手元にあるとは限らな
い。

のんきに長風呂で大汗をかいて、「喉かわいた―！」というとき、炎天
下を汗みずくで帰宅した途端、あるいは予期せぬ下痢や発熱で、脱水症状
を防ごうと緊急に思い立ったとき、あるはずの生のレモンが切れていると
いうのは、往々にして起こることなのだ。

けれど、ビタミンCの粉末の買い置きがあれば、いつでもさっと我が家

Spoonful of Honey　　074

の点滴「はちみつ水」（手作りイオン飲料）が作れる。生の果物と違って、はちみつ同様、備蓄しておくことができるので、緊急災害時の備えとしても置いておくと安心感が違う。

はちみつが日本薬局方に指定されていることはすでにふれたが、ビタミンCの粉末もそうで、「アスコルビン酸（またはLアスコルビン酸）」という名称で薬局で手に入る。これはビタミンC入りのサプリメントや化粧品、食品などを作るときの原料として使われているもので、サラサラとした白くてすっぱい粉末（「原末」と称されていることが多い）だ。

ビタミンCがインフルエンザやがんの治療に役立つということを提唱したアメリカのノーベル賞受賞生化学者、ライナス・ポーリング博士が、93歳で亡くなるまで体調管理のために毎日摂っていたというのも、このビタミンCの原末だ。

以前は私も、ビタミンCの錠剤をサプリメントとして買い置きしていたときもあったが、この原末の方がうんと経済的だし、からだへの吸収も早いし、余分なものが何も入っていないし、何より粉状のため、使い回しや調整が自由にしやすいので、今ではもっぱら原末を使うようになった。

はちみつ水を作るときには、レシピにあるように、好みに合わせて、5００ミリリットルの水に対して小さじ4分の1から2分の1杯のビタミンCの原末を溶かして使うといいだろう。小さじ4分の1杯は、ビタミンC１２００ミリグラムぐらいに相当するということを目安として覚えておくと自分に合った量を探すのに便利だ。[*4]

季節や体調によって、好みの味を楽しもう

手作りのはちみつ水の場合、使うはちみつや天然塩の種類によって、味や見た目がまるで変わるのが、また楽しい。お気に入りの味のはちみつや塩を季節や体調によって使い分けるといいだろう。

アカシアのはちみつは、さらりとしていて味もとってもあっさりしている。できあがりの色も淡く上品だ。特別に美味しくて新鮮な柑橘が手に入って、そちらの風味を優雅に楽しみたいなら、迷わずアカシアだ。

風邪気味のときについつい手が伸びるのは、北海道の菩提樹（シナノキ）のはちみつ。味にもバターのようなコクがあり、見た目もこっくり。菩提

*4 ビタミンCについて詳しくは、「はちみつとビタミンCで、見えない敵と闘う──1」（135ページ参照）。

Spoonful of Honey　076

樹の花は、ドイツやフランスで昔から風邪薬とされ、ハーブティーとして処方されることもある。ハーブ屋さんで「リンデン」の名で手に入るのは、菩提樹の花と葉だ。その花粉が溶け込んだ天然はちみつは、風邪のときの優しくて強い援軍になる。

濃い茶色でしっかりとしたミネラルの味がする、黒蜜のような甘露蜜のはちみつ（Honeydew honey　ハニーデュー・ハニー）は、生きた酵素がたっぷりの栄養爆弾。栄養ドリンクの材料としては申し分ない。

こんなふうに、バリエーションにはきりがないのだが、まずは好みの味で手頃で使いやすい、便利な「自分の定番はちみつ」を探してみるといいと思う。うちの場合は何年も変遷を重ねて、今のところはニュージーランドのクローバーのはちみつ。

でも、はちみつの旅には終わりがないことは重々わかっている。まだ出会わぬはちみつとの未来を思うだけで、ほおがゆるんでしまうのである。

5　大汗かいたら、「はちみつ水」（手作りイオン飲料）

はちみつ化粧水と
はちみつのお風呂

Spoonful
of
Honey
6

はちみつを摂りなさい……

容姿を美しくし、頭脳を明晰にし、身体を強くするために。

――ヴェーダ（紀元前千年頃のインド最古の聖典*1）

古代インドでも、エジプトでも、はたまたローマでも、はちみつは、最良の薬として扱われていた。外用、内用、それぞれの用途に合わせ、いろいろな薬草とどう組み合わせるか、古い医学書の中に多くの処方が残っている。

香料や化粧品の基剤として使われていることも多い。

クレオパトラは美容のために、はちみつをこの上なく愛用したそうだが、「はちみつ風呂」の言い伝えは、王妃の地位の高さとその威光を広めるのに、一役買っていたのかもしれないねえと、湯船の中でぼーっとしながら想像してみる。

確かに、お医者さんが薬として扱う貴重なはちみつの壺を浴室の化粧棚からひょいと取り出されたら、招き入れられたローマ皇帝だって不意を突かれて「ほほー」と思うだろう。

その上、間髪入れず壺の中身を浴槽にぶちまけ、寝室にバラの花びらを振りまかれでもしたら、幻惑されるか、見ているお付きだって「？」と言葉に困るから、いずれにしても言い伝えとしては、「クレオパトラのはちみつ風呂。ははー」という感じなのかもしれない。

*1 主要参考文献⑲

当時のアレクサンドリアは地中海世界の中心で、豪華絢爛（けんらん）の街だった。

今の時代に生きていたら、彼女は何をお風呂に入れるのかしらん。

それはさておき、その時代から、さまざまな皮膚病や傷、やけどに対して、何よりの治療薬であるとされてきたはちみつだが、今も変わらず肌にいいことだけは、どうも間違いなさそうだ。

はちみつの薬効が現代医学でも再確認されて、「医療用はちみつ」という概念が南半球やヨーロッパからお医者さんたちの間に広まり始めたというお話をしたけれど、そのきっかけとなったのも、ひどい傷ややけどなどの皮膚の外傷治療にはちみつを使う研究の数々だったようなのだ。

日焼けの手入れに、はちみつを

はちみつが、現代でもやけどの薬として再発見されつつあるという内容の文献をよく見るようになってから、我が家では「はちみつ化粧水」＝「ハニーウォーター」の出番がずいぶん増えた。

特にがんの放射線治療の副作用で傷んだ皮膚や粘膜の治療に、はちみつ

を使って高い効果があったという臨床報告の論文がいくつかあることを知ってからは、はちみつの化粧水を、日焼け対策としてたっぷりと使うようになった。

放射線と紫外線には波長の長さやエネルギーの大きさの違いはあれど、肌を傷める基本の仕組み自体は、ほとんど変わりがないからだ。

作り方はとっても簡単で、100ミリリットルの水に小さじ2分の1杯の好みの天然はちみつと耳かき1杯のビタミンC（アスコルビン酸）の原末を入れて溶かし、化粧水のびんに入れるだけ。

いや、これがほんとうに、紫外線に当たってほてってしまった肌に気持ちいいのです。　特に、冷蔵庫で冷やしておくと、とてもいい。

いずれにしても、はちみつの化粧水は冷蔵庫に入れて保管し、1ヵ月以内に使い切らなければならないので、新鮮なうちに惜しげなくというつもりで、たっぷりと全身に使える。

そういえば、葡萄畑の仕事に毎日はちみつ水を持って行くエフランは、炎天下の作業の合間にホースの水で頭や手をゆすいでは、はちみつ水を首筋や腕や顔にパタパタはたいていたものだっけ。

実は、15年以上前に私が書いた本の中でも、お気に入りの基本の化粧水

*2　参考文献参照㊼、㊽、㊾。

083　6　はちみつ化粧水とはちみつのお風呂

のひとつとしてはちみつ化粧水の自家用レシピを紹介している。でもその頃はまだ、はちみつ化粧水の効能として客観的にはっきりわかっていて伝えられるのは、「糖分によるやわらかでしっとりとした保湿力」という認識だった。

ただ、当時も自分で「夏から秋への季節の変わり目、日焼けした肌が退色していく頃に、特に効果があります」と所感を書いているところを見ると、使い心地の感覚として、日焼けの手入れにいいなという実感は確かにあったらしい。

実は、私は軽い紫外線アレルギーなので、その頃から、はちみつの化粧水が自然とお気に入りのひとつになっていたのかもしれないと思う。

当時は、やけどの薬としては、第一にラベンダーの精油だと思っていたから、強い陽ざしに当たってひりひりしたり、プップツと湿疹が出るようなときには、もっぱらラベンダーの化粧水＝「ラベンダーウォーター」を使っていた。

しかし、やけどにはちみつが効くという研究がいくつも出ている今となっては、自分の弱点に対して、うれしい選択肢が増え、万々歳なのだ（日

Spoonful of Honey　084

焼けでなくて、やけどそのものの手当てについては別途ふれるので、93ページ参照のほどを）。

化粧水で、はちみつの香りを愉しむ

はちみつ化粧水＝ハニーウォーターは、18世紀にも大人気だったらしい。

「ジェームズ2世の薬剤師だったジョージ・ウィルソンによると、これは肌をなめらかにし、その香りは最も快いもののひとつだったという」という記述のある本がある。*3 けれども、その処方を見てみると、そこにはいろいろな芳香成分の含まれた精油が使われているので、はちみつ自体の香りをそのまま愉しんだというわけではなさそうだ。

私は化粧水にしたときの、はちみつそのものの甘くて野の花のような香りが大好きなので、はちみつの化粧水に精油を加えることはまずない。

はちみつそのものをかいだときの香りと、化粧水を顔や腕やからだにぬいたときの香りの感じはまるで違う。腕をくんくんとかいだときに香るほのかで自然な健やかさは他にはないし、はちみつの種類を変えれば、化

*3 参考文献参照⑬。

085 　　6 はちみつ化粧水とはちみつのお風呂

粧水の色も香りも変わって楽しい。

はちみつの香りをよりしっかりと愉しみたかったのと、日焼けの手入れの効果をアップしたかったので、今回ご紹介した新しいバージョンのレシピは、15年前とは少し変わっている。

はちみつの分量は、小さじ4分の1杯から小さじ2分の1杯になって濃度が上がったし、クエン酸の代わりに酸化防止剤として、ビタミンCの原末（アスコルビン酸）を入れることになった。保湿力という観点からも、はちみつの分量がアップしているわけだが、この量が心地よくなったというその差が、もしかすると15年の歳月の流れを表しているのだろう。

というわけで、はちみつの量は、ご自分の肌に合わせて、どうぞお好きな使い心地の頃合いを探してみてください。

紫外線ケアには、はちみつとラベンダーのお風呂

はちみつを入浴剤としてお風呂に入れるというのは、言ってみれば、は

Spoonful of Honey　086

ちみつの化粧水にそのまま全身つかるということだ。

うーん、なんと豊かな気分!

湯船の大きさにもよるけれど、大さじ2杯から3杯ほどのはちみつをティーカップなどに取り、そのままスプーンを添えて浴室に持ち込む。

はちみつをお風呂に入れると、そのままベタベタしないの? と思われるかもしれないが、ご心配なく。しっとりすべすべの保湿効果に驚かれるはずだ。

お風呂に入れる場合は、浴室全体にはちみつの香りが広がるというわけではないので、はちみつにはスキンケア効果だけを担ってもらうようにして、香りは好みの精油を合わせることが多い。はちみつの上にそのまま垂らして、スプーンでよく混ぜ合わせてから湯に溶かす。

紫外線ケアに焦点を当てるなら、はちみつの入浴剤に合わせるのは、やけどや傷の薬であるラベンダーの精油で相乗効果を狙うのが、何と言ってもおすすめだ。

湯船いっぱいに対して、4、5滴をはちみつによく混ぜ合わせるといいだろう。

もっと凝るなら、ラベンダーの花のはちみつと合わせてもよい。

087　🥄　6 はちみつ化粧水とはちみつのお風呂

強い陽ざしにちょっとまいってしまったからだを湯船にゆったり横たえ
て目を閉じれば、はちみつの溶けこんだ湯のやわらかな肌当たりが心地よ
く、ミツバチの楽しげな羽音が飛び交う満開のラベンダー畑が見えてくる。
澄んだ空気と清々しい香りにすっぽりと包まれる。

これはたぶん、クレオパトラも見たことのない景色かな、とふと思う。

はちみつと花のむこうに、余計なことを忘れ、ひたすら見たい景色を見
られる幸運。

ああ、今日も一日悪くなかった、と思えるお風呂の時間だ。

はちみつ軟膏と
はちみつの絆創膏

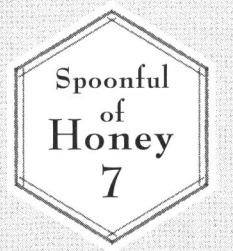

Spoonful
of
Honey
7

はちみつは炎症や潰瘍をきれいにし、
硬化した唇の潰瘍を軟らかくし、
吹き出物や膿の出る傷を癒やす

——ヒポクラテス

「唇があれたら、はちみつをそのまま塗っておきなさいね」と子どもの頃、祖母に言われたのを、今でもはっきり覚えている。

それ以来、「あれた唇にはちみつ」というのは、典型的「おばあちゃんの智恵」みたいな家庭療法なのかな、と思っていた。

ところが、天然はちみつは今でも日本薬局方でれっきとした「医薬品」に指定されていると知ってから、ものは試しと手に入れてみた薬局方はちみつの説明書を見て、それはそれは驚いた。そこには、「口唇の亀裂・あれには、そのまま患部に塗る」と、昔、祖母の言ったことがそのまま書かれていたからだ。

もしかすると、あれた唇治療情報の出典はおばあちゃんたちではないかもしれないぞ、と思ったのはそのときだ。だって、薬局方を制定した医薬品の専門家やお役人さんたちが、おばあちゃんたちの言うことを薬局方にそのまま記載して公表したと考えるのは、やっぱり無理があるでしょう？

で、はちみつの「あれた唇治癒効果」について書かれたものを探してたどっていったら、なんと、古代ギリシャの医学の父に行き当たった。

はちみつは、いろいろな外傷、皮膚、粘膜の損傷、炎症にすばらしい治

癒効果を持つことが、近年になって、科学的にもはっきりとわかってきている。

そして、はちみつの傷に対する治癒効果は実際には、からだの表面どこでもござれという勢いなのに、なぜか「唇」をことさら強調した言説を残しているらしいのが、ヒポクラテス先生なのだ。[*1]

勝手に夢想をたくましくして、「能力と判断のかぎり、患者に利益すると思う養生法をとり、悪くて有害と知る方法を決してとらない」という「ヒポクラテスの誓い・第3」が、日本薬局方の先生方に今でも絶大な威光を持っていたとしてみよう。

医学の父から現代まで子々孫々、「はちみつは最上のリップクリーム」と規定されてきた、ということになる。

実をいうと、子どもの頃の私にとっては、はちみつは最上の唇治療薬にはならなかった。甘くて美味しすぎるのだ。ついペロペロなめてしまうから、薬は唇からすぐに消えて、かえって乾燥してしまい、あれがなかなか治らない。

大人が苦い薬を飲ませようとするときに、もったいぶって言うのは「良

*1
主要参考文献⑲。

Spoonful of Honey　092

「薬は口に苦し」だ。こんなに甘いものが薬だなんて、やっぱりおかしいよ

ねえ、と思っていた。

以後、何十年も経って自分が大の大人になり、はちみつが傷に効く理屈

を理解して初めて、やっと理性を働かせてなめるのをがまんし、はちみつ

をリップクリームとして活用できるようになったわけである。

唇があれたときだけでなく、予防のための普段のリップクリームとして

も、手軽だ。唇が柔らかくなって乾燥せず、つやも出ていい感じである。

もしかするとヒポクラテス先生は、はちみつで手入れをした柔らかくな

めらかな甘い唇を眺めるのが、ことにお好きだったのではあるまいか。

はちみつが特に効く傷・やけど

ただ我が家の場合、普段の生活を思い返してみると、はちみつを「治療

薬」として一番活用しているのは、水ぶくれのできたやけどや、リンパ液

が滲出（しんしゅつ）するようなタイプの傷を作ってしまったときである（もちろん、大

きなけがをしたときには、迷わずお医者さんに行ってください）。

子どものころのように走り回ったあげく盛大に転んでひざを擦りむいたりはさすがにないが、料理中の不注意で、やけどや切り傷、どこかにぶつけて皮がむけてしまう擦り傷などは、もちろん今でもたまにある。

たとえば、料理中に熱湯や油がはね飛んで皮膚に着地し、やけどしてしまったら、我が家の場合、「治療法」として基本的にあるのは３つの選択肢だ。

冷水でよく冷やしたあと、

1　「はっかのバーム」を塗る

2　ラベンダーの精油を綿棒で直接つける

3　絆創膏にはちみつを塗って患部にはる

「はっかのバーム」は、以前に『はっか油の愉しみ』という本の中でレシピを紹介したことがあるが、10グラムのワセリンに60滴の薬局方のはっか油を混ぜ合わせたメンタムのようなものだ。切り傷、やけど、虫刺され、虫除け、鼻づまり、乗り物酔いの緩和そのほか、いろいろ使えるとっても重宝な軟膏である。これの作り置きがあれば、ちょいちょいと塗っておく。

ラベンダーの精油は原液のままで、切り傷、やけどの薬として使えるの

＊2　肌への刺激がないので、薬効成分を練りこむ基剤としてよく使われる。薬局で薬局方ワセリンが手に入る。

Spoonful of Honey　094

で、これも綿棒やガーゼなどにしみこませ、患部につける。あるいは、患部に原液をぽたりぽたりと落としてもいい。

いずれもよく効くのは何度も体験済みである。が、やけどの場合、一番治りが速いのは、やはり、はちみつなのだ。特に、水ぶくれができたときに抜群にきれいに跡形なく治るのは、はちみつの軟膏、絆創膏（または包帯）だと思う。[*3]

豆粒大ぐらいのやけどの水ぶくれなら、きちんと消毒した針でぷつんと刺して中のリンパ液をやさしく出し、拭き取って、患部を覆うようにはちみつを塗って、絆創膏やガーゼを当て、留めておく。これを寝る前と朝に取り替えれば、1、2日で患部はきれいに乾燥してしまう。その後は、放っておいてかまわない。

やけどの水ぶくれだけではない。ヒポクラテスが「膿の出る傷を癒やす」と言っているように、また、それを確認したお医者さんたちが近年報告してくれているように、傷口が乾かず濡れていたり、じゅくじゅくしたりするようなタイプの傷に、軟膏として断然いいとされているのが、はちみつなのだ。

*3 軟膏として外用にするはちみつは、食用のものから取り分けておくと、清潔を保ちながら使いやすい。口絵参照。

はちみつの抗菌作用の仕組み

はっかやラベンダーなどの精油がもつ芳香成分には、菌の繁殖作用を抑え、からだの免疫機能を高める働きがあるとされているが、はちみつにも、非常に高い抗菌、殺菌作用がある。そしてその仕組みは、最近になって詳しく解明されてきた。

はちみつの80パーセントという高濃度の糖分の中で、バクテリアは体液を浸透圧で吸い取られてしまうため、死んでしまうというのが、長らくその抗菌作用の説明だった。またその他に、はちみつのpHが3・2から4・9で、薄めの酢ぐらいの酸性度なので、その中で菌が繁殖できないということも言われてきた。

けれども、それだけでは説明できない殺菌力がはちみつにはあり、それは、はちみつに含まれるグルコン酸の殺菌力に加え、グルコースオキシダーゼという酵素が強い殺菌力を持つ「過酸化水素」*4を作るからだということが明らかになったのだ。

*4　過酸化水素の抗菌作用は、光や空気、熱に対して不安定なので、はちみつは遮光びんに保存するか、暗い戸棚の中に保管するのがポイント。

Spoonful of Honey　096

過酸化水素といえば、消毒液のオキシドールの成分である。小学生の頃、ひざを擦りむいて保健室へ行くと、オキシドールで消毒してもらい、傷口から白い泡がブクブク出るのを見ながら、しみるのが痛くて身をよじっていたのを思い出す。ところが同じ過酸化水素による消毒でもあら不思議、はちみつの場合は、傷口にそんなにひどくしみない。

しかも、先ほど言ったはちみつの糖分による保水性が、老廃物を含んだリンパ液の排出を促してくれる。水ぶくれができる前に素早く冷水で冷やしてはちみつを塗り、絆創膏か包帯をしておけば、水疱ができるのを防ぐことができる場合も少なくないが、たとえ不愉快な水ぶくれになってしまった場合でも、針穴から丁寧に水疱をぬいて「はちみつ包帯」をすれば、素早く治って跡形もなくなる。

膿やリンパ液を吸収して傷口を清潔に保ってくれる上、絆創膏や包帯を傷口からはずすときも、痛くないという優れものなのである。

そして、傷ややけどに限らず、膿やリンパ液が関係するような湿疹の症状を和らげるのにも、役立つ場合が多いようだ。我が家も、恩恵にあずかっている。

夫は子どもの頃から、手にプップッとごく小さなかゆみのある水疱を伴った湿疹がときどきできる人なのだが、最近では、どんな薬よりも、はちみつをつけて絆創膏をはっておくのが、治りが速いと言う。すぐに乾いてかゆみが止まるよと言うのだ。

抗生物質が、効かなくなった耐性菌をやっつけるはちみつパワー

近年はちみつの抗菌作用に注目が集まるようになったのは、抗生物質が効かなくなった感染症による潰瘍で手足を失いかけていた糖尿病患者の治療に、思案投げ首の末「ヒポクラテスが言うように」はちみつ包帯を使ってみた医師たちから、きれいに治ってしまった！　という臨床報告がいくつも相次いだことが大きい。

細菌がはちみつへの耐性を持つようにならないかと実験してみても、そのメカニズムはまだはっきりとは解明されていないのだが、そうはならないのだという。*5

＊5　主要参考文献㊼。

Spoonful of Honey　098

糖尿病にかぎらず、耐性菌による感染症は、今では世界中で大問題になっていて、毎年、とても多くの人が命を落としているらしい。応用の可能性はまだまだこれからの楽しみだが、今世紀に入ってはちみつは、まるで救世主のように、現代医療の現場に舞い降りてきたのだ。おばあちゃんたちが愛用していた、あのはちみつが。

ヒポクラテス先生の見解と感想、今後の医療への展望を今こそ聞いてみたいと思うのだが、それは叶わない。

未来の医療がどんなふうになっていくのか、少しでも見届けたいと思ったら、できるだけ長生きするよりないのかもしれないねえ、と思いつつ、ぺろりとひとさじのはちみつをなめる日々なのである。

はちみつパックと
はちみつクレンジング

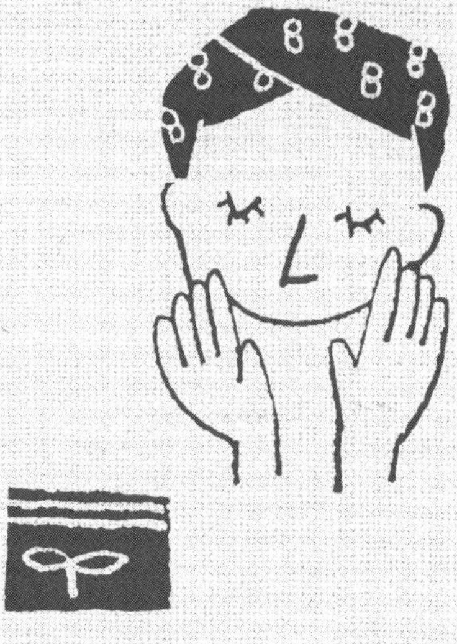

Spoonful
of
Honey
8

蜂蜜入藥之功有五。清熱也。補中也。解毒也。潤燥也。止痛也。生則性涼、故能清熱。熟則性溫、故能補中。甘而和平、故能解毒。柔而濡澤、故能潤燥。緩可去急、故能止心腹、肌肉、瘡瘍之痛。和可以致中、故能調和百藥而與甘草同功。

——『本草綱目』[*1]

25年ほど前の新婚旅行は、2ヵ月ほどかけて、東南アジア、中国で過ごした。

アメリカ人の夫は当時ドイツ文学が専門で、ヨーロッパで過ごした時間は長かったけれど、それまで日本を含めてアジアには全く縁遠かった。そこで、今までと違う場所をちょっと時間をかけて見てみよう、ということになったのである。

香港から広州に入ったときに、夫が微妙に身構える気配がわかった。シンガポール、マレーシア、インドネシア、香港のあたりまで時折目にしていた横文字がなくなった。漢字だけの世界に突入し、初めての異な感覚に、いきなりぞわぞわと襲われたようなのだ。

「まかせなさい!」と私は太鼓判を押して見せた。

「中国語はわからないけど、私は漢字は読めるんですからね。レストランでも食べたいものを何でもどんどん言って。ちゃんと注文してあげるから」

鴨料理が食べたいという夫の要望に応えてメニューに「鴨」の一字を探し出し、出てきたのがあひるの水かきの煮付けを山盛りにしたひと皿だっ

*1 明朝の開業医、薬草学者であった李時珍（1518〜1593）の編纂による本草学の集大成ともいえるもので、没後の1596年に出版された。日本には1607年に入ってきたが、本草学者の小野蘭山がまとめ、『本草綱目啓蒙』として1803年に刊行され、江戸期の薬学の発展に大きな影響を与えた。

たとき以来、夫の結婚生活への覚悟は決まったと言う。「まかせてはいられない」と。

確かにあのときは、功をあせってしくじった。

けれど、やはりそこは我々日本人。落ち着いてじっくり当たれば、漢文の謎解きにかけて、全く漢字を知らない欧米人に比べれば一日の長がある。

それが証拠に、冒頭にあげた16世紀、明の時代に書かれた生薬学の古典『本草綱目』の中の「蜂蜜」の説明箇所を、お茶でも飲みながらゆっくりながめてみてください。

たとえ、すべてを読み解くことができなくても、はちみつがいかに健康や美容に役立つか、脳みそにしみわたって来るような気がしませんか？

悪玉菌を殺し、肌を清浄にするはちみつ

洋の東西を問わず、古い文献に同様の効能が淡々と述べられているのを確認すると、ありがたみが増すのは確かなことだが、それに加えて科学的にその理屈が今日的に解明されてきているのを知ると、なるほどねえ、と

Spoonful of Honey　104

肌にいい理由がますます腑に落ちる。

はちみつ軟膏のところで、耐性菌にも打ち勝つはちみつの抗菌作用についてふれたが、はちみつが発生させる過酸化水素による殺菌力は、悪玉菌だけを退治して、肌の上の善玉常在菌を傷めないとされている。

これって、にきびや吹き出物のケアにとっては、とってもすばらしい効用と言えるのではあるまいか。だって、原因となるアクネ菌や黄色ブドウ球菌とのあくなき闘いが、にきびや吹き出物退治の要諦であると段々わかってきたのだから。

このことを意識するようになってから私も、何かの拍子にごく小さな吹き出物がぷつんと白い頭を見せたりしたときには、慌てずすかさず、洗顔後、指先ではちみつを付け、吹き出物の頭をはちみつの中におぼれさせるようにしている。

顔の一点をはちみつで光らせたまま外出するわけにいかないというときには、ラベンダーの精油を綿棒でつけて対処するが、どちらもきれいに治るものの、はちみつの方が治りがスピーディなのは確かだ。

きれいに跡形なくなるまで、私の場合、ラベンダーが2日、はちみつの

場合1日という感じである。

そしてたとえ、にきびや吹き出物に全く悩まされていないとしても、はちみつを、汚れを落とすクレンジングに使ったり、はちみつパックやトリートメントをしたりするのが、肌を清潔に保つのに役立つことは、もはや、不思議でもなんでもないだろう。

とてもシンプルな
はちみつクレンジングの方法ふたつ

一番てっとりばやいのは、普段の自分に一番合った洗顔のあとで、引き続き2度目のクレンジングに純粋な天然はちみつをそのまま使うことだ。

ざらざらしては気持ちよくないので、結晶化していないとろーりとした液状のはちみつを使う。お気に入りのはちみつが結晶しかけているなら、60度の湯で湯煎（ゆせん）にかけるか、びんごと60度ぐらいの湯につけて気長に待つ。

いずれにしても、生のはちみつの、生きた酵素の働きを殺してしまわないためにも、はちみつ自体の温度が40度を超えないように気をつけたい。

Spoonful of Honey　　106

適量（小さじ2杯ほど）を手に取って、顔全体にたっぷり塗りのばし、手のひら全体で隅々まで、残った汚れを浮かせるようによくなじませながら、ゆっくりとなめらかな感触を楽しもう。

こんなに気持ちいいのに、肌の上にいるやもしれぬ目に見えない悪玉菌を強力に退治してくれているとは！

頃合いをみて洗い流せば、はちみつクレンジングは終了だ。

はちみつの糖分の保湿力で、洗い上がりは柔らかく、きめ細かな感じになる。

肌の表面が細かくあれていたりすると、すこーしヒリヒリした感じがするかもしれない。あるいは、目にはちみつが入ると、しみることもある。

でも、ご心配なく。はちみつは粘膜の炎症にも抜群にいいとされていて、後でふれるが、目薬として使われることもあるぐらいなのだ。

もう一つ、別の簡単な方法は、普段の洗顔、クレンジングに使っている石けんやオイルを手に取り、そこに小さじ1杯ほどのはちみつを足して混ぜて使うというものだ。必要な時は、これを2度繰り返す。

この場合、はちみつ化粧水（82ページ）で仕上げるといいだろう。

107　8 はちみつパックとはちみつクレンジング

はちみつが、しみ、そばかすに効き、肌を白くすると言われてきたわけは？

ヨーロッパでは、「はちみつがそばかすにいい」とか、「はちみつには漂白作用がある」というのは、「昔から女たちに伝わる美容の智恵」レベルでは、実はよく言われることである。

だから、金髪のトリートメントにはちみつ、黒髪のトリートメントには糖みつ（黒みつ）がいいとは広く知られていることだし、日に当たったあと、はちみつ化粧水＝ハニーウォーターでケアをするといいというのも、考えてみれば、同じ言い伝えにまつわることなのかもしれない。

でも、「漂白作用」とまで彼女たちが言い伝えてきたのはどういうことなのか？　まさか、はちみつが過酸化水素を発生させるからと言って、過酸化水素で漂白させる「酸性漂白剤」みたいな作用のことを指していたわけではないだろうねえ、とは思うのだが……。

いずれにしても、しみやそばかすが消えるにしろ、あれた肌が元通りに

Spoonful of Honey　　108

なるにしろ、傷んだ古い細胞が代謝され、再生した健康な新しい細胞にとって代わられることが不可欠だ。肌のきめがなめらかに整えば、でこぼこのないきれいなカーブを描く肌の表面は、光を反射して白く見える。

はちみつが傷を速く治すということは、細胞の再生を促すパワーにあふれているということだから、それが女たちに言い伝わる「はちみつの美白作用」の秘密かな？　と今のところは考えているのですが、どうでしょう。

はちみつフェイシャルパックの即効性とお風呂でのはちみつトリートメント

これからすぐに出かけなければならないのに、どうも今日はお化粧ののりがよくなさそうだな、うーん、困った！　というようなときの救急パックが、たった1、2分でできる「はちみつのフェイシャルパック」だ。

洗顔後、まず化粧水を肌にしっかりしみこませる。好みの天然はちみつ小さじ1杯にオリーブオイル（乾燥肌向き）やローズヒップオイル（脂性肌向き）など、好みの美容オイルを5滴、手のひらで合わせ、よく混ぜる。

そして、たっぷりと水分を含んだ肌全体に塗りのばす。1、2分置いてからぬるま湯で洗い流せば、肌のきめがとりあえず整って、メイクがちゃんとのるようになる。この即効フェイシャルパックで、今まで何百回助けられてきたかわからない。

でも、大好きなはちみつを心ゆくまでゆっくり味わいつくしたいと思ったら、そんなバタバタしたシチュエーションではなく、やっぱりお風呂だ。

湯船にからだを伸ばしてのんびり。

洗顔をすませた顔には、とっておきの天然はちみつが塗ってある。先週はシチリアのレモンのはちみつだったが、今日は熊野の日本ミツバチが集めた和蜜だ。このマスカットのようなみずみずしい香りと味を、ハチたちはいったいどうやって醸し出すのかしらねえ、と夢見心地で目を閉じてぼーっとしている間に、肌の表面では善玉常在菌がさぞや元気に飛び跳ねているのであろう。

湯船から出るときに、顔の上のはちみつをからだ全体に塗りのばし、軽くすすいでから上がれば、湯上がりの肌はすべすべだ。

温泉に行ってもこれはできない。我が家ならではの贅沢なのです。

Spoonful of Honey　　110

はちみつ目薬

Spoonful
of
Honey
9

白内障治療のための点眼薬としてハリナシバチハチミツが伝統的に使われてきたとは、なんと思いがけなく、魅力的な事実でしょうか。これはマヤ文明の薬局方にも言及されている古代アメリカ先住民の伝統なのです。

——パトリシア・ヴィット

はちみつが、昔から世界中いろいろなところで目の薬とされてきたといっていた。

うことは、手元の本をぱらぱらめくったときに目にしたり、耳学問では知っていた。

たとえば、紀元前千七百年頃のエジプトの文献に、「目の治療薬として、イナゴマメのさやを発酵した蜂蜜に入れて挽きつぶし、それを目につける」とある。これを『ファラオの秘薬　古代エジプト植物誌*1』という本の中で初めて見た20年ほど前には、「イナゴマメって何?」と頭の中をハテナがたくさん駆け巡ったものだ。

ところが8年ほど前になってやっとそれは、カロリーが低く、鉄分やカルシウムなど栄養価の高いスーパーフードとして、アメリカのグルメ自然食ブームの中で話題になっていた「キャロブ」という地中海地方原産のマメ科の植物のさやの果肉だということがわかった。

甘みがあり、カフェインを含まないのに風味や色がチョコレートに似ているということで、砂糖を使わなくてもココアやチョコレートの代替品になる美味しいお菓子の材料として大人気。最近は日本でも、挽いたパウダー状のものが自然食品や製菓材料として手に入るようになっている。ココ

*1　主要参考文献⑫。

アパウダーみたいなキャロブパウダーは、そのままでも食べられるし、確かにお菓子作りに使うとなかなか楽しい。

しかし、その正体がわかったからと言って、これを発酵したはちみつと混ぜてつけると目がよくなるよ、ファラオの秘薬だし……と言われても、「そうかそうか」と目に入れてみる勇気はなかなか出ないものである。

古代エジプトの医学文献には現代医学に照らし合わせてなるほど、と理解できるものも多いが、医術と呪術にあんまり境のないところもあったのでは、と思えるところも少なくない。「昔からいいというものは、やっぱりいいんだね!」と単純に言えないことも多いのである。

いや、そもそも、イナゴマメの粉を省いてはちみつだけにしたところで、それをどろりと目に入れるのは蛮勇だとしか思われないのだった。

しかし、古代エジプトばかりでなく、インドのアーユルヴェーダでも、ピュアな天然はちみつそのものを、白内障や目のけが、疲れ目などの治療に目薬として使うという。

はちみつは、食べても入れてもいかにも目によさそうですよと、いろいろなところから繰り返し、漏れ聞こえてくるのである。

Spoonful of Honey　　114

白内障、角膜炎、結膜炎の治療報告、
そして目の老化現象や充血、疲れ目に

私も、仕事でパソコンのモニターの真ん前に座って過ごす時間は長く、目は常に乾燥しがちだし、「慢性的に疲れがたまっていることは間違いない。

生理食塩水を目薬にしてドライアイに水分を補給する以外に、いいケアの方法はないだろうか、もともと近眼だし、これから段々年をとって、もっと見えにくくなっていったら困るよねえ、と常々気にはなっていた。

「はちみつは粘膜の修復にいい」ということは知っている。

それでも今風の目薬しか実際に見たことがなかった私には、どろっとしたはちみつを目に入れてみる勇気はどうしても出なかった。

はちみつを使った現代の医師たちによる目の治療報告がまとめられていたある本にじっくりと向き合うまで、そして、疲れ目や視力の低下をなんとかしたいという自覚が、いよいよつのってくるまでは。

あるとき、視力がガタッと落ちたのを自覚するできごとがあった。

ひょんなことで目に異物が入って表面に傷ができてしまったのだ。それ自体は大事にいたるようなけがではなかったが、眼帯をしているので、パソコンのモニターを見ていても、元気な方の目もすぐに疲れてしまう。

「はちみつは傷や疲れ目にいいんだよねえ」と例によって思い出しはしたものの、この段階でも正直、けがした目の中にはちみつを入れてみようとは、とても思えなかった。

ところが1週間ほどしてけががすっかり治ってから、私は改めて愕然とした。けがの前からこの数日で、両目とも確実に視力が落ちている！

このまま放置はよくないかも……。

私はある一冊の本を引っ張り出した。ずっと手元にあったとはいえ、これまではこの本を耳学問で読んでいた。今度はもしかすると、実践者になるかもしれない構えで改めて読んでみるのだ。

『ハチミツと代替医療　医療現場での可能性を探る』[*2]というその本には、主に傷や粘膜の治療に病院でどのようにはちみつが使われているかの報告や、はちみつが持つ抗菌作用、免疫増強作用、抗炎症、抗酸化作用、細胞増進促進作用の仕組みなどが研究論文としてまとめられている。タイトル

[*2] 主要参考文献⑲。

に「代替療法」とあるが、はちみつを使った治療に科学的な視点を当てようとする医療研究者たちの試みの例と言っていい。日本語訳も、ちゃんと医学的な校閲を経ている。

目の病気や傷害に関する情報を探しながら読んでいく。目も粘膜の話だからか、やはり胃の潰瘍や口内炎と同じぐらい、はちみつの得意範囲であるらしい。

冒頭に引用したパトリシア・ヴィットさんは、この本の著者のひとりである。彼女は、南アメリカでは古代から白内障にはちみつが使われてきたと述べているわけだが、現代でもベネズエラやメキシコ、ブラジルでは白内障治療に病院ではちみつが使われていると言っている。

ハリナシミツバチとはあまり聞かない種類だが、その貯蜜ポットである巣房は、普通のミツバチのようにみつろうでできているのとは違って、プロポリスでできているらしい。そのためにプロポリスの抗菌性有効成分がはちみつにしみこんでいて、一般のミツバチのはちみつより、病気の治癒効果が高いとされている。[*3]

ニュージーランドのマヌカハニーを「医療用はちみつ」として金字塔の

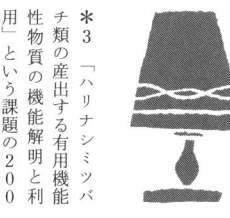

*3 「ハリナシミツバチ類の産出する有用機能性物質の機能解明と利用」という課題の2006年の研究について、国立研究開発法人農業・食品産業技術総合研究機構のホームページに概要が報告されている。

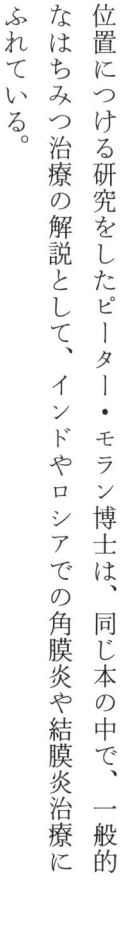

位置につける研究をしたピーター・モラン博士は、同じ本の中で、一般的なはちみつ治療の解説として、インドやロシアでの角膜炎や結膜炎治療にふれている。

インドやロシアで使われているのは、ハリナシミツバチやマヌカの蜜ではなく、地域で通常手に入るミツバチの天然はちみつだろうと思うが、それでも抗菌、抗炎症、抗カビ作用がちゃんとあり、結膜炎や角膜の感染炎、目のやけどなどに処方されているとある。

なんと言っても、それまで試してみる勇気の出なかった私の背中を「ほうらね」と押してくれたのは、そこに載っていた一枚の写真であった。結膜炎の患者の大きく開いた目に、はちみつを点眼しているところだ。

エジプト、インド、南米、ロシア、ニュージーランド。こんなにあちこちの大陸で、古代から今まで綿々と、人々が目にはちみつを入れてきたと言うのだ。やってみてどうなったとしても、きっと大事にはいたるまい。

何より今や、我が両眼はよれよれの状態だ。そうでなくても最近目の疲れが少しずつひどくなってきたし、あんまり遅くまで仕事をすると、朝起

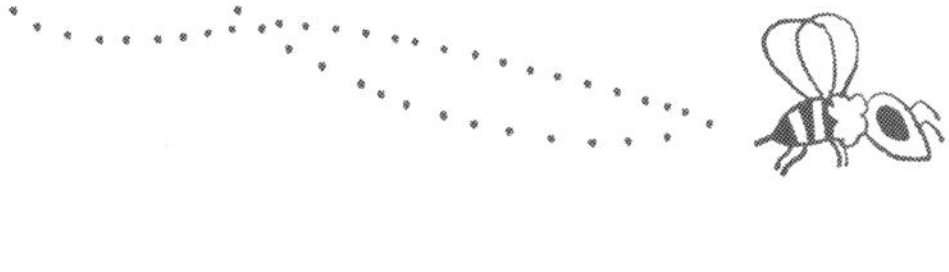

Spoonful of Honey　　118

きたとき、まだ目が重く感じられることもある。「若年性白内障」などといることばもあるぐらいだし、突破口があるなら、そうなる前に、できる用心はするべきかも。

そういえば、アメリカ西海岸のある自然食品店に置いてあった雑誌の特集で、アーユルヴェーダのお医者さんが、

「別に目のけがや病気でなくても、単なる疲れ目や充血、白内障の予防にもとてもいいのですよ。白目をきれいな白にする美容効果もあります。かなりしみてたくさん涙が流れ出ますが、それが目にいいのです。目を洗浄、解毒し、水晶体に栄養分を与える効果もあります」

とインタビューに答えている記事を見たことがあった。その時は「ふーん」ですませてしまったが、一生のうち、私の目とはちみつが出会う機は、今こそ熟したのではないだろうか、よし！

目に湿布をしたような気持ちよさ

ロシアの方法だと、はちみつを20パーセントから50パーセントほどに水

で薄めて使うことが多いようである。市販されているアーユルヴェーダの
はちみつ目薬も、はちみつの分量は50パーセントから70パーセントぐらい
で、あとはハーブなどが加えられていることが多い。

一方でベネズエラでは、はちみつを薄めず、そのまま使うという。
私は、できるだけ準備や保存などに手間のかからない方法を選択するく
せがあるので、はちみつそのままをストレートに点眼することにした。手
順や道具を省く方が、清潔も保ちやすい。

ハリナシミツバチのはちみつに、独特のプラスアルファの抗菌作用（プ
ロポリスによる）があるように、マヌカハニーにも、他のはちみつにはな
いメチルグリオキサール（MGO）という独特な抗菌成分があり、それが
治癒力の高さの理由とされている。そこで、目薬としては、日本でも手に
入りやすくなってきた医療グレードのマヌカハニー[*4]を使うことにした。ミ
ネラルが多く含まれていることも目にいいようである。

点眼の方法として一番簡単で確実なのは、綿棒を使うことだ。ただし、
綿棒はくれぐれも清潔に保管し、はちみつも食べるものとは容器を分けて、
暗い戸棚の中にしまうか、点眼用はちみつ専用の遮光びんを用意する。

*4 活性度10+以上のマ
ヌカハニーが一般に医療
グレードとされている。

Spoonful of Honey　　120

綿棒の先の方にはちみつをのせ、鏡を見ながら下のまぶたか眼球の下側の表面に、ちょんちょんと1、2滴を、当てるように、置くようにしてつける。そして目をぱちぱちさせて全体によくなじませる。

「わー、しみる!」という感じが、さーっと広がり、そして涙がぽろぽろと流れ出す。目に湿布を当てたような感じなのだが、そのしみ方が不思議にすばらしく気持ちいいのだ。くせになる感覚である。

しばらくは目が赤くなるが、5〜10分ほどで、しみるのと充血がおさまってくると、目がすっきりはっきりし、白目の透明感が増す。目の中の汚れや不純物が清しく(すが)さっぱり流されて、眼球が奥まで洗浄されてきれいになったような気がするのだ。

自分の涙で目を洗う

ドライアイに生理食塩水や一般的な目薬などでいつも水分を補給する癖がついてしまうと、目は自力で涙を出す能力が衰えてしまうと言われる。

その点、はちみつ点眼なら、自然に涙を出してそれで目をうるおすこと

ができるし、目の洗浄まで自分の涙でまかなえるわけだ。紫外線や放射線で目が弱りかけても、炎症を修復する働きがあるので、粘膜を癒やし、楽にしてくれるというわけである。

朝起きたときは目を洗うためにはちみつ点眼をし、夜寝る前には昼間の汚れを洗い流して水晶体への栄養補給をするためにはちみつ点眼をする。

調子がよくなってくると、朝か寝る前のどちらか１回だけでも、十分間に合っている感じである。今や、目の酷使の程度によって、感覚で頻度を調節できるまでになった。

いやー、あの時、決心してよかったな、としみじみ思えることが一生のうちにいくつかあるとすると、私にとって、迷いを振り切ってはちみつ点眼に踏み切ったのは、確実にそのひとつであったと言える。

眼精疲労はほぼ過去のものとなり、起床時のまぶたも確実に軽くなった。私の様子をしばらく横目でじーっと見ていた母をはじめ、幾人かの知り合いたちも、効果を目の当たりにするや、はちみつのついた綿棒を手に、鏡の前に立つようになった。はちみつ目薬のファンは日々確実に増えつつある。

ただですね、我が夫はまだためらっていて、はちみつ点眼に踏み切れないでいるのです。私が綿棒を使う様子を見ながら、いまだに「うーん、こわい」と言う。ぽろぽろ涙を流すのを見て首をふる。

あなたも泣いちゃえばいいのに。気持ちいいのになあ。

ともに泣ける日はいつ、と思い描く毎日なのだ。

はちみつの胃薬

Spoonful
of
Honey
10

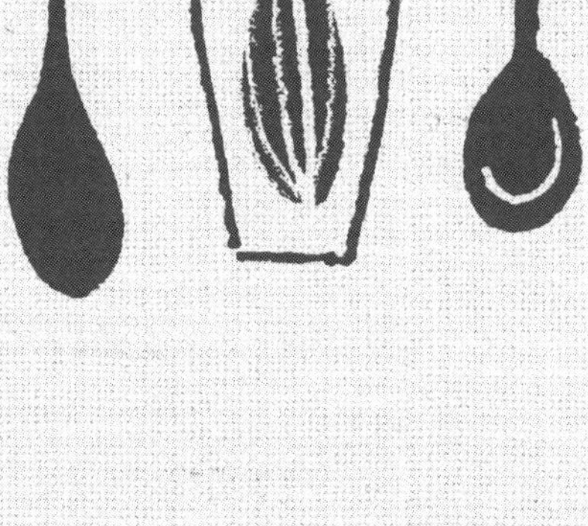

多種類のはちみつの中で、胃炎・胃十二指腸潰瘍の改善に強い効果を示すのが、「そば」や「栗」、「冬青*1」のはちみつと言われています、これは、亜鉛の含有量が多いからと言えるでしょう。現在、効果的な医薬品が開発されているため、はちみつで治そうというかたはほとんどいませんが、はちみつで胃潰瘍が治ったと喜びの声を聞くことは、20年前まではそうめずらしいことではありませんでした。

――養蜂家・医師・宇津田舎博士

「医療用はちみつ」というジャンルが、近年急速に注目を集めるようにな
った流れを、大きなできごとを柱に、ざっと振り返ってみよう。

ニュージーランド、ワイカト大学のピーター・モラン博士が、「マヌカ[*2]
ハニーは、他のどんなはちみつにもない特別な治癒成分を持っている」と[*3]
いうことをプレスリリースで発表したのは、一九九一年のことだった。

二〇〇〇年には、イギリスの五つの病院で行われていた難治性潰瘍の治
療の取り組みについてリポートされたBBCのテレビ番組の放送があっ
た。これは、イギリス中に旋風を巻き起こしたという。

と言うのも、番組中インタビューを受けたアーロン君という少年がいて、
髄膜炎による感染症で足先と手の指先のほとんどを失うという経験をして
いた。

九ヵ月間、どんな治療を施しても進行を止められないと医師団も行き詰
まったあげくに、マヌカハニーを塗ることで九週間のうちに完治したとい
う、そのエピソードが驚きをさらったのだ。

折しも抗生物質が効かなくなってしまった耐性菌の問題が大きくなりつ
つあった最中のこと。耐性菌による感染症や、薬の副作用の問題に救いの

[*1] モチノキ科の常緑樹で関東より南の山地で六月頃開花する。雑木林で他の花と混ざることが多いので百花蜜になるのがほとんどだが、単花蜜は結晶しやすく、コクのある味わい。

[*2] 主要参考文献①。

[*3] このマヌカ特有の成分「ユニークマヌカファクター（UMF）」から来る抗菌能力を特に数値化し、特有の活性度指数として、マヌカハニーのパッケージに5[+]、10[+]、20[+]などと表示されるようになった。例えば、「10[+]」とは、消毒液であるフェノールの10パーセント希釈液と同等以上の抗菌作用を持つことを示す。病院で皮膚や医療器具の殺菌消毒に使われる消毒液は2パーセントのフェノール希釈液。

127 🥄 10 はちみつの胃薬

手を差し伸べるように登場したのが、「医療用はちみつ」だった。

その後数年間に、ドイツのボン大学付属小児病院で、小児がん治療の化学療法で免疫力が弱ってしまった子どもたちの傷の治癒に、通常の消毒方法や抗生剤よりもはちみつの方が効果を上げているということが知られるようになったのも、大きい[*4]。

その上、2008年にマヌカハニー独特の強力な抗菌作用を持つ成分がメチルグリオキサール（MGO）という物質であるということをつきとめたのが、ドレスデン工科大学のトーマス・ヘンレ博士だったから、以降、ドイツはニュージーランドと並んで、「医療用はちみつ」研究の先頭に立つことになる。

病院や診療所で使うためにマヌカハニーを塗布して包装した包帯や絆創膏、はちみつを薬として摂りやすいパッケージに詰めたり、トローチにしたものなど、医薬品としての製品も次々開発されるようになった。

また、マヌカハニーに限らず、はちみつを昔から医薬品として扱っていた伝統のある中近東やネパール、インドなどでも、地域で手に入る良質な天然はちみつの成分や効能を科学的に明らかにし、積極的に医療に応用し

[*4] 主要参考文献㊿。

[*5] 「ユニークマヌカファクター」の実体が、「メチルグリオキサール（MGO）であると判明してからは、マヌカハニーのパッケージの表示には、実際に含まれているMGOの分量を示す数値を表示する方法へ移行しつつある。ちなみに、MGOは、光にも熱にも強い。また、マヌカ以外のはちみつでは、特有の成分があるのか、あればその分は何なのかが、まだ区別ができないことが多い。そのため、はちみつが一般に共有する「過酸化水素」などによる抗菌作用をすべて含め、そのはちみつ「全体の活性度」を示す数値としてTA（トータルな活性度）を表示した製品もある。

Spoonful of Honey　128

ていこうという動きが、活発になってきたようだ。

伝統医学や薬草学の分野ではもちろんだが、2008年以降、ざっと見ただけでも、口内炎、特にがんの放射線治療の副作用で起こる難治性口内炎、咽喉内潰瘍の予防や治癒や治療に、はちみつを内用、外用で処方し、成果を上げたといった医学論文などが、こうした国々から出てきている。[*6]

日本のはちみつ博士はいずこ

こんなふうに「医療用はちみつ」の流れを追ってみると、日本にも、いろんな病気の治療にはちみつを使うことについて一家言あるお医者さんが、いてくれたらなあ、と思わずにはいられない。

今でもはちみつは一応、日本薬局方にも指定された立派な医薬品なのだし、使い方も難しくない。

専門的な研究成果や臨床報告の例が日本でもいっぱい出てきたら、私たちが普段の健康管理、ちょっとした不調をいなすための、ヒントの宝庫になるんだけどな……と思う。

[*6] 主要参考文献⑱、⑲。

日本だって今、医療現場で抗生物質が効かない耐性菌による感染症の問題は深刻になっていると聞く。はちみつの出番はいろいろありそうな気がするのだが。

現代に現れし日本のヒポクラテスみたいな、はちみつ博士出よ！

……と思ったときに思い出したのが、冒頭の文章だ。

10年ほど前、ある友人が「あなた、こういうの好きそうよ」と言ってプレゼントしてくれた『はちみつで元気を手に入れる』（「家庭画報別冊」2004年刊）の中で見たもので、その医療監修を担当された先生の見解である。

この方は医学博士でご自分も養蜂をされている。ヨーロッパには、お医者さんで養蜂が趣味、という人はけっこういるが、この先生は養蜂家の2代目ということで、ハチのことは本格的だ。はちみつを使った患者さんのケア、生活指導の知識、経験などを豊富にお持ちのようである。その証拠に、はちみつの内服の仕方のアドバイスがとっても具体的で腑に落ちる。

胃炎や胃・十二指腸潰瘍の症状を改善するためにはちみつを摂るなら、胃壁全体にはちみつを行き渡らせるのがポイントだという。そのためには、

Spoonful of Honey　　130

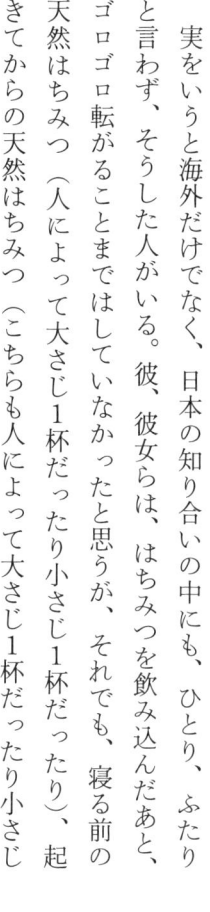

「起床後、空きっ腹におちょこ１杯のはちみつを生のままのみほします。そして横になり、はちみつを胃壁全体に塗りつけるようにゴロゴロとゆっくり転がります。そして30分は何も口にしないことが肝心です」と丁寧にアドバイスされている。

この時期（2004年）に、「現在、効果的な医薬品が開発されているため、はちみつで治そうというかたはほとんどいませんが……」と言っておられるのは、時代の変化が感じられて、とても面白い。今思えば、この先生の治療法は時代をうんと先取りしたものだったのだ。

というのも、10年後の今や、病院で処方された抗生物質では胃の中のピロリ菌を退治することができずに、はちみつに頼って治す人が、世界中でどんどん増えつつあることは疑いようがないからだ。

実をいうと海外だけでなく、日本の知り合いの中にも、ひとり、ふたりと言わず、そうした人がいる。彼、彼女らは、はちみつを飲み込んだあと、ゴロゴロ転がることまではしていなかったと思うが、それでも、寝る前の天然はちみつ（人によって大さじ１杯だったり小さじ１杯だったり）、起きてからの天然はちみつ（こちらも人によって大さじ１杯だったり小さじ

1杯だったり）を続けることで、抗生物質で退治できなかったピロリ菌を見事にやっつけた。

「検査したら、なくなってたよー！　お医者さんに、何かした？　って聞かれちゃった」と、何度かきいたから、たぶんお医者さんたちも、うすうす、はちみつパワーの存在には気づいていらっしゃるのではないかしらん。

ただの消化不良や胃もたれにも

私自身は胃潰瘍になりかけたことはない。だが、たまの消化不良や胃痛、胃もたれ、あるいは、このまま寝ちゃったら明日は胃が重いぞ、というようなときに、天然はちみつのひとさじが大活躍することは何度も体験して知っている。

また、小さじ1杯の天然はちみつに薬局方のはっか油を1滴落として爪楊枝などでよくよく混ぜてから飲みくだす「ひとさじのはっかのはちみつシロップ」は、我が家では、食べ過ぎで胃が重いときの頓服的な胃薬だ。口も胃も、すーっとして、胸の中まで軽くなる。

Spoonful of Honey　132

ピロリ菌退治には「医療用はちみつの草分け」マヌカハニーが大人気のようだ。

けれども、ものによって多少の程度の差はあれ、加熱や添加物のない純粋な天然はちみつであれば、胃薬としてちゃんと効き目があるというのが実感だ。

宇津田先生が胃薬としてすすめておられる「そば」や「栗」、「冬青（そよご）」のはちみつというのは、天然はちみつの中でも、胃の粘膜を強くすると言われる亜鉛をはじめ、ミネラル分を豊富に含んでいる仲間である。天然はちみつも最近はよりどりみどりだが、同じものでなくても、求める効能を考えて性質の似たものを選ぶように意識するのがコツだと言える。

はちみつは環境の忠実な鏡でもあるから、薬として摂るなら、産地の公害や農薬の状況、製造過程などにも、心配りをする必要があるだろう。

夢見る日本のメディカルハニー

南米の熱帯地域にいるハリナシミツバチというちょっと変わったハチの

133　　10　はちみつの胃薬

話に「目薬」のところでふれた。みつろうでなくプロポリスでできた貯蜜庫の中にはちみつを貯めるので、飛び抜けた抗菌作用と効能を持ち、白内障に抜群に効くらしいという話である。

それを言うなら日本にだって、国内でも少数派の変わったミツバチがいる。西洋ミツバチとはまるで性格も違うという日本ミツバチだ。西洋ミツバチよりずっとおとなしいのに、害虫や病気にはとても強いという。

のんびりと時間をかけて花蜜を集めるので採蜜量は少なめだが、結果的に蜜が長い時間巣にとどまるため、水分がよく飛んで熟成が進み、旨みの増した美味しい蜜が採れる。

それに、日本独特の植物や産地で摂れたはちみつには、西洋ミツバチのはちみつであっても、知られざる特徴があったとしてもおかしくない。

もしかすると世界がびっくりするような、すごくユニークですばらしい効能の「医療用はちみつ」が、日本にも隠れているのではないか。

そんなワクワクする夢想をやめられないのだ。

Spoonful of Honey　134

はちみつとビタミンCで、見えない敵と闘う——*1*

Spoonful
of
Honey
11

世界をもっと幸せで、
うんと明るい場所にできるだろうと信じているの。
「化学」という自然の道具箱を生かし切ることで。

――ハニーレモン 「Disney wiki」英語版より

古い本に伝わる伝統料理の作り方を、ページを繰りながらじっくり読む
のはとっても楽しい。

だが、世界のどこかで誰かが今日も、飛びきりの新しい味を編みだして
はいないだろうかと、舌なめずりをしながら食材の名前でレシピの検索を
するのも、大好きな余暇の過ごし方のひとつだ。

ネット上で、はちみつ（honey）とレモン（lemon）の組み合わせで検
索したら、ある時期、ヒーロー物のアニメ映画に登場するらしい「ハニー
レモン」*1という名前のキャラクターに遭遇するようになった。

すらりとした、ちょっぴり猫背のかわいい女の子でいつも前向き。明る
く冒険好きな化学の天才という設定らしい。世界に散らばるアニメファン
たちが、ブログ上で工夫を凝らしたハニーレモン嬢のコスプレや、人形な
ど自作のグッズを披露したりしている。

そして、冒頭のことば（日本語訳は筆者）が彼女のせりふなのだろうか、
英文でよく引用されているのだった。

興味を引かれ、へー、どれどれ、いったいどんなシーンでこのせりふが
飛び出すのかなと、ちょっぴりワクワクしながら原作のアニメを見てみた。

*1 2014年、アメ
リカ、ディズニー制作の
アニメーション・ファン
タジー映画で、邦題は『ベ
イマックス』。原題は、
（Big Hero 6）。

すると、確かにハニーレモン嬢はいきいきとかわいらしいキャラクターだったが、ファンの子たちが盛んに引用しているのに、残念！　肝心のせりふが一度も映画の中には出てこない。

不思議に思って出典を確かめてみると、映画会社のキャラクター紹介ページにたどり着いた。どうやら例のせりふは、キャラクターの設定をする中で、考え出されたことばのように見える。

いずれにしろ、ストーリーはロボット工学や化学研究の最前線という舞台設定なのに、「はちみつとレモン」という古風な組み合わせが、悪と闘うスーパーヒーローの名前になっているのが面白い。

昔から伝わる暮らしの智恵が持つ底力は、いつの時代も侮れないわけである。

「病気の予防や治療にビタミンC」という一般的な習慣

明るく元気でへこたれず、人の痛みに共感する優しさと、スリルと実験

Spoonful of Honey　138

大好きの旺盛な好奇心を併せ持つハニーレモン嬢が、冒頭のせりふを体現していることは間違いない。

彼女が信じていると言うように、化学という自然の道具箱を生かし切ることで、世界をもっと幸せで明るい場所にしようと志した人は、これまできっと少なくなかっただろう。

たとえば、「ビタミンC博士」と呼ばれるアメリカの生化学者、ライナス・ポーリング博士が残してくれた功績の輝きはとても大きい。

博士はその他にも化学者としてさまざまな業績を残した人だが、ごく普段の私たちの生活にシンプルに役立つありがたさという意味では、ビタミンCの研究は、ほんとうに希有な偉業と言えるのではないだろうか。

ポーリング博士が1970年に『ビタミンCと風邪[*2]』、1976年に『ビタミンCとかぜ、インフルエンザ[*3]』を出版して以来、ビタミンCをサプリメントとして摂ることを習慣にする人が世界中に増えたのは確かなことだ。

その後、博士によってビタミンCの抗がん作用に関する論文や本[*4]が発表され、風邪ばかりでなく他の病気の予防や治療にまで研究が広がったこと

[*2] 原題『Vitamin C and the Common Cold』（邦題『さらば風邪薬！ビタミンCで風邪を追放』）。

[*3] 主要参考文献㉑。

[*4] 主要参考文献㉒。

が知られるようになり、関心は世界中でさらに高まった。

思い返してみると、日本でも80年代半ばの一時期はビタミンCブームの最中。通学、通勤途中の電車の中吊り雑誌広告や本などで、その効用を謳う文句をよく見かけたような気がする。

今ではビタミンCは心臓病やその他さまざまな病気の予防にもいいということが広く知られるようになって、実際、アメリカにいる身内や友人、知り合いは、ほとんどの人が病気の予防のためにビタミンCのサプリメントを摂っている。

ビタミンCを上手に摂ることができれば、うっかり風邪をひきかけてもひどいことにはならず、お医者にかからなくても乗り越えられるとみんなが知っているからだ。

医療費がべらぼうと言っていいアメリカでは、そう気軽に病院に行くわけにいかず、おちおちひどい風邪もひけない。

心臓病などになったら、請求書のことを考えただけで心臓マヒを起こしてしまうから、自己管理して防衛しなければ、と考えている人も冗談抜きにたくさんいる。

Spoonful of Honey　140

何しろあちらは高額治療で破産するという中産階級もそう珍しくない、病気と医療に関しては荒野の世界。

ビタミンCはそんな中、荒野でうっかりのたれ死なないために、病魔に繰り出す手裏剣みたいなものなのだ。

ビタミンCの「適量」は自分で見つける

アメリカでは、自分がひょいとガムやキャンディを口に放りこむついでに、「あなたもどう?」というような感じで、ビタミンCの錠剤を勧められる場にたまに出くわす。どれだけ摂っても害がなくからだにいいもの、とみんなが認識している点では、ビタミンCは「安全な食品」扱いだ。

私自身の体験を思い起こせば、はじめにビタミンCと印象的な出会いをしたのは、やはりブームの最中の日本で、25年以上前のことだった。

ビタミンCの摂り方について、ポーリング博士来日時のインタビュー記事[*5]を読んだとき、なんだかすごく面白そう! とワクワクしたのを覚えている。

*5 主要参考文献㉔。

アメリカでのビタミンCの1日当たりの摂取推奨量がたったの60ミリグラムだった時代（当時の日本は50ミリグラム）に、ポーリング博士は何年間も、ビタミンCのグラム単位での摂取を提唱、実践していた。それは、もっとたくさんのビタミンCを摂れば、病気の予防や治療が効果的にできるのだという理論の発見に基づいた摂取量なのだ。

85歳当時は、普段、日に18グラム（1万8000ミリグラム）を摂っていたと言う。

風邪をひきかけたりしたら、さらにもっと量を増やすということらしい。

もともと、国の摂取推奨量というのは、あくまでビタミンC欠乏症である「壊血病」にならないための数字なのだ。

ちなみにビタミンCの別名「アスコルビン酸」は、「壊血病＝スコルビュティック（scorbutic）」の前に、それを否定する「a」をつけることから生まれたことばなので、「壊血病防止ビタミン」というわけで、確かに命名の理屈は通っている。

しかし、壊血病というのは死と隣り合わせの病であって、壊血病になるほどビタミンCが不足したら、それは大変な非常事態だということだ。

ポーリング博士の発見のポイントは、ビタミンCは、その何倍にも摂取

＊6　現在の推奨量は、アメリカ90ミリグラム、日本は100ミリグラムになっている。

Spoonful of Honey　142

量を増やしても安全だし、増やすことによって、壊血病だけではなく、もっとさまざまな病気を未然に防ぎ、また治療することができる力を持っているということだった。

18グラムというのは正直ちょっとびっくりしたが、適量の数字は人によってまるで違うし、また同じ人でも年齢や体調によって全然違ってくるので、ちょうどの頃合いを自分で探し出すのが賢い使い方だと言う。

当時85歳のポーリング博士も、60代の頃は、一日2、3グラムから始めたらしい。*7。

水溶性のビタミンは、摂りすぎても余分は尿に出てしまうから副作用の心配はいらないし、やや軟便になることが十分足りているという目安になるので、適量の判断を自分でするのも簡単だと言う。

なるほど、いずれにしても、理論がシャープなだけではなく、研究を我が身で実践している先生の話は、聞いていて安心感があり、やってみようという気になりやすいのである。

何より「自分のからだで確かめながらポイントを探す」というのは、普段の私の遊びのつぼ、ど真ん中だ。

*7
主要参考文献㉖。

143　11　はちみつとビタミンCで、見えない敵と闘う——1

そこで我が身をじっくり観察しつつ、500ミリグラムのビタミンCと、それと組み合わせるといいとおすすめのマルチビタミン・ミネラルの錠剤とともに、春夏秋冬をひとまわり過ごしてみることにした。

その結果、毎日の量とタイミングをある程度うまく調整できるようになるまで1、2ヵ月。

1年が経過する頃には、風邪を素早く治すのにも、ストレスがたまりがちなときも、タイミングよく量を増やすことでうまくしのいでいくコツと、絶対風邪をひきたくない！　というときの予防の術を、まがりなりにも身につけた。

個人的には、我が家では家族も含めて、ビタミンCの効果をからだでめでたく納得し、うん、なるほど役に立つんだねえ、という実感を得たのは確かなことだ。

元気なときとひどい風邪をひいて体調が悪いときの適量の差は、当時の私の場合、1日2グラムから10グラムぐらいの間だということもわかった。ああ懐かしい。あれは、やってみて、ほんとうに面白かった。

風邪やストレスとの新しい闘い方を習得し、とってもためになったこと

も事実だ。

はちみつを通して再会したビタミンC

ただ、そのあとのことを言えば、私は、サプリメントの錠剤を毎日摂り続けるのはやめてしまった。

ポーリング博士は、健康維持のために、毎日かなりの量（4グラムから10グラムほど）のビタミンCを、ビタミンEやマルチビタミン、ミネラルのサプリメントと一緒に摂ることを勧めておられたし、本を読めばその理論はよくよく納得できるものだ。

だが、そもそも自分も家族も基本的にすこぶる健康で、持病もなく、特にからだの不調を感じていなかったこと。そのため、ビタミンCをがんや心臓病のような病気の治療に役立てられないかというような、さしせまった動機がなかったからかもしれない。

それに、食い意地が張っていて、口に入れるものは何でも美味しいほうがいい、栄養もできれば美味しいものから摂りたい、という趣味だったか

ら、風邪の予防と治療に「効く」という実感とコツをつかんだら、それだけで好奇心が満たされて、気がすんでしまったのだ。

そこで、当時の個人的な結論としては、「体調を崩しかけたりして急に必要なときに、タイミングよく集中的に使えるように、ビタミンCの買い置きだけはしておく」という使用法に落ち着いていたのである。

ところがそれから何年も経って、まえがきで初めに書いた原因不明、喉のしつこいイガイガを経験することになった。「医療用はちみつ」のすばらしい世界に招き入れてくれるきっかけとなったイガイガである。

すると今度はその巡り合わせで、まったく違った角度から、あらためてビタミンCと向き合うことになったのだ。

というのも、何人ものはちみつ療法の専門家が、はちみつを「医薬品」として治療目的を持って摂るときには、その効果を高めるためにビタミンCを補ったり、ビタミンCを含んだ食品と積極的に組み合わせるのがいいですよ、とすすめていたからである。

人は他のほとんどの哺乳動物と違い、体内でビタミンCを作ることができない。

前にも何度かふれたように、ほぼ完全食品のはちみつだが、ビタミンC
だけは、含まれている量だけでは必要量を十全に満たせないということも
ある。

だが、それ以上に、はちみつとビタミンCを合わせると、さまざまな症
状に効くはちみつの治癒効果を増すだけでなく、基本的な免疫力をアップ
させ、病気を防ぐことにつながるのだというのだ。

そう聞いたときふと、ちょっと待てよ、と考えた。

ビタミンCの摂り方のコツとして、以前からマルチビタミンとミネラル
のサプリメントを一緒に摂ることが勧められていたのを思い出したのだ。

「‼」

マルチビタミンとマルチミネラルのサプリメントというのは、生のはち
みつそのものではないか。しかも、はちみつは、市販の錠剤にはまねでき
ない活性ビタミンの爆弾だ。うーむ、なるほど。

「はちみつとレモン」という古典的な組み合わせには、私などからすれば、
「だって、美味しいもん」という何よりの大義があるとは思っていたが、
実はそれ以外にも、ちゃんとした生化学的な理があったらしいのである。

147 　　11　はちみつとビタミンCで、見えない敵と闘う──1

はちみつとビタミンCは同じ武器を手に
ウイルスやがん細胞をやっつける

はちみつとビタミンCの美味しくて簡単な組み合わせ方の話に入る前に、ビタミンCのすばらしいパワーについて、ちょっとばかり突っ込んだ話を、もう少しだけさせてほしい。

はちみつに対する新しい興味を頭の隅に置きながら、いざ改めて最近のビタミンC関連の資料を当たってみると、またずいぶんと面白いことがわかってきた。

1994年にポーリング博士が93歳で亡くなって以降も、ビタミンCに関しては、さまざまな研究、議論や論争が続いている。一時期など、「ビタミンCが風邪やがんに効くということがはっきり証明できるわけではない」と、ビタミンCの効き目自体を疑問視する風潮まであったのだ。

けれど長い経緯を端折って言うと、2005年にある画期的な研究論文[*8]が発表されて、「ビタミンCはがんに効く」というポーリング博士の主張

*8 主要参考文献㊾。

Spoonful of Honey　148

がやはり正しかったことが明らかになった。

その内容は、高濃度のビタミンCが、がん細胞だけを殺し、正常細胞にはダメージを与えないという「仕組み」をはっきりと説明し、それを証明するものだったから、実際、この論文をきっかけに、ビタミンCの高濃度点滴や経口投与を、本格的にがん治療に使って効果をあげるお医者さんは続々と増え、アメリカでは今では1万人にもなったのだと言う。

で、その論文のキモの部分なのだが、ビタミンCの抗がん作用は、ビタミンCが血管内で作り出す「過酸化水素」によるのだと言う。過酸化水素は強い酸化作用によってがん細胞を殺す働きをするが、正常な細胞内では生体の酵素が過酸化水素を分解するため、健康な細胞は無傷でいられる、というのだ。

さて「はちみつ軟膏と絆創膏」、「はちみつパックとクレンジング」のところで、はちみつの抗菌作用の鍵として「過酸化水素」ということばが出てきたのを覚えておられるだろうか（96ページ、105ページ）。

はちみつオタクにとっては、「過酸化水素」とは、はちみつの抗菌殺菌作用に関わる大事な成分。耳にすればピピッと反応するキーワードなのだ。

インフルエンザウイルスや胃がんのピロリ菌、虫歯のミュータンス菌、にきびのアクネ菌そのほか悪玉菌に対しては、はちみつも強力な殺傷剤「過酸化水素」でやっつける。だけど、はちみつが発生させる過酸化水素が、健康な細胞や正常な善玉常在菌を傷つけることはない。

その場面を想像してみると、これってまるで、邪悪な菌の軍団に対して、はちみつとビタミンCが、同じすごい威力の秘密兵器を使うみたいな、胸のすくヒーロー物の世界ではありませんか。

はちみつとビタミンCを混ぜた「ハニーレモンキャンディ」は最強のサプリメント

はちみつを大さじ1杯すくいとり、はちみつをのせたまま、スプーンを小皿に置く。そこに、薬局方にもなっているビタミンCの原末（アスコルビン酸[*9]）の白い粉を小さじ4分の1杯のせる。はちみつがあまりこぼれ出さないように注意しながら、竹串などの細い棒ではちみつとビタミンC原末をこちょこちょと混ぜ合わせる。

[*9]　薬局で扱われているビタミンCの原末（アスコルビン酸、またはL—アスコルビン酸）と同じものが、簡易包装でお手頃にインターネット通販など（「食品グレード」の表示）で、手に入る。

現在のビタミンC原末の世界でのシェアは、医薬品表示、食品表示を問わず、ほぼ9割が中国産で約1割がイギリスとなっている。

販売時に「国産」とあるのは、原末を輸入の上で国内で包装したということで、事情はどの国でも同様。

純粋な原末であるかぎり、品質の心配はいらない。

よく混ざったら、スプーンをそのまま口に入れてペロリ。

わー、すっぱい！ でも甘くて美味しい。はちみつレモンキャンディの味だ。小皿にこぼれたはちみつも、余さずすくいにきれいになめてしまいましょう。これが、我が家の最強のサプリメント、「ハニーレモンキャンディ」の標準版だ。

このサプリメントのポイントは、はちみつや混ぜるビタミンCの分量を、自分で細かく調節できること。一日の中で、体調や場面に合わせて、自分なりの分量や配分を細かく工夫できるのがとても便利なのです。

薬局方のはちみつは、「滋養、栄養剤」としてはちみつを摂る場合（これって、サプリとしてってことですよね）、摂り方を詳しく解説してくれているわけではないが、1日に30グラムから60グラムという目安をくれているものもある。

種類にもよるけれど、はちみつは、小さじ1杯がだいたい7グラムで、大さじ1杯は約21グラム。100グラムで294キロカロリーということを頭に入れておくと便利だ。

そして、ビタミンCの原末（アスコルビン酸）は、イオン飲料の作り方

のところでも言ったが、小さじ4分の1杯で約1200ミリグラムのビタミンCが摂れるというのが目安である。

「大さじ1杯のはちみつに小さじ4分の1杯のビタミンC」というのがご紹介した標準版の分量だが、流動体や粉末の強みで、好みの味や摂りたいビタミンCの分量に合わせて、これも自在に増減して調節できる。

ビタミンCの摂取量をもっと細かく管理したいなら、もっと小さな計量スプーンを使ったり、0・1グラム単位で計れるデジタル秤を使うのも手だ。石けんやクリーム作りのハーブやクレイ、粉のラピスラズリや、パンを作るときのドライイーストなど、細かいものを計量するのに使っているが、何かと役立つ秤である。

何はともあれ、この「ハニーレモンキャンディ」、こんなに簡単に、体力作りや免疫力増強、病気の予防ができるなんて、今でも何だか信じられないほどなのだ。なんといってもおやつのような美味しいサプリメントで、しかも効能を発揮する成分以外に何の余分な混ぜ物もないのがうれしい。

しかもこれは、よく効く風邪薬でもある。

このレシピに使うはちみつは、できあがりの味としてはどうしてもビタ

＊10　1928年にビタミンCを発見し、それが壊血病を防ぐことを解明した功績により、後にノーベル生理学・医学賞を受賞したハンガリー人の科学者、アルベルト・セント＝ジェルジ博士（1893―1986）は、晩年、熱心にがん治療の研究をしていた。その同じ博士が、（2008年にマヌカハニーの特有有効成分であることが判明した）メチルグリオキサール（MGO）の発見者でもある（発見は1963年）。病気治癒のプロセスにおける、はちみつとビタミンCの働きを考えるとき、「過酸化水素」に加えて、「MGO」という共通のキーワードが登場するとは、何と興味深いことだろうか。

Spoonful of Honey

ミンCの酸味が勝ってしまうので、繊細な風味が魅力だというタイプのも

のはおすすめしない。料理やお菓子作りに使う日常用のはちみつで十分だ。

ただ、それでも必ず、混ぜものや加熱や汚染のない生の純粋なはちみつを

使ってください。ミツバチがせっせと集めてくれた元気の素をそのまま

ただくことが、このサプリが抜群にいい理由なのだから。

ところで、発明品をハンドバッグに詰め込んで飛び回る化学の天才ハニ

ーレモン嬢だが、アニメの中ではちみつとレモンを実験素材にしたりする

わけではない。ところが何の偶然か、超硬合金を一瞬でバラバラにくだい

てしまう薬品を作る実験で、「過酸化水素」を扱っていたりする。

たぶん、アニメを作った人たちは、はちみつとビタミンCの秘密兵器が

過酸化水素だなんて、考えていたわけではないだろうけど……。

*10

はちみつとビタミンCで、見えない敵と闘う——2

Spoonful
of
Honey
12

ひとつの公害汚染をどう解決するか
を論じることは、
慢性の病気の根元が化膿し続けているのに、
対症療法をしているようなものなのです。

――福岡正信 『わら一本の革命』ローデイルプレス版[*]より

アメリカ有数の小麦とワイン用葡萄の産地、醸造地である、ワシントンとオレゴン州境の小さな田舎町に住んでいたある夏のことだ。

友人のジェナが、自分が運営に関わった近くの大学で開かれる環境保全のイベントを是非見に来て、と誘ってくれた。ほとんど稀少品種になりかけだという原種の小麦を石臼で挽いて、彼女が最近せっせとパンを焼いていたのは、このためだったのかもしれない。

会場に行ってみると、中庭に設えた青空市場のかなり大きな一角に、農業や園芸、畜産、養蜂、自然環境に関する本を古書から新しいものまでたくさん集めた移動書店が出ていた。ひょろりと背の高い四、五十代の店主の男性に聞いてみると、こうしたタイプのイベントは多く開かれるので、そうした所をいろいろ回ると地域の農業や環境の様子が垣間見られて興味深いのだという。

ふと気づくと、「The One-Straw Revolution」という文字を背にした本がざっと7、8冊はある。しかも、古いのから新しいのまで、ハードカバーからペーパーバックまで、装丁もいろいろだ。

福岡正信著『わら一本の革命』の英訳版。

＊1　日本語原書初版は1975年だが、アメリカでは1978年に英語版が刊行された。西洋の読者のために章の冒頭に見える短い解説が加えられており、日本語版にない福岡自身のことばもある。これはそのひとつで、英文から筆者が翻訳したもの。

「この本、いっぱいそろえてるのね」ときくと、

「もちろん。自然農法や有機農法の世界でフクオカを読んでいないのはモ

グリだからね」とウィンクが返ってきた。

なぜ、おかしな循環が止まらないのか

ここは１００年以上前からアメリカのパンかごと呼ばれる地域の中心

で、古くから小麦を作る豪農を中心に築かれてきた町だ。最近はカリフォ

ルニアをはじめ、近場のシアトルやポートランドからも、都会を離れて有

機農業を始めたいと移住してくる若者や転職組も増えている。すばらしい

葡萄ができるので、フランスやドイツ、スイス、インドなどからはるばる、

ワイン関係の仕事をするためにやってくる人も多い。けれども地域一帯の

産業の根幹はまだ、戦後広まった穀物や果物の大規模農法だ。

農薬を使わない有機農業でみごとな野菜を作る若い名人のキムが畑で作

物の世話をしている様子を見ていると、まるで元気いっぱいの彼女は保育

園の先生で、みずみずしいレタスやズッキーニが、やんちゃな子どもたち

Spoonful of Honey 158

に見えてくる。

　彼女の畑の土と、従来の農法で普通に農薬や除草剤を使う近隣の土は、見るからに違う。

「この辺は、周りはぐるっとまだ普通のやり方でしょ？　だからどうしたって隣が農薬を撒くと風で飛んでくるの。完璧とはいかないわね」と彼女は首をふる。

「でも、私は自分の畑を元気にすることしかできないわけだし、ここの土がちゃんと呼吸ができるようになれば、少なくともその分だけは世界が元気になるわけだから……」

　キムの話を聞いているとなんだか、畑と人のからだも、同じもののように思えてくる。

　自分が直接耕せるのは自分のからだだけ。

　でも、自分が身を養う食べものを選び、ちゃんとその土を作れば、もしかするとその分は、世界も元気になるのかもしれない。

　人のからだは言わば、空気や地面や水と、食べものや呼吸でつながりながら、環境に浮かんでいるようなものである。世界が病むとき多少なりと

159　　12　はちみつとビタミンＣで、見えない敵と闘う——2

も人は病み、人が病むときには世界が病むように思える。そこには、あまり境目がないように思える。

日常的に土に近い人たちは、そのことを敏感に感じているので、何かの異変があるとさっと身構える。

アメリカ全土でミツバチが大量に死に始めたとき、その不気味さはこの上なかった。あるとき、近くの高速道路で、ワシントン州の巨大なリンゴ農園に受粉の労働のために遠路はるばる東部から送り込まれたトラック一杯のミツバチたちが、横転事故で投げ出されて一匹残らず飛び去ったというとんでもない事件があった。農にかかわる友人たちはみなショックを受けていた。

工場へ大量に卸される安い加工用のリンゴを得るために、私たちは、いったい何をしているのだろう。

「ビタミンＣを摂りなさい」

東日本大震災の原発事故の直後、オレゴン州の酪農家たちは一時期、出

Spoonful of Honey 160

荷停止に追い込まれた。偏西風に乗ってやってきた放射性物質が原乳から検出されたからだ。

海の向こうから遥々やってくるのは想定外だったと思うが、ワシントンとオレゴンの州境を流れるコロンビア川一帯の人々にとって、今後いつあるかもしれない放射能被害を危惧すること自体は、決して新しい問題ではない。稼働はストップしているとはいえ、世界最大の廃炉事業、かつ環境問題である、ハンフォード核施設を抱えているからだ。

そのせいか震災のあったその年、アメリカの家にいたときも、3・11直後の日本の悲痛な状況に対する地域の友人たちの配慮のまなざしには、救われる思いをすることも多かった。

知り合いの父親は、この核施設でクリーンアップのプロジェクトに携わる物理学専門の技術者のひとりだ。ある集まりで、なごやかなカクテルタイムに会話を交わしたとき、

「ビタミンCを摂りなさい」と彼は言った。

「身を守るためには、ちゃんとビタミンCをたくさん摂ることだよ」

実をいうとそれを聞いたとき、私はそのことばを大して深く気にとめな

かった。ビタミンCはあまりにもありふれたものだったから、これはきっと彼一流の言いまわしで、からだをいたわってくれたのだと思った。だから気持ちだけを心からうれしく受け止めて思わずにっこりし、「ありがとう」と、お礼を言ってすませてしまったのだ。

ああ、あのとき、もうちょっとよく話を聞いておくのだったと地団駄踏んだのは、後にビタミンCの経口投与が被曝対策に役立つという内容の研究が確かにあるということを知ったときだ。

あのとき「え？　なぜなぜ、どうして？　あなたは毎日仕事場で、どんな風に摂っているの？」と問い詰めておけば、きっともっと早くに丸腰の不安をなだめることができたかもしれないのに！

中でも、「人が朝食時に体重1キロ当たりで35ミリグラムのビタミンCを摂った上で1時間後に採血し、分離した白血球に放射線を浴びせたら、ビタミンCを摂らないときよりもDNAの損傷が著しく少なくなった」という内容のイギリスの論文 *2 などは、わかりやすくて、その結果はいかにも普段の生活にストレートに役立ちそうではないか。

*2　主要参考文献㊿。

Spoonful of Honey　　162

紫外線対策と放射線対策の共通点

そもそも、こうした研究があることを教えてくれたお医者さん方が、事故後の日常の低線量被曝に対応できるようにと勧めておられるビタミンCの摂取量や摂り方は（たとえば、成人は1回1〜2グラムを1日3〜4回、子どもは1日で体重1キログラム当たり60ミリグラムを2〜3回に分けて）、ポーリング博士が本来インフルエンザ、がん、心臓病などさまざまな病気の予防や治癒に役立つと勧めていた方法（たとえば成人1日4グラムから10グラムを数回に分けて）とほとんど変わらない。

そしてやっぱり、ビタミンC単独で摂るのではなく、他のビタミンやミネラルをちゃんと組み合わせた方がいいとされている。

ほらね、ここでまた我が家では、はちみつの出番です。

ビタミンCを摂るときは、はちみつと組み合わせると、活性マルチビタミン、マルチミネラルを合わせることになるので、効果が高まり、しかも美味しい。

[*3] 主要参考文献㉙。

163　12　はちみつとビタミンCで、見えない敵と闘う——2

また、前にも少し触れたが、実は、紫外線と放射線が細胞を老化させ、DNAを傷つける仕組み自体は、波長の短い放射線の方がエネルギーが強いということを除けば、そう変わらない。美容情報として紫外線ケアのためにビタミンCを摂ることが勧められるというのも納得だが、上手にコツを押さえれば、理屈としては確かに、美容どころでなく、被曝対策もできることになる。

ただ、ビタミンCというのは前にも言ったように、人によって効果の出る摂取量がまるで違うから、1日で摂る量、1回に摂る量は、やはり自分でしばらくやってみて、頃合いを探し出すしかないのだ。

ビタミンCは、重大な副作用は全くないとされているが、摂りはじめは胃腸にガスがたまったり、胃が重くなり、違和感を覚える人もいる。だから、大人の場合も、はじめは500ミリグラムや1グラムから始めて様子を見た方がいいとすすめられていることが多い。[*4]。

そして、その適量を探し出したら、はちみつとビタミンC（アスコルビン酸）の原末で、「ハニーレモンキャンディ」（150ページ）を調合し、10時と3時のおやつというのも悪くない。

[*4] 少しずつ摂り始めると、すぐに慣れて調子をつかむ人が多いようだが、特に胃が敏感な人のために、カルシウムやマグネシウムを加えてpHを穏やかに調整した粉末状、または錠剤の「バッファードビタミンC」もある。アメリカではスーパーで手に入る。日本でもサプリメントとして手に入れることができる。

Spoonful of Honey　164

それ以外にビタミンCの原末を上手に摂る他の方法としては、オレンジジュースや黒酢ドリンクのような、もともと甘酸っぱい飲みものに適量を溶かすのが、濃縮レモン果汁をプラスした感じになって、意外と飲みやすい。水に溶くとかえって酸味がきつく感じられる。

もちろんそこに、はちみつを適量溶かしこんで、たとえば「ハニーオレンジビタミンC」ジュースにすると、もっともっと美味しくなる。

まず自分が健やかになること

あのいまいましい原発事故で膨大な量の放射性物質が空や海や地面の上に派手にばらまかれてしまった。そして今も湯気をふく煮立った釜に蓋ができない。

こんなことにしてしまって、いったい私たちはどうしたらいいのだろう？　再び間違わないために、今日何をすればいいのだろう。

その上「ひとつの公害汚染をどう解決するかを論じることは、慢性の病気の根元が化膿し続けているのに、対症療法をしているようなもの」なの

165　　12　はちみつとビタミンCで、見えない敵と闘う——2

だ。問題は複雑に絡み合う。

世界には地獄の釜がいくつもぱっくり口を開けている。

世界中で誰もがみな、風、水、塵が流れ、舞い、循環するこの空間で呼吸をし、土が産み出してくれるものを今日も食べて生きている。

どこにいようと、この空間の頸木に私たちを繋ぐものこそが、絆なのだ。生きているかぎり誰ひとりとして、この空間からは自由になれない。

対症療法では駄目なのだ。だから、持ち場をこれと決めたら、今日、目の前の自分の土を蘇らせるしかない。土と同じようにこのからだを耕し、へこたれず健やかになっていくしかない。

働きバチが無心に飛び、花に飛び込み、花蜜を吸うように。

Spoonful of Honey　166

はちみつで
おなかすっきり

Spoonful
of
Honey
13

「はちみつを混ぜた海水」は、強い下剤となる。

はちみつ、雨水、海水を1対1対1で合わせて漉し、

犬の星（シリウス）の灼熱の季節の間に、

防水剤を施した壺に入れて発酵させる。

沸騰させた海水2に対してはちみつ1を加え、

瓶詰めするやり方もある。

これは（下剤としては）「海水」よりも穏やかである。

──ディオスコリデス『マテリア・メディカ（薬物誌）*1』より

ディオスコリデス先生は、ローマ時代のお医者さま、植物学者で、薬草学の父と言われる。現代でもヒポクラテス先生と並んで、医学、薬学、植物学の分野で大変な尊敬を集めるお方だ。

皇帝ネロの侍医であったらしいから、もしも朝、皇帝が思うように用を足せずにじれていたら、処方したのは、この「はちみつを混ぜた海水」だったのだろうか。

ネロの軍隊の軍医として各地をまわったとも言われているが、長旅の途中、先々でトイレタイムのリズムがつかめず困った兵士は少なくなかっただろうねえ、と、いささかの同情をこめて想像できるから、この処方はおそらく、豊富な臨床経験に基づいた、かなり効きめの確かなものではないかしらんと思うのだ。

とは言っても、最近は悲しいことに、薬の材料にしようと思えるほどのきれいな雨水や海水がなかなか手に入らない。だからもちろん実際に、自分でこの通りにやってみたことがあるわけではないのです。

でも、古代ローマのものだというのに、なぜか、そう違和感を抱かせないこのレシピをよくよくながめてみると、レモンやビタミンCこそ入って

＊1　主要参考文献⑪。英語版のテキストから抜粋。翻訳は筆者。

いないけど、これって言わば、ベースは天然塩を材料にした72ページの「は
ちみつ水（手作りイオン飲料）」で、そのはちみつと塩分の濃度をうんと
上げたものですよねえ、と気づく。

そういえば、ディオスコリデス先生は、この処方の一つ前に、「海水」
はそのままで、非常に強力な、かなりからだに負担のかかる、き
つい下剤となると言っておられる。それに整腸作用のある、はちみつを加
えることで、より優しい「緩下剤（かんげ）」となるというニュアンスだ。

はちみつ水でデトックス

夏、あまりの暑さに、72ページの「はちみつ水（手作りイオン飲料）」
を1日1リットルは摂っているという友人がいた。

「滋養補給になるし、とっても美味しいし、夏バテや熱中症予防にいいか
らって、がんがん飲んでいたのよね。そしたら突然、下痢しちゃったわよ
う、しゃーしゃーと！　でも不思議なことに、体調も全く悪くないし、い
つもと違ってお腹（なか）は全然痛くなかったのよねえ」と、親しい仲でなければ

Spoonful of Honey　170

決してできないであろう、味な報告をくれたことがあった。

友人の話を聞いて、「どういうことか?」とディオスコリデス先生の文章を改めてながめ、さらにつらつらと考えた。

「はちみつ水」の栄養剤や水分補給としての効果を確かに享受していたから、彼女は元気いっぱいだったのだと思う。

ただ、この「はちみつ水」はもともと、農作業やスポーツで汗をいっぱいかいたり、熱中症寸前だったりで、塩分補給が絶対不可欠な場合のためにと、適量の天然塩を加えたイオン飲料のレシピである。

だから彼女のように、それほど発汗による塩分の喪失のないデスクワーク中心の生活で、レシピどおりの天然塩入りはちみつ水を一定量以上摂れば、夏といえども穏やかな下剤として働く場合もあるかもしれないねぇ、と思ったわけである。

その上、ライナス・ポーリング博士も言うように、ビタミンCにも緩下作用がある。ビタミンCがからだの中に必要十分量蓄えられたとき、人は軟便になり、それが健康な状態だというのだ。それならば、ビタミンCの粉末もたっぷり入っているはちみつ水をたくさん摂ったとき、相乗効

171 　🥄 ─　13 はちみつでおなかすっきり

果でデトックス作用があるというのは確かにあり得ることである。

「はちみつ水」はそれまで自分の中では、汗だくになる特別なときのためのレシピだった。だから、普段、そんなにたくさん飲むことはなかったのだけど、もしかして多めに飲んだら実際影響があるだろうか（平たく言えば、下剤になるだろうか）と実際に飲み方をいろいろ試してみると、お腹をすっきりさせる効果は確かにあるようだ。

それで私はこの手作りイオン飲料、「はちみつ水」を、デトックス用途で使う場合には、ディオスコリデスとデトックスのDを取り、「ハニーウォーターDD」と名づけることにした。

72ページにあげた標準的なレシピは、はちみつ、天然塩、ビタミンC原末の分量に関しては、あくまで我が家での上限としての定番の量であり、これを出発点の目安にして、心地よい適量を工夫し、探していただけたらと思う。

繰り返すようだが、気候や汗のかき方、体調も日によって違うし、効果がある分量がどれだけで、摂るのは一日のいつがいいというポイントなど、自分でも「いつもこれ！」とは、なかなか決めがたいからだ。

お腹が重くなってきて、何らかの必要を感じたときに適宜、状況に応じて摂ることで、穏やかに行き詰まった事態の進行を促す働きがあるということは、実感として言えると思う。

実は、はちみつ自体にすばらしい整腸作用がある理由は、現代的な知見から見てもちゃんとある。はちみつのすごいところは、便秘にも、下痢にも、どちらにも、根本的に効くということなのである。日々の食習慣に継続的に上手に取り入れることで、対症療法ではない、根本的な腸の健康を手に入れることができる。

ひとつには、はちみつに含まれるオリゴ糖やグルコン酸は、善玉の腸内細菌を増加させ、悪玉菌を減少させるとされている。継続的にはちみつを摂取すると、大腸がんの予防効果があるという研究結果を、腸内細菌研究の第一人者である光岡知足先生が示しておられるということを、126ページでふれた宇津田博士は紹介し、便秘でなく「下痢をしている場合には大さじ3杯が有効です」と書いておられる。

実際に大さじ3杯のはちみつを一度に食べるのは甘くてかなり大変だと思うが、経験のあるお医者さんによるこうした具体的なアドバイスは、私

たちが自分で試してみようとするとき、目安としてほんとうにありがたい。

また、オリゴ糖やグルコン酸以外にも、はちみつが発生させる過酸化水素による抗菌作用が悪玉菌を殺し、善玉菌を傷つけないということは、前にもふれた。考えてみれば、朝食、または夜のデザートに、「ヨーグルトにはちみつ」というのは、「腸内フローラ（腸内のお花畑）」と言われる腸内環境を整えるには最良の食べ合わせであることは間違いない。

はちみつを上手に肥やしにすれば、お腹の畑を蘇らせ、元気な花を一面に咲かせることができる。そうすれば、不快な便秘や下痢とはおさらば、日々健康な堆肥を生み出せる！　というわけだ。

「はちみつ水でデトックス」を試す場合の注意に話を戻そう。

ディオスコリデス先生が「非常に強力なきつい下剤」だという海水の塩分濃度は約3パーセントで、考えてみれば、私がはちみつ水のレシピに使う天然塩の分量は、その10分の1ほどにすぎない。だが、それでも500ミリリットルで1・5グラムの塩を摂ることになるには違いないので、うっかり塩分の摂りすぎにならないようには、留意しなければならないだろう。

友人にこのレシピの成り立ちを説明し、運動してよほど汗をかいたとき以外は、暑いからといって、はちみつ水を冷やしすぎないほうがいいんじゃないかということと、あまり汗をかかないのに栄養剤として多めに飲むのなら、天然塩の分量は減らした方がいい。でも、特にお通じをよくしたいときには、1日のカロリーや塩分量を調整しながら、飲む分量を、ちょっと多めにしてもいいみたいだねえということを伝えた。

その後、もともと便秘気味だったという彼女だが、「ハニーウォーターDDね、はちみつと塩とビタミンCの量を体調に合わせて調整したら、今や快腸、快便よー。なんだかちょっぴりやせたでしょ?」とご機嫌だ。

ある猛暑の夏、犬の星の下で女たちが、古代ローマのお医者さんごっこで楽しんだ顛末(てんまつ)である。

断食クリニックで学んだことと、お腹(なか)の畑の土作り

ちなみに、15年近く前のことだが、ある断食クリニックに行ったとき、

先生に教えていただいた、今も忘れられない智恵のことばがある。

「病気で下痢が止まらないという、よからぬ場合を除き、たまの一発下痢（ああ、開けっぴろげすぎて、ほんとうにすみません！）は、悪い、余計なものを体外に排出してすっきりできる貴重な機会。だから、決して不安になる必要はないのです。そんなときにはこれ幸い、ありがとうと、ゆっくり熱いお茶でも飲んでお腹を温め、失った水分をささっと補給しておけばよろしい」とのことであった。

「たまに上手に風邪をひき、たまに上手に下痢をしてください。便秘はだめ。それが悪いものをため込まず、大病をしない秘訣です」

なるほど、なるほど……。

お腹がすいているとき人は素直に頭を垂れる。そもそも、断食のため3度の食事をしないと、1日24時間とは、信じられないほどの長さなのである。お腹に何も入れられない分、脳みそはいつになくいろいろなものを吸収し、それを咀嚼し、身につけようとする。

見上げる空はひたすらに青く、流れる雲を目でずっと追っていても、なぜか時の歩みは遅い。ああ、鳥はいいなあ、あそこで自由に木の実をつい

Spoonful of Honey 176

ばんでいる……。

5日間、石清水だけの完全断食。大変面白かったが、ごめんなさい、食いしん坊の私には、もうたぶんできないだろうと思う。でも、あのときはほんとうにいろんなことを、頭でなくからだで考えた。

「長く断食すると、その人の弱い部分に反応が出ます。だから、人によっては、胃が痛んだり、腰が痛んだりします。少々は我慢してもいいのですが、我慢できないと思ったら、言ってください。顔を見ていればだいたい様子はわかりますが、その時にはイオン飲料をあげますから」と先生に初めに言われた。

いやー、面白い。自分はいったいどこが痛くなるだろう、と興味津々で待ち構えていたら、完全断食5日めの最終日、朝から両目の奥ががんがんして、頭全体に広がってきた。夫の方は何ともない。

ははあ、やっぱり普段酷使している目に来ましたか、面白いものですね、と思いながら、我慢できるかとがんばってみたが、どこかが痛いとか、かゆいとか、ちょっとしたことでもからだの不調への耐性が全然ない不甲斐ない人なので、30分ほどでギブアップ。いただいたのは500ミリリッ

トルの市販のイオン飲料だったが、それで頭痛がうそのように消えていったのにも驚いた。

面白かったのは、夫のアメリカ人の同僚がそのしばらく後で同じ施設に行ったとき、2日めに癇癪を起こして「こんなこと、やってられっか！」と飛び出して家へ帰ってしまったというエピソードだ。

「いやあ、彼はさ、気はいいやつなんだけど、普段からものすごくせっかちで短気なんだよ。先生がイオン飲料をあげる間もなく、あれよとあれよと飛び出して行ってしまったんだねえ」と、まだ怒っている本人から直接経緯を聞いた夫は、その話をしながら笑いをかみころしていた。

うーむ、弱いところが露わになるとは気質のことまでだったのか！

断食、恐るべし、である。自分を知るにはいいが、一緒にやる人を選ぶかも。もしかすると普段も、人前で弱点が露わになりそうなときごくりと飲むため、はちみつイオン飲料を用意しておくのも手かもしれないですね。

断食つながりで言えば、この手作りはちみつ水を使って、折を見て、夫婦そろってたまに1日断食をする。最近、食べ過ぎでからだが重いね、という時期が続くと、1日ひとり当たり2リットルまでを目安にして、ここ

Spoonful of Honey　178

ら辺で内臓に休日を、というわけである。

丸1日食べないとは言っても、実際には、はちみつを160グラムぐらい摂ることになるわけだから、厳密には断食とは言えない。

でも、固形物を全く摂らないことで、胃腸は休める上、はちみつによる粘膜修復効果の助けも全く摂らないことで、胃腸は休める上、はちみつによる粘膜修復効果の助けも得られる。これだけの分量を摂れば、「ハニーウォーターＤＤ」の「下からデトックス」効果も期待できるというわけである。

ちなみに当日消費を前提に、はちみつ水を冷蔵庫に入れない方が、からだを冷やさない。たまに1日食事の支度や後片付けがないと、なんだか気分が新鮮だ。時間がたっぷりあってうれしい。お風呂にもゆっくり入れる。

丸1日でなくとも、夕食だけ抜いて、寝るまではちみつ水1本（500ミリグラム）にすることもある。それでも胃腸はちゃんと休めて、翌日のからだが軽い。手軽なようだが胃腸の調子を整えるという目的のためには、立派にプチ断食となるのである。

ディオスコリデスは、はちみつと雨水と海水を発酵させて解毒剤を作った。からだに毒がたまると、人は病気になるからだ。

でも、毒をぬいただけでは、人は元気にならない。

健康なエネルギーの源はどこかと考えてみれば、それは、取り入れた食べものを耕し、発酵させ、微生物と共生し、栄養を循環させる、腸内フローラが育つお腹の畑の中だ。お腹の中にきれいな花を満開に咲かせることができたとき、からだに元気がみなぎる。

肥料や薬を選ぶのは私たちだ。

あなたはどんな農法で花を咲かせますか？

はちみつは健康な土作りの大きな助けになってくれる。だから私はときどき畑に「はちみつ水」を撒く。はちみつを肥やしにする。

ちなみに、はちみつと水を混ぜたもの＝はちみつ水を発酵させると、「ミード」という美味しいはちみつのお酒になる。

元気になったら、おいしいお酒を飲もう。

ミツバチの羽音を聞きながら。

Spoonful of Honey　　180

あとがき ❁

はちみつミルクか、はちみつワインで
おやすみなさい

　寝る前と朝起きてからひとさじずつ、マヌカのはちみつをゆっくりと味

わうようにしたら、それまで長らく私の喉に居座っていた、嫌なイガイガ、

ひりひりが、そして、他のはちみつで退治しきれなかった最後のちりちり

が、どこかにするすると退却していった。それも1日、2日のうちに。

　集めた花蜜を酵素と混ぜ合わせ、巣房に詰め込み、羽ばたきで水分を飛

ばして濃縮し、頃合いになったらふたをして熟成させる。このすばらしい

ひとさじを作りあげたハチたちは、いったいどんなところにいるのだろう。

そしてその蜜源の花はどんな空の下で、どんなふうに咲いているのだろう。

日本が初冬へと向かう11月の第4週、私は春爛漫（らんまん）のニュージーランド、北島のコロマンデル半島へやってきた。　満開のマヌカの花と忙しく飛びまわるミツバチたちを見るために。

ワンガヌイ海洋保護区域の端にあるハーヘイの町の、エメラルド・グリーンの海を見下ろす丘の上から、木立の中を海岸まで続く道をハイキングしていたら、視界が開けた内陸側の向こうの丘一面に、白や淡いピンクの薄もやが見えた。マヌカの花だ。　山桜に比べると、そのもやは、うんとはかなく、まぶしい陽光とあたりを満たす潮の香りの中で、山がごく薄いガーゼのストールを羽織っているかのように見える。

ビーチへのハイキングを終えたあと、マヌカの樹をあちらこちらに見ながら森林地帯の309ロードをドライブしていたら、くねくねとした道端に、ハチの巣箱がいくつも置いてあるのが見えた。　働きバチがあたりをブンブン行き交っている。　車を止めて飛び出すと、あたりの空気はマヌカのはちみつの甘く健やかで力強い香りに満たされていた。喉のひりひりを治そうと家の台所でスプーンを握りしめ、びんのふたを開けるたびにふわりと広がった、あの香りの元がここにある。

Spoonful of Honey　182

「マヌカハニーなんて、風味が強いし色は黒いからって、前は見向きもされなかったんだ」と養蜂家のアンドリューさんは面白そうに笑った。

「よくて加工用に回すか、捨てるしかなかったのに、今じゃラボで効き目のグレード検査を受けて、病院へ行くか海外でも引っ張りだこだ。こうして遥々日本から、ハチを見に自分が飛んで来る人までいる」

切断を免れないと言われた手足や、ときとして命そのものを救うパワーを秘めていたこの甘露を、不遜にも一時期、人は捨てていた。命を養うその力の代わりに、私たちは何を手に入れたかったのか。

収穫された蜜ごとに検査機関でその治癒力が証明され、グレードを明記した証明書が発行されるということなどは、こうしてせっせと忙しく花蜜を運び続けるハチたちの関心の埒外だ。彼女たちは昔からずっと変わらず、無心にひたすらはちみつを作る。それは、その行為が、自分たちの大家族を養う大事な仕事だからである。

「あったよ、あったよ！」と腰を振り、パワー全開のダンスをして、その

はちみつの素材となる美味しい花蜜をたたえた花の群れを発見したら、その

情報を仲間たちに正確に伝達しようとする。それは、巣のなかで眠るみんなの大切な子どもたち、そして、自分たち自身を養うためだ。

一生懸命働いて、貯めた蜜を誰かがごっそりもらいにきても、彼女たちは太っ腹だ。熊のプーさんであれ、人であれ、ほしいと言うならいらっしゃい。私は今日もまた花を見に行く。

この本は、ずっと身近にあって大好きだったのに、何十年もの間、はちみつの底力に気づかなかったうっかり者が、ひょんなことからその秘めたるパワーに魅せられ、夢中であれこれ冒険してみた、経験や覚え書きを個人的にまとめたものだ。はちみつに、あれもできる、これもできるとその再発見にうれしくなったあまり、思わず遊び場に走り出て、「はちみつ好きはこの指とまれ！」と言っているようなものである。

一読して、自分もはちみつの効き目を実際に試してみたいと思ってくだされば、美味しいはちみつが、世の中にもっと増えることになるだろうと思うので、とてもうれしい。この本でご紹介した使い方を目安の一例として役立て、自分に合った方法を工夫し、楽しんでいただけたらと思う。

Spoonful of Honey　　184

そして、世界中にはまだ、数え切れない種類のはちみつがある。その治癒的効能に着目するファンが増えれば、各種はちみつの秘めたるパワーについて、学術的発見がさらに進むことになるのでは、と期待がはずむ。

「医療用のはちみつ」や、この本でははちみつと組み合わせて使う方法を提案したビタミンCなどについては、近年興味深い研究が進み、専門家の間でもさまざまな情報が行き交っているようだ。

他のどんな分野でも同じだと思うが、科学の議論も社会的存在である人がする以上、そこは証拠の有無や理論の整合性だけですいすいと進んではいけない荒野のようだ。私たちの目に普段あまり触れなくとも、そこには常に手に汗握るドラマがある。

一話ごとのドラマの結末を引き受けていくのは、私たちだ。だからそんな議論を観戦し、私たちのためにと無心に研究をしてくれている方々に陰ながら声援を送り、その貴重な成果を普段の暮らしにどう活かしていけるか、あれこれ頭をひねるのも、素材好きの生活者の醍醐味である。

　各項目の冒頭にあげた引用文は、それぞれのお話をするときの、お茶会の掛け軸のようなつもりである。本や文献からのものもあれば、交流のあ

った身近な人のことばもあり、その引用の仕方は、とりとめなく統一感に欠けて見えるかもしれない。ただ、これまで私がはちみつを愛し、はちみつについて考えるとき、大きな印象や示唆を与えてくれた心の師ばかりだ。古代に生きた方々も、面識のない方もいらっしゃるから直接御礼を申し上げられないが、どの方にも心からの敬意を捧げたい。

そして、この本を作るにあたって、直接お世話になった方々への感謝の気持ちを言い尽くすことばを私は持たない。同じ巣のチームの中で、持ち場を分担してせっせとはちみつを作りあげてくださった働きバチのお姉さま方と、いっしょに羽ばたいてくださった雄バチのお兄さま方である。特に、司令塔の広瀬桂子さんと、花蜜を集めに行ったら、花の香りにふらふらと寄り道して皆さんをハラハラさせてばかりの筆者を、直接監督しなければならなかった編集担当の島口典子さん。胃が痛くならないように、どんなにか、たくさんのはちみつを、なめなければならなかったろうと思う。

それから応援し続けてくれた家族、友人たちも。

ほんとうにありがとうございました。

Spoonful of Honey　186

古来、甘いものは人にかぎりない幸福感を与えてくれた。

中でもはちみつは、急激な血糖上昇やアドレナリン分泌を抑えるので、幸福感が長続きすると言われている。アセチルコリンが副交感神経を優位にして鎮静作用をもたらしてくれるので、興奮はおさまり、気持ちもからだもリラックスできるらしい。

今晩悲しくて、あるいはうれしすぎて、眠れないかもと思ったら、少しだけ温めたミルクか、夕飯の飲み残しの美味しいワインにひとさじのはちみつを溶かしいれ、ベッドに持ち込もう。

花の中で甘い香りにからだごとすっぽり包まれるミツバチになった夢がみられるかもしれない。

2015年　秋

前田京子

㉔『おいしく治そう・栄養療法の権威が答える健康ハンドブック』丸元淑生著　1986 文藝春秋

㉕『壊血病とビタミンCの歴史・「権威主義」と「思いこみ」の科学史』K.J.カーペンター著　北村二朗・川上倫子訳　1998　北海道大学図書刊行会

㉖『新・ビタミンCと健康・21世紀のヘルスケア』村田晃著　1999　共立出版

㉗『ビタミンCがガン細胞を殺す』柳澤厚生著　2007　角川SSC新書

㉘『ビタミンCの大量摂取がカゼを防ぎ、がんに効く』生田哲著　2010　講談社＋α新書

㉙『今、注目の超高濃度ビタミンC点滴療法』水野春芳著　2013　日本文芸社

㉚ The One-Straw Revolution: An Introduction to Natural Farming, M. Fukuoka, edited by L. Korn, 1978. Rodale Press. (『自然農法・わら一本の革命』福岡正信著　1975　柏樹社)

㉛『腸内細菌学』光岡知足著　1990　朝倉書店

㉜『健康長寿のための食生活・腸内細菌と機能性食品』光岡知足著　2002　岩波アクティブ新書

㉝『免疫と腸内細菌』上野川修一著　2003　平凡社新書

㉞『人体常在菌のはなし・美人は菌でつくられる』青木皐著　2004　集英社新書

㉟『根の活力と根圏微生物』小林達治著　2013　〔初版は1986〕　農文協

㊱『光合成細菌で環境保全』小林達治著　2012　〔初版は1993〕　農文協

㊲ Fruitless Fall: The Collapse of the Honey Bee and the Coming Agricultural Crisis, R. Jacobsen, 2008. Bloomsbury. (『ハチはなぜ大量死したのか』R.ジェイコブセン著　中里京子訳　2009　文藝春秋)

㊳『ミツバチの不足と日本農業のこれから』吉田忠晴著　2009　飛鳥新社

㊴『見捨てられた初期被曝』study2007著　2015　岩波科学ライブラリー

㊵『死の灰と闘う科学者』三宅泰雄著　2014　〔初版は1972〕　岩波新書

㊶ Zumla, A. and A. Lulat. Honey: A remedy rediscovered. Journal of the Royal Society of Medicine. 1989;82:384-85.

㊷ Molan, P. Selection of honey for use as a medicine. http://waikato.academia.edu/PeterMolan. 2012;1-5.

㊸ Irish, J. et al. The antibacterial activity of honey derived from Australian flora. PLoS One. 2011;6(3):e18229.

㊹ Nightingale, K. Native honey a sweet antibacterial. Australian Geographic (online). 2011 Mar 3 (www.australiangeographic.com.au/news/2011/03/native-honey-a-sweet-antibacterial).

㊺ Haydak, M.H. et al. A clinical and biochemical study of cow's milk and honey as an essentially exclusive diet for adult humans. American Journal of Medical Sciences. 1944;207(2):209-18.

㊻ Paul, I.M. et al. Effect of honey, dextromethorphan, and no treatment on nocturnal cough and sleep quality for coughing children and their parents. Archives of Pediatrics and Adolescent Medicine. 2007;161(12):1140-46.

主要参考文献

① Manuka: The Biography of an Extraordinary Honey, C. Van Eaton, 2014. Exisle Publishing.

② Manuka-Honig: Ein Naturprodukt mit außergewöhnlicher Heilkraft, D. Mix, 2014. 360°
meidien gbr mettmann.

③ Practical Beekeeping in New Zealand, A. Matheson and M. Reid, 2011. Exisle Publishing.

④『ミツバチの世界・個を超えた驚きの行動を解く』J.タウツ著　丸野内棣　訳　2012　丸
善出版

⑤『ミツバチ・飼育、生産の実際と蜜源植物』角田公次著　1997　農文協

⑥『日本ミツバチ・在来種養蜂の実際』日本在来種みつばちの会編　2000　農文協

⑦『我が家にミツバチがやって来た』久志冨士男著　2010　高文研

⑧『ミツバチの生活』M.メーテルリンク著　山下知夫・橋本綱訳　2000　工作舎

⑨『ミツバチの文化史』渡辺孝著　1994　筑摩書房

⑩『ミツバチの文学誌』渡辺孝著　1997　筑摩書房

⑪ De materia medica, Pedanius Dioscorides of Anarzarbus, translated by L.Y. Beck, 2005.
Olms-Weidmann.

⑫『ファラオの秘薬・古代エジプト植物誌』L.マニカ著　編集部訳　1994　八坂書房

⑬『香料文化誌・香りの謎と魅力』C.J.S.トンプソン著　駒崎雄司訳　1998　八坂書房

⑭『アーユルヴェーダ・日常と季節の過ごし方』V.B.アタヴァレー著　稲村晃江訳　1987　平
河出版社

⑮『アーユルヴェーダのハーブ医学』D.フローリー、V.ラッド共著　上馬場和夫監訳・編著
2000　出帆新社

⑯ The New Standard Formulary, A.E. Hiss, Ph.G., and A.E. Ebert, Ph.M., Ph.D., c.1910.
G.P. Engelhard & Company.

⑰『歴代日本薬局方収載生薬大事典』木下武司著　2015　ガイアブックス

⑱『ハチミツの百科・新装版』渡辺孝著　2003　真珠書院

⑲ Honey and Healing, edited by P. Munn and R. Jones, 2001. International Bee Research
Association.（『ハチミツと代替医療・医療現場での可能性を探る』P.マン、R.ジョーンズ編
［国際ミツバチ研究協会］　松香光夫監訳　2002フレグランスジャーナル）

⑳『はちみつで元気を手に入れる』(別冊家庭画報)宇津田含監修　2004　世界文化社

㉑ Vitamin C, the Common Cold and the Flu, L. Pauling, 1976. W.H. Freeman & Company.
（『ライナス・ポーリングのビタミンCとかぜ、インフルエンザ』L.ポーリング著　村田晃訳
1977　共立出版)

㉒ Cancer and Vitamin C: A Discussion of the Nature, Causes, Prevention, and Treatment of
Cancer with Special Reference to the Value of Vitamin C, E. Cameron and L. Pauling, 1979.
W.W. Norton & Company.（『がんとビタミンC』L.ポーリング、E.キャメロン共著　村田晃、
木本英治、森重福美共訳　2015〔初版は1977〕共立出版)

㉓ How to Live Longer and Feel Better, L. Pauling, 1996. Avon Books.

㊼ El-Haddad, S.A. et al. Efficacy of honey in comparison to topical corticosteroid for treatment of recurrent minor aphthous ulceration: A randomized, blind, controlled, parallel, double-center clinical trial. Quintessence International. 2014;45(8):691-701.

㊽ Motallebnejad, M. et al. The effect of topical application of pure honey on radiation-induced mucositis: A randomized clinical trial. Journal of Contemporary Dental Practice. 2008;9(3):40-7.

㊾ Khanal, B. et al. Effect of topical honey on limitation of radiation-induced oral mucositis: An intervention study. International Journal of Oral and Maxillofacial Surgery. 2010;39(12):1181-5.

㊿ Green, M.H. et al. Effect of diet and vitamin C on DNA strand breakage in freshly-isolated human white blood cells. Mutation Research. 1994;316(2):91-102.

(51) Yamamoto, T. et al. Pretreatment with ascorbic acid prevents lethal gastrointestinal syndrome in mice receiving a massive amount of radiation. Journal of Radiation Research. 2010;51(2):145-56.

(52) Chen, Q. et al. Pharmacologic ascorbic acid concentrations selectively kill cancer cells: Actions as a pro-drug to deliver hydrogen peroxide to tissues. Proceedings of the National Academy of Sciences. 2005;104:8749-54.

(53) Keim, B. Honey remedy could save limbs. Wired (online). 2006 Oct 11 (http://archive.wired.com/medtech/health/new/2006/10/71925).（『抗生物質が効かない細菌に、蜂蜜で対抗』 http://wired.jp/2007/06/21/抗生物質が効かない細菌に、蜂蜜で対抗/）

著者からのお願い

この本では、これまでに専門的な研究によって一般的な安全性や効用が発表され、広く確認されてきた素材やその活用法について、著者の経験を合わせながら紹介しています。しかし、どんなに安全性が高いとされる素材も、全ての人に相性がよいということはありません。「自分との相性」を注意深く確かめながら、自己判断の上で、活用するようにしてください。また、はちみつは、幼児の発達と健康に大変よいとされているものの、過去にはちみつの中にボツリヌス菌が見つかったことがあることから、腸内細菌叢が未発達な1歳未満の乳児には与えるべきではないとされています。これについては、参考文献⑲の巻末に大変興味深い報告があります。

前田京子――まえだ・きょうこ

1962年生まれ。国際基督教大学教養学部、東京大学法学部卒業。
手作り石けん・ボディケアブームの先駆けとなったベストセラー
『お風呂の愉しみ』『オリーブ石けん、マルセイユ石けんを作る』(共に飛鳥新社)、
『石けんのレシピ絵本』(主婦と生活社)などの他、
2014年に出版された『はっか油の愉しみ』(マガジンハウス)も話題となった。
この他にも著書多数。横浜市在住。

ひとさじのはちみつ
自然がくれた家庭医薬品の知恵

2015年9月24日　第1刷発行
2015年12月18日　第6刷発行

著　者　前田京子
発行者　石﨑　孟
発行所　株式会社マガジンハウス
東京都中央区銀座3-13-10　〒104-8003
書籍編集部　☎03-3545-7030
受注センター　☎049-275-1811

印刷・製本　中央精版印刷株式会社

Ⓒ 2015 kyoko Maeda, Printed in Japan
ISBN978-4-8387-2776-6 C0095
乱丁本、落丁本は購入書店明記のうえ、小社制作管理部宛にお送りください。
送料小社負担にてお取り替えいたします。定価はカバーと帯に表示してあります。
本書の無断複製(コピー、スキャン、デジタル化等)は禁じられています(但し、
著作権法上での例外は除く)。断りなくスキャンやデジタル化することは
著作権法違反に問われる可能性があります。
マガジンハウスのホームページ　http://magazineworld.jp/

マガジンハウスの本

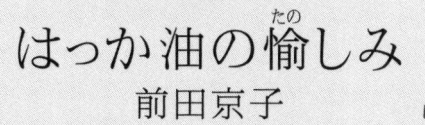

はっか油の愉しみ
前田京子

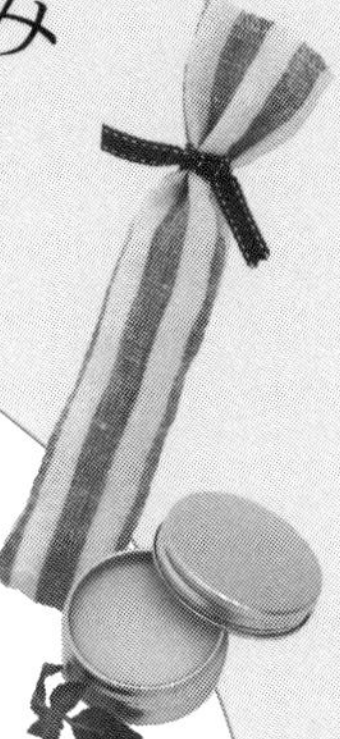

薬局で簡単に手に入る
「魔法の液体」

マウスウォッシュ、クレンザー、
入浴剤などが手作りできる34の
レシピ＆エッセイ

「もうはっか油のない暮らしなど考えられない」
愛用20年、熱い思いを込めた書き下ろし！

定価 本体1389円（税別）